"Hooper brings her A-game in Sacred Seas, tying all of her tales together in an exciting, inevitable finale. The kind of book that keeps you up all night, racing to find out how it ends."

Marie Jaskulka ~ Author of *The Lost Marble Notebook of Forgotten Girl & Random Boy*

"With its stellar fast-paced plot, multifaceted story, wonderful character growth, and a healthy dose of magic, myth, and finding that delicate balance between love and loss, triumph and tragedy, and light and dark, Sacred Seas is the ending that we deserve. This series has solidly placed itself in my list of favorites."

Sarah Quick ~ *Exploring All Genres*

Sacred Seas

Starry Sky Publishing

Copyright © 2017 Karen Amanda Hooper

ISBN ebook: 978-0-9961470-2-6
ISBN paperback: 978-0-9961470-3-3

Cover art by Melissa Williams
mwbookdesign.com

Interior art by Steve Graham
theinfinitycreative.com

Formatted by Shayne Leighton
parliamentbookdesign.wordpress.com

Edited by Rebecca Brown

Visit author Karen Amanda Hooper on the Web at
http://www.karenamandahooper.com

Sacred Seas

The Sea Monster Memoirs, #3

KAREN AMANDA HOOPER

Starry Sky Publishing

Sacred Seas

The Sea Monster Memoirs, #3

KAREN AMANDA HOOPER

1

Rowan

My brother wasn't his usual self.

Treygan had been quiet for most of the boat ride. He seemed worlds away. That wasn't the unusual part—he'd always been on the stoic, broody side—but he was so spaced out he didn't even notice that Lloyd and I were trying to have a conversation with him. On the horizon, the late morning sun highlighted the outlying islands of Key West. We were nearing our destination, and I had a feeling that whatever was bothering Treygan shouldn't be discussed where we might be overheard by humans.

I slowed our boat and the engine quieted to a low rumble. Lloyd glanced at me, but Treygan continued staring straight ahead, shoulders hunched forward and tense. I walked over and stood beside him. No reaction. Mentally, he wasn't even in the same boat as Lloyd and me. It wasn't until I leaned across him and my face blocked his view that he snapped out of his deep thoughts.

"Why did we slow down?" he asked.

Like his mood, his eyes seemed darker than usual. We were in human territory, so his mer traits were submerged, but I didn't need to see his skin turn blue or his hallmarks ripple to know he was upset.

I wasn't a fan of pointless conversation. "Let's discuss whatever's bugging you now because I'd like you fully present when we reach land."

He rubbed the back of his neck then raked his hand through his hair. "I'm worried about Yara."

"Why?" Lloyd asked. "You're all back home and everyone can live happily ever after."

"Something's weighing heavy on her," Treygan explained, "and she won't talk to me about it. She dances around the real issue by complaining about other problems, but there's something tormenting her."

"Otabia warned us no one is ever the same after visiting Harte," I reminded him. "That place left its mark on all of us. You can't expect Yara to be unaffected."

Treygan sighed and lifted his face into the wind, closing his eyes like he did when he was enjoying himself, but his deep frown said the opposite.

Lloyd gripped his shoulder. "Do you think maybe she's homesick?"

Treygan considered that possibility. "Perhaps. She claims to love Rathe, but Earth's realm is where she seems most comfortable."

"She's been through a lot of changes in a very short time," Lloyd reminded him. "And it isn't like she moved a few miles away. She relocated to a different world. A world that expects a lot from her."

"I wish I could make the transition easier on her." As always, my selfless brother wanted to fix something beyond his control.

"I'm sure you'll find a way," I assured him. "You always do."

He stared out at the water again.

"Something else is weighing heavy on you too," Lloyd said.

He shrugged. "Our focus should be Yara."

"We're family, Treygan," I said. It was a fact that was too easy to forget because of our recent years of fighting and not speaking to each other. "Talk to us."

Slumping into his seat, he explained, "I'm wondering if it's me that's the problem. I feel like we've become disconnected.

What if she and I aren't meant to be together?"

"Don't be ridiculous," I huffed. "You're perfect together."

"Maybe Harte changed us too much, or maybe we just haven't been facing the reality that Yara is now a ruler of Rathe. When it comes to power, she's the new Medusa."

"So?" Lloyd asked. "How does that change what you two have together?"

"It changes everything because—" Treygan lowered his eyes. "Because I'm no Poseidon."

I scoffed. "You're as close as any male sea monster could be without being a god."

"I'm far from a god," Treygan argued. "And Yara is now essentially a goddess. What if I'm not a worthy partner for her?"

Lloyd said exactly what I was thinking. "Don't make me smack some sense into you. You love her, and she loves you."

"She loves every creature of Rathe," Treygan grumbled.

"True." I returned to the wheel to adjust our course. "But she's only *in* love with you."

Lloyd nudged Treygan's knee. "Together, you two opened the gate between Earth and Rathe. You led everyone home and saved many lives. And then you went and completed a seemingly impossible quest in the depths of hell. Don't underestimate yourself."

"I worry about her," Treygan said. "For years I was responsible for protecting her, keeping our kind supplied with plants to keep them alive, and ensuring the gate opened. At the time, it felt like a lot. I constantly worried what would happen if I failed at even one of those tasks. Yara's responsibilities are endless and they affect our whole realm. That seems unfair. It's too much for one soul to handle."

"Yara will do what she has always done," Lloyd said. "She will adjust to her circumstances and thrive. However, a ruler of Rathe, especially a new inexperienced ruler, needs a supportive partner. She wants her partner to be you."

"Indulge us," I said, steering us northeast so we'd have a

straight shot between the two barrier islands. "Even if you were to end things with Yara—which, by the way, would be the stupidest move you've ever made—who would you suggest as a better match for her?"

Treygan glanced at me, then at Lloyd, then at the floor.

"Exactly," Lloyd grunted. "You're not suggesting anyone because there is no better match."

"I'm glad you think so." Treygan didn't sound any happier than when this conversation started, but I couldn't think of anything else to say to ease his worries. Every person had their insecurities. Every relationship had its growing pains.

"I don't *think* so." Lloyd shifted in his seat and rubbed his knees. "I *know* so. Now, grab my wheelchair and get ready to help your old man. We need a lot of stuff and I hate shopping."

Mine and Vienna's vow renewal ceremony was at sunrise tomorrow at Eden's Hammock. I had asked Lloyd to lead our ceremony, which meant a lot to him, and to me. My father was finally an important part of my life and that felt good.

We were having a small party at Lloyd's place—mainly because he couldn't go to the celebration Vienna and Yara were planning in Rathe. Several times a day I wished our worlds didn't have to be divided. Traveling back and forth to see Lloyd wasn't exactly convenient.

Once upon a time, our father had called Rathe home, but he gave it all up so he could be human and marry the mermaid he loved. Sometimes I wondered if, given the choice, he would do it all over again.

I hoped so, because without him and his sacrifices, Treygan and I wouldn't exist.

We had finished shopping and were walking back to the boat when one of my plastic bags ripped. Boxes of pastries and a loaf of bread hit my feet as a jar of peanut butter rolled down the street.

Treygan smirked at me and held up his canvas bags. "Told you these were the way to go."

I set down my other bags on top of the existing pile in Lloyd's wheelchair. He was walking, using the handles of the wheelchair for support, because he claimed his legs needed exercise to get stronger.

I hustled along the sidewalk to retrieve the peanut butter, which had rolled to a stop against the curb. As I bent down to pick it up, an elderly woman came out of the store directly in front of me. I stood upright and then froze right there in the street. She also paused, and after a moment of staring at me with wide eyes, her wrinkles softened and she smiled.

"Rownan," she said sort of breathlessly. "My goodness, what a happy surprise crossing paths with you."

What were the odds? The High Priestess who had married Vienna and me decades ago, and whom I hadn't seen since that night, popped up out of nowhere the day before we were about to renew our wedding vows.

"Hello," I said as Treygan and Lloyd walked up behind me.

The High Priestess stepped closer, offering a pleasant greeting to Lloyd, and then she turned to Treygan. Her green eyes seemed to sparkle when she looked at him. "Treygan, so nice to also see you here."

Treygan narrowed his eyes in a way that worried me. "Yes, as you can see, both my brother and I are alive and well."

Before we entered Harte, Treygan had told me that the High Priestess warned him about our future at my wedding reception. She told him I would be in danger, and asked him how far he would go to protect me. For almost two decades he worried about what she meant, but when the time came to accompany me to Harte, he went without hesitation. I had no idea why he was getting so uptight about it now.

I started babbling to break the weird tension between Treygan and the High Priestess. "Treygan told me you saw something terrible during the reading at my wedding, and you were right, we had to go through hell and back. Treygan risked his life to protect me. We saved Vienna and brought her home, so it all worked out."

Lloyd didn't seem surprised by my explanation. Maybe Treygan had already told him too.

"Splendid. How momentous." The High Priestess's smile didn't waver. She pulled her wrap-around blouse tighter around her waist as she glanced up the street. "I have an appointment, so I must be on my way, but I'm so glad that your choices led you here and we had the pleasure of encountering each other again."

"Me too." We nodded at each other before she turned and walked away.

Treygan and I started in the opposite direction, but after a few steps he looked over his shoulder and stopped. I turned around too. Lloyd still stood in place, leaning on the handles of his wheelchair, watching the High Priestess glide up the street.

"What about ripple effects?" he called out.

I glanced at Treygan, but his gaze was locked on them.

The High Priestess stopped and slowly pivoted to face us. Her smile had been replaced with a frown. "Ripple effects are a given. Always. With every choice."

Lloyd pushed his chair a couple of steps closer to her. "I know that. I'm asking if you can foresee any effects from the choices they made. Do you know what happens next?"

Treygan and I were both moving closer so we wouldn't miss her reply.

She kept her focus on Lloyd. "It's not my place to say."

"Please. They're my sons."

Her piercing green eyes momentarily flickered to Treygan and me, and then she sighed. "The darkness I saw has not passed. The veil still covers both of them."

My grip on the peanut butter jar tightened. "What's going to happen?"

"You have suffered great hardships and come through the darkness, but the darkness has followed you." Sadness softened her tone. "Further hardships are ahead. For both of you."

She had to be kidding. We had literally been through hell and back. That wasn't just a euphemism. We had overcome more than our fair share of hardships.

"What about Yara?" Treygan asked.

"Yara?" The High Priestess's gaze flickered to the sky. "My apologies, but I'm not familiar with anyone by that name."

I almost laughed. "Well, there you have it. If you didn't see Yara in your visions, then you're way off. She changed everything."

The High Priestess gave me a faint smile and shrugged. I couldn't tell if she was offended by what I had said or if she was thrown off by the mention of an important person that she, with all of her prophet power, didn't know about. "As I said, I have an appointment to keep and now I will be late. I wish you both the best."

"Wait." Lloyd reached one hand toward her. "Perhaps we could schedule a new reading with you."

"No," I said. "All due respect, High Priestess, but we'll create our own fate. Carry on to your appointment. We're sorry for making you late."

With a final bow, she turned and walked away again.

Lloyd grunted. "I'd like to know what she meant by a dark veil covering both of you."

"It's a standard fortune teller's scam. She got lucky by guessing Treygan would have to protect me at some point in my life. She's forecasting more bad news now because she knows everyone has problems." I turned to my brother. "Right?"

He hesitantly nodded.

"Come on," I said. "Let's get all this stuff to the boat. We're behind schedule too."

We walked in silence back to the dock. No one spoke as we loaded all of the bags onto the boat. Treygan and I helped Lloyd on board, and then I took the helm as Treygan untied our ropes. My brother and father stared back at the town as we pulled away.

"Stop worrying," I shouted over the engine and waves. "We're fine. Nothing can be worse than what we survived in Harte."

2

Hiking up the long skirt of my sundress, I sat on the edge of the hammock then shimmied into it and let the netting cradle me. Sadly, returning home and trying to feel like my old self was not helping me relax like I had hoped. Even the tranquil blue sky and swaying palm trees of Eden's Hammock didn't calm my whirlwind of thoughts.

Sage slithered down my shoulder and turned to look at me. Her silver tongue flickered in and out as I went over my mental checklist again.

Invitations extended to all species to the celebration in Rathe. "Check," I mumbled, unsure if I was updating myself or Sage.

Meeting with the rest of the gorgon kin to make them feel like an appreciated part of Rathe instead of pariahs. "Check. I think." Only time would tell if the gorgon kin would be able to reintegrate with sea creature society after years of isolation, but I had faith.

Finally obtain permission from Stheno and Euryale to appoint a new siren. "Check. Halle-freaking-lujah."

Trying to discuss anything with Stheno and Euryale was nearly impossible. After days of relentlessly begging, my spiteful gorgon co-rulers only agreed so I'd shut up and leave them alone. Now Otabia and Mariza could stop nagging me about replacing Nixie—as if anyone could ever replace her.

I set the rest of my checklist aside when I heard Uncle Lloyd's boat engine humming in the distance. I didn't need to look to confirm the guys were returning from their trip to town. Even if I didn't recognize the sound, my sea creature senses told me that two of my kind were approaching.

I stroked Sage's chin and whispered to her, "Get some rest. Retreat."

She recoiled to the back of my head then dissolved into her ethereal plane of existence. Sometimes I wished I could do that too. At least I could do the next best thing.

I used my new blending ability to make myself invisible. I didn't fully understand my unique skill yet, but being able to camouflage myself with my surroundings had its perks. From the comfort of my hammock, I secretly watched Treygan, Rownan, and Uncle Lloyd unload the boat and carry everything inside. I debated revealing myself and helping, but the long swim to Eden's Hammock, combined with the endless management of affairs in Rathe, had left me exhausted.

"Yara?" Treygan called from Uncle Lloyd's deck a few minutes later. "You're here somewhere, I sense you."

Staying perfectly still so my hammock wouldn't sway and reveal my location, I sidled a glance through the holes in the netting. In a beautiful blend of mer and human, Treygan wore shorts and nothing else, showing off the black, blue, and indigo hallmarks decorating his skin. He ran his hand through his dark hair as he turned in a slow circle, scanning the beach and water.

"I give up," he shouted. "Show yourself."

I turned my head so I could see him better. Only a few feet away, my hammock was within his peripheral vision, so I lifted one arm straight up. I concentrated on my selkie side, and then my camouflaged arm changed to skin so white and silvery it appeared frosted. My selkie claws glistened in the sunlight as I wiggled my fingers. For fun, I channeled my energy and connected with the humidity in the air. Bolts of heat lightning

Sacred Seas

flashed from my fingertips and up into the sky. "Over here."

Treygan turned, smiling at my little light show. The lightning fizzled to a dull buzzing as I let my mer side surface. Colorful hallmarks of vines and other symbols appeared on my pearly skin. He walked over and stood above me. The sun was behind him, so his face was only a silhouette. "Playing hide and seek?"

"You knew I was here." The hammock was usually my hiding place of choice.

He lifted my hand and kissed my wrist. "Maybe, but sometimes I like reassurance that you want to be found."

"Found by you? Always."

He climbed in with me, causing the hammock to sway. I turned on my side to face him, not only so I could look into his indigo eyes, but because I missed being in his arms. As I traced the Canis Major constellation of freckles on his face, he asked, "How is everything in Rathe?"

"Busy and busier. I almost feel guilty for taking a break. It's one of those days when I'd like to pretend I'm just an insignificant island girl and relax in a bubble of ignorant bliss."

"Technically, we are in a bubble."

Uncle Lloyd had cloaked the whole island in a spell so we wouldn't have to hide who and what we were anymore. We were free to be ourselves until he reopened Eden's Hammock for vacationers again. *If* he ever did.

Treygan stroked my cheek and looked at me with so much love that it warmed every part of me, monster and human. "No matter how hard you try, you could never be insignificant."

There it was. Another of the never-ending reminders that I was the new co-ruler of Rathe—a job which entailed a lot of drama and overwhelming responsibility. I sighed, frustrated with myself that I wasn't transitioning into my role with more grace and confidence. Medusa was the confident and graceful one. How could I ever meet the expectations of a legendary goddess?

"Call me selfish," I told Treygan, "but I'd like to put everything else on pause while I reconnect with you."

He stared at me for a long moment, his lashes fluttering as unreadable thoughts raced through his mind. In a sad voice, he asked, "So you feel like we've become disconnected?"

"That's not what I meant." I pressed my forehead to his. "We've had so much to deal with, and the burden never seems to lighten. Whenever I think we're going to have some quality alone time, someone interrupts because they need something."

He tucked my head under his chin and wrapped his arms around me. I relaxed against him, inhaling his comforting smell and savoring the solidity of him.

"Rathe is in a state of flux," he said. "Once everything is stable again we'll have more alone time. Until then, whenever we can, we'll steal private moments like this to tide us over."

I curled into a ball, hoping he'd find a way to cocoon himself around me and hide us from the rest of the worlds.

He kissed the top of my head. "We're still connected, Yara. We always will be. Our bond is unbreakable."

I kissed the stone anchor hallmark above his heart. Treygan was my anchor. He didn't let me go adrift in Harte. I almost gave myself over to the darkness in that evil place, but Treygan kept me tethered to the light. Hell had tried to separate us, and it had failed.

"Unbreakable," I agreed in a whisper.

Right on cue, I sensed unwelcomed company approaching. I closed my eyes and focused on my camouflage ability, letting myself blend with Treygan and the hammock.

He groaned when he realized what I was doing. "Who is it this time?"

"Otabia and Mariza."

"I wish you could make me invisible too."

My concealing powers wouldn't hide me from the sirens because they could also sense me, but I still tried my best. Seconds later, their flapping wings blew my hair back as they landed steps away from our hammock.

"Go away," Treygan grunted at them, still holding me tight.

I didn't look up, but I could see Otabia's black boots as she stomped toward us. Mere inches from my face, her long talons grabbed the edge of the hammock. I dropped my camouflage and tried to sit up just as she yanked hard and flipped Treygan and me into the sand.

Otabia didn't bat a glaring eye. "Stop lounging around and give us a replacement!"

I sprang to my feet as my wings formed and flew open. They made me feel bigger and more powerful, which helped during arguments with Otabia and Mariza. I extended my hand to help Treygan up, but he was already standing and brushing sand from his shorts.

My head tingled as Sage shot forward and hissed. She was emotionally connected with me even when she wasn't physically present and she always materialized to defend me when I felt attacked. I squared my shoulders and glared at my pesky siren sisters. "I told you, selecting someone is not that simple."

Mariza flung her long brown hair behind her. "Stheno said they gave you their approval."

"Yes, but I still need to choose the right candidate," I countered. "We don't exactly have applicants waiting in line to fill the position."

Otabia glowered at me with her cold ebony eyes. "You are a ruler of Rathe. It is your duty to maintain the balance of our realm and its creatures. We are out of balance. Fix it."

"I'm trying my best."

"By spending so much time here in the human realm? Go back to Rathe and do your job."

Otabia was getting in my face, but I knew she was holding back. Since our return from Harte, she had been speaking to me with a little more respect. Not much more, but it was an improvement. I huffed and relaxed my wings. Sage settled on my shoulder. "Nixie hasn't even been gone a month. Why are you in such a rush?"

"We are growing weaker the longer we are without a third,"

Otabia explained. "Our trinity has never been incomplete this long. It's unacceptable."

Even though I was part siren, it wasn't enough to fill the vacancy left by Nixie's physical death. It also meant I wasn't affected by their trinity being incomplete. Unless that was the reason I was always so tired lately.

"What about when my mother left you?" I picked sand from my wings. The topic of my mom made me fidgety, especially around Otabia and Mariza. They knew so much about her, and I knew so little. "Weren't you short one siren until Nixie was promoted?"

"Cleo was smart," Otabia said. "She planned ahead. Nixie was ready to take her new position the day Cleo deserted us. Your mother was a lovesick fool, but she never would have left us incomplete."

Mariza poked me in the chest with a mud-colored talon. "Apparently, you didn't inherit her wisdom or consideration."

"Hey, watch it." Treygan stepped to my side.

I motioned for him to stay out of it with one hand while slapping Mariza's talon away with the other. "I didn't know Nixie would die."

"But she did, and you haven't done anything to replace her."

"She can never be replaced." I hated how they made Nixie sound so disposable. She died to save me, Treygan, Rownan, Vienna, Jenna, and Keeley. She deserved better, especially from her two sisters. Rubbing the sore spot on my chest, I said, "We should allow time to grieve."

Mariza flipped her shimmering brown hair over her shoulder with a huff. "Why impose your human bereavement customs on us? So we can feel sick and miserable?"

"For most people, that's the gist of grieving."

"We are not *most people*," Otabia quipped. "We are sirens. We grieve our fallen in our own way. Select a third for us by the Eve of Poseidon or we will kidnap those precious little sprites of yours and terrorize them."

Part of me knew they were right and it wasn't fair of me to judge them by human standards. A bigger part of me was furious they would drag Nixie's sprite family into this. When I replied, my tone was icier than the selkie side of Rathe. "You wouldn't."

"Wouldn't I?" Otabia kept her gaze locked with mine as she lifted her ebony wings. "Don't test me, Yara. You won't like the outcome."

My wings lifted higher and wider than hers. "Ditto to you, sister of mine. Do I need to remind you that I'm one of Rathe's rulers?"

She threw me a look of utter disdain and Mariza snickered. The two of them strutted away and took off, flying out over the water without a glance back at me.

"The Eve of Poseidon," I groaned. "She has to be joking!"

The Eve of Poseidon was a sort of holiday in Rathe. Treygan had told me that for eight days at the end of Stheno's season, Rathe's suns and moons stopped moving in the skies, giving Stheno, Euryale, and Medusa's energy a renewal period. Poseidon's energy would take over, and Rathe's residents believed he watched them closely during that time. Treygan said that resulted in everyone behaving better than usual and praying to Poseidon to grant their hearts' desires, like human kids being extra good at Christmastime and writing letters to Santa. Apparently, most sea creatures thought they had a better chance of receiving help from Poseidon or Medusa than from Stheno and Euryale. I understood and agreed with that assessment. The holiday spirit of the Eve of Poseidon was why we chose it for our reunion celebration.

In Rathe, time was measured by tide cycles: low, mid, and high. After high tide the cycle started over again, signaling the beginning of a new day. The Eve of Poseidon was one full cycle away, or tomorrow night based on Florida time. On top of everything else going on, Otabia was insisting I find a fill-in for Nixie by tomorrow night.

I rubbed one of my temples as Sage soothed the other. Finding a new third siren was one of the unchecked items on my list, but I had been trying. None of the mermaids were willing to trade their existence of sun and warmth for a life of hunting morally challenged human men, stealing their memories, and then regurgitating their blood for Stheno and Euryale. Even the gorgon kin, who I thought wouldn't be grossed out by the job description, politely declined.

"Looks like your break is over," Treygan said gingerly.

Hiking up the long skirt of my sundress so I wouldn't trip, I walked up the beach to Uncle Lloyd's house. "Maybe a selkie will want the job. They're used to drinking blood." Treygan followed me as I continued. "But I don't know any of the females very well except for Vienna, and she won't want to do anything except make up for lost time with Rownan."

"True," he agreed. "If I were you, I'd start with Eve. All those years she spent helping Jack run the bar, she dealt with her share of unsavory human men. She might enjoy a bit of vengeance as a siren."

"Good idea." I sped up, excited by Treygan's suggestion, but he caught me by the wrist and made me stop and turn to face him.

"Or . . ." He tucked a strand of my wind-blown hair behind my ear. "I know you were respectfully avoiding discussing her replacement with her, but perhaps it's time to consult Nixie. Maybe she knows someone who would want the job."

Nixie hadn't fully crossed over. As my mother had done, Nixie chose to stay in the Inbetween so she could help me. Her reasoning was that, dead or alive, she was my assigned siren and it was her duty to protect me. As much as I loved still having her around, I didn't want her stuck in limbo for years like my mother. I wanted her to enter the Eternal Falls and have the peace she so greatly deserved. I wasn't ready for her to leave me yet, but the day would eventually come when we'd have to say goodbye to each other. "No one could ever replace Nixie."

"I agree wholeheartedly." He grinned, knowing as I did that

Nixie—in invisible spirit form—was most likely eavesdropping on our conversation.

We climbed the ramp to Uncle Lloyd's back deck. He was maneuvering his wheelchair with one hand while he watered his potted plants. He paused to look at me then lowered his watering can. "Your wings are out. I take it that wasn't a friendly visit from Otabia and Mariza?"

I morphed back into human form and adjusted the back of my dress where my wings had bunched down the fabric. "They want a third siren appointed. I understand why it's important to them, but they're being unreasonable about how fast they want it done."

Uncle Lloyd returned to watering his flowers. "Those two have never been reasonable about much of anything."

"I second that," Treygan said. "Moving on to a different topic, what's the verdict on relocating the gateway?"

My fatigued muscles twitched at the reminder. "Denied."

The gateway to Earth was on the far outskirts of Rathe, so even flying there required extra travel time. Those who needed to swim took longer. Ages ago, when Medusa and Poseidon created Rathe, they hadn't planned on commuting to the world from which they'd been banished, but my situation was different. I needed to check on Uncle Lloyd regularly, and Eden's Hammock still felt like my true home. Traveling back and forth every day was exhausting and took valuable time out of my crammed schedule. I tried rationalizing with Stheno and Euryale about how moving the gateway closer to Gorgon Rock would be beneficial for everyone, but they refused to even listen to me.

I flopped down in a patio chair and sighed. "How am I supposed to get anything done when I need Stheno and Euryale to approve any and all changes? It's impossible."

"Appeal to their greedy side." Uncle Lloyd rolled himself over to the spigot and refilled his can. "Offer them something in exchange for their cooperation."

I grunted at the suggestion. I had already offered the gorgon sisters more horrible memories in exchange for the power to approve decisions on my own. Given how much they liked to see me suffer, I thought they'd jump at the chance to experience more of my trip to literal hell. But they had no interest in any of my other memories of Harte. I had lost my bargaining power by giving them a memory that had them acting like drug addicts.

Uncle Lloyd patted my knee as he rolled past me. "You'll find a way to make it work."

He had more faith than I did. Hands down, I had the worst sisters in all the worlds. Growing up an only child, I had always wished for a sibling, but now that I had inherited two gorgon sisters who hated me and two siren sisters who bossed me around, I wanted to retract my wish.

Whistling happily, Uncle Lloyd rolled down the ramp and into his garden.

"He's been out of Rathe for too long," I quietly told Treygan. "He doesn't remember how horrible Stheno and Euryale are. I wish a rogue wave would swallow them and carry them away. For good."

Treygan chuckled. "The sea isn't always bluer on the other side."

"I know that. But I thought Stheno and Euryale were rude and spiteful before we went to Harte. Now they're ten times worse and practically useless."

Treygan walked through the open door to the kitchen. Bottles clanged together, and the cupboard doors squeaked open then shut. A few seconds later he returned with two glasses of juice and handed one to me. "I still don't understand their obsession. Harte's evil and twisted world is really that enticing to them?"

"Apparently."

"It would be interesting to know what memory you gave them."

I took a few gulps of my drink. "I'm sure it was something scary and horrible."

I shivered thinking about our dreadful experiences in Harte. I would have been happy to give all those memories away, but Stheno and Euryale only wanted the one they currently fought and obsessed over.

I hadn't told Treygan the whole truth about the problem. Mainly because I refused to believe what Nixie had told me. According to her, I'd given the gorgon sisters memories of my encounter with a kraken. Not some huge squid-ish monster like the name implied. Nixie had heard Stheno and Euryale describe him as exquisite, intoxicating, exotically beautiful, and soul-shatteringly seductive. Which, so Nixie claimed, is why I'd had a hot and heavy makeout session with him.

Thinking about it made my stomach hurt. I didn't want it to be true. I couldn't even imagine cheating on Treygan. Why would I have made out with a morally depraved monster from Harte who apparently had tentacles? Yuck.

But Stheno and Euryale weren't faking their obsession. Disturbing and disgusting as it was, they took turns regurgitating and drinking my blood that contained the memory of the kraken encounter.

"Whatever you gave them," Treygan said, sitting beside me and motioning to Uncle Lloyd, "it was worth it, right?"

Uncle Lloyd rolled his wheelchair along the garden path. Still whistling a cheery tune, he stopped to prune his gardenia shrubs.

In exchange for giving Stheno and Euryale all of my kraken memories, they had lifted the curse on Uncle Lloyd and reversed the damage they had done to his health. Uncle Lloyd could see again. No more kidney dialysis. No more hacking up his lungs. Even his legs were gradually getting stronger.

I wanted him to let Indrea and Caspian attempt to completely heal him, but he claimed their powers wouldn't work on him since he had turned human. He said his weak legs were nothing compared to how good he felt everywhere else, and he was determined to be rid of his wheelchair soon.

He glanced up at us and caught me staring at him. Smiling, he held up a beautiful white flower. I smiled back and lifted my cup of juice in salute.

Treygan wrapped his arm around my waist and rested his chin on the top of my shoulder. "Look how happy he is. You gave him the greatest gift of all. Well worth whatever price you paid."

I wanted to tell Treygan the truth, but like a hundred other times, I couldn't find the courage. We had just returned from hell. I didn't want to put more strain on our relationship by confessing I had cheated on him. I tried making myself feel better by arguing that I didn't remember it, so as far as I was concerned it never happened. But truthfully, my guilt and worry ate away at me every day and night.

My focus shifted to the beach where Rownan and Vienna were decorating for their ceremony. Keeley and Jenna flitted around them adding flowers, seashells, sea glass, and sparkles to anything and everything.

I had no idea what happened at a selkie wedding, or in this case a vow renewal, but I was glad to celebrate a joyful occasion. Watching Rownan and Vienna together made me smile, but then something caught my attention on the other side of the beach near my favorite hammock.

Squinting to see it better, I realized it was a shabby vessel made of half-rotted wood. "Looks like a raft or some kind of debris washed up on the beach."

"Probably remnants from an old shipwreck," Treygan said. "The tide will take it back out soon."

I shuddered. "Will you please get rid of it? It reminds me of the raft we floated around on while we were in Harte. It gives me the creeps."

He stood and kissed my forehead. "Consider it gone."

As he walked down the ramp, I admired the view of him. His confident, strong gait, his broad and muscular back, even his calves were sexy. Besides being physically ideal, he had every mental, emotional, and moral attribute I could ever ask for in a guy. I had fallen so deeply in love with him. I had no reason to ever want anyone else.

3

Koraline

Losing someone is infinitely harder than loving them. I came to that realization while I was in a coma.

After the sharks attacked me, I faded into unconsciousness and ended up in the Inbetween. I had to make an impossibly difficult decision: fight to live, or pass through the Eternal Falls. The lure of peace tempted me, but I considered all the people I would leave behind. They weren't ready to lose me, and I wasn't ready to be lost.

I used Harriet Stowe's famous words as my mantra. "Never give up, for that is just the place and time that the tide will turn."

I turned my back on the magnificent waterfall. I chose to cling to life, regardless of how fast it sifted through my ghostly fingers. When I made my decision, I didn't realize I'd be able to watch over the living in spirit form. It seemed like a miraculous gift. At first, anyway.

During my healing ceremony, every mermaid and merman in Paragon Hall touched me body and soul. Even though my soul wasn't in my body, I felt them. Every pair of fingers against my eyelids, every bit of love, hope, and healing energy gave me more strength. By the end of the ceremony when Yara made the final pledge, I truly believed I would pull through. Their love and prayers gave me the strength to survive.

I found myself wanting to be everywhere at once: making sure Pango was okay, giving Treygan and Yara signs that they should be together, and swinging my ethereal fists at Rownan's head to keep him away from Yara. Not that anything I had tried actually worked. I was a spirit. Nothing solid about me except my will to live.

It didn't take long for the Inbetween to become less of a gift and more like a curse. Watching and listening to people be upset, make bad decisions, fight feelings they shouldn't be fighting, and focus their energy on pointless stuff was beyond frustrating.

One part was worse than all of that combined—being unable to make contact with Joel.

Joel was my best-kept and most treasured secret.

He was the guy who put a bounce in my step and set my soul aglow. I hadn't told anyone else about him, so he had no way of knowing I had been attacked by sharks and was in a coma.

I visited him many times. I tried splashing water on him, moving objects around his house, turning the pages of his books as he read them. None of it worked. I was an invisible presence no one could sense.

Joel started suspecting something had happened to me when I didn't show up at our planned picnic on an uninhabited island a few miles off the coast of Key Largo. He took his boat out and searched all of our favorite places from sunrise until sunset. When the sun melted into the ocean, so did my heart. If I didn't survive, Joel would never know what had happened to me. He would think I had abandoned him.

That night, I stayed beside him after he anchored his boat. He took off his glasses and sat there for hours, silent and staring at the lapping waves. Even though he couldn't feel me, I curled up against him and listened to him breathe. It's amazing how the quiet sound of the breath of someone you love can be more beautiful than any song or poetry.

"I love you," I told him. "If I could go back and do it all over, I would marry you. I wouldn't care that it was forbidden."

Knowing he couldn't hear me only intensified my guilt over saying no to his proposal. I had wanted to say yes. I had wanted to scream yes and jump into his arms, but I had followed the rules instead of my heart. As always, when soul-deep instincts are ignored, regret inevitably follows.

As I clung to him in my spirit form, my heartache suffocated me. If I lived, I vowed to never again regret any choice I made. I needed that moment of clarity. The desire to correct my mistake was one of my most powerful reasons to survive.

One bleak day, my life force felt extremely low so I blipped over to Pango to see how he was holding up. I didn't have to blip very far. When the fog cleared, I was with Pango on the mainland, heading directly for Joel's bookstore.

My worlds were about to collide and all I could do was watch, wait for the explosion, and hope the wreckage would be minimal.

The rusty bells above the door jingled as Pango entered the store. The welcoming potpourri of old books, coffee, and tea that had flooded over me every time I walked through that door was now painfully absent. Another thing I missed about living: smells.

My brother didn't seem to notice the heavenly scent. He simply walked ahead, scanning the aisles. I saw Joel before Pango did.

Joel stood on a stepladder, stocking the Local Interests section. He didn't have to look down very far when Pango walked up to him. Pango was almost as tall as him even with Joel standing on the second step of the ladder.

"May I help you?" Joel asked him, friendly and polite as always.

"Your name is Joel, is it not?"

Joel grinned and pointed to his name tag. "According to this it is."

"We need to have a chat. Can you take a break?"

Joel slid the last book in its slot. "I don't know what you—" He froze and looked at Pango again. "Are you Koraline's brother?"

Pango nodded, and Joel nearly jumped off the ladder.

"I'm so sorry. I had no idea." Joel leaned in and whispered, "Koraline said you had green hair. The blond threw me off." He shook his hand while Pango evaluated his every word. "I've wanted to meet you for so long, but Koraline would never introduce us. I haven't seen her in over a week. Where is she? Is she okay?"

Pango glanced around at customers with their noses in books. "Can we step outside?"

"Absolutely. Right through here."

As soon as they stepped through the back door, Joel looked up at him with eager eyes. "Please, tell me she's all right."

Pango saw the genuine concern on Joel's face. He motioned to the steps. "You should sit down."

Joel declined, anxiously rocking from foot to foot, a dozen different emotions crossing his face. I was so worried about him that I could barely process what Pango was saying. "Attacked . . . sharks . . . coma . . . I'm sorry."

Joel put his hands over his chest and dropped to his knees. I hovered in front of him, trying to caress his face and comfort him, but of course I couldn't. Meanwhile, Pango kept piling on the dismal news.

According to my brother, I had gone downhill rapidly in the last couple of days. My lungs had collapsed. I was only alive because of a machine.

"Stop!" I shouted to my thickheaded brother. "No more details!"

No one heard me. Pango told Joel everything: how I almost died protecting Yara from sharks, the extent of my injuries, and my slim chances for survival.

The update was a shock to me too. I had been so worried about everyone else that I had forgotten to check on my own body.

Joel begged my brother to take me to a hospital. Pango and I both shook our heads. Caspian and Indrea had far more medical experience than any human doctor, and much more power to heal. If they couldn't fix me, no one could. Pango told Joel they didn't think I'd live, and my only hope for survival was the gateway opening soon. And if I couldn't be healed in Rathe, at least I could have a proper mer funeral.

Pango tried to help Joel to his feet, but Joel swayed sideways until he caught hold of the stair railing and sank down again.

For a long time they sat together on the back steps of the store. Neither one cried or spoke a word. They didn't make eye contact. Pango looked at the ground then the sky. Joel took off his glasses and stared at his hands.

"*We the Living*," Joel muttered.

My heart burst with love and remorse.

Pango glanced at him, confused. "Come again?"

"That's how we met," Joel explained. "Koraline came into the store, asking me if we had a book called *We the Living* by Ayn Rand. I knew I didn't have it in stock, but Koraline captivated me from the second she spoke. I asked her what the story was about so I could hear her talk more. She told me the plot so passionately, even quoted a couple lines. I had to see her again, but didn't have the guts to ask her out, so I promised I'd order a copy for her and told her to come back in a week." His shoulders bounced and his head bobbed with silent laughter. "I really overdid it. A collector in Arizona had a signed first edition from 1936. A thousand dollars later I had the book, wrapped in tissue paper, waiting for her."

"She paid a thousand dollars for a book?"

"No, she expected the reprinted anniversary edition for twenty bucks, but man, you should have seen her face light up when she unwrapped the first edition." Joel leaned back and closed his eyes. "I told her she could have it for free if she'd go on a date with me. She said no. I felt like the biggest loser in the world. Then she came back a few days later and told me she'd go out with me, but she couldn't accept the book. She knew roughly what I'd paid for it." Joel smiled sadly. "She said she liked me because I was thoughtful and kept promises, not because I had a collectible book she wanted."

Grinning at the memory, I stared at Joel, feeling that new-love rush all over again. I had wanted to kiss him so badly then. But I hadn't because I didn't want to seem too easy, and I couldn't now because it was impossible.

Pango sighed, sadness and heartache blending in one whoosh of breath. "You two met about three years ago, correct?"

"How'd you know?"

"That's when she changed. She sang a lot, went on more research trips, didn't check in as much, and stopped looking at all the hot mermen like she used to. I suspected she had a secret beau, but I assumed she'd tell me when she was ready. When it started to look like she wouldn't come out of the coma, I realized her special someone might not know. I felt awful snooping, but I read her journals to find out who she was seeing. She had written volumes about you. I had to find you and explain what's happened. Koraline wouldn't want you to think she abandoned you." Pango patted Joel's hand. "I wish we could have met under better circumstances."

Bless my barely beating heart. I had the best brother in the worlds. A snoop, yes, but a caring snoop with honorable intentions.

Joel nodded. "Me too. I don't know how many times I've asked her if we could meet. The last dozen or so were because I wanted to ask you for your blessing. She always refused, so I proposed anyway."

If I had solid hands, I would have covered my eyes. Joel proposing to me was such a big secret that I hadn't even written it in my journal.

"Proposed?" Pango choked.

Joel shrugged. "Don't worry, she said no. Told me it wasn't allowed in your world—a mermaid marrying a human."

"It's true," Pango sighed. "Sad but true."

"Why isn't it allowed?"

"A few wormy apples ruined the bunch. You know how it goes."

Joel grunted in understanding and looked at the sky. "Do you think there's one afterlife for everyone? Humans, merfolk, whatever else is out there?"

Oh, how I wished there could be. Watching my brother and the man I loved together, I wished our worlds and heavens weren't divided. But I had seen what awaited me if I passed through the waterfall. It was for sea creatures only.

"I don't know what awaits us after this life," Pango answered.

"I hope there's only one heaven." Joel fiddled with his glasses. "Maybe she'll wait for me."

"No, Joel," I said, moving closer and trying to caress his face. "Don't let my death crush your brave spirit."

"Koraline would want you to love again," Pango told him. "You're how old? Mid-twenties or so? You've got a long life ahead of you."

I cringed. That was the worst thing my oblivious brother could have said.

Joel had an undiagnosed disease that resembled cystic fibrosis. His doctors estimated he'd live to thirty, forty if he was lucky. I had prepared myself for losing him first, but watching him lose me, hurting him so deeply, was much worse.

"I wish I could see her one last time." Joel spun his glasses, clenching his eyes shut and fighting back tears.

He quoted one of my favorite lines from *We The Living*. He said it so quietly that Pango didn't hear him over the garbage truck passing through the alleyway, but I heard him. "'When a person dies, one does not stop loving him, does one?'"

"No," I answered, sitting between the two men I cherished most. I tried to hold their hands. "One never does. I will love you both eternally."

Between that and hearing Pango tell Joel how bad off I was, I had no hope left. Together, over those next few days, Joel and

I sank into a deep depression.

I spent most of my time with him, curling up beside him while he slept, hovering so close I could almost imagine the way his breath used to feel on my skin, wanting to kiss his lips, trying to wipe tears from his eyes as he stared at the ocean telling me he loved me again and again.

And then, the day after the Triple Eighteen, the tide turned.

One moment I was with Joel, pretending he could feel me running my fingers through his hair. The next moment, I fidgeted awake, disoriented and questioning why I was staring at a periwinkle tree with stardust twinkling among its leaves. The rays of three suns stretched far and wide above me.

Pango leaned over me and smiled. "Welcome back to Oz, my brave and precious Dorothy."

I was in Rathe.

Alive. In Rathe. Our glorious, magical, sight-for-sore-eyes Rathe. Yara and Treygan had done it. The gateway had opened. After almost two decades of being locked out, we were home.

I should have been ecstatic, but my body and heart felt so heavy. The physical pain was enough to bring me to my knees—if my knees hadn't been eaten by sharks. How would I ever swim back to Joel with only half of my tail? How would I ever swim again at all? All I wanted was to swim back through the gateway and into Joel's arms, but I couldn't.

Instead, I lifted my arms, which felt like two bags of wet sand, and I hugged my brother.

His huge hands cradled me as he lifted me into a sitting position. I wanted to assess the damage to my tail, but I was covered with large leaves from the waist down.

"How bad is it?" My voice came out gruff and scratchy.

Pango's emerald lips curved into a pitiful but positive smile. "It doesn't matter. You're still the most enchanting mermaid in all the worlds."

My throat and mouth were so dry, but I managed to swallow before voicing my biggest fear out loud. "Will I ever swim again?"

Pango sighed and held my face in his hands. "That's like asking if the sun will ever shine again."

Fast forward through my excruciating recovery, countless healing sessions with the Violets, Yara, Treygan, and Rownan's journey to Harte, and the agonizingly long days of waiting for the mechanism that would allow me to see Joel again.

The big day had finally arrived.

Pango finished helping me attach the engineered fluke over the stretchy sleeve cinching my waist and what was left of my tail.

"It feels unnatural," I told Pango.

"Of course it does," he laughed. "It's a prosthetic tail. But if that darling dolphin in Florida can make it work, so can you."

I had been trying to remain optimistic about the fact that I'd never feel my fins again, or walk on human legs. I only cried when no one else was around, and even then I'd only cry for a few minutes before reminding myself that self-pity wouldn't get me anywhere. It wouldn't help me swim again. It wouldn't reunite me with Joel any quicker.

"If you need help, I'll be right by your side," Pango assured me. Even though he had recently been promoted and his hair and eyes had changed to electric blue, his heart was still the same—hero-sized.

I smiled at him, recalling a memory from when we were kids. He'd wanted so badly to learn how to ride a bicycle. I'd run beside him, holding the back of his seat, assuring him he could keep going if I let go. He'd always squealed and told me he couldn't do it without me. Now I felt the same about him.

"You're making great progress," Pango continued. "However, my offer still stands if you'd rather—"

"No." I cut him off. "Our reunion will not consist of me

rolling up in a wheelchair." I had imagined reuniting with Joel a million times. Daydreams of us running into each other's outstretched arms were shattered by the realization that we'd never even stroll down a street together again. I'd never ride a bike again. I had a long and growing list of Never Agains. "We have to meet in the water."

Pango nodded. "As it should be."

I rubbed the slick sleeve wrapped around my hips. "He's human. How is our relationship supposed to last if I can't ever go on land again?"

"We can get you back on land too. Don't worry your pretty little head."

"What am I going to do? Swim around with prosthetic legs strapped to my back and swap them with my mechanical tail every time I want to go for a walk? What a nightmare."

"Hey, sweet sister of mine." He tugged on one of my pigtails. "The situation is not ideal, I'll give you that, but you two love each other. You'll find a way to make it work."

"What if he doesn't want to be with me anymore?"

"Then perhaps I'll rip off his legs and you two will be a perfect match."

I glared at him and he chuckled.

"Kidding!" He repositioned a flower in my hair as if it wasn't going to get ruined during our long swim. "Joel is an intelligent young man who knows you're the best thing that has or will ever happen to him. He most definitely wants to be with you. He still can't believe you're making him wait. He doesn't care about your injury."

"He can say that now because he hasn't seen it. Once he does, everything will be different."

"Koraline, he truly loves you. True love accepts you as you are. All of you. The best parts and the broken ones."

Biting my lip, I nodded. Joel did love me. I didn't doubt that. But my confidence was lacking. Losing limbs will do that to a person.

Pango tugged on my hair again. "At least you don't have to keep him a secret from me anymore."

I swallowed hard and stared out the window toward Indrea and Caspian's home nearby. "True, but what happens if anyone else finds out?"

"Innocent until proven guilty. Now, slide into the water and let's make sure everything feels comfortable for our long sea voyage."

We both knew I wasn't innocent. I had a forbidden relationship with a human. The sweetest, smartest, and kindest human I'd ever encountered. I was about to see him again for the first time since the day before the shark attack. No matter what my punishment, I would never again feel guilty for being in love with Joel.

My almost-death had changed me. In spirit form, I saw things people thought were private. I discovered truths that I would use to protect myself if needed. I was no longer ashamed of my love for a human because I had learned one thing for certain while observing from the Inbetween: Everyone has secrets.

4

"Nixie?" I ran my fingertips over the smooth wood of her enchanted wall panel.

Seeing Nixie's carved image reminded me of happier days when she still flew by my side as a living being, instead of a spirit lingering in the Inbetween as my messenger to Medusa.

"I need your help." I stared at her teak eyes until they glowed ruby red. She seemed to transform from inanimate wood to a radiant ghostly version of herself, and I took a quick step back. I was still trying to get used to seeing her in spirit form.

Since Nixie swore it was still her duty to protect me, she watched over me more than I thought was necessary, so it was safe to assume she had witnessed my conversation with Mariza and Otabia. "What do I do about Otabia's threat?"

"Find my replacement." Her high-heeled boots made no sound on the floor as she strutted to the front door and passed through it. She liked to go outside during our talks. She claimed the fresh air made her feel better, but I always wondered if she actually felt anything in her current state.

I followed, opening the door and joining her on the porch. "Your soul is still here. Can't you keep your position as their third?"

"That's not how it works. They need a physical sister to connect with."

"Do you know anyone who would want the job?"

"No one comes to mind."

"What about when you were chosen? Weren't there other candidates?"

"A couple selkies, but Cleo never told me their names. And a few other sprites volunteered, but . . ." Her bright eyes dimmed to a chilling garnet. "Promise me right now that you will not give a sprite the position."

"If one of them wants it, then—"

"No! I thought I wanted it too, but it wasn't like I thought it would be. I don't want to see any of my sisters feeling that alone and homesick." She jabbed her finger at my chest, but it went through me. "You can't do that to them. They are too innocent, too good-natured. Don't change them from something so beautiful to something so sinister."

"Nixie, you weren't sinister."

"You don't know a fraction of the things I did. Promise me no sprite will ever be transformed into a siren."

I didn't want to make a promise if there was a possibility I'd have to break it out of desperation. What would I do if no one else wanted the position?

"Yara," Nixie growled. "Promise me or I will find a way to tell Treygan about your dirty secret."

"That's not fair."

She scoffed at me. "See? Sinister. I never would have black-mailed anyone when I was a sprite."

I didn't like limiting my options, but I owed it to Nixie. I owed my life—and the lives of several others—to her. "Fine. I promise. No sprite will be chosen for the job."

"Thank you. Now, I suggest asking Rownan and Vienna if any selkies have expressed interest. Every sea creature in Rathe knows a new siren must be selected. I'm sure the whole realm has been buzzing with gossip about possible candidates."

"I haven't heard any mention of it except from Mariza and Otabia."

"No one talks about the boss when she's around. They wait until your back is turned." She sat on the porch railing, swinging one boot as she examined her long red fingernails. I had asked her how she managed to look so alive and real, aside from the fact that I could see through her as if she were a hologram. She claimed to have a knack for projecting her old physical form in great detail, but she also gave credit to Medusa being a fantastic coach.

I sat on the railing across from her. "I want all the sea creatures to feel comfortable talking to me."

"They won't. You're their ruler. Rulers are feared."

"I don't want to be feared."

"You do want that. Fear will lead to respect."

"I'd rather be respected without the fear."

"Earning that kind of respect will take time. Currently, you've only proven that you were willing to die to open the gateway, and that you can survive a trip to Harte. You must also prove that you can keep Rathe running smoothly, and you have a lot to learn about successfully running a world. Especially one so magical."

"I know. Sometimes I think I'm not cut out for the job."

"You can say that again. Medusa is not impressed with your performance so far."

"Thanks." I hopped off the railing and sat in a porch chair. "That makes me feel even worse. What happened to your deep desire to help people?"

"Not people," she corrected. "You. And I am helping by telling you the hard, cold truth before you drown in self-pity and there's no way to resuscitate you."

I sighed. "I feel so inadequate compared to Medusa."

She glided over and sat in the seat beside me. "You have incredible power, abilities that most sea creatures would kill for, and a hot sea stud who is enamored with you. Can you buck up and be more grateful and confident?"

"I am grateful, but my confidence needs some serious work."

"No kidding. I'm surprised Treygan hasn't ditched you yet. Males don't like insecurity, you know. Keep this up and you'll be mermanless."

"And then there's that," I said. "Maybe he's too good for me."

"Oh, good gods, I did not agree to attend a pity party. Snap out of it."

Even though I was sure we were alone, I glanced around the property and at the living room window behind us before whispering, "That memory I gave to Stheno and Euryale is proof that I cheated on him."

"You don't even remember it." Nixie didn't bother lowering her voice because I was the only one who could hear her.

"Just because I don't remember it, doesn't change the fact that I did it."

"It was in Harte. Treygan would never hold you accountable for anything that happened in that hellish place."

I slumped back in my chair, rubbing my aching neck muscles. "Then why was I so afraid to tell him? Why did I give the memory to the gorgon sisters instead of admitting what I had done and begging for his forgiveness?"

"Because you didn't want to hurt him."

That truth gave me some small amount of comfort. I never wanted to hurt Treygan, but using that excuse seemed like the easy way out. Disappointment in myself plagued me like a virus I couldn't shake.

Nixie leaned toward me, examining my head. "Where is Sage? Why isn't she hissing some sense into you?"

"She's resting."

Nixie's brows rose. "Sage wouldn't want to rest while you're like this. You sent her away."

I shrugged. "I don't want to bother Sage with my stress and worrying."

"Oh, but you'll summon me and force me to deal with it?" She said it playfully. We both knew she loved that I always turned to her, which is why she appeared whenever I called. Nixie still thrived on being needed. And I needed her more than ever. "You're letting it get the best of you."

"Letting what get the best of me?" I asked.

"Harte. That twisted realm messes up every soul who enters it. You wouldn't be acting this pathetic if you'd fight the Harte Hangover a little harder."

"Harte Hangover?"

She shrugged. "Best name I could give it. You're glum, negative, and whiney. Plus, you're getting too skinny. You need to eat more. Come on, to the kitchen we go."

She passed through the bay window before I could argue, so I begrudgingly pushed myself out of my chair and went back inside. "Maybe you're right. I have a lot to be grateful for, right?"

"A whole lot." She ran her fingers over her portrait. "You received a second chance at life. You're already one step ahead of me." She pointed at her wooden corset. "My cleavage looked much better when I was alive. This carving is misleading."

"You're still here," I reminded her, ignoring any discussion about her cleavage. "You should be grateful too."

"I miss being solid, though. Existing in spirit form is for the birds."

"You're part bird."

"Not anymore." Nixie's grin mirrored mine. "There we go. Let's have more of that. Smile. Be happy. Live your life. Rule Rathe! But be sure to let me help. Yesterday I was so bored I almost jumped into the Eternal Falls just for something to do."

"Don't you dare," I warned her. "I need you."

"So you claim. Start proving it."

I walked past her into the kitchen. "You helped me choose a location for the big party."

"I still say you should have had it at The Divide. Party directly outside of Gorgon Rock and irritate Stheno and Euryale for the pure joy of it."

The Divide was the place where the selkie and mer sides of

Rathe met. Sunlight on the mer side, darkness on the selkie side, with Gorgon Rock sitting directly on the dividing line.

"This is a celebration of everyone returning home and re-uniting. The last place I'd have it is a place called The Divide. I hate that name."

"Why?"

"Because of the war that went on for almost two decades between the mer and selk."

"But thanks to you that's over."

I opened the refrigerator door, reviewed my options, and settled on starfruit. "A name like The Divide reminds everyone of their differences instead of embracing what we all have in common."

"Which is what?"

"Our love for Rathe. And each other. *All* the species of sea monsters."

"That reminds me, some of the gorgon kin accepted my invitation to the party."

Nixie shook her head. "Only you would insist on inviting the most introverted of all sea creatures. The gorgon kin aren't social by nature."

"Talus seemed happy to accept. Did anyone ever invite them to parties before?"

Nixie considered my question then shrugged. "I honestly don't know, but probably not since we like to avoid turning the majority of Rathe's residents to stone."

"Pshhh." I waved my hand. "Treygan and I can control our gorgon abilities. I'm sure after all this time they've learned to control theirs too. It's a new dawn for Rathe, and I'm glad that we're all coming together as one big family."

Nixie sighed. "Okay, but remember I warned you they aren't social. Don't take it personally if things go horribly wrong at this little get-together."

Rowman

"Hey, we need the boat again," I told Treygan. "Lloyd got a call from an old friend. He has to pick up something in town."

"We can all go together. I'm planning on heading back out in a few minutes."

I had found him on the dock, wearing gardening gloves and breaking boards over his knee. He tossed a couple of pieces into a pile on a tarp.

"What's with all the wood?" I asked.

"It washed up on the beach. I'm taking it to the Dumpsters behind Jack Frost's."

"Why don't you dump it on the other side of the island?"

"Smell it and then tell me you want it anywhere near your vow renewal ceremony." He waved a broken plank under my nose.

"Good gods! What's it made of, rotting fish?" The putrid smell reminded me of the graveyard beach in Harte where I had found Vienna. "If Jack catches you dumping that crap at his bar, he'll kill you."

"Jack could never catch me. Besides, I promised Yara I'd get rid of it for good. I don't want to chance the tide carrying it back here."

"Agreed." I didn't want Vienna getting a whiff of that stench. The last thing she needed was reminders of Harte. "Let's get moving. It's smelling worse by the second."

Our trip back into town was uneventful. Lloyd went off on his mystery errand while Treygan and I tossed the rotted wood into a Dumpster. When we finished, we washed our hands using a spigot behind Jack's bar. Then we washed them three more times at the boat slip while waiting for Lloyd.

"Seriously, what's with this smell?" I sprayed more boat cleaner on my fingers and scrubbed them with a deck brush. "It's relentless."

"I don't know, but I'm glad to be rid of the source." Treygan started the boat's blowers then gestured behind me. "There's Lloyd. Let's go home."

I turned around to see our father rolling himself down the dock, but I didn't see any bags. "Thought you were getting something?"

"I did."

I helped him onboard while Treygan loaded his wheelchair and stowed it away. "What'd you get?"

"Don't you worry about that." Lloyd scrunched his nose and jerked his head back. "You sure you threw everything out? I can still smell it."

"Even trashed the tarp," Treygan told him.

"I should have bought some bionic air freshener. Sorry that I didn't." Lloyd motioned for Treygan to start the engine. "Let's get this boat moving so we can air it out."

Hopefully, by the time I got back to Vienna I wouldn't smell like I'd been digging through a rotting whale corpse.

Several miles from shore, I was leaning over the side of the boat, letting the spray of water beat against my smelly hands, when Treygan snapped his head up and narrowed his eyes.

"What is it?" Lloyd asked him.

"I'm sensing two merfolk nearby. Two very familiar mer-folk." Turning around, he scanned the water as our boat slowed.

"Unless I'm reading her energy wrong, one of them is Koraline."

I straightened, searching with him. "How could that be?"

"I'm wondering the same thing."

"Should we check on them?" Lloyd asked.

"I feel obligated." Treygan turned to me. "I know you're eager to get back to Vienna, but would you mind?"

"Not at all."

We turned westward and spotted two swimmers in the far distance, heading toward the town we had just departed. The larger one was most definitely Pango.

Lloyd shut off the motor. "What's she doing out here? And how did she swim all this way?"

"We won't find answers standing around here." I nudged Treygan. "Go. You'll catch up to them faster if you swim."

"I won't be gone long." As he was pulling off his T-shirt, I spotted another boat on the horizon.

"More company heading directly toward them," I warned. "They aren't changing their course."

Treygan dropped his shirt then dove into the water.

"Should we be worried?" I asked my father.

"Probably. It's a full moon. That's usually when all hell breaks loose." Lloyd rubbed his knees as if they ached. "The High Priestess said to be cautious of rings around the moon."

"The High Priestess?" My gaze tightened on him. "Is that why you came back to town? To find her again?"

"No. Like I told you, I had to meet up with an old friend. She happened to be in the same place and gave me some useful information."

"Dad, she's a very old woman who is probably going senile. Don't take her doomsday predictions so seriously."

He smirked. "Son, don't forget that I'm a very old soul as well, and any predictions about dark veils over my sons will be considered with the utmost seriousness. Speaking of which, she gave me a message for you."

I rolled my eyes. "What message was that?"

"She said to tell you this time you'll be the one to help Treygan. That you'll have to act before it's too late."

"Too late for what?"

"That part she couldn't see, but she said changes were brewing that would end for better or worse based on the choices of two souls. I'm assuming those two souls are you and Treygan, but she couldn't confirm that. She did say the consequences would be life changing. Actually, I think the exact phrase she used was world changing."

The wind had picked up, so maybe the raised hair on my arms was simply a result of the weather and not the creeped-out feeling crawling up and down my spine. "It's like I said before. Psychic predictions are always vague so they'll fit nearly any situation." I wasn't sure who I was trying to convince, me or Lloyd. I looked away and searched the water for Treygan. "We make our own fate and determine our own future."

"You get that determination from your mother."

The mention of my mom made my throat tighten. I missed her more than I ever thought possible.

"Since we're alone, now is probably a good time to give you this." Lloyd pulled out a leather pouch and untied it. "Call it an early vow renewal present."

"You didn't need to get us anything."

He dumped a small object into his hand. I caught a flash of vibrant blue before he closed his fingers over it.

"Is this another gorgon bloodstone? How many of those do you have hidden away?"

"This is the only stone of its kind. It's only recently been returned to me, and I'll be damned if I let it go missing again on my watch, so you listen to me. Guard it with your life. I'm entrusting it to you because, well, because you are precious to me."

We had spent so many years not speaking. I'd made so many wrong assumptions about the man sitting in front of me. For a long time I thought he hated me, that he considered me a mistake he wished he could erase. I had wasted irreplaceable time and energy being angry at him instead of simply asking him for the truth.

Treygan was his planned son, born from the mermaid he loved and married. I was the bastard, born of the selkie woman who tricked him into giving her a child.

It wasn't a contest or a way to gauge who he loved more, but I had to ask. "Did you also give one to Treygan?"

He kept his eyes on the hand holding the rock. "This isn't about him. I'm entrusting it to protect *you*."

"Protect me from what?"

"From whatever is coming. It will also protect all the souls you love."

If the stone would protect Vienna, then I was sold. No further explanation required. "Do I need to do anything special for it to work?"

"Keep it safe."

I held out my hand, but he closed his eyes and began speaking in ancient gorgon. It always sounded like he was reciting a poem when he was casting a spell. Beams of bright blue light flowed like tiny rivers through the cracks between his fingers. The light faded when he stopped chanting, and he opened his hand to reveal a simple gray rock etched with blue veins.

He placed it in my palm and closed my fingers around it. "What I just did is our secret, understood?"

Still paranoid about meddling and being punished by our gods, even though Yara had released him from that curse. Poor guy. "Understood."

"Don't lose it. Keep it in your armband so it's on you at all times."

I unzipped the middle compartment of my armband and slid the stone inside. "Is this what you did for Yara?"

"What do you mean?"

"That necklace you gave her with gorgon blood. Did you cast a protective spell over it?"

"I did, but it turned out she didn't need my protection."

"That's not true. You protected her for years."

"I did what I could with my limited resources. I've done the same for you and Treygan. It's what you do for those you love. You do whatever is within your power to keep them safe."

In my father's own way, he had just told me he loved me. A rare sentiment for him.

"So this rock," I clarified, "will protect me and Vienna from harm?"

"And then some."

"Thanks, old man." I pressed my armband and the treasured stone inside it against my chest. "This means a lot to me."

Koraline

As I struggled to keep up with Pango, I cursed my prosthetic tail. I hated that I couldn't travel at my old speed. Pango had to swim slower than usual for my sake.

However, the energy of the day made up for all of that. The water was clear and shimmering as Earth's sun beat down from above. The coral below us seemed brighter. A pod of dolphins swam behind us, sensing my physical strain and giving me emotional support. They would give me physical support if needed, but I was determined to make it without assistance.

Pango's eyes met mine. *You okay?*

I'm holding up.

We're almost there.

Joel was meeting us at a specific intersection of longitude and latitude in a harbored span of water. The odds of another boater being there and seeing us in the middle of the ocean— with no vessel of our own—were slim, but we had to be safe. I didn't want to contribute to another mermaid sighting, and I couldn't simply morph into human form like before. Traveling to Earth's realm had become much more complicated for me.

Pango squeezed my hand, and even though he pretended he wasn't, he helped by pulling me along.

Please let Joel be there, I prayed.

The dull roar of a boat engine was music to my ears. I pumped my mechanical tail harder. We dove deep as a precaution in case it wasn't Joel, but as we swam closer, I saw familiar colorful artwork painted on the bottom of the boat.

I practically yanked Pango to the surface with me. The moment our heads burst through the water, Joel's engine shut off.

I breathed his name as sunlight reflected off his glasses. "Joel."

I smiled so big I thought my cheeks would tear in half. Joel leapt to his feet, waving at us as his boat coasted forward with the current. My smile faltered when I noticed the oxygen tubes attached to his nose, but I shook off my worry. Health hindrances—mine and his—would not ruin this happy reunion.

I swam closer until my fingertips trailed along the bow of *Jokor*. He had named his boat after us a little over a year ago. His artistic rendition of a colorful joker with an emerald mer tail smiled down at me. I had missed *Jokor*'s mischievous grin, but I'd missed Joel infinitely more.

I had waited an eternity for this moment, but it felt as if not even one day had passed when he reached over the side and our hands touched.

"Kor," he whispered, leaning down as far as he could until the plastic tubes tugged him back. I grabbed the side of the boat and lifted myself out of the water up to my waist. Our lips met and a squeal of glee caught in my throat.

Pango clapped as the dolphins whistled, clicked, and chattered around us, sharing in our happy reunion. Joel cradled my face and pulled back to look at me. "I almost forgot how radiant you are."

"You better not have forgotten anything about me," I teased.

He kissed me again and my heart soared straight up into the sky. I didn't care that Pango was watching. I could have clung to the side of that boat forever if it meant being able to kiss Joel.

But then Pango's words startled me. "Pardon my interruption, little love fishies, but we have a visitor approaching."

I tensed, lowering myself back into the water, and turned around to see Treygan's dark hair breaching the surface several feet away. I hadn't planned on getting caught, but of all people to get caught by, I was grateful it was Treygan.

"Well, hello," he said, greeting all of us as he slicked back his wet hair.

Pango's cheerful reply sounded forced and guilty. "Treygan! Imagine running into you out here in the wild blue yonder."

"Hi," I muttered.

Treygan looked over my head. "Joel, nice to see you again."

Joel had helped Treygan and the others get into Harte, so I knew they had spent time together, but actually seeing them interact still rattled me.

Joel wore a genuine smile as though nothing about Treygan's interruption worried him. "Always a pleasure, Treygan."

Treygan glanced between Pango and me. "I see you have a new development, Koraline. Mind if we dip below the surface so you can tell me about it?"

The intense look in his eyes said he wanted to know about more than just my new tail.

"Sure." I turned to Joel and flashed him an "it will be okay" grin. "We'll be back in a couple minutes."

He didn't seem one bit concerned as he adjusted his glasses over his twinkling eyes.

Once we were underwater, Treygan admired my new tail. *When and where did you get that?*

I rubbed the tight sleeve of the back-breaking contraption. *Pango had it made for me. The Violets approved it.*

He circled me, studying it, but like a gentleman didn't ask to touch it. *Why didn't you tell me about it?*

We haven't seen you since it arrived, and I didn't tell anyone ahead of time because I was afraid it wouldn't work. Plus, I wanted to surprise everyone by showing them I could swim again. I hoped my answer would be enough to keep him from asking me why I was so far from home, with such a new and risky device, and meeting with Joel.

Koraline, it's brilliant. And you already appear to be mas-

tering it. I'm so happy for you.

Thank you. I massaged my lower back. *This thing isn't exactly easy to operate, but it'll get better the more I use it.* I tried steering the topic away from me so he wouldn't ask the question I didn't want to answer. *Where's Yara?*

Eden's Hammock, destressing. He looked up at the surface then said, *Enough dancing around the issue. Why is Joel the bookstore owner waiting up there to meet with you two?*

So much for stalling. My focus darted to Pango, but he shrugged and pretended to examine his fingernails. Getting in trouble was the last thing Pango needed after his recent promotion to Blue.

Pango came with me in case I had issues with my new tail. I'm the one who wanted to meet with Joel.

Treygan's brow creased. *Why are you acting guilty?*

I glanced away again, but he dipped sideways and forced me to look at him. *Koraline?*

If anyone would understand that I couldn't help how I felt about Joel, it would be Treygan. He could have turned Yara to stone, but he still fought to be with her because he loved her. Joel was feet away, waiting for me to surface. I couldn't lie, and I didn't want to twist my words into something that would belittle my feelings for him. *We were together before my coma. This is the first time we've seen each other.*

Together? Treygan was far from stupid. The flash of shock on his face was gone in an instant, but I knew he understood.

Yes.

You've been having a forbidden relationship with a human?

Pango extended his sight so we could both hear his thoughts. *Treygan, you know as well as we do that we can't control who we fall in love with.*

In love? Treygan's eyes widened. *You're in love with him?*

I am, I declared, unashamed. *I have been for quite a while.*

Shades of gray and purple tinted his skin as he crossed his arms over his chest and went still. Nearly impossible to pull off underwater, Treygan's stony stance usually happened when he was angry, but those purple patches meant he was worried. *When do you plan on telling the Violets?*

I'm not planning on telling them. Please promise me you won't say anything.

Do you realize how serious this is? You're breaking one of our highest laws.

May I remind you, Pango said, *of a time not long ago when the Violets thought they knew what was best for you and Yara and tried separating the two of you.*

Treygan's tensed muscles relaxed.

Mm-hmm, Pango continued. *And let me also remind you that yours truly helped you defy the Violets so that you and Yara could spend time together and save all of your fellow sea creatures who had been so cruelly locked out of our realm.*

That was different, Treygan argued.

Not much different. We broke the rules for you and risked our necks in the name of love. The love you share with Yara. I'm sure your karmic debt could be repaid by doing the same for Koraline and Joel.

Treygan sighed, sending bubbles floating all around his head. *I wish I'd never witnessed any of this. I won't volunteer the information, but if anyone asks me directly, I will answer.*

That's all I ask. Thank you! I rushed forward and hugged him. *Thank you so much.*

Just be careful, he warned. *It's not only Caspian and Indrea deciding our fate anymore. Some of the elders are old-fashioned and won't be so lenient with your punishment if they find out about this.*

I'll be careful, I assured him. *Thank you again.*

I darted toward the surface, hoping Pango and Treygan would stay down there and chat for a while so I could have alone time with Joel.

It wasn't quite the uninhibited reunion I'd hoped for. I had to stay in the water because I couldn't risk being seen in my current state by anyone but Joel. He had to remain in the boat since he was attached to a portable oxygen tank—a new development since I had last seen him, and one I was concerned about.

After spending a few minutes gushing about how happy we were to see each other again and catching up on what had happened in the last few weeks, I asked, "Are you getting worse?"

"Yeah," he said, somehow still smiling, "but we knew that would happen."

I hoped worrying about me hadn't contributed to his decline. "I didn't expect it to happen so soon."

"Me either, but this disease is unpredictable."

"But you'll be okay, right? As long as you have the tank?"

He leaned down and stroked my cheek. "I'll be perfect now that I know you're safe."

Pango rejoined us and cleared his throat. "I'm popping up to tell you that Treygan has departed and I'm going for a swim." He winked at me. "How long would you like me to be gone?"

I started to reply, but Joel beat me to it.

"Actually," Joel said to Pango, "I'd like to talk with you too."

"Oh? Well, isn't that sweet of you." Pango said it nicely, but I could tell he was confused.

Joel pointed at his own eyes. "I noticed your eyes have changed. I take it you've been promoted?"

I grinned proudly at my brother. We were in human territory, so when his head was above the water his hair was sandy blond, but his eyes were a definite change from green to blue.

Pango blushed. "Indeed. I was promoted after my heroic assistance with the Harte shenanigans."

"I'm glad to hear it." Joel fidgeted with his nose tubes. "It greatly increases the odds of my plan working."

"What plan?" I asked.

Joel nervously glanced between my brother and me. He cleaned his glasses with the bottom of his T-shirt then put them back on. "Pango, I wish to be turned mer."

I stiffened.

Pango gasped and his hand flew to his throat. "Beg your brazen pardon?"

"You're a Blue. I'm human. You have to grant me a wish. I wish to be mer."

Pango's jaw dropped and he turned to me. "You told him about the genie curse?"

I shook my head, still in shock. "No! I would never."

"She didn't tell me," Joel said. "My grandfather did." His gaze lowered to his hands as he fidgeted with his oxygen tube. "And if you don't grant my wish soon, you might remain a Blue forever."

I stopped breathing. My ears rang. "Why does he have to grant your wish soon?"

Joel's comforting smile was long gone. "Because my doctors think I may only have a few weeks left to live."

I spent the next two hours alternating between crying, kissing Joel, and grilling him about exactly what his doctors had said, what tests they'd run, what treatments they'd tried. Pango was uncharacteristically quiet and had a funny look on his face the whole time, like he was torn between feeling sorry for Joel and wanting to throttle him for invoking the genie curse. His giant heart won out in the end, like always. He was the one who noticed Joel's oxygen tank was running low, and he gently insisted Joel head back to port for his own safety. Joel wouldn't leave before I did, so I gave him one more kiss and slipped under the waves with Pango.

Swimming away from Joel was one of the hardest things I had ever done.

What if his doctors were wrong and he had less than a few weeks left? Every time I saw him, I would worry it might be the last.

After only a few minutes of swimming, I needed a break. My back and stomach muscles ached, but not nearly as painfully as my heart.

Pango circled and hovered in front of me. *Everything will work out as it's meant to.*

The Violets won't approve his transformation. A part of my soul shriveled up thinking about it. *You know they won't.*

They have to. I refuse to be a victim of the genie curse and be stuck as a Blue forever. I'd look much better in indigo or violet. He was trying to lighten the mood to make me feel better, but it wasn't working. *We'll discuss it with Treygan and Yara before we present it to the Violets.*

Yara is a ruler now. She could issue me a punishment that would prevent me from coming back to see him.

He swam closer and lifted my chin. *Or maybe, just maybe, our new formerly-human ruler would sympathize and help us grant his wish.*

I blinked several times, trying to understand what my brother was suggesting. Then it dawned on me. *You mean, ask her to approve a transformation for Joel?*

I'm fairly sure she has authority over the Violets.

You're right! Why didn't I think of that?

Pango tilted his head. *But is that what you truly want? It would be a drastic change for him.*

Of course it's what I want. I loved Joel and I wanted to spend the rest of my life with him. If that time could be spent together in Rathe, it would make everything that much more perfect. I squeezed my brother's arms with excitement as I imagined Joel joining our world. *A drastically changed life is better than no life at all.*

6

After the family party at Uncle Lloyd's, Treygan and I sat on the deck of my old house, watching the moonlight dance across the water. When I was a child, my mother had sat in the same chair, staring at the same ocean, missing my father and Rathe so much that her depression eventually killed her. She had sacrificed her own happiness to give me life and a future of sunlight and freedom instead of eternal confinement in the gorgon grotto.

Treygan's deep voice cut through the silence. "Is there anything you'd like to bring from here to Rathe?"

"What do you mean?"

"Any personal belongings that would make you feel like a part of Eden's Hammock is with you in your new home."

He was implying the obvious without saying it out loud. I needed to spend more time in Rathe doing my job. I needed to stop clinging to Eden's Hammock and settle into my new home. *Our* new home. At least, I hoped he still wanted us to live together. "Do you mean home as in a place where you and I live together?"

"Of course I do. I asked you to move in with me before we went to Harte."

I looked past Treygan, down the beach to Uncle Lloyd's house. The house where I lived after my mother died. The house where I learned what *home* meant. "I'm worried about being so far from Uncle Lloyd."

"He's doing a million times better now that the curse has been lifted. He even walked around town today."

"Walked? Without his chair?"

Treygan grinned. "Well, he used his chair like a walker, but he said his legs have been aching less and he's been doing physical therapy. He walked around town for a solid ten to fifteen minutes at a time before he needed to rest."

"That's wonderful news! Why didn't he tell me?"

"He wants it to be a surprise. He plans to officiate at Rownan and Vienna's vow renewal while standing, not sitting in his wheelchair."

I was so proud of him, and so relieved that he might make a full recovery. I gazed out at the beach again, reflecting on how happy I was about Uncle Lloyd's health, but then my focus shifted to the shoreline and I bolted upright.

"What's wrong?" Treygan asked.

"I thought you got rid of that raft?"

"I did." He stood and followed my gaze. "I broke that thing into pieces, loaded it in the boat, and disposed of it in the Keys."

I stood too. Both of us stared at the waves lapping against the beached raft. Moments ago, it hadn't been there. I was sure of it. "It can't be. Right? No way could that be the same one from Harte."

"The one from Harte?" Treygan's head jerked back like the idea not only surprised him, but disgusted him. He wrapped his arm around me. "I highly doubt that. The tides must still be carrying in debris from somewhere."

I wanted to believe that, but my nagging intuition wouldn't let me. "Let's burn it."

"Burn it?"

"Yes." I hiked up my skirt and plowed forward. "Now."

"I'll grab matches," he called from behind me.

"No need," I shouted over my shoulder. "I've got my own fire."

I stomped through the sand and dragged the raft out of the

sea foam and onto dry land. I pushed my hair out of my face to examine the wet, rotting wood and caught a strong scent of vanilla and licorice. The raft looked exactly the same. Same as the one in Harte. Same as the one from this morning.

Treygan came up behind me and put his hands on my shoulders. "Breathe. Everything will be okay."

My instincts were telling me otherwise. Instead of replying, I summoned my siren side and kindled my inner fire. With a wave of my talons, the raft ignited and started to burn. The slats of wood turned black and smoke billowed so thick and fast that we stumbled backward.

Treygan gagged and waved away the smoke. "Good gods, that stinks. Come on, let's get some fresh air."

Strange that he thought the strong wafts of vanilla and licorice smelled bad. I thought the opposite as they warmed my nose and tugged at a memory that wouldn't surface.

Holding hands, we turned and walked down the beach. I glanced over my shoulder, making sure the raft still burned. The entire thing was engulfed in flames. *Take that, Harte.*

Treygan made small talk in an attempt to take my mind off of the burning mystery behind us. We were approaching Uncle Lloyd's house when he stopped and turned to face the water. He stared out at the moonlit waves and smiled. "Wait until you see this phenomenal bit of good news."

"What are you talking about?"

"Koraline and Pango are approaching."

"Koraline?" Now I sensed them too. My radar seemed to be on the fritz lately. "How could she travel all this way?"

"You'll have to see for yourself."

We waded into the water up to our knees. Pango's thick head of curls surfaced first and he waved to us. Pango looked good as a Blue. As much as I liked him as a Green, his sapphire coloring suited him even better.

Sure enough, Koraline's pigtails poked through the water next.

"How are you here right now?" I asked her once they were within hearing range. "Don't get me wrong, I'm excited to see you, but how?"

She grinned, but in a sad and tired way. "I have a new prosthetic tail."

"Like the dolphin in Florida!" Pango added joyfully.

Years ago, Uncle Lloyd had read me news articles about a dolphin named Winter and the mechanical tail that saved her life. I had no idea where or how Pango had gotten his hands on Koraline's, which had to be custom made. He was making a serious run for the title of Best Brother in Both Realms. "That's amazing. So you're good as new?"

"Not quite." Koraline grimaced, leaning on Pango. "It's taking some getting used to, and strengthening of muscles I didn't know I had. I'm exhausted."

"We didn't want to crash Lloyd's little soirée, so we were hoping we could rest here for the night," Pango said. "Give Koraline a chance to recuperate from the long swim."

I almost offered her a bedroom, but what she needed was a resting pool. "Uncle Lloyd won't mind a couple of party crashers," I said. "He has a huge tank in his living room. I'm sure he'd be happy to let you rest there."

"Well." Treygan smirked. "As long as you don't mind sharing it with his fish."

Replacing Uncle Lloyd's floor to ceiling aquarium was also on my To Do list. Rownan had shattered it to pieces in a fit of rage over Vienna being trapped in Harte. Treygan's emergency fix of using his gorgon ability to create a new tank for the fish was innovative, but it wasn't practical to have a massive stone tub sitting in the living room.

"Those accommodations sound delightful." Pango answered for Koraline, even though she looked uneasy about the idea. "We could use some good quality time with Lloyd anyway."

Without any warning, Pango scooped up Koraline and carried her onto the beach. I tried not to stare at her fake tail, but when she was close enough, she reached out and touched my arm. "It's okay. You can look at it. The design is impressively clever."

I still felt beyond guilty that she'd almost died. Thank the heavens above that she'd survived, but she was severely and permanently injured because of me. Seeing her almost whole again brought bittersweet tears to my eyes. "It's even green."

Koraline grinned. "Pango had some of the green sprites color it for me."

"It's perfect," Treygan said, and I agreed. I didn't want to jinx anything by saying my thoughts out loud, but after weeks of battling one nightmare after the next, things were starting to look up.

I led the way into Uncle Lloyd's house and Pango followed carrying Koraline. It was nice not having to worry about being seen by outsiders. No one had to maintain a human appearance, but for some reason, most of the time I still did.

I glanced behind me and my chest ached because of the sadness on Koraline's face. She stared at her tail with a vacant look like she was mentally miles away. Apparently, I wasn't the only one having a hard time accepting a new way of life. The barbs of my guilt dug a little deeper.

We entered the house and Pango gently placed Koraline in the stone tank then reached over the edge to help her remove her tail. She sighed with relief as Pango lifted the prosthetic out of the tub and set it on the floor.

"Uncle Lloyd's helping Rownan and Vienna with their vows right now," I told them, "but he'll be thrilled to see you when he's through."

Pango glanced between Koraline and me. "Actually, we're glad we have you and Treygan alone. Koraline has a request. An important one."

"A request for me?" I asked.

Koraline gripped the edge of the tank as she stared at me with what almost seemed like desperation. She bit her lime-colored lip then said, "I'd like to nominate a human for transformation to mer."

My lips parted, but my brain couldn't recover from the shock fast enough to reply.

"He's an amazing person," she continued. "I've known him for years. He's super smart and kind. He'd make a great addition to our realm."

"Have you lost your mind?" Treygan asked her. "We agreed this should remain a secret."

"What?" I gaped at him. "You knew about this?"

"Our paths crossed earlier today, but clearly a lot has changed between then and now because turning Joel mer was never mentioned."

"Joel? The bookstore owner?" I shouldn't have been surprised. I had suspected Koraline had feelings for him when she told me to ask him about Harte.

Koraline started to speak again, but Treygan cut her off. "Don't involve Yara in this. Your request has to go through the Violets."

Koraline lifted herself higher, stretching her chin over the edge of the stone tank. "That policy only exists because Stheno and Euryale never wanted to hear from us, and we couldn't ask Medusa. Now that Yara has taken Medusa's place"—Koraline turned to me and slightly bowed her head—"I'm asking you."

I stroked the end of my ponytail, glancing between all three of them as they waited for me to answer. "I don't know what to say. Obviously this is my first time dealing with this sort of thing."

Treygan was stern and dismissive. "Now isn't a good time."

"There won't be a better time." Koraline's voice hitched with urgency. "His lungs are failing. Changing him to mer might save his life."

"And," Pango said all singsong, "he officially wished to be turned through me, which means if I don't grant it and he does pass away, I will never be able to excel to my destined position as a Violet."

"Pango," Koraline hissed. "Isn't Joel's life more important than your rank?"

Treygan interrupted again. "Sea creatures are forbidden to have romantic relationships with humans. We have laws about that."

"I was human," I reminded him.

"You were an extremely complex exception. If we approve one request without a strong reason, then we'll have requests pouring in every time a sea creature finds a human appealing."

I crossed my arms over my chest. "As one of Rathe's rulers, I don't see a problem with it."

Treygan's eyes bugged. "Yara, you can't make a decision like that. We have a system. Defined, detailed procedures that end in a majority-rules vote."

I stepped closer to the tank. I was almost one hundred percent sure now that Koraline loved Joel. As a former-human-turned-mer who fell deeply in forbidden love with Treygan, I wanted to defend Koraline and Joel's relationship. "Who votes?"

"The Violets," Treygan said. "They understand the consequences and impact of changing a human and allowing them into our world."

"The same Violets who ordered you and I be separated when they found out we loved each other?"

The stubborn wrinkles in his brow relaxed for a brief moment, but they returned when he pinched the bridge of his nose. "They did what they felt was right to protect the wellbeing of all sea creatures trapped in this realm."

"Treygan, we disobeyed their orders and opened the gateway. We succeeded because, against their so-called better judgment, we fought to be together."

"Yes, but—"

"Correct me if I'm wrong," I continued, "but wasn't it you who knocked out a guard so you could get to me?"

"You are wrong. Delmar punched Enzo, not me."

"Don't pretend you wouldn't have done it if Delmar hadn't gotten there first."

He took a deep breath and glanced at Pango, possibly searching for some support, but didn't get any. Pango would do anything to see his sister happy.

"Yara," Treygan said calmly. "You are just starting to settle into your role. Most of Rathe's residents barely know you and have little to no trust in you yet. Do you really want your first major act to be a blatant disregard for a law and system that has been in place for centuries?"

He had a point. I hardly knew all of my job requirements, much less how to perform them. I needed to gain the trust of the creatures of Rathe, not make them doubt my ability to rule or make responsible decisions. I turned back to Koraline. "Let me discuss this with the Violets and get back to you."

Koraline reached out and gripped my hand. "Please hurry. He doesn't have much time left."

My heart hurt for her. And for Joel. "How long?"

"Maybe a few weeks, but he's struggling to breathe. Each day that passes, he'll probably get worse."

I knew how she felt. If Uncle Lloyd were still suffering, I would be desperate to help him too. I squeezed Koraline's wet hand. "Everyone is busy preparing for tomorrow, but as soon as the celebrations are over, I'll speak with Indrea and schedule a formal meeting with the Violets."

Pango placed one hand on my shoulder. "Please remind them that Joel is the one who educated us on the Devil's Triangle and how to enter Harte. *He* is one of the main reasons you, Treygan, Rownan, and Vienna, are still alive."

"That's true," I said optimistically. "We might not be here today if not for Joel."

Treygan uncrossed his arms from his chest and his tone softened when he said, "I can't argue that fact. We owe him more than we could ever repay. I'll go with Yara to the meeting and fight for his transformation."

At last, the sweet, caring, romantic-even-though-he-denied-it side of him had broken through.

"Thank you," Koraline said to Treygan. "Now get over here so I can hug both of you."

7

Koraline

I floated in Lloyd's tank, staring up at his living room ceiling, but I had stopped seeing the plaster. My thoughts had been consumed by daydreams of Joel being mer and us living together in Rathe. He was going to love Rathe so much.

A shadow fell over me and fingers snapped in front of my face. My daydream of Joel with a deep red tail faded away as Rownan's goatee came into focus.

I rubbed my eyes and pulled myself up to the ledge. He and Vienna stood outside the stone tub, smiling at me.

"Good evening, sunshine," Rownan said. "Fancy seeing you on this side of the gateway."

I splashed water on my face and smoothed down my hair. "Hi, Rownan. Hi, V."

"I can't tell you how happy I am to see you out and about, Koraline." Only Vienna could live in hell for over a decade and remain the same sweet soul she always was.

I leaned over the edge of the tub and peered into the kitchen. Pango was making his famous midnight pancakes. Lloyd had parked his wheelchair at the kitchen table and sat in a regular chair sipping milk.

"Why didn't you wake me?" I shouted to my brother.

Pango set down his spatula then pushed the wheelchair through the kitchen doorway. "You looked so content that I didn't want to interrupt whatever you were fantasizing about."

My cheeks tingled at the reminder of my visions of Joel. Pango produced a big fluffy towel and spread it over the wheelchair's seat. Rownan and Vienna headed into the kitchen as my brother reached in to help me out of the tank. I didn't like needing assistance, but the dynamics of the tank left me no choice.

Pango placed me in the seat and I folded the towel so it covered what was left of my tail. Per usual, I stayed in mer form because human form was much more painful. The Violets kept telling me the more time I spent in human form the less painful it would be, but I'd chosen to focus on rehabilitating in mer form first. I felt like I could only deal with so much pain at once, and the Violets respected my decision.

I rolled myself to the kitchen table and kissed Lloyd on the cheek. "Sorry for crashing your family gathering, but thank you for letting us recharge here."

"You and Pango are welcome here any time and for any reason."

"We can be on our way before the ceremony."

"Oh no," Vienna said, sounding genuinely disappointed. "Please stay. It would be so nice to have you and Pango attend."

My brother clapped two oven mitts together. "Yay! We were hoping for an invitation. There's nothing better than witnessing soul mates officially declaring their eternal commitment to each other—again."

"We would be honored to attend," I agreed. "Thank you."

Pango pinched my cheek. "Now, sensational sister of mine, eat before you wither away."

Pango had made his signature sand dollar pancakes. I devoured four of them while everyone else engaged in conversations about Rownan and Vienna's vow renewal.

Leaning closer to Lloyd, I spoke quietly out of respect. I was about to bring up a very personal topic that no one discussed. "Would you mind if I asked you some questions about your transformation?"

Everyone who had been talking paused. Lloyd's milk glass

hovered in front of his mouth. Pango's loaded fork hung above his plate with syrup dripping from his pancakes. Vienna's dark eyes slid sideways in slow motion.

Rownan was the first to speak. He leaned back in his chair and tossed his napkin on the table. "Oh, I would love to hear this."

Lloyd cleared his throat. "My transformation, hmm? I don't see why not. Most of my secrets are out in the open by now, so fire away."

"What was it like?" I rested my elbows on the table. "Changing from gorgon to human?"

"It was so long ago that I can hardly remember the details."

"Do you remember if it was painful?"

"Yes, but well worth the pain."

"Because you could be with Liora?"

He smiled so blissfully that I could have sworn his eyes twinkled. "I would have endured any amount of agony for the time Liora and I spent together."

The romantic in me wanted to ask him more about how they met, and at what point they decided to break the rules and change their entire lives so they could be together, but I stuck to the necessary questions. "How did you get the gorgon sisters to approve your transformation?"

His brows rose. "This seems like a peculiar question coming from someone so proud of her mer heritage. Are you thinking of asking to be human?"

"Absolutely not."

"Then why all the questions?" Lloyd probed.

I fiddled with my braids and looked away from the staring audience waiting for me to elaborate. As if on cue, there was a knock at the front door.

"Who on Earth could that be?" Lloyd asked. "None of you knock anymore."

Rownan pushed his seat back from the table and went to check. I forgot all about our conversation when Joel walked into the room, toting his oxygen tank on wheels behind him.

"Hello, everyone." Joel politely nodded to each person at the table. "Sorry to interrupt your meal."

I couldn't hide my shock at seeing him on Eden's Hammock. "What are you doing here?"

I pulled my towel tighter around me. Joel had seen me in mer form before, but not since I'd lost most of my tail. Even if he had caught a glance of me yesterday in the water, the prosthetic tail would have made me appear whole. Sitting in a wheelchair with no legs or tail dangling over the seat made me feel embarrassed and awkward.

"Something important is bothering me. I needed to discuss it with you as soon as possible." He adjusted the tubes hanging from his tank and fixed his attention on Lloyd. "I'm sorry for showing up at your home unannounced and uninvited."

Lloyd raised his glass and winked at him. "Any friend of Koraline's is welcome here, but how did you get through my harboring spell?"

Joel answered with a nervous smile. "My grandfather was a learned man. He taught me a few tricks. Koraline, may I speak with you in private?"

I clenched my towel even tighter, not wanting to roll myself away from the table that kept my lower body—or lack thereof—hidden from his view. "Umm. . . ."

Pango stepped in to save me. "Joel, why don't you have a seat in the den? It's to the left of the foyer where you entered. Koraline will meet you in there lickety-split."

Joel agreed and Rownan stepped aside to let him pass.

As soon as he was out of earshot I turned to Pango, panicking. "He can't see me like this!"

"He saw you yesterday, my dear."

"He saw me in the water, not like this." I motioned to the wheelchair and the towel covering my lap.

"He knows what happened to you, fancy fins. He's a big boy and fully capable of handling the change."

Rownan sat in the empty chair beside me. "Koraline, I don't fully understand what's going on here, but I have a hunch. As an outside observer, may I point out an obvious fact you may be overlooking?"

I hesitantly nodded.

"Joel has tubes in his nose," Rownan noted. "He's wheeling that oxygen tank around like he's had a lot of practice. The guy knows what it's like to have a disability. Of all the people in this room, he can probably best relate to your worries and insecurities. Also, when he looked at you, I could practically feel his love for you pulsing from him like sonar waves. To be blunt, I don't think he even notices you're missing part of your tail."

I glanced at the doorway that Joel had gone through, and then I leaned over and kissed Rownan's cheek. "I forgot how sweet you are when Vienna's around to bring out the best in you."

Vienna grabbed a few flowers from the vase on the table. She moved behind me and said, "Let's tidy up your braids and add these. I know you feel better when you have flowers in your hair."

They knew about my feelings for Joel without me telling them. They knew and they were being supportive.

"Thank you," I told them as Vienna beautified me the best she could with her limited resources. I turned to Lloyd. "Are you okay with him being here? With us spending time together in your home even though it's against the law?"

Lloyd sipped his milk. "Darling, you're forgetting that I was the king of breaking Rathe's laws." He shrugged. "Besides, this isn't Rathe. What happens on Eden's Hammock stays on Eden's Hammock."

"You look gorgeous." Vienna pulled my chair back from the table. "Go get him."

I took a shaky breath to calm my nerves then rolled myself out of the kitchen and into the den. I paused before rounding the wall separating Joel and me. As I tugged on the bottom of my towel to make sure my scarred tail was hidden, Joel called out, "Please stop worrying so much and get in here."

I inched forward and peeked through the open doors.

He smiled so sweetly I thought my insides would melt out of me. "Hello, beautiful."

"Hey, handsome," I said, rolling into the room. He stood and reached for his tank, but I held up my hands. "No, sit. I'll come to you. I'm not helpless."

He flashed me a reassuring grin and sat down. "Neither am I."

What a lovely mess we were.

I started to park my chair beside him, but he pulled me around so that we faced each other. His eyes never flickered from mine.

"I didn't want you to go back to Rathe before I had a chance to clear my conscience. I asked Pango to grant my wish, but . . ." He blinked fast—one of his nervous habits.

"But what?" I pressed.

"I'm here to retract my wish."

"Why would you retract it? I think it's the most marvelous idea I've ever heard."

"If something does happen to me sooner than predicted, I don't want to leave your brother cursed."

"Don't talk like that. We need to stay positive."

"I'm a rational guy. I like to be prepared for any and all scenarios." He seemed to struggle for his next breath. "But most importantly, I want you to be with me because you choose to be, and because you love me, not because I forced you to with a wish or my declining health."

I clutched his hand. "Almost dying changed my whole perspective on life. Love between two souls is a gift. It shouldn't matter that you're human and I'm mer. If turning you mer extends your life, then that's an epic bonus, but I don't want you to be a secret anymore. Wish or no wish, I would do practically anything for us to be together. I love you."

"I was hoping you'd say something along those lines." He kissed the top of my hand then pressed my fingers to his cheek. "When will the Violets give their answer?"

"I'm not sure how long it will take. Maybe a day or two? Your case will be presented and then they'll vote."

He nodded firmly and said, "They'll approve it."

I wanted to be as confident as him, but I knew how old-fashioned many of the Violets were. We did need to stay positive, but I also needed to be honest with him. "In Rathe, no request for human transformation has been approved for over a hundred years."

His eyebrows pulled inward so tightly his glasses slid down his nose. "They approved Yara."

"She was the child of two former sea creatures. She was never pure human. And her transformation was necessary. Part of a deal made with our gods. She didn't need approval."

"I helped Yara and the others save Vienna from Harte. That has to be worth something."

"Pango reminded Yara and Treygan of that. They said they will plead that point."

His thumb rubbed circles on the top of my hand. "Why do you sound so worried?"

"Because no matter what they decide, I'll still have to stand trial for having a forbidden relationship with you."

His grip on my hand loosened and he sat up straight. "Are you ashamed of your relationship with me?"

"No, I'm not one bit ashamed. Being with you is worth any punishment they issue."

"People should never be punished for being in love with each other."

"I agree wholeheartedly."

"I'm sorry it has to be this way."

"Me too."

He squeezed my hand again then asked, "How does it work? The transformation process. That's one thing my grandfather could never figure out."

"An Indigo has to turn you. I've heard the process is complex and dangerous, but merfolk aren't given details until they've reached Indigo rank." I stroked a flower in my hair while choosing my next words carefully. What I was about to say would hurt him, but not telling him could put his life at risk. "My main concern is that your lungs might not be strong enough for the transformation."

He flinched and stared down at his oxygen tank with sadness filling his eyes. My lungs ached with sympathy as I watched him fight the acceptance of his own fragility. We all wish to be stronger than we are. No living creature is an exception to limitations. Regardless of how brave, beautiful, or brilliant, we are all breakable.

"My lungs may be weak," Joel said, "but the strength of my mind and heart make up for it."

I admired his confidence, and I wasn't trying to be a pessimist, but now it was my turn to be rational. I figured we should discuss all the negatives to get them out of the way. "When Yara was turned, she lost a lot of her memories of being human. It's part of the process somehow."

His head bobbed as he considered that fact. "I'm okay with that. All that matters is I remember you."

"What if you don't?"

"You said a lot of memories, but not all of them, correct?"

"Treygan told me they leave the most crucial ones, memories that contribute to your deepest self and make you who you are. That probably doesn't include times with me."

"I'm sure it most certainly does." He lifted my chin so our eyes met. "You're the most important person in my life. A few years ago, when I became the last surviving member of my family, I welcomed an early death. I figured my condition was my ticket out of this lonely world. Then I met you and my zest for life was restored. I've prayed every single night for my lungs to grow stronger so that I don't have to leave you. I dream of us creating a family of our own and growing old together. Of course the crucial memories of my deepest self include you. You're as deep as I get, Koraline."

My heart overflowed. "Like you said, I'm trying to prepare us for any and all scenarios."

"Fair enough. If by some chance they take my memories of you, then you can make me remember. I'll be mer. You can do that amazing soul sharing thing you've told me about. Show me everything we've been through. Give me back all of the important moments."

"Every moment with you is important to me."

"They are to me too. But you know what I mean."

"They'd all be secondhand. You might not emotionally connect to them the way you do now."

"I don't believe that. My lungs may fail, my memories may be taken away, but my soul is connected with yours. No matter what happens, the bond between us can't be broken."

My throat tightened as I fought back tears. "I hope with all my being that they say yes."

"They will. They have to. We're destined to be together."

Pango knocked on the wall behind me. "Pardon the intrusion, but speaking of destiny, did I overhear someone wanting to retract a wish that would leave me free to excel to my destined rank of Violet?"

I rolled my eyes and smiled over my shoulder at him. "Eavesdropping much?"

He gave an exaggerated shrug, feigning the innocence he couldn't speak aloud.

"Yes," Joel said. "I want to retract it. Pretend I never asked you to grant me a wish."

"It doesn't work that way." He brushed flour from his apron and leaned against the doorframe. "You've activated the launch sequence, so now I must grant you a wish before I'm freed of obligation to you."

"What if I changed my wish?"

"Please do, but make it something I can actually grant."

Joel contemplated his options and then pulled the oxygen tubes out of his nose so he could sniff the air. "Those pancakes smell delicious. I wish for you to make me some pancakes."

Pango victoriously raised his spatula. "Yes! Wise fellow, you are. My pancakes are so scrumptious they've been rumored to improve moods, restore health, and ensure lifelong happiness."

"You're such a good guy," I told him after Pango dashed away to play chef and grant Joel's revised wish. "Add this to the infinite list of reasons why I love you so much."

Joel pulled me closer to him and then sweetly kissed me. "Let's hope those rumors about his pancakes are true. I need all the help I can get."

8

Rowman

Our vow renewals were perfect. In contrast to our large wedding, the gathering was small and intimate. We were surrounded by the people who loved us most. Those who had sacrificed their lives to protect ours. Having our closest friends and family gathered around us while we officially declared our bond again was one of the highlights of my life.

The ceremony took place at sunrise to represent the dawn of a new era in our relationship. Our wedding had taken place in Norway while the Northern Lights danced in the midnight sky. Both events were beautiful in their own way, but what made them both breathtaking was Vienna.

Her black hair was curled in wavy tendrils that didn't quite reach her pale shoulders. She wore a white sundress trimmed with silver pearls that glistened in the sunlight. A bouquet of white moonflowers—her favorite—matched the crown of flowers Keeley and Jenna made for her hair. In all honesty, she could have worn a burlap sack and still been gorgeous.

Lloyd led the ceremony while standing on his own. It was one of the best gifts anyone could have given me—seeing my father healthy and self-sufficient, and being part of such a special day for Vienna and me.

He spoke a lot about the miracle of love and how we had already weathered bad times so we should now be blessed with good times and joy. He said some other meaningful stuff, but I kept getting distracted by Vienna's smile.

When the time came to bind our wrists together, Lloyd used

a rope of various iridescent shades of black, gray, silver, white, and brown. It felt cool and slick.

"What is that?" I asked him.

"Serpetugon vine. Stronger than any material this realm has ever created. It's to symbolize how your marriage will never be broken. Not that the two of you need it, but I like the sentiment."

"I love that sentiment," Vienna said. "We're honored."

I examined it closer. "What's it made of?"

"Skin shed from the serpents of a gorgon's head. That's what makes it so strong."

I did a double take. Up until this morning, Lloyd had rarely discussed or even mentioned details about his life as a gorgon. Had the snakeskin wrapped around our wrists come from his snakes? From serpents that had been part of him before he gave up that existence?

I didn't have the nerve to ask, but believing it could have been part of his past as a sea creature made his gesture that much more meaningful.

When the ceremony ended and Lloyd untied the vine, I paid close attention to what he did with it. He placed it in a box that resembled an old treasure chest and locked it.

"Shall we head back to Rathe for the party?" Yara asked.

"Yes, go," Lloyd insisted. "I'm sure the natives are restless."

The ceremony had made me feel drunk on love and happiness, so I didn't try hiding my feelings like usual. I clutched my father's shoulders then hugged him. "I wish you could come with us, old man."

He hugged me tight. "My place is here now, but thank you for allowing me to be part of this."

"I wish I could rewind time and get back all those years I wasted being angry at you."

He waved me off. "Stop dwelling on the past when you're living such a glorious present."

"You're going to make an awesome grandfather."

His face lit up. "I'd sure love the chance to prove you right."

I hugged him again, really hugged him, proud that such a strong and brave man was my father. "We'll be back soon."

"I'm counting on it."

Treygan approached as Joel helped Koraline wheel her chair back into the house.

"Koraline will be staying here for a while," Treygan informed us.

Vienna glanced at them as they disappeared through the back door. "Can't say I blame her. They seem quite smitten with each other."

"Are you staying too?" I asked Pango. "Or coming back with us?"

"You think I'd miss the first big Rathe extravaganza in almost two decades?" He shook his head. "Even the soap opera that is currently my sister's life couldn't keep me away."

Everyone else said their goodbyes to Lloyd, but as I turned away he called me back. He reached out and patted my armband. "Don't lose that stone. Remember, keep it on you at all times."

"I will."

As if he knew I had planned on giving it to Vienna, he said, "You, Rownan. Keep it on *you*." He squeezed my arm tighter and nodded toward everyone on the beach. "It will allow you to protect them too."

Vienna, Treygan, Yara, and Pango waited for me in the surf. Vienna's loving eyes met mine and she smiled brighter than the moons of Rathe.

"I'll guard it with my life," I assured him. "See you soon."

I joined the others and we waded into the water to start the long swim home.

Macawfish swarmed the entrance of the gateway. They were gossipers and mostly a nuisance, but because they were repeating the same few words, their chatter was impossible to ignore.

Sisters! Gone! Where?

What are they going on about? Vienna asked me.

I don't know. I turned to my brother, who was watching Yara as if in awe of her.

Yara floated in place with her arms held open at her sides. Macawfish lined each arm and she stared at them intently. She had told me about her affinity for Rathe's creatures since becoming ruler, but seeing that it extended to all species—even the irksome macawfish—earned her even more of my respect.

They're nervous, Yara said. *Worry is coming off them in waves.*

That's their nature, Treygan told her. *They're busybodies.*

Yara studied them with concern. *I wish they could speak in full sentences.*

Treygan and I both smirked. *Let's be grateful that wish will never come true.*

Must I remind everyone that we have a celebration to attend? Pango swam ahead.

Yara gently rolled her arms. The macawfish dispersed and followed in her wake as she swam toward the surface. The rest of us couldn't get within five feet of her because of the colorful school surrounding her. The sight was a reminder that power had shifted in Rathe. Treygan was no longer the only one who worshipped Yara.

9

My encounter with the macawfish worried me, but I couldn't let it spoil the party. I would find them again afterward and try to decipher what they were upset about. Even though Treygan assured me that getting any sense out of them was next to impossible.

The reunion celebration took place at Hieros Cove. It was neutral ground for all the species and a popular choice for parties. I'd missed out on the decorating to be at the vow renewal and I couldn't wait to see it. Twinkling lights shone through the water and grew brighter the closer we swam. I turned to look at Treygan.

He watched me with a smile. *You're going to love this.*

Treygan held my hand as we surfaced. I had planned on not gasping no matter what I saw. As one of Rathe's rulers, I thought I should keep my composure. But there was no controlling it. I gasped so hard I swallowed water.

Lightsing bugs filled the dark purple sky, twinkling and collectively singing a beautiful song. At first I thought glowing streamers were draped from tree to tree, but looking closer I realized they were bands of water filled with colorful glowing fish like the ones used in the lanterns during Koraline's healing ceremony.

During my moment of awe, Rownan, Vienna, and Pango transitioned to legs and waded up the beach onto the mint-green sand.

"Come on, Majesty of the Macawfish," Pango shouted to me. "Your realm of sea monsters has been awaiting this party for nearly two decades!"

"The water streamers," I said to Treygan, watching one ripple as dozens of glowing fish swam through it. "How do they stay that way?"

"Some of the older merfolk and sprites are able to manipulate water into lasting forms. They use water to decorate as easily as humans use paper."

"It's so pretty."

Creatures trickled in from every direction. Otabia and Mariza flew in, followed soon after by all of the water sprites. The sprites seemed as delighted to see me as I was to see them. Keeley and Jenna acted like my bouncers as their sprite kin converged and covered me in hugs and kisses.

"Back off!" Jenna shouted. "Give her some breathing room."

"It's okay," I assured her. "I'll never turn down affection from you sprites."

"Well, in that case." Jenna rushed forward and hugged and kissed my nose. "We've missed you so much."

I giggled as more of the sprites hugged and kissed me then darted off to enjoy the party.

As I strolled around welcoming everyone, I noticed that none of the gorgon kin had shown. My high spirits sank a little. I'd really hoped this celebration could be a chance to bring everyone together.

When Eve arrived I pulled her aside and asked her if she had any interest in becoming a siren. She had questions I couldn't even begin to answer, so I called Otabia and Mariza over to tell her everything she wanted to know and more. When Mariza got much too graphic about their blood-drinking escapades, I told Eve to let me know her decision and excused myself. Considering the disturbing excitement in Eve's eyes, I was pretty sure that Treygan was right and she may actually accept.

Only a few minutes later, Vienna and Rownan were telling me a funny story when suddenly Rownan stopped in mid-sentence. He stared past me, an amused grin tugging at his lips.

"I'll be damned. Look what the waves washed in."

I turned to see several gorgons swimming toward us. The snakes on their heads dove in and out of the water. Instead of transitioning to legs, they used their serpent bodies to slither up the beach.

A female I hadn't met yet led the group. In many ways she reminded me of Stheno and Euryale: mossy-colored skin, eyebrows that looked like seaweed, fangs protruding from her bottom lip, and pinwheel eyes that spiraled into solid black as she fixed her gaze on me.

I was so happy to see the gorgon that I practically skipped down the beach to greet them. Intending to shake hands, I stuck out mine and said, "Hi, I'm Yara. We're so glad you came."

She looked down at my hand and tilted her head.

"Yara," Treygan said quietly as he walked up behind me, "shaking hands is foreign to them." I let my arm fall to my side as Treygan continued warmly, "Hello, Messina. Welcome."

Messina, the friendliest of the gorgon kin according to Koraline, smiled at me. Even though it revealed more of her fangs, she looked beautiful. Sage bobbed up and down in greeting and Messina's serpents did the same.

"My apologies, dearest Yara." Each of Messina's words was spoken with a slight hiss. "Most of my kin respectfully declined your invitation, but a few such as myself were intrigued." She turned and motioned to a familiar gorgon behind her. "Talus seems to have grown fond of you."

Talus had dragged me through the gateway on the Triple Eighteen and delivered me to Stheno and Euryale. He hadn't been gentle, either, gripping me so tight it should have left bruises. He never said one word to me or looked at my face during that encounter. But two days ago, when I had visited gorgon territory to invite them to our celebration, Talus had been downright gentlemanly.

Just as he had then, he took my hand and lifted it to his face, but his lips never touched my skin. His nostrils flared and I realized he was smelling me. "Greetings, Yara. Lovely to see you again."

"You too, Talus. Thank you for coming." I turned back to Messina. "It's so nice to meet you. Koraline told me great things about you, including the poem you wrote." Her brow wrinkled with confusion, so I elaborated. "Beauty hidden under a veil of tragedy. Sorry if I'm misquoting it."

Her mossy-colored skin blushed even darker. "That was my grandmother's poem."

"Oh, I'm sorry."

"No harm or foul. I share her beliefs, but I am not as eloquent."

I began to reply, but my skin prickled with a strange sensation I had never felt before. My hallmarks swirled fast across my skin. Searching through the countless sea creatures moving all around me, I zeroed in on one shadow in the distance.

I sensed him so strongly that my fingers flexed to relieve the tension.

His full head of black braids broke through the water first. No serpents, so he wasn't a gorgon. As his face appeared, I felt guilty for thinking how strikingly handsome he was. His lean, muscular chest had no hallmarks, so he wasn't mer, which only left selkie.

As he strutted onto land, I couldn't see the usual faded scars or smooth fur of selkies. From the waist down, a dark, shiny, blue-black substance covered his sculpted legs. I glanced around, waiting for someone to greet him, but a strange change had come over the crowd.

Most of the females had stopped to watch the new guest approach. Almost every male watched the women with confused or concerned expressions—including Treygan.

"What's wrong?" he asked me.

Over my left shoulder, Pango whispered into my ear, "Who is that delectable creature approaching us? Please, for the love of giggles and goosebumps, let him be sauntering over to me. Merrick will just have to deal with it."

I watched the tall, dark, and handsome guest confidently approach us. "Who is he?"

Treygan stepped closer to me. "I don't know. I've never seen him before."

Pango hummed. "Remember, I called first dibs."

Everyone watched as the newest party guest stopped directly in front of me and flashed the most seductive yet wicked smile I had ever seen.

"You've ignored my requests." His voice was deep and smooth as silk.

"I don't believe we've met," Treygan said to him. "Who are you?"

The stranger's penetrating stare didn't flicker from mine.

"I'm sorry," I said, feeling like I had been tranquilized by his intense black eyes. "I've gotten lots of requests lately and haven't been able to respond to all of them yet. Can you tell me what yours was?"

The scent of vanilla and licorice washed over me before the words escaped his lips. "I sent my raft to you. Twice."

My pulse pounded in my ears. My hands tensed again. Treygan's muscles flexed and he spread his shoulders wide. "This is the last time I'll ask. Who are you?"

I couldn't have moved even if I wanted to. Fear had rooted me in place. The stranger standing in front of me had sent the raft from Harte. Even though I couldn't remember, my instincts were certain who he was. I couldn't believe he was here in Rathe.

"How?" I muttered.

He leaned so close that his breath chilled my ear as he whispered, "I told you that you would return to me for eternity. I'm here to collect."

Treygan shoved him and stepped between us. "Back away

from her."

Rownan, Delmar, and Merrick all rushed over and flanked Treygan. Pango pulled me backward so fast I stumbled. I was grateful that so many large, strong bodies now stood between me and the stranger I didn't want to believe could be real.

"Gentlemen," the stranger said calmly. "This doesn't concern you. I am only here for Yara."

Treygan seemed to grow taller. "You have no right to be here."

His deep laugh made my whole body tingle. I pushed the exquisite feeling away, hating my own reaction.

"Tell them, Yara," the handsome, laughing stranger said. "Tell them who I am and why I'm here."

I closed my eyes, like a scared child who believed if I couldn't see him then he wasn't real. I forced out the lie. "I don't know who you are."

He tsked. "A pity to hear untruths from such perfect lips. Allow me to remind you."

With a supernaturally fast wave of what appeared to be several arms, Treygan and the rest of the guys were thrown through the air like leaves blowing in the wind. I didn't even have time to gasp or see where they landed before the stranger had me pulled tight against him.

His lips closed over mine and assaulted me with the taste of vanilla. I tried to push him away, but a rush of ecstasy surged through me and I lost the ability to think or resist.

Suddenly, the warm arms wrapped around me turned hard and cold. The stranger pulled back, releasing me from his intoxicating kiss, but his arms stayed locked around me. I glanced down and saw his arms encased in stone. But only two of them. To my horror, he had six more.

Treygan ran toward us, rage burning in his eyes. The moment he reached us, stone exploded all around me and the stranger let go, his arms breaking free from his stone constraints.

Messina and the rest of the gorgons slithered forward.

Treygan moved to stand in front of me, his arms reaching back protectively.

Rownan stood behind me. "Don't move, Yara. Stay between us."

The stranger's dreadlocks twisted and hardened into black and blue coral as his legs and extra arms morphed into long, shiny tentacles. It should have been repulsive, but I stared in astonishment.

Messina shouted, "Merciless gods, he's a kraken!"

No, I thought. *Not* a *kraken*. The *kraken*.

"All sea creatures were invited to this occasion," he purred. "Am I not a sea creature?"

"Only sea creatures of Rathe," Treygan hissed. "You're not welcome in our realm."

The kraken looked past Treygan directly into my eyes. "Do you feel the same, young ruler? Even after all we have shared?"

My mouth opened, but I couldn't find my voice. I wiped my lips, hating that they still tingled from his kiss. My dark secret had come back to haunt me. I fought to regain my composure and speak with assertiveness. "I don't remember anything about you except this moment. You're not welcome here."

He narrowed his eyes and tsked again. "Clearly you need a stronger reminder of the bond we share." His tentacles stretched toward me.

"Now!" Treygan shouted.

He and the other gorgons petrified the kraken again. Every inch of him crackled and turned to stone. His face was the last bit of him to turn gray and solid, and his eyes glowed black and blue as he stared at me. He was still staring at me as his eyes turned to solid rock.

Treygan spun and took my face in his hands. "Are you all right? Did he hurt you?"

Before I could answer, there was a sound like thunder and a shower of debris made me duck and throw my arms over my head. The kraken had obliterated every piece of stone the gorgons and Treygan had created. I stumbled backward until Rowan caught me and steadied me. Treygan shook stone shards out of his hair and turned to face off with the monster again.

The kraken nonchalantly brushed the rock dust from his torso. "Not a particularly welcoming bunch, are you?"

He flashed a sinister sneer at everyone, and then he locked his focus on me again. "Say your goodbyes and make the necessary arrangements. I would like us to return to Harte as soon as possible."

"I'm not going anywhere with you," I declared, wishing I sounded firmer than I did.

He stepped closer. Treygan lifted his hands.

"No need," the kraken told Treygan. "The stone spectacle has grown tiresome. I won't touch her again. At least not right now." He grinned at me. "We have all of eternity for that."

I shook my head.

"You will return with me," he insisted. "The longer you refuse, the more your people will suffer."

"Go back to hell where you belong," Rownan snapped.

"Happily," the kraken said. His tentacles stretched and lifted him high above the crowd. "But not without Yara."

I clutched Treygan. His muscles were so taut I worried he had turned to stone.

"In the meantime, I'll be acquainting myself with your realm," the kraken said. "See you again soon."

He dissolved right before our eyes. I blinked several times. Then I looked at the spot where he had just been. Multiple grooves formed in the sand, leading into the surf. The water splashed as if someone were wading through it, and then the splashing stopped.

He hadn't vanished. He had made himself invisible.

"I take it back," Pango said. "I don't care how pretty he is, I don't associate with krakens from hell."

"What was all of that about?" Treygan asked me.

Thankfully, everyone else had broken out into chaotic conversations around us, so our discussion felt somewhat private.

"I don't know," I lied. "All I know is we need to send him back to Harte."

"How?" Rownan asked from the other side of me.

Vienna stepped up beside him and grabbed Rownan's hand. "How did he get into Rathe?"

"The same way we entered Harte," I guessed. "He must have discovered another gateway."

Treygan's eyes bored into me. He probably wanted to know what the kraken meant about our time together in Harte. Or maybe he wanted to scold me for allowing the kraken to kiss me, but I'd have to deal with that later.

The elders of every species circled in on me, demanding to know what I intended to do, how this had happened, why the kraken wanted me, and more. All of their questions made my head swirl.

"Yara." Indrea's voice cut through all of the chatter. "Tell us how we can help you."

She sent calming energy through me and it helped steady me so I could think clearer. I nodded, realizing she wanted me to step up and handle this crisis because that's what a good ruler would do.

"Send scouts to the gateway at Trident Rock to make sure no other Harte creatures are coming through," I said. "I need to speak with Stheno and Euryale right away. They may know something that will help."

I turned to Treygan. "We'll talk soon. I realize I owe you a lot of answers."

"I'm coming with you," he insisted. "You can't be alone. Not with that *thing* lurking and making himself invisible."

"I'll take the siren sisters with me. Flying is the fastest way to get there and you'll slow me down."

Treygan winced.

"I'm sorry, I didn't mean it that way." I rubbed my forehead, hoping to ease my sudden headache.

"It's fine," he said. "Go. I'll be waiting outside of the grotto when you're finished."

I lifted my wings and screeched out a call to Otabia and Mariza. They swooped through the sky above me and I rose to join them.

"To the Gorgon Grotto," I ordered.

"I warned you not to enter Harte," Otabia hissed. "Now look what you've done."

I glared at her, but I couldn't argue. I looked up at the three suns and moons. Faint rings of fog that I'd never seen before surrounded all of them.

Holy Poseidon, what *had* I done?

The flight to Gorgon Grotto made me even more anxious than I already was. The macawfish weren't the only inhabitants of Rathe who were agitated now. Everywhere I looked sea creatures of all sorts were behaving erratically. By the time the sirens and I got to the grotto, my stomach was doing summersaults.

"Let me go in alone," I told Otabia and Mariza.

Neither one argued. In my heron form, I entered the secret passageway and navigated the tight corridors until I burst through the water and landed inside the grotto.

Only one torch burned on the wall, which was troubling. Sometimes Stheno and Euryale's torches burned dimly, but I had never seen them completely out.

I morphed back to normal and called out, "Stheno? Euryale?"

No reply. No snoring, no tails rattling. Nothing but dripping stalactites.

Sage slithered against my cheek.

"They have to be here," I told her. "There's nowhere else they can go."

The sisters had been sentenced to the grotto for eternity, so they had to be lurking somewhere. A thought crossed my mind that maybe they were dead, which would explain their torches not burning, but how could two immortal gorgons die? Had they killed each other over the kraken memory? *Could* they kill each other?

No, Sage assured me. *Or they would have done so long before now.*

Sage didn't always provide such clear answers. I had tried asking her many times why her mental communications were so sporadic, but she wouldn't answer me, which made me question if the whispers in my mind were really her or my own subconscious.

A bottle floated in one of the tide pools. I bent over and picked it up, examining the dark liquid inside. "What is this?"

Gorgon blood, Sage whispered.

"It's from Stheno or Euryale, isn't it?"

She slithered down my shoulder and her tongue flickered out and tapped the glass.

"A message in a bottle. How cliché." I looked down one of the tunnels. "Why can't they just talk to me in person?"

Sage didn't reply. With a wave of my hand, I made the flames of my grotto torch burn brighter so I could examine the bottle's contents. I grimaced as the thick blue blood sloshed around inside.

I hadn't been visiting the grotto as often as I should, so it was understandable that Stheno and Euryale might need to speak with me about something, but to leave me a bottle of their blood? Not a classy calling card.

I searched every cavern, every dark tunnel, and even their private dens, calling out their names, but they were nowhere to be found.

"I don't understand," I told Sage. "How could they vanish?"

The message.

"You really expect me to drink this?" I forced back a gag.

She only hissed, but I knew what she was thinking because I

was thinking it too. Their blood message might be the only way for me to get answers.

I took a deep breath of moldy, stagnant air. I'd promised Treygan and myself I'd never drink blood again. I certainly didn't want to—even with my selkie and siren instincts I didn't crave it—but if it was my only way of finding out Euryale and Stheno's whereabouts, then it was a necessary evil. I grabbed the neck of the bottle. "Treygan will understand, right? There are exceptions to every promise."

Sage didn't reply. I ignored the spasms in my stomach and pierced the cork with one of my selkie claws. Air hissed from the hole. The metallic scent of blood made my stomach turn.

"Down the hatch," I grunted, lifting the bottle to my lips. I threw it back and took a gulp, silently cursing the parts of myself that enjoyed the taste.

The memory sucked me from the present and into a scene from Euryale's not-so-distant past.

Stheno stood in front of me, her tail rattling as she stared into a large piece of the all-seeing mirror.

"I see her."

Experiencing the moment as Euryale, I rushed forward, staring into the mirror with Stheno. Medusa's serene face peered back at us.

"I have discussed your request with Poseidon," Medusa said. "After much debate, we are granting it."

As I watched, it was so difficult to remember that I was experiencing Euryale's memory. I felt her excitement and her desire to be with the kraken. He was a drug and she would have done anything to get another dose of him.

Euryale turned to Stheno and they gazed into each other's pinwheel eyes. Both of them were so full of joy they were shaking.

"After all this time," Stheno hissed. "We'll be free."

"Free," Euryale repeated. "And with him."

Stheno looked around the cave walls. "I will not miss this place."

"Nor will I."

Medusa spoke from the mirror. "The gateway at Trident Rock will only be open during low tide. If you do not cross through before Poseidon's white waves ebb back through the black spires, then you will have missed your opportunity."

"How do we get there?" Stheno asked in a panic. "We can't leave the grotto."

"I will create a portal that connects you to the cliffs near Trident Rock, but first you must leave word of your abdication for Yara. Once that is done, exit through the tide pool. If you happen to encounter any other sea creatures at Trident Rock, do not look them in the eye or speak to them. If either of you do so, we will revoke permission to enter Harte and never consider it again."

Stheno and Euryale nodded fervently. "Thank you, sister. Thank you. Eternal thanks."

Medusa shook her head of flowers and vines as two shimmering tears rolled down her cheeks. "May you embrace your chosen eternity in darkness."

A tide pool to Euryale's left began to bubble and then a light from deep within it grew brighter.

"The portal!" Euryale exclaimed.

"Quick," Stheno urged, her eyes pinwheeling with fire. "We must leave Yara a message first."

I snapped myself free from the memory and stumbled backward. Sage rubbed her nose against my cheek, trying to comfort me. I unclenched my eyelids and turned to meet her silver stare.

"They left us and entered Harte," I muttered in disbelief. "On their way in, they must have let the kraken out." Panic filled me. "I'm alone. My co-rulers abandoned me."

Stheno and Euryale had ruled from the grotto since Rathe's creation. What would happen now that both of them were gone? I was still in training. I didn't know nearly enough to rule this realm by myself.

On the ground, not far from where I stood, was the piece of mirror Stheno and Euryale had used. I walked over and picked it up. My hands were trembling. "Medusa?"

I waited, but nothing happened.

"Medusa, please." My voice shook. "Can you hear me?"

Stheno and Euryale were able to communicate with her using the mirror. Shouldn't the same rules apply to me?

No. Very different rules. I didn't know if that was Sage or my self-doubt talking.

"Medusa?" I tried again. The mirror remained unchanged. Not even a wave or blur of motion.

Sage was silent, but I could feel her disappointment. No matter how long I stared into the mirror, Medusa would never answer.

Quietly, I gave voice to the dreadful truth simmering inside of me. "I did this. They never would have left if I hadn't given them my memory of him. It's my fault the kraken is here. It's my fault Stheno and Euryale abandoned Rathe."

I was so angry at myself that I threw the mirror against the cave wall. It shattered and Sage recoiled.

"We need Nixie."

I scrambled to get out of Gorgon Grotto as fast as possible. I had to fix the dire mess that I had created, but I needed Medusa's help to figure out how. Nixie was my only way to communicate with her, and I couldn't communicate with Nixie unless I had Uncle Lloyd's charmed wall panel.

As I flew out of the grotto, I didn't stop to tell Otabia and Mariza what I had learned. I raced past them to find Treygan. He needed to get Nixie's portrait and bring her into Rathe. I didn't know if that was possible, or if Uncle Lloyd's spell would even work in Rathe, but we had to try.

In the meantime, I had to stop the kraken from doing anything I would regret.

10

Koraline

Joel finished reading a chapter of *Gulliver's Travels* and closed the book.

"You can't stop there," I whined. "You ended on a cliffhang-er."

He inhaled some oxygen before setting his mask on the end table. He assured me he didn't need to be connected to the tank at all times, but I suspected he was trying to be tough instead of safe. "Every chapter ends with us wanting to know more."

"Then stop in the middle of a chapter. If you don't, I'll be wondering what happens next."

"Exactly. Imagining all the possibilities is half of the fun."

I squinted at him and reached for the book. "You call it fun. I call it torture."

He smirked and shoved the book behind one of the sofa cushions. "Speaking of imagining possibilities, if they do agree to let me become mer, I'm worried I won't look good as a Red."

I pictured him in a deep ruby tone, but every rank had a wide variety of shades and variations and they were impossible to predict. "You'll look great in any color."

How long does it usually take to be promoted to Yellow?"

Before I could answer, Rownan burst through the door, fol-lowed by Delmar. They rushed past the den without a word, so I unlocked the brakes of my wheelchair and rolled after them. Joel followed as Rownan's troubled voice carried from the kitchen.

"Yara needs Nixie's portrait."

"What's wrong?" Lloyd asked him.

"A kraken from Harte got into Rathe."

We rounded the corner. I couldn't have heard him correctly. "A kraken in Rathe?"

Delmar gave a confirming nod as Lloyd sat dumbfounded looking up at Rownan.

Joel stood at my side, wheezing slightly. "Creatures from Harte can't enter other realms."

"What makes you say that?" Rownan asked.

"Every book and paper I have on the subject. They all say the same thing. Creatures of Harte are trapped there forever with no way out."

Delmar spoke grimly. "Then your sources are wrong. We had a very unpleasant encounter with him."

"He wants Yara," Rownan said.

Lloyd shook his head. "I don't understand."

"Back up a bit," I said, still in disbelief. "A kraken, as in a giant squid?"

"Yes," Rownan said. "Except this squid can appear human like us and he's a powerful S-O-B."

Joel leaned against the back of a chair. I motioned to the den where he'd left his oxygen tank, silently asking if he needed it, but he shook his head and mouthed, "I'm fine."

He wasn't fine and we both knew it. "What about Joel's transformation?"

"Koraline!" Joel chided. "Now is not the time."

He didn't understand. I wasn't being entirely selfish here. "You're the only one of us who has done research on the creatures of Harte. If you were mer you could travel to Rathe and help. And Yara was going to discuss your transformation with the Violets after the party. There's a chance she already got an answer."

"She never got the chance," Delmar said. "Our unwelcomed visitor caused quite a panic."

I turned to Joel. "Could you leave us to talk in private for a few minutes?"

Joel dipped his head and whispered in my ear, "Research or not, I don't think this is a good time to bring up my request."

"Just give us a few minutes," I whispered back. "Perfect opportunity for you to get some air."

Joel sighed then offered everyone an apologetic shrug and left the room.

I rolled myself closer to the group. "Obviously I'm concerned for the safety of Rathe." I lowered my voice so Joel wouldn't overhear me. "But I'm also terrified that Joel could die any day."

"I understand." Rownan said. "But our first priority right now is helping Yara fix this mess."

"I told you, *Joel can help.* He has been studying sea creatures and everything related to the ocean since he was a child. He has a whole secret family library of documents and artifacts that date back more than a hundred years."

Delmar glanced sideways at Rownan.

Rownan shrugged. "He was a big help getting us into Harte, maybe he can get the kraken back there too."

"Perhaps," Delmar agreed. "But the timing is awful, Koraline. I'm not sure if any of the Violets will be open to even considering this right now."

"Would you vote yes?" I asked him.

Rownan snapped his head up as if he'd forgotten Delmar was now a Violet despite his new plum-colored eyes and hair.

"Do you truly love him?" Delmar asked me.

"Absolutely."

"Then I will vote yes."

Eyes wide, Rownan asked, "Really?"

Delmar ran a hand through his wet hair. "I supported Yara and Treygan when they were forbidden to be together, didn't I? Helping star-crossed lovers seems to be a new hobby of mine."

If he were within reach, I would have hugged him.

Lloyd cleared his throat. "Back to why you boys came storming in here. . . ."

Rownan returned his attention to his father. "Will Nixie's portal still work if we take it to Rathe?"

Lloyd rubbed the white stubble covering his jaw. "I believe so, as long as Nixie is still willing and knows where the portal is located."

"How do we make sure she knows?" Rownan asked.

I knew the answer to this one.

"Nixie helps Yara," I explained. "She watches over her the same way your mother watches over you, and Yara's mother watched over her. She's in spirit form, so she can travel anywhere in the physical world in the blink of an eye."

They all studied me with fascination, probably realizing how I'd learned the rules of being in spirit form. I had been where Nixie was, but I'd returned to tell the tale.

"So she could be here right now listening to us?" Delmar asked me.

"It's possible," I said. "But it's more likely she's watching over Yara, given the circumstances."

Rownan walked over to Nixie's carved panel and Delmar followed.

Lloyd was right behind them. "I can't change its size without compromising its power."

"That's all right," Delmar said. "We can handle it."

They started to lift her off the wall, but Lloyd said, "Wait. Let me put a spell on it so it's easier to carry underwater."

As Lloyd worked his ancient gorgon magic on Nixie's panel, Rownan paced in the foyer waiting for him to finish. I thought I heard him say something like, "Damn the High Priestess and her predictions," but I was too scared to ask him what he meant.

After the guys left, I decided I couldn't wait for Yara to find the time to talk to the Violets. Joel's health was declining too quickly. What if his doctors were wrong about how much time he had left? That question kept haunting me, getting more urgent with every minute that ticked by.

Pango had promised he would return to Eden's Hammock to swim me home after the party, so I waited for him. Lloyd was a good and generous man, but I didn't want to leave him with the responsibility of looking after Joel alone.

When Pango arrived, Merrick was with him. He claimed he'd brought Merrick along to help with some post-party clean-up, but I think Pango just missed his soul mate. My brother had been spending much more time with me than usual lately.

I told them my decision, explained how Joel might be able to help Rathe, and asked if they'd stay with him until I returned.

Merrick ran his hands through his floppy green bangs and gave me a disapproving frown. "Koraline, I don't think now is the time. I suspect the Violets are a bit preoccupied."

"I know that." I was well aware that Rathe was in a state of emergency. However, an unstoppable clock was counting down the breaths left in the man I loved. "But Joel's time is running out."

"I'm okay," Joel said from behind me.

I turned to find him lurking in the doorway, oxygen tank in tow. "You're struggling to breathe."

He wanted to argue with me, I could tell, but instead he sighed and sat in the chair beside me. He took my hand then softly kissed my knuckles. "What if you ask them and they say no and forbid you to see me again?"

My insides ached at the thought. "If that happens, then I'll find a way back to you no matter what."

Quietly, as if reluctant to interrupt our moment, Pango said, "I doubt they would forbid her from coming back. Especially since your time is—"

"Don't." I glared at him with such intensity that his mouth snapped shut. He was about to tell Joel they'd let me come back because it could be my only chance to say goodbye. I refused to think about it.

Frustration and disappointment tugged on Joel's beautiful lips. "This feels all wrong."

I kissed him. "I'll be back soon, and hopefully everything will feel right again."

Pango stood. "I'm going with you."

"I can go alone. You and Merrick just arrived. You should stay."

"I'm not letting you travel through Rathe alone while a beast from Harte taints our oceans. Merrick can stay here and keep Joel and Lloyd company. You and I will tag team the Violets and attempt to obtain permission to turn a human mer for the first time in, what, a century or more?"

Merrick shook his head. "Dreamers, both of you."

Pango winked at me. "Realists never make the history books."

11

Rownan

After the fiasco at the party, I'd had a moment of panic that the kraken would also try to take Vienna back to Harte, but she calmed me down. She'd said in all the time she had spent in Harte, she had never encountered any kraken, and the one at the party hadn't even looked at her.

Still, as Delmar and I swam through the gateway to Rathe, I let my mind slip into shadowing mode so I could check on her. Just to be safe.

She was at Moonstone Beach helping patrol the waterways for the kraken. She looked calm and focused. Most importantly, she was with a group of selkies and safe. No signs of a kraken anywhere, so I opened my eyes and focused solely on the task at hand.

Treygan had asked Delmar and me to get Nixie's panel because he refused to leave Yara. He and Yara had been pretty much inseparable before, but with the kraken coming for her, he was insisting that she never be alone. I would do the same in his place.

I don't know if I was just nervous thinking about it or what, but the farther we swam into merfolk territory, the more I sensed something was off.

The water is cloudier than usual, Delmar said.

Is that it? I asked. I knew something seemed different. *What causes that?*

His gaze darted all around, assessing the underwater trees we swam past, and then he looked at me. The worry in his eyes made me tighten my grip on Nixie's panel.

Nothing I know of has ever had this effect on our water. Between this and the strange rings that recently appeared around our suns, I'm assuming Rathe is being tainted by the kraken.

I cursed under my breath and pumped my tail harder. *Hurry. We need to discuss this with Yara and Treygan as soon as possible.*

"Treygan?" I called as Delmar and I swam through the rivulet into Treygan's house. "Yara?"

Delmar swam ahead and walked up the steps into the living room. He did a quick scan of each room. "No one's here."

"Let's get Nixie out of the water and then I'll shadow Treygan and find out where they are." I pushed Nixie's portrait toward Delmar.

He pulled it out of the rivulet as I morphed my tail into legs and climbed out.

"Where should we put her?" Delmar tilted the panel upright and we each grabbed a side.

"Over there against the wall. That way Yara and Treygan will see her as soon as they get back."

We set her down and leaned her against the wall that separated us from the kitchen. I stood back and admired my father's craftsmanship.

"She looks good," I said. "She's back in Rathe where she belongs."

I missed Nixie. A big part of me was still consumed with guilt over her death. If she hadn't entered Harte to rescue us, she'd still be alive.

Delmar must have read my mind because he squeezed my shoulder. "We all miss her. But her spirit lives on. We can be grateful for that."

A loud bang in the resting room startled both of us. "Thought you said no one was here?"

"I didn't see anyone." Delmar opened the double doors and froze, staring straight ahead.

"What is it?" I asked.

"You tell me."

I joined him and peered inside. The rocks surrounding the pool were covered with black streaks. I glanced around and noticed more on the walls. "What is it?"

"I don't know." Delmar walked inside and hesitantly touched his finger to a large symbol on the wall shaped like an eye. "It's wet."

"Is it ink?" The second I spoke the word we both went rigid and stared at each other. Ink. Cephalopod. Kraken.

I spun around and searched the living room and kitchen again. "That bastard was here."

Delmar looked out the windows. "I don't see him anywhere."

"He's sneaky but messy." I scanned the floors, the walls, every doorway, but I didn't find one more trace of ink. Delmar was right behind me most of the time. We were searching for a trail to follow, but none existed.

"Or," Delmar said, "he left his mark on purpose to toy with us."

I had tried assuring Treygan that the kraken was harmless. That we'd find a way to get rid of him before he even saw Yara again. At the time, Treygan had only grunted in reply, unconvinced by my fake optimism. The truth was that a living, breathing part of Harte had followed us home to Rathe. And he had been in my brother's house.

I headed for the back door. "I'm shadowing Treygan right now. Let's go."

At Paragon Castle, dozens of selkies and merfolk guarded the perimeter. We were meeting in one of the underwater rooms, hoping that would make it harder for the kraken to eavesdrop on our conversation. Since he could make himself invisible, we assigned guards to watch for any signs of disturbance in the water surrounding us.

After Yara updated us on Stheno and Euryale leaving and the kraken sneaking in, Delmar and I told Yara and Treygan about the kraken's home invasion.

They were silent for a few seconds, shooting sideways glances at each other. Yara let out a whoosh of breath.

He knows where you live, Yara said to Treygan.

Where we *live,* Treygan corrected.

I haven't officially moved in yet, and it's probably best that I don't until the kraken is gone.

I disagree. Treygan crossed his arms over his chest. *We're safer together than we are apart.*

He'll know where to find me.

He'll find you no matter where you go. I'd prefer you stay with me.

Vienna chimed in. *This is only a suggestion, but maybe you two could temporarily stay in Forbidden Apple Lagoon. Odds are he can't enter there, right?*

I thought it was a good idea, but Yara's face scrunched up. *I'm not going to hide from him. It's my fault that he's here. I have to figure out how to send him back.*

I searched the arched windows for the sirens, who I had assumed would be guarding Yara, but didn't see them anywhere. *Where are Otabia and Mariza?*

They're with Eve, Yara explained. *She's going through an intense transformation process and they have to be with her.*

Vienna looked as shocked as me. *Eve is the new siren?*

I nudged her to be quiet. One of our own giving up life as a selkie and becoming a siren was a big deal, but now wasn't the time for gossip.

Yara turned to Indrea and Caspian and said, *We need to talk about the cloudy water and the rings around the suns and moons. Has anyone reported any other strange stuff?*

I looked at Treygan, wondering if it should be him or me to tell her about the High Priestess and her ominous warning about rings around the moon. Then I remembered Treygan hadn't been there when Lloyd told me about that. I started to mention it, but Indrea spoke first.

We should address the changes in you as well. Indrea's amethyst eyes scanned Yara from head to toe.

Me? Yara looked down at herself. *How have I changed?*

Of course, now everyone was looking at Yara. I couldn't see any changes, and Treygan also looked perplexed.

Your hallmarks and coloring have slightly faded, Indrea told her. *You look like a muted version of your usual self.*

Yara held her hands up in front of her, studying her skin. *Are you sure?*

Indrea drifted closer to Yara and held up her arm. *Look at the vine hallmark that runs down your shoulder. Remember how it used to glisten like the inside of an oyster? Most of your hallmarks have lost their vibrancy.*

Perhaps it's due to stress? Treygan suggested.

Caspian shrugged. *We've seen Yara in plenty of stressful situations. It has never affected her coloring before.*

Do you feel healthy? I asked Yara. *Any symptoms of illness?*

I don't think so. Yara pressed the back of her hand to her forehead. *Have there been coloring changes in any others?*

Not yet, Indrea replied. *But we are keeping a close eye on everyone. Also, teams of selkie and merfolk researchers are investigating the cloudy water issue. And we're working on figuring out why the suns and moons are fading, including yours.*

Stheno's and Euryale's suns and moons had faded to the point where they could hardly be seen, but we assumed it was because they'd left Rathe. I hadn't paid enough attention to Yara's sun and moon to notice a change.

Do we think it's kraken-related? Yara asked. *Or a result of Rathe losing two of its rulers?*

We can't be certain of anything yet, Caspian replied, *but we'll let you know as soon as we have more information.*

Please do. Yara straightened and pushed back the hair floating in front of her face. *In the meantime, I'll meet with Nixie and figure out how to restore the ruling trinity of Rathe.*

And the kraken? I asked.

Yara swallowed hard.

You and I are in charge of dealing with him, Treygan answered. *Yara's top priority is the wellbeing of Rathe.*

I scanned the room and the silent guards around us. The mood was tense and I could feel everyone's worry, even if no one was openly expressing it. I didn't want to make it worse by pointing out to my brother that it would be difficult for him to deal with the kraken and protect Yara at the same time. I'd have to step up and take the reins on this one.

This must have been what the High Priestess saw in her vision. The kraken was the darkness that followed us home. I hated that I was suddenly believing in fortune telling, but if my brother needed me, I was absolutely going to be there for him.

Sounds good, I told him. Whatever you need.

12

Guards waited outside of Treygan's resting room. We had scrubbed away all traces of ink on the rocks and walls, but the creepy eye drawing wouldn't wash off no matter what we tried.

"I still say you should stay at our place until the kraken is gone," Rownan told me for the third time. "Safety in numbers, right?"

I had already explained my logic to Treygan and he mostly agreed, but Rownan wasn't getting it. "The kraken won't hurt me. He can't drag me back to Harte with him or he would have already. Even if I set up somewhere else, he'd find me. I'm staying here."

Treygan set a potted bamboo palm in front of the eye symbol. Since we couldn't wash it off, we were screening it with plants. The thick leaves of the palms completely covered all traces of the ink on the wall.

"Perfect," I told him. "Thank you."

He brushed dirt from his hands. "If it still bothers you, tell me and I'll figure out a different solution."

"It's fine," I assured him. "Would you and Rownan mind giving me some privacy for a few minutes? I need to speak with Nixie."

"Of course." He kissed my cheek before he and Rownan left and shut the doors behind them.

I had moved Nixie's wall panel into the resting room because it was more private than the living room. The carved wood hadn't even dried out yet, but the magic still worked. I was relieved when Nixie's ruby eyes came to life and her spirit stepped through.

"I'm sorry," I said, immediately feeling guilty about Eve.

"For what?"

"For replacing you so soon."

"It wasn't 'soon' in siren terms. Apologize to Otabia and Mariza for taking so long. And then apologize to Eve. The transformation is insanely painful. I'm surprised you can't hear the screaming from here."

I shivered. "It's that bad?"

"Worse. I don't want to talk about it. Don't need reminders of my past mistakes."

Poor Eve. At least she was in good hands with Mariza and Otabia. They'd make sure their new third was safe no matter what.

Nixie walked to the pool then appeared to step on its surface. She looked around, examining the plants covering the kraken's graffiti. "The place cleaned up nicely."

"Did you see him do it, by any chance?"

She shook her head. "I was with you." She stopped in front of her panel and smiled. "It's nice to officially be back in Rathe. I mean, I'm enjoying this experience of being an angel of sorts and going wherever I please whenever I want, but having my portal here feels right."

"You make a wonderful angel," I told her.

"Tell me something I don't know."

"How about something is polluting our water, there are rings around our fading suns and moons, and the kraken is toying with us."

"I know all of that. And of course he's toying with you. Medusa says that's one of the things he does best."

I didn't ask what other things he did best. I had an idea what the answer would be and it made me sick thinking about it. "Stheno and Euryale are gone."

"Duh. Even the macawfish knew that."

"Why did Medusa let them go?"

Nixie's lips puckered. "I'm not sure. I didn't ask."

"How could you not ask that? It's the most important question I can think of!"

"No, the most important question is how do you get the kraken back into Harte where he belongs?"

"Do you have the answer to that?"

She looked pleased with herself. "First, you must choose two new rulers to restore the power of the trinity."

My lips parted, the weight of yet another paramount decision tugging my mouth open. "I barely managed to find a replacement for you. How am I supposed to choose two people to help me rule a realm I'm still learning about?"

"You're first problem is you said *people*. Obviously that won't work. They have to be sea creatures."

"Now is not the time to be a smart ass. Who does Medusa want me to choose?"

"I asked for suggestions, but she said it wasn't her place. You have to decide who is worthy of the job and who you could reign with for eternity."

"I can't make a choice that huge."

"What does your gut tell you? Medusa says that's almost always the right answer."

My gut told me Treygan, but as we learned during the Triple Eighteen, the three rulers had to be female. I mentally went through all the female sea creatures I knew and trusted. One person did stick out among all the others. Even as I said her name, it felt right. "Indrea."

Nixie's transparent red brows rose. "A mer candidate. I can't say I'm surprised. You always liked them best."

I ignored her sassy remark. "She's wise, level-headed, genuinely cares about others, and she voluntarily sacrificed her life in Rathe to stay with those who'd be trapped in Earth's realm when the gate closed. Plus, we get along. She seems like the perfect choice."

"Sounds like you've made up your mind. Now, who will be the third?"

Again, I reviewed my options. None felt as certain as Indrea. I could think of a few reasons why some would make a great leader, but they all had negatives working against them too. Not that I was perfect by any means, but it was an impossibly difficult choice. "I don't know."

"Maybe you need to get Indrea on board and then ask for her opinion. After all, she has to rule with them too."

"What if Indrea doesn't accept?"

"Then she wasn't the right choice."

A horrible thought occurred to me. "Medusa doesn't expect the two new leaders to be cursed to live in the grotto like Stheno and Euryale, does she?"

"I didn't think to ask." Thoroughness was not one of Nixie's strengths.

"She has to agree to change that condition. I won't sentence anyone to that dark, lonely way of life."

"What if she won't allow it?"

My own confidence surprised me as my answer surged out of me without hesitation. "Then you change her mind."

"What if it's not within her power to decide that on her own?"

"Then you tell her to summon Poseidon and make him agree."

Nixie's lips pursed and she strutted closer. "He wouldn't approve it for her own sisters. What makes you think he'll approve it now?"

I didn't have an answer. The best I could come up with was, "If they both say no, tell them the world they created will fall to ruin because I can't run it on my own. I won't even try."

Nixie shot me an unimpressed look. "You were almost talking like a true ruler. What happened?"

"I'm scared, that's what's happened. How could she let her

sisters abandon our world?"

Nixie eyed me up and down. Her expression was hard to read. Concern? Disappointment?

She raised her chin and said, "I'll return as soon as I have answers from Medusa."

"Hurry," I urged. "I'll wait here."

She stepped through the wall panel, leaving as quickly as she'd come. I could feel Treygan lurking close to the doors. He couldn't see or hear Nixie, but he had probably heard most of my end of the conversation. Not that he was eavesdropping. He was just staying within earshot in case the kraken stopped by again.

I called for him to come in, and he entered the room looking worried.

I started pacing. "It turns out that I have to appoint two new leaders to rule with me."

Treygan's brows shot up. "That's a massive responsibility."

"No kidding. I am not prepared for this."

He leaned against the wall and watched me prowl from one edge of the pool to the other. I had done three laps before he asked, "Whom are you choosing?"

"My gut is telling me to offer it to Indrea."

He nodded. "Wise choice. And the second?"

"I don't know. I considered Koraline, Kimber, even one of the sprites, but none feel as right as Indrea."

"Have you considered offering it to a selkie? One mer, one selkie, one"—he motioned to me—"mixture of everything."

"Do you think Vienna would want the position?"

Treygan shook his head. "No. After all she's been through, she isn't mentally or emotionally fit for such a responsibility."

"You're right." I thought of all the selkies I knew besides Eve. "Maybe Dina?"

"Dina is much too young and immature."

I rubbed my forehead. "This is like a high stakes poker game, and I've never played poker."

"Discuss it with Indrea. Together, the two of you will make

the right choice. I have faith in you."

I wrapped my arms around myself, knowing the moment I had been dreading was closing in on us.

Treygan cleared his throat. "Are you ready to tell me?"

I sighed and closed my eyes. There was no denying the fact that I was hiding a secret anymore. That secret had followed us home.

"You can tell me the truth, no matter how bad it might be."

"The thing is—" I turned to face him. The sadness in his eyes felt like jellyfish stinging my heart. I despised myself for whatever I had done to cause his pain, and for inadvertently bringing the kraken into Rathe. "The thing is, I don't know what happened because I gave those memories to Stheno and Euryale."

Relief and confusion washed over his face all at once. "You honestly have no memory of him from Harte?"

Finally, a question I could answer truthfully. "No, none."

"But something did happen. He made that clear."

I looked away, ashamed.

"Stheno and Euryale must have said something to you," he probed. "You must have some idea of what the memories were. You told me they were obsessively consuming them over and over again."

I nodded timidly. Every second our conversation continued was a second closer to me losing Treygan. He was about to discover that I was a cheater. He'd never be able to trust me again, and no one should stay with a person they couldn't trust.

As I struggled to find adequate words to confess to doing something so bad I'd given the memory away so I wouldn't have to face it, I was spared. Nixie's wall panel glowed bright red, casting shadows on the floor between us. Saved by my angel siren.

"I'm sorry," I told Treygan, "Nixie's back with Medusa's answer."

He looked so defeated, so anguished. He pinched the bridge of his nose and squeezed his eyes shut then let out a breath.

"Right. Go ahead."

I turned away from him and Nixie appeared in front of me wearing a huge smile. "Mission completed. No one will have to live in the grotto."

"You're certain?" I asked her.

"She gave her word." Nixie rubbed one ghostly talon across her lips. "I also asked why she freed Stheno and Euryale."

"And?"

"You won't like her answer."

My guilty conscience was about to be validated. "I still need to hear it."

Nixie sighed. "She said you left her no choice. You made them obsessed with the kraken. They were becoming useless as co-rulers because they were losing their sanity. They were even threatening to create krakens of their own. Rathe didn't stand a chance if Medusa left them in charge."

In a selfish effort, I attempted to defend myself. "Did they even have the power to do that? They didn't do anything except reject practically everything I proposed."

"Apparently they had *a lot* of power and totally could've created a sexy kraken army, but they mostly used it to control the seasons, maintain the balance of light and dark, and a bunch of other stuff we take for granted."

I was flabbergasted. "They never left the grotto. How could they do any of that?"

"They didn't have to leave the grotto. Rathe draws on the power of its rulers to keep things running. It just needs little directional nudges every now and then, and they had the all-seeing mirror for that."

"The mirror you broke and stole from the grotto to help find us in Harte."

"Yes," Nixie said, sounding a little guilty. "I thought Medusa would be angry about that, but she didn't even yell at me. And anyway, I only took one piece. The other pieces still worked. I'd do it all over again to save your life. And Treygan's. And

Rownan's and Vienna's."

Conversations I'd had with Treygan about Rathe's history swirled in my brain. Medusa had used the all-seeing mirror to rule when she was alive and restricted to the grotto. Why hadn't it occurred to me that her sisters might do the same?

I closed my eyes and resisted the urge to slam my own head against the wall. Medusa didn't stop ruling Rathe with her sisters until I came along. After I took her place, she still watched over me to be safe. She probably considered it my supervised training period while Stheno and Euryale still ran Rathe using the mirror as always.

Until I unloaded my filthy secret on them and made them so obsessed with a kraken that they begged to live in Harte for eternity. Now I was ruling Rathe alone, and my power wasn't enough to keep it going.

I was stunned. Speechless. I already knew it was my fault, but now I realized how thoroughly and epically I had screwed up. I had bartered with Stheno and Euryale, but hadn't considered the consequences. Yes, Uncle Lloyd was healthy again and the curse was lifted from him, but in exchange I may have single-handedly doomed Rathe. My knees felt like they might give out, so I sat down on one of the boulders beside the pool.

Nixie sat beside me. "Told you that you wouldn't like it."

"The rings, the cloudy water, fading colors; it's all happening because Stheno and Euryale left."

"Yes."

"They left because of me. He's here because of me. All of it is my fault." My head dropped into my hands. "Medusa must think I'm a worthless idiot."

"No, she doesn't. But Poseidon does."

I peered at her from between my fingers. "Medusa told you that?"

"Not in so many words. She did say that ever since your transformation to mer, your actions have caused her to fight with him more than ever."

I closed my eyes and groaned. "Great. In addition to everything else, I'm also breaking up the eternal marriage of our creators."

"Nooo," Nixie cooed.

I sat up and looked at her, waiting for support or encouragement, anything to make me feel the tiniest bit better.

She waved her hand dismissively. "They aren't married. At worst, you're breaking up a centuries-old love affair."

"Thanks for the clarification."

"I'm here to help keep things in perspective."

I rolled my eyes and stood. "Rathe will keep deteriorating unless I do something fast. I'm going to see Indrea and ask her to rule with me. Hopefully she accepts and has a great suggestion for our third. See if you can find the kraken. Spy on him and let me know what he's doing. Once the power of the trinity is restored, we can send him back to Harte and get Rathe back to normal."

"You've got it, boss." Nixie strutted over to her wall panel. "Good luck."

I opened the resting room doors to update Treygan, but he was gone. Delmar stood in his place. Motion outside the front window caught my eye.

Treygan was wading into the waves. He hadn't left my side since the kraken's arrival, but now he was.

"Where's he going?" I asked Delmar.

"I'm not sure."

I looked at Rownan, but he just shrugged. "He said he needed to clear his head."

Had Treygan put together the pieces of our earlier conversation? He seemed upset when Nixie had interrupted us. Did he figure out I had cheated on him with the kraken?

He dove beneath the surface and swam away. Never once did he look back at me. I was terrified he never would again.

14

Koraline

The long swim to Paragon Castle was exhausting. My back and ribs ached and I wanted to yank my prosthetic tail off to get rid of the extra weight, but the physical pain paled in comparison to my fear for Joel. I was so preoccupied rehearsing over and over what I wanted to say to the Violets that it took me ages to realize something was wrong.

Why do I remember it being more beautiful? I asked my brother as we approached the towering palace.

Our real castle was much taller than the replica we had built in Earth's realm, and it had expansive wings on each side. Elaborate detail work had been added over the centuries, including countless pieces of colorful sea glass, which were my favorite. Today they seemed dull.

It does look lackluster, Pango said quizzically. *Like it's in need of a good cleaning or the suns aren't shining enough light on it. Everything has looked like that since we came through the gateway. Very peculiar.*

I squeezed his arm so he'd look at me again. When our eyes met, he asked, *What's wrong? Are you in pain?*

I was, but that's not what I wanted to talk about. *I'm scared. What if the Violets say no?*

What if they say yes? You won't know until you ask.

Indigo guards surrounded the castle. At first I thought nothing of it because we'd always guarded the replica in Earth's realm, but then it hit me that we were in Rathe and guards had never been necessary here. The kraken's appearance had obviously changed our peaceful way of life.

We're here to speak with Caspian and Indrea, Pango told the two guards at the main entrance.

They're in Whelk Hall with the other Violets, one of them said as they let us pass. *Best to wait until the meeting is concluded.*

Pango held my hand as we swam through the wide corridors.

A few Violets and selkie elders exited Whelk Hall as we approached. At least we wouldn't have to wait for the meeting to finish. We swam inside and approached Caspian and Indrea.

I donned my brave girl face and asked, *Caspian, Indrea, may we speak to you in private?*

Indrea flashed me one of her motherly grins. *Certainly. Come this way.*

We swam out of the hall and into a smaller room nearby. I wrung my hands and weaved back and forth a few times before Caspian stopped me.

Koraline, is everything okay?

I'd like to make a formal request.

Go on, Indrea said.

Pango gave me an encouraging nod, but my stomach felt like it was home to a dozen electric eels. My mind went blank. I had practiced my speech so many times, but I couldn't remember where to start. Pango made eye contact with me and privately said, *Poseidon's quote.*

Yes. The quote. Awkwardly, I began. *First, I'd like you to ponder the wise words of Poseidon, who long ago said, "We are creatures of the sea, masters of the ebb and flow. Like the suns and moons that give us life, we will shine for eternity because we allow nature to change us how it wishes, and carry us where it may."*

Wise words indeed, Caspian agreed, *but what is your request?*

I bit my lip and grabbed the end of one of my braids as it

floated in front of my face. Why couldn't I remember the rest of it?

Suddenly, I relaxed and let go of my hair. Indrea was sending me calming energy, bless her. Gathering my thoughts, I pictured Joel's face and found my courage.

I'd like to request that a very worthy human be transformed to mer.

Caspian and Indrea glanced at each other. It felt like days passed before Caspian asked, *Who is this human?*

Joel. The bookshop owner who helped us with the Devil's Triangle.

Caspian lowered his head. *I knew that was a bad idea.*

I didn't realize you knew each other, Indrea said.

Pango stepped in. *Koraline loves books and she loves to learn. It makes sense that she'd befriend a bookshop owner who has literal volumes of knowledge to share.*

Indrea's purple brows rose when Pango finished a bit too convincingly with, *They're dear friends.*

Caspian did not look pleased. *We worried about him knowing we existed for this very reason. We can't transform every human who thinks they would enjoy life with the merfolk.*

He's dying, I blurted out. *Turning him is his only chance of survival.*

Dying? Indrea asked. *From what?*

He has a rare condition similar to cystic fibrosis. His lungs are giving out.

His lungs? Caspian repeated. *That reason alone is enough to disqualify him. The transformation would kill him.*

If we don't try, he's guaranteed to die. At least this gives him a chance.

A slim chance at best, Caspian argued.

Indrea's chin dipped. I could tell she was disappointed in me. *This is a horrible time for this sort of request.*

I know, and I apologize for that, but as I said, he doesn't have much time. Otherwise, I wouldn't be asking. Another rea-

son for turning him would be so he could help with the kraken situation.

How could a sick human help with that?

He's been studying ocean folklore since he was a child.

Clearly offended, Caspian said, *We aren't folklore.*

You know what I mean. Myths and fairy tales were created to keep our existence secret, but Joel's family saw through that. For generations they've studied everything they could about sea creatures and ocean legends. Don't forget, Joel is the main reason that Yara and the rest of Vienna's rescue party succeeded. Joel told them how to enter Harte, how the flow of time worked, when they needed to return, and more. His knowledge helped save their lives. Shouldn't we offer him the same in return? We owe it to him.

Caspian and Indrea glanced at each other. I couldn't tell if I was getting through to them.

Pango chimed in again. *Also, he knew about the genie curse. When he realized I was promoted to Blue, he wished to be turned mer.* Caspian jerked back, and Pango held up his hands. *Wait, allow me to finish. Mere hours later, he changed his wish to something simpler. He felt guilty and didn't want to leave me cursed. That's more proof of his upstanding character.*

I quickly added, *It also proves that he knows more about our kind than most humans and even some sea creatures.*

Indrea gave a slight nod. *We will give it thorough consideration. But as you know, it isn't up to only us. This has to be presented for consideration to all of the Violets.*

I know, I said. *But if you explain how helpful Joel is, what a great person he is, and what an asset he could be to Rathe, how could anyone say no?*

Before we agree to move forward, Caspian said, *we need to ask you something. Are you more than friends with this human?*

It felt like coral was lodged in my throat. No matter how hard I tried, I couldn't swallow.

Disappointment flashed in Indrea's eyes. *Koraline?*

Screw keeping secrets. Look where it had gotten me in the past.

I love him. Admitting it had felt good the last couple of times, but this was different. This confession could have terrible consequences.

Caspian's brows furrowed. *You've been having a forbidden relationship with a human?*

Meekly, and so slowly it seemed the water tried to keep me from confessing my crime, I nodded.

Oh, Koraline. Indrea's tone was laced with sorrow. *This complicates your request in a very big way.*

I know, I admitted. *But it doesn't change the fact that he could help us, and he will die if we don't help him.*

Indrea touched her forehead and sighed. Bubbles floated between her and Caspian. I didn't know if it was on purpose or an oversight because they were so stressed and tired, but they kept their sight extended so I heard their conversation.

We'll have to call a meeting, Indrea told Caspian. *No one has requested a transformation in a long time. With all that's going on, everyone is already nervous.*

We can't go to the others with this now, Caspian argued. *How can you even consider this request knowing Koraline broke the law?*

Caspian. Indrea's tone carried a hint of exasperation. *We were locked in Earth's realm for almost two decades. Most of us interacted with humans much more than we ever had in the past. Frankly, I'm surprised more sea creatures haven't admitted to being tangled up in relationships with humans.*

It sounds like you're supportive of her decision to break one of our laws.

I'm not supportive of it, but I understand how easily it could have happened.

I can't back you up on this in front of the others, he told her.

Indrea straightened, her tail stiffened, and she squared her shoulders. *I didn't ask, nor would I expect you to.*

Yara swam into the room. *I'm sorry for the interruption, but I need to discuss an urgent matter with Indrea.*

Of course, Indrea said. *One moment, please.*

Yara looked past Indrea and her eyes widened when she saw me and Pango. *Sorry, I didn't know you were here. I promise I haven't forgotten about your request, Koraline.*

It's okay. I already requested it myself.

Her shocked gaze darted back to Caspian and Indrea.

I swam forward and held Indrea's hands. *Please help him.*

Caspian answered for both of them. *After this kraken situation has been handled, we can discuss it further. But not before then, Koraline. I'm disappointed in you for pressing the issue now, given the threat to Rathe.*

He can help! I argued.

Caspian bristled. *I don't see how. Has he provided you with any useful information about the kraken? Anything at all that might be beneficial?*

The only thing Joel had mentioned was that he had read the kraken couldn't leave Harte, which was obviously incorrect. I didn't want to discredit him, so I answered carefully. *Not yet, but he has a lot of resources in his family library. Resources we don't have.*

I doubt any of the Violets will see that as a good reason for transforming a sick human in a time of realm-wide crisis.

Indrea gave a reluctant nod of agreement. *I'm sorry, but he's right.*

So you're not even going to propose it? I asked her. Moments ago, she had seemed so close to siding with me.

Her amethyst eyes filled with sadness. *I understand how badly you want this, but the odds of persuading any of the Violets to agree will be much better once the current crisis has passed. We cannot be selfish at a time like this, dear one.*

Ashamed, but still desperate and determined, I turned and swam away.

They weren't the only ones I could ask for help.

15

Rownan

Vienna and I reached Harp's Back Falls and approached the roaring waterfall. A public meeting was being held so we could discuss the strange rings around our moons, or at least the one moon we could still see. The other two were pretty much gone and the lack of moonlight was starting to worry us. Some even claimed to be feeling physical effects like headaches, weak muscles, and dizziness.

I couldn't help noticing that as loud and powerful as it was, the flow of the falls seemed weaker than usual. Vienna locked her arm with mine as we dipped behind the waterfall curtain and headed down the short tunnel that led to the ice park where many of our selkie social gatherings took place.

We were early, but so were many others. A few pessimists voiced their doomsday theories while small groups gathered around, listening and nodding. Our world coming to an end. The kraken becoming our new ruler. A Harte plague that would wipe out everyone. Others spoke privately in hushed but frantic voices. The fear and tension were palpable as we waited for the meeting to begin.

"This isn't good," Vienna whispered to me. "They're already starting to panic."

"I know, but the elders will calm everyone down and give us assignments. That will help." I hoped.

A familiar thwapping sound caused me to spin around. Much to my surprise, Eve landed on the ice near some of her cousins. *Landed.* As in, she had wings and came down from the sky instead of up from the water. Her grand entrance offered a welcome distraction for the distressed crowd. All the talking stopped for a second as every selkie focused their attention on her.

I knew Eve had accepted Yara's offer to become a siren, but seeing it with my own eyes was still a shock. Her eyes had changed color to match her new steel-gray wings. She strutted around wearing a signature siren corset and high-heeled boots. Selkies swarmed her, asking to feel her feathers, and she obliged all of them while flashing seductive smiles and biting her silver lips.

"Wow," Vienna said. "Look at her."

"You sound envious."

"I am." She stared unblinking at Eve until I snapped my fingers in front of her. She smacked my hand playfully. "Not that I'd ever give up being a selkie, but you have to admit, being able to fly would be incredible."

I raised a brow and smirked at her. "Flying is the only good part of being a siren?"

She blushed. "Being irresistible might be fun too."

I kissed her hand. "Sirens have nothing on you and never will."

"You're the only male in all the worlds who believes that." She leaned in and kissed me. "But you're the only one who matters to me, so it all works out."

Eve saw us and waved. Maybe waved wasn't an accurate term. More like she slowly wiggled her talons in the air like she was tickling us from a distance and enjoying every second of it. She practically purred as she approached us. "Hello, you two."

"You look breathtaking," Vienna told her.

"I wish I could take credit," Eve said, "but this new package is the design of our gods."

"I still can't believe you're a siren."

"Believe it, because here I am." She raised her hands above her head and spun in place while rolling her hips. Vienna blushed and gripped my arm tighter. As if she had anything to worry about.

"So, just like that?" I asked. "Yara offered and you accepted?"

Eve shrugged. "I needed a change of pace."

"Do you feel different?" Vienna asked her.

"In too many ways to count. I'm sure it will take time to get used to it all, but so far I'm enjoying it more than I anticipated. Aside from the pain of the transformation, of course."

"Bad?" Vienna asked.

"You can't imagine. Like someone cut every tendon in my body, shattered my bones, boiled my blood, and then stabbed new parts into places where they didn't fit."

Vienna shook her head. "No thank you. Have you gone hunting with Otabia and Mariza yet?"

"It was a requirement to complete the transformation."

"What was *that* like?"

I did not want to hear about Eve's first soul-sucking encounter with crappy human men. Luckily, one of my neighbors had slipped back into his Kraken-plague-will-kill-us-all speech, giving me a good excuse to go shut him up.

"You ladies have fun with your girl talk. I see someone I need to talk down from a ledge." I ran my fingers through Vienna's hair as I passed behind her. She and Eve continued their discussion without skipping a beat.

I crossed the park and had almost reached my target when a collective gasp rippled through the crowd around me. I turned to see the kraken strolling in like he owned the place. He had legs instead of tentacles and was only sporting two arms. I was debating the best way to rip them off when Dina hurried to his side and clung to him like a lovesick pup.

I tensed and rushed over to him. "Get out."

He grinned down at Dina. "My dear, will you please excuse us while Rownan and I chat?"

The bastard knew my name. Dina looked crushed and

backed away. I glared at her. Traitor.

"We weren't properly introduced at the party," the kraken said, as if we were a handshake away from being best buds. "My name is Luska."

"I don't care what your name is. This is selkie territory and no one invited you."

"On the contrary, I received several invitations." He waved at Ebony, who stood a few feet away from us. She looked star struck as she waved back then blew him a kiss. Another traitor.

"Luska! I've missed you!" Shona started making her way toward us, but her brother grabbed her by the waist and pulled her back. What was it with this guy and his effect on women?

Most of the selkie males were gathering and closing in around him. We were like a pack of wild and angry dogs eager to protect our own.

"Stay away from my people," I warned him.

He smirked. "Too late for that."

I balled my fist and pulled back, intending to rearrange his pretty-boy face, but Vienna caught my arm.

"Don't," she said calmly. "This isn't the time or place."

I almost ripped out Luska's tongue when he licked his lips and said, "Hello, prized pet."

"Don't speak to her," I snarled.

She glared at him then looked me steadily in the eye. "Let's get out of here."

All Vienna had to do was bat her lashes at me and I would have followed her anywhere. Reluctantly, I nodded and she pulled me away, but the bastard opened his mouth again.

"Your wife does look delectable. I don't blame you for wanting her all to yourself."

My claws were out and I had spun back around before Vienna could stop me. I slashed his chest with one hand and served him a jaw-splitting right hook with the other. An eruption of shouting and chaos broke out around us.

My beatdown was rudely interrupted by multiple selkie females grabbing me and pulling me away from him. Dresden, Vienna's brother, took over where I left off. He managed a solid punch to the back of Luska's head and slashed his back before he was pulled away too. One of Vienna's cousins got in a few kicks to the kraken's ribs. I thrashed and squirmed, trying to break free so I could hit him again, but the girls held tight as Vienna shouted at all of us to calm down.

Luska glanced at his chest where blood black as ink oozed from his wounds. His eyes flared with rage and he stepped forward. His two arms morphed into multiple black tentacles that whipped around him, lashing out at his attackers. I tried to duck, but the girls held me in place. One tentacle hit the left side of my face harder than any set of knuckles ever had. My knees buckled on impact.

I tried shaking away my blurry vision to check on Dresden and Vienna's cousin, but gray wings separated us. The girls tugging at my arms cried out and let go as Eve grabbed me out of their hands and threw me backward. I crashed into an ice boulder so hard that it cracked. I grunted in pain as I tried finding the wind that had been knocked out of me.

"Sorry, Rownan," Eve shouted. "I'm not used to my own strength yet."

She had the kraken lifted in the air by his throat. He wasn't kicking or struggling. He actually smiled at Eve then licked his lips. I couldn't hear what he said to her, but she let out several shrill notes of her siren song before flying up and out of sight, taking him with her.

Vienna was at my side, crouched down and examining me for injuries. "Row, are you all right?"

I rubbed my aching back as I stood. "I'm fine."

Vienna glared at the lust-sick selkie females who stared at the sky, searching for the worthless pond scum they had tried to protect. "I can't believe they acted that way over him. It's like he bewitched them into drooling puppets."

A gut-wrenching worry hit me harder than the kraken had.

What if his pull over females was some sort of supernatural ability that they couldn't resist? "You aren't bewitched by him, are you?"

She looked disgusted. "Absolutely not!"

I prayed she'd stay that way.

16

Watching Caspian and Indrea through the doorway, I wondered if I'd ever get used to the sight of two sea creatures having a private underwater argument. I could tell from their expressions that something kind of intense was going down, but they both just floated there, staring into each other's eyes and making occasional hand gestures. After what seemed like ages, Caspian turned away and swam off.

My apologies, Indrea said, beckoning for me to join her. *That man can be so stubborn.*

I waved aside her apology, eager to tell her what I had learned. *Nixie spoke with Medusa. Power needs to be restored to the trinity before things get worse.*

Indrea was all business. *How do you restore power?*

I have to replace them with new rulers.

Her eyes went wide. *To live in the grotto for eternity?*

No. I made sure of that. I didn't want to dance around the subject. The sooner I had co-rulers, the sooner Rathe would stop deteriorating. *You are my first choice.*

Indrea's hands flew to her chest. *Me?*

Medusa said to trust my instincts, and you were the first person that came to mind. I realize it's a lot to—

I accept.

I blinked a few times, surprised she had agreed so easily. I had prepared a whole speech to convince her. *You do? Just like that? Don't you need to discuss it with Caspian?*

I make my own decisions. Caspian will fully support this one.

We stared at each other as smiles spread across both of our faces. The reality of having a co-ruler whom I loved and respected shined a brighter light on the future. No more Stheno and Euryale making every conversation impossible. Indrea was the most easygoing person in the worlds.

Thank you, I said. *You have no idea how happy this makes me.*

What happens next? Indrea asked.

We need another co-ruler. I was hoping you might have a suggestion.

Hmm. She tapped her chin as she floated back and forth. *It's a paramount decision which deserves careful consideration.*

Yeah, but we're kind of crunched for time.

Yes we are, Indrea agreed. *The deterioration of Rathe is starting to affect its inhabitants. Some merfolk and selkies are reporting ailments such as weakness, shortness of breath, and dizziness.*

How many?

The most recent count including both species is over two dozen.

My stomach turned. Our people were getting sick and it was my fault. *What about the sprites?*

I sent someone to check on them. They should be back soon.

Part of me wanted to race to Echo Bayou and check on them myself, but I needed to stay on task. *What should we do about those who are sick?*

Violets are healing our people on a case by case basis and the selkie healers are doing the same. It's the best we can do without the Waterstone.

The what?

Indrea flinched, and I realized she hadn't meant to say that last part.

Indrea, what is the Waterstone? I tried to put some stern authority in my tone, and to my surprise it worked.

She sighed and rubbed her temples. *It is of no help to us now, but you should know the story. The Waterstone is an ancient artifact that can be used for healing and protection. Caspian and I took it to Earth's realm when we knew we'd be trapped there. We believe it played a role in keeping us alive until Treygan discovered the C-weed. We suspect it was stolen from us during the chaos of the Triple Eighteen and we do not currently know its whereabouts. We only discovered its theft after Koraline was injured.*

I stared at her, my eyes wide. *Why didn't anyone tell me this before?*

Otabia told the council that Stheno and Euryale forbade it. My eyebrows shot up and she shifted uncomfortably, looking almost like she'd rather swim out the window than keep talking. *They said you would want to go in search of it, and they couldn't have a co-ruler of Rathe continually haring off on mad quests.*

I made a strange noise between a grunt and a laugh, wondering if they'd said that before or after the trip to Harte. *Thank you for telling me now. Obviously, I can't go 'haring off' to find this Waterstone at the moment, so let's focus on what we can do. The wellbeing of Rathe and its residents is our top priority. Once we choose our third, things should go back to normal and we can deal with the rest of our problems.*

Indrea didn't look convinced. *I fear restoring power won't be as simple as announcing your choices.*

It won't be. We have to get the blessing of the gods, and I'm not exactly sure how to do that. Stheno and Euryale kind of glossed over that part when I was made a ruler.

Follow up with Nixie and ask Medusa for clarification while I weigh possible candidates. Meet me back here once you're certain how we proceed.

I nodded and turned to leave, but then paused. *Indrea, what does the Waterstone look like?*

The odds were slim that I'd stumble upon it, especially if it had gone missing in Earth's realm, but better to be educated than ignorant.

Her gaze drifted upward, searching for the right words to describe it. *It is a small stone, quite beautiful, more like a gem. Do you remember the color of Treygan's eyes before he turned Indigo?*

How could I forget? They were the eyes that pulled me into his soul for the first time and made me fall deeply into eternal love. I nodded. *So, the Waterstone is almost as beautiful as him?*

She grinned. *Almost.*

Much to my relief, Treygan had been waiting for me at his house when I returned. He had greeted me and kissed me when I arrived, but I had been in a rush to speak with Nixie and couldn't stop to talk. Now that my meeting with her was done I had to clear the air between us.

I opened the double doors to find Treygan and Rownan in the kitchen speaking in intense whispers. Treygan looked up at me and I knew something was wrong. When Rownan turned his head I saw a spectacular bruise forming on the side of his face.

Treygan walked over to me, radiating tension. "I have to go, but you'll have plenty of protection until I return."

"Again? Where are you going? What happened to Rownan?"

"The kraken showed up at Harp's Back Falls and a fight broke out. He's seducing the female selkies."

"And you two are planning to stop him? How? You saw what he did at the celebration. And if a group of gorgons can't stop him, what makes you think the two of you can?"

"We don't know how to stop him yet, but we will find a way."

My heart sped up. "Treygan, please don't get involved."

"How can I not? He said he was here to take you away, and

now he's attacked my brother. I can't sit back and do nothing."

"I can protect myself."

"I don't doubt that, but Rathe is my home. You are my partner. Rownan is my brother. I will do whatever is required to protect all three."

I knew trying to talk him out of it would be a losing battle. He had his mind made up and there'd be no changing it. Our uncomfortable conversation from earlier had been forgotten, or at least pushed aside. Even though I felt like it caused a bigger disconnect between us, reconnecting would have to wait. "Promise me you'll be careful. Remember, you're still my guardian."

He kissed my forehead. "Always."

I looked over Treygan's shoulder at Rownan waiting by the rivulet. "You two better protect each other. If any harm comes to him, I'm holding you accountable."

"So am I," Rownan said.

They left together and my stomach churned into a dark pit of worry. I went from window to window, counting eight guards outside surrounding the house and lining the beach. Next to Paragon Castle, Treygan's house was now the best defended building in Rathe.

While waiting impatiently for Nixie to return with answers, I scanned Treygan's bookshelves. I wasn't sure what I was looking for, but I couldn't just sit there or I'd go nuts. Maybe I could find helpful information about the Waterstone. I selected a few history books and set them on the kitchen table. I had only been reading for a few minutes when I heard someone entering through the rivulet.

I turned around to see Treygan rising out of the water.

"You weren't gone long," I said. "Did you forget something?"

"Yes."

He swept me into his arms and kissed me so passionately that my siren side stirred awake. With all the recent stress and drama, we'd had barely any alone time. I didn't realize how much I missed the feel of him until he pulled my body against his.

We clutched each other and fell to the floor, rolling a few times as we both struggled to be on top. He slammed my hips to the floor a little too roughly. I chalked it up to the heat of the moment and was going to let it slide, but when he pinned me down and bit my neck I reared up. "Ouch!" I jerked back to look at him. "What has gotten into you?"

He released one of my wrists and wrapped his hand around my neck, practically choking me.

Forget the heat of the moment. His out-of-nowhere roughness left me cold and angry. I shoved him off me and jumped to my feet. He reached for me, but I backed up. "Stop! This is a major turnoff. You're acting like a sex-crazed lunatic."

"What's wrong with that?" He sounded strange, different.

I gaped at him as he crawled toward me. I continued backing away. "What happened to finding a way to protect the people of Rathe and defending your brother? Making out should be the last thing on your mind."

He stood slowly, inches separating us. "I plan to do much more than make out."

I opened my mouth to call him a selfish numskull, but my breath hitched as the scent of vanilla hit me. His indigo eyes turned an eerie shade of dark purple then black. I froze with shock as he kissed me again and jammed his tongue so far into my mouth that I almost gagged.

My intuition screamed the truth until my ears rang. I broke the kiss, placed my hands on his chest, and whispered, "Kraken."

He groaned with pleasure. "I'd much prefer you call me by name. Luska."

Summoning all the siren strength within me, I heaved him off me. He landed on his feet and dropped his Treygan disguise, morphing into the same humanesque form he'd taken at the party.

I screamed to the guards for help, but my voice echoed back at me as if I were surrounded by steel. I looked around us and noticed a layer of dark, transparent material surrounding the room like a bubble. I reached out and touched a cold liquid wall. "What is this?"

Luska stepped closer. "An ink cloud."

I glared at him. How many more tricks did he have up his sleeves?

"A protective barrier." He lifted one arm that morphed into a black tentacle. With the tip, he tapped the barrier and shimmers of light snaked off in all directions. "It's soundproof for young rulers who like to shout for help when I come near."

I unsheathed my selkie claws and tried slashing my way through it, but it appeared to be indestructible. "How did you make yourself look like Treygan?"

His eyes glimmered in a way that made me dizzy. "Call it magic, if you will."

"You have no right to deceive me and violate me that way."

"Deception and violation is part of what makes it so erotic." He stepped closer, opening his hands as if I'd slide right into them.

I sidestepped out of his reach. "You're a monster."

He followed me slowly but confidently. Too confidently. "So are you. A lovely and addicting one."

"Go back to Harte where you belong."

"I will. When you return with me." He caressed my shoulder and I shoved him away.

"Clearly you have no respect for boundaries. Why haven't you just taken me back to Harte against my will?"

"You're a ruler of this realm. I can't remove you from it. You have to go willingly."

So I was right about that. Thank Poseidon and Medusa for small miracles. "That will never happen."

"Then I stay here." He sat on the sofa and kicked up his feet on the coffee table. "Harte has become a bore anyway. I'm having a much more savory time here in Rathe."

I hated his nonchalant arrogance, as if this was all a game to him. "If you harm any of my people, I swear—" I couldn't think of an adequate threat.

"What do you swear?" He licked his lips and scanned my body from head to toe, then back up to my chest where his eyes lingered. Leftover remnants of my human modesty made my mer skin and hallmarks feel like inadequate coverage. "My goal is to please you, not anger you, young ruler. Perhaps you can persuade me to spend my time participating in *other* activities."

"Go to hell."

"As I previously stated, I'll only return if you accompany me."

"Why would you want to be with me when I don't want to be with you? I have no memory of our time together. I gave it away."

"We will create new memories."

"No, we won't. I'm not yours."

"You will be. You gave away the memory of us because it frightened you to feel something so powerful. You knew that silly merman of yours would never again be able to satisfy you."

"That's not true."

"Isn't it?" His dark eyes scanned me again as a lazy grin parted his lips. "You felt exquisite. Like your body was created to meld with mine. We were combustible together."

I winced, praying he was lying.

"A mortal wouldn't be able to handle such ecstasy, but you are a goddess. The only reason for ridding yourself of such a blissful memory is to protect that inadequate half-breed mate you've so poorly chosen." He rose and strutted toward the kitchen then turned around, meeting my gaze with an intensity that sent chills through me. "Lie to yourself for as long as you wish, but it is the truth. Eventually you will require more than he can offer. You will succumb to me because only I can fulfill your deepest, darkest desires."

He walked away, opened the back door, and then dissolved into thin air again. In that instant I realized the ink cloud no longer surrounded me.

"The kraken!" I shouted. The guards outside turned to look at me. "He's here. He's invisible!"

They scurried, panicking, trying to figure out how to find an invisible intruder, but Luska was gone.

I slammed the door, angry at him and myself. I couldn't remember what we had or hadn't done together in Harte, but as far as I was concerned it had never happened. It certainly would never happen again. I was a creature of the sun, the light. I didn't need some evil kraken to fulfill any deep, dark desires because I didn't have any.

Sage slithered over my shoulder and caressed my cheek. Her cold scales reminded me that I was also a creature of the moon, the darkness. So yes, I did have a light side and dark side, but they were balanced. And Treygan, my partner and true soul mate, was mer and gorgon. Light and dark. He was balanced too. We were a perfect match.

The kraken would never convince me otherwise.

17

Koraline

Pango was spending time with Merrick, so I swam to Delmar and Kimber's house alone. I hated to ask Kimber for such a weighty favor, but she was one of my oldest friends. She had to know I would do it for her if our situations were reversed.

And it wasn't really a favor, I reminded myself. I was collecting on a debt she owed me. Never in a million years would I have ever thought I would use our past as a way to get her to do something against the law, but I was desperate to save Joel.

As soon as she sensed me coming, Kimber leaned out the window and waved. I steeled my nerves and swam into the rivulet entrance.

Delmar and Kimber's rivulet was deeper than most. They had more deep-water areas throughout their home because Kimber could only communicate underwater. Except with Delmar. He seemed to be able to read her mind no matter where they were.

I had always thought their system of communication had been good enough for them—unique and special, even—but after my time in the Inbetween, I knew differently. They wanted more, and they had broken laws in an attempt to make that happen. They were hiding their crimes, and I didn't think I would ever use it against them, but my current predicament left me clutching their secret as my unthinkable backup plan.

I had barely made it inside when Kimber dove in and greeted me underwater with a hug.

Let me see, she said, turning me to check out my new tail. Even with her stone lips, I could tell she was smiling. *Delmar told me about it. It looks wonderful.*

Thank you. It's taking some getting used to, that's for sure. I studied her dark hair and fins. *Look at you as an Indigo. It's different, but it suits you.*

Thanks, but I'm not sure I like it. I miss my light blue coloring.

You couldn't stay a Blue forever.

She nodded sadly. *I'm hoping when I reach Violet status, I will be a soft shade of lavender.*

It won't take you long, I assured her. Currently, I was grateful she was an Indigo. If not, she wouldn't be able to help me.

Would you like something to eat or drink? she offered.

No, I'm fine, thanks.

Did you hear about Stheno and Euryale abandoning Rathe? And now the kraken is out there seducing selkies. Isn't it awful?

I had no idea what she was talking about with the selkies, but I'd worry about that later.

It's very worrisome. I hesitated, fidgeting with my necklace and hoping Plan A would work because Plan B made me sick. *Kimber, do you remember the day the gate closed, when I gave up my seat on the airplane so your mother could make it back in time?*

One of the selkies had mysted a private pilot into flying a load of merfolk and selkies to Key West before the gateway closed. I didn't want to be trapped in Earth's realm, but Kimber's mom had two other children in Rathe who needed their mother. She made it back in time. I didn't. I've never once regretted my decision.

How could I forget? Kimber replied. *I am forever grateful for what you did for my family.*

You told me if there was ever anything you could do to repay me, to just ask and it would be done.

Her eyes flashed with apprehension. *I think I know where*

this is leading. Delmar told me about Joel.

I wasn't surprised. She and Delmar told each other every-thing. *I'm hoping with all of my heart and soul that you'll agree to turn him mer.*

She drifted backward and glanced around as if searching for an answer in the water. *I'm honored, but I've had no training. Delmar said Joel has weak lungs. I'm not qualified whatsoever for such a delicate transformation. I'm sure there are much bet-ter choices.*

You're my only choice.

She squinted, confused, and then her eyes widened. *The Vi-olets did approve this, right?*

They won't even consider it until the kraken crisis has been resolved.

Kimber's shock rippled through the water. Her hands spread at her sides. *You're asking me to turn a human without authori-zation?*

I would never ask such a thing if it wasn't a life or death situation.

Koraline! She gripped my upper arms. *Do you not under-stand the ramifications? You'll be punished and so will I. Se-verely punished.*

I'm willing to endure any punishment to save his life. My stomach churned thinking about how badly I didn't want it to reach that level of ugliness.

Her grip loosened and her brow wrinkled. Due to her stone lips, it was hard to read her expression, and then she closed her eyes so I couldn't hear her thoughts either. When she looked at me again, she asked, *What about Yara? Can't she grant permis-sion?*

Treygan told her she has to follow protocol to earn the trust of the merfolk. And now with the kraken showing up and Stheno and Euryale leaving, she has much bigger things to worry about. She can't help me right now, and I'm running out of time.

How much time do we have?

I couldn't tell if she was seriously considering saying yes or assessing how long she had to figure out an alternative. *I'm not sure. Days? Maybe weeks, but the odds of him being strong enough to survive decrease with every tick of the clock.*

She blinked rapidly, looking around us again, perhaps searching for the right thing to do.

I held her hands. *Please, Kimber, I would never ask for something like this if it didn't mean the worlds to me. I would never want to see you punished, but I am desperate and you're the only one I can ask. If I still had knees, I would get down on them and beg.*

She squeezed my hands and gave me the look of pity that I hated so much, but in this situation pity might work in my favor. *Koraline, I've never done a transformation before.*

Most Indigos haven't and never will. But you are married to someone who did the most important turning of our lifetime. Delmar must have told you everything about how he turned Yara. Knowing you two, you probably helped him study and learned the specifics even better than he did.

It's true, slipped from her mind before she closed off her thoughts. Kimber wasn't just my only hope, she was our best chance of Joel surviving the transformation. When she lost her ability to physically speak, Kimber became more sensitive to the energy of others. She would be much gentler than any other merfolk.

When her gaze met mine again her tone was genuinely sad. *I'm so sorry, but I can't do it without permission from the elders.*

My insides shriveled with self-loathing. I truly despised myself for what I was about to do.

Please don't hate me for this, Kimber, but if you don't turn Joel—

I could barely maintain eye contact with her. I was about to blackmail one of my best friends. I had no right, but I also had no other options. Guilt swirled through my gut like a riptide.

If you don't help us, I'll tell the Violets that you and Delmar have been conjuring illegal spells in attempt to turn your mouth back to normal.

Her eyes went so wide with shock that I had to look away. I was the worst friend in this world or any other.

Completely aghast, she asked, *How could you possibly know about that?*

The Inbetween. I checked in on you several times while I was in my coma. I can tell the Violets at least two of the spells you've tried, what the results were, where you hide your research notes and spell components.

She shook her head slowly as she placed her hands at her temples. She was trying to absorb the impact of being so violated, but there was no way to soften the blow. I finished as fast as I could. I wanted to get through the most despicable act of my life as quickly as possible.

Believe it or not, I was rooting for you every time, begging for it to work, but it didn't, and you'd cry, and Delmar would say—

Stop it! I don't want to hear anymore. Her skin swirled with anger and sadness. *You had no right to spy on us!*

I know. I only wanted to make sure the people I loved were okay. I had no idea I'd discover you doing something illegal. That was the worst part about learning someone's secrets. You couldn't unlearn them.

She turned her back to me. I could imagine the horrible things she must have been thinking about me. I extended my sight so she could hear me without having to look at me. I couldn't bear to see the repulsion in her eyes anyway.

If you help Joel, I'll never mention anything to anyone about the spells. I swear it on my life. I couldn't believe I was about to say more mean and terrible things to her, but it was far too late to turn back. *Helping Joel wouldn't be a selfish crime. You and Delmar casting illegals spells to make you normal again would have a worse punishment for both of you.*

She whipped around to face me, her dark eyes filled with so

much hurt that I felt it like a physical blow.

I had to keep going. No matter how violently my heart—and hers—was breaking, I had to finish. *Turning Joel will most likely have less severe consequences because you'd be doing it to help someone else and possibly our realm. Indrea and Caspian wouldn't let anything bad happen to you. And since Delmar's a Violet now, I'm sure they'll all fight for the lightest punishment possible.*

Mentioning Delmar's rank was a not-so-subtle reminder that his new promotion would surely be taken away if the other Violets knew about the illegal spells. Bubbles from Kimber's nose filled the space between us. She was huffing like an angry bull and I didn't blame her. I wouldn't even blame her if she strangled me to shut me up.

After several agonizing minutes of her silently drifting with the slight current and hugging herself, her arms finally dropped to her sides. Our eyes met, and in that moment I knew I had demolished one of my most treasured friendships.

She blinked one more time, slowly and deliberately, and then said, *Fine.*

I tensed, afraid that I might have misinterpreted. I needed to be certain. *Does that mean you'll do it?*

It seems I have no choice. I won't allow Delmar to be punished for something that only I so badly wanted.

Oh, Kimber! Thank you! I surged forward to hug her, but she held up her hands.

Don't touch me.

I lowered my arms and clasped them behind my back. *You may not believe it, but I didn't want to do this. I almost couldn't go through with it. I will never forgive myself, so I don't expect you to either, but please understand that I only did it to save Joel's life. If there were any other possible way, I wouldn't have involved you. It's probably difficult to believe right now, but I truly love you. If it were your life at risk, I would have stopped at nothing to help you too.*

Her eyes were narrow slits, but they didn't seem as cold anymore. The green tones of her skin were fading and a faint shade of purple tinted her chest and neck. The color changes meant that, as heinous as the situation was, she still felt some small amount of love. *Maybe I could forgive you one day if you had only threatened me, but you also threatened my husband. I'm not sure if I can ever forgive you for that.*

I understand, and I'll apologize until my dying day. I will owe you a million favors for this.

No. No more owing anyone anything. She drifted backward, putting more physical distance between us. Emotionally, she had already pulled miles away from me. *I will do my best to change Joel, but I'm worried it's not going to turn out like you hope.*

I'm keeping faith that it will all be okay in the end. I have to believe that or I wouldn't be able to do any of this.

We need to bring Delmar. As you so cunningly reminded me, he's now a Violet. If anything goes wrong after Joel is turned, then Delmar can heal him.

Even after the pain I had just put her through she was still being considerate of Joel. *Won't Delmar tell you not to do it?*

Probably, but then I'll explain why and he'll see we have no choice. But be ready for his wrath. I hope you're motto of "love until it kills you" doesn't become literal after he finds out you're blackmailing us.

I swallowed hard at the thought of Delmar finding out what I had done. He wouldn't kill me, Kimber and I both knew that, but losing him and Kimber as my friends would be more painful than death. *I still stand by my motto. There's nothing better worth dying for.*

18

Rownan

Treygan and I gave up trying to find the kraken in selkie territory. Everyone swore they hadn't seen him since Eve carried him away after our fight. We had no luck locating Eve, either. Our next stop was Gorgon Rock. Located in the center of our two oceans, it was the tallest landmark in Rathe, so we would be able to see the greatest distance from one viewpoint.

We began our climb and I looked up at the sea of gray above us. Precipitation should have been falling over both oceans daily, warm rain on the mer side and snow for the selkies. But not one drop or flake had fallen in almost two days.

"It's like our entire sky is dying," I said.

Treygan was climbing above me, and he paused to look up. "It should come alive again once Yara assigns her new co-rulers."

I worried what would happen to Rathe with everything being so out of balance. "I hope she does it soon."

"She will."

"Who do you think she'll choose? Besides Indrea?"

"I don't know." Treygan sounded annoyed, like he couldn't be bothered to discuss the huge decision that would forever change our realm and shape the future. "I suggested a selkie."

"Wow. That was kind of you."

"Seems logical. One light, one dark, and then Yara is a balance of both."

"Maybe she'll ask Vienna."

Treygan stopped again and turned to face me. "Vienna has

suffered more than any soul should over the years. I don't think she needs that amount of pressure or responsibility right now."

"She could handle it."

"And what about you?" His voice took on an unexpected edge. "Could you handle knowing that she'd become immortal? You'd get old and eventually pass on, but she'd still be here without you, ruling for eternity."

A sad wave of realization washed through me. "Damn," I murmured. "No wonder you've been so depressed. I never even considered that."

His brow furrowed. "We're talking about you."

"No, we're not. Yara will live forever. You're worried about what will happen to her when you die."

He turned away and continued to climb. "She's strong. She'll be fine."

I followed, quickening my pace to keep up. "What about you? It kills you to know that one day you'll have to leave her."

"Of course it does, but that's how life works." Gruffly, he said, "We can't all live forever. Keep that in mind before you go nominating Vienna for a position she wouldn't want."

"You still have over two hundred years with Yara," I pointed out.

He didn't say anything for a few moments, but then he quietly grumbled, "That isn't nearly enough."

I stayed silent for the rest of our trek. I couldn't think of anything helpful to say.

A few minutes later, we reached the top of the cliffs. Treygan and I stared out at the oceans, searching for any sign of the kraken. Besides the dull sky and not-so-clear water, everything looked normal. No sign of the cephalopod from hell.

I squatted down, hesitating to voice my idea, but decided it was better than standing around moping together. I stretched out on the rocky ground. "Join me."

Treygan turned and found me sprawled on my back. I patted the ground beside me. "Come on, like when we were kids."

He shook his head. "We aren't kids anymore."

"Maybe that's the problem. We've taken life too seriously for way too long. Get down here and stare up at the sky with me until we find a solution to this problem."

"I doubt that's going to work."

"But you didn't say it won't work, which means part of you believes it might. So swallow your pride and get down here."

He huffed, but then he gave in and stretched out beside me. We were a couple of inches apart.

"That's not how it works," I reminded him.

He huffed as he scooted closer and pressed the top of his head to mine.

I knocked on his forehead. "You're the one who always said two minds are better than one, remember?"

"I made up some really stupid theories."

"Agreed, but this wasn't one of them. We had some of our best ideas while brainstorming out here together."

Staring up at Rathe's sky with my brother made me nostalgic. Our lives were so much simpler back then. We were full of imagination and innocence.

"You focus on the suns," I instructed. "I'll stare at the moons. Eventually, we'll come up with a perfect blend of light and dark, and that will balance out our problem and give us a solution."

They were his words, and I'm sure he was touched that I remembered them, but he only said, "Let's hope so."

For a few minutes we lay there in silence. I didn't wonder what he was thinking. I let my own thoughts wander wherever they wanted.

I studied Yara's moon in detail. Only several tides ago it had looked like a magical pearl, subtly pulsing with pastel colors of the rainbow. Now the rippling waves of color had stilled, and the gray ring around it seemed to be growing thicker, casting a shadow on it that blocked out some of its light. It reminded me of the gift Lloyd had given me.

"I almost forgot." I unzipped my wristband and pulled out

the stone. "Lloyd gave me this."

Treygan turned his head then sat up quickly, staring at the rock in my hand. "Lloyd gave you that?"

I mentally cursed myself. Lloyd must have wanted me to keep the stone a secret because he knew it might hurt Treygan's feelings, and I was too thoughtless to realize it. "I guess he figured he gave one to you and Yara, so he wanted Vienna and me to have one too."

Treygan's scowl softened. One stone per couple. That seemed logical and much easier for Treygan to accept than our father giving Yara and me precious stones and not him. If it wouldn't sacrifice the power and integrity of the stone, I'd break it in half and give him the biggest piece. But it wouldn't be the same, or mean nearly as much as Lloyd personally giving it to him.

I added a bit more verbal ointment to his wound. "He said it would protect everyone."

One of Treygan's brows rose. "All of Rathe's creatures?"

"Well, no, I doubt that, but all of the people I love."

He flashed me a disapproving frown, like I should love every single creature in Rathe.

"Give me a break," I said. "I don't even know every soul in our realm. How can I possibly love all of them?"

"Because we're all connected."

"Whatever. Anyway, when we fight the kraken, this will protect us."

"Did Lloyd specify that?"

"He didn't use those exact words, but my gut says it will."

I hadn't heard anyone approaching, which is why I nearly dropped the stone when Yara suddenly landed beside us. All three sirens landed seconds after her.

Somewhat out of breath, Yara said, "Oh, thank gods."

Treygan was already on his feet. "What's wrong?"

"The kraken snuck into the house while I was there. The guards never saw him."

My brother went still as a statue, which meant he was at an intense level of anger. "Did he hurt you?"

"No." Yara hesitated. "But he can change forms. He can look like anyone." She wiped her mouth. "He was disguised as you, Treygan."

Treygan's hallmarks swirled so fast I thought they might leap from his skin. Through clenched teeth, he said, "I'll shatter him to pieces."

"Please calm down," Yara told him. "It didn't take long for me to realize it wasn't you. He acted nothing like you. But we have to warn everyone in Rathe. They need to know he could be disguised as anyone."

I needed to find Vienna and get her out of Rathe. I'd take her to Eden's Hammock and she could stay with Lloyd until the kraken was gone. We needed to send that bastard back to hell ASAP.

19

Treygan stared at me, scanning my body as he blinked kind of frantically. Impossible as it was, I felt like he could see the kraken's fingerprints all over me. I hated that I had kissed him and let him touch me for so long before I figured out he was an impostor. I wanted to beg for Treygan's forgiveness, but with so many others gathered around us, I opted for guilty silence.

"That has to be it," Treygan said.

"What has to be what?" I asked.

"Your strange ability. The way you can blend with objects and make yourself seem to disappear. Cephalopods do that. You began doing it after we came back from Harte."

"What are you implying?"

"Somehow you inherited his ability."

Treygan said something else, but I didn't hear him. An ocean of truth roared in my ears, muffling everything except a soul-chilling realization.

My newest ability to camouflage myself—to appear invisible—was the trait of a cephalopod. An ability I had acquired from the kraken. I closed my eyes, feeling sick all over. What must we have done together for me to inherit his power? If he had somehow tainted me with his creepy ability, I was determined to use it against him for revenge.

Treygan put a hand on my arm. "Yara, are you all right? You're trembling."

Sickness had quickly escalated into anger. I was angry at myself for ever going near the kraken, but I was furious with him for everything else: coming to Rathe, the harm he was caus- ing, seducing and attacking selkies, invading Treygan's home, and violating me by pretending to be Treygan.

"You're right. I must have gotten it from him." I uncurled my balled fists. "So I'll use it to beat him at his own game."

"How?" Treygan asked.

"I don't know yet, but I will figure out a way."

Rownan stepped toward Eve. "What happened after you flew off with him? Any insider tips on how to destroy him?"

Eve was new, but it already felt like she'd been a siren for- ever. "Sorry, but no. I had to fight a powerful urge to *be* with him. Seeing him harm my former selkie kin kept my will strong. Once he realized his smooth-talking wasn't working, he choked me with a tentacle and broke out of my grip. I dropped him in the ocean a few miles from Harp's Back Falls."

"Bastard," Rownan huffed. "Anyone else have any ideas?"

Mariza had nothing to say, which was a rarity. Otabia's black eyes darted aimlessly. I scanned each of my siren sisters again, and a notion hit me so hard that I couldn't believe I hadn't thought of it sooner.

Otabia instantly picked up on my excitement. "What, Yara? Tell us what you're thinking."

My wings lifted high. "We can't discuss it here on the chance we'll be overheard."

My sea creature sensing ability had been hit or miss late- ly, and Luska's power of invisibility meant he might be lurking anywhere at any time, except for the areas of Rathe that only a select few could access.

"The grotto," I said.

Otabia flew off the cliff and dove toward the underwater en- trance. Mariza and Eve followed, both transforming into bird form on their way down.

I pulled Treygan close to me and whispered, "I'll share my

idea with you as soon as I finish speaking with them."

He nodded his understanding. "I'll wait for you outside of the entrance. Go conjure up a genius plan."

Inside the grotto, my siren sisters and I could speak freely.

Eve looked around with a mixed expression. "It's beautiful in an eerie kind of way, but how could Stheno and Euryale live trapped in here for so long?"

Mariza started to reply, but I cut her off and jumped right into the more important topic.

"I have to remove his memories of me." I don't know why I didn't think of it the moment I realized he was impersonating Treygan. I could have done it already.

"Yes! Brilliant!" Otabia agreed, her wings fluttering. "If he doesn't remember you, he'll have no reason to stay here."

"Remove it all," Mariza added. "Memories of everyone he has encountered while here."

Eve's gray eyes softened. "Please make sure that includes the selkies."

We needed to think this through. I didn't want to screw it up. "He'll fight me. The moment he realizes what I'm doing, he'll try to stop me. I won't be able to remove much in such a short time."

Otabia preened her black wings while humming, contemplating. "He won't be able to stop you if he's asleep."

"Asleep? Do krakens sleep?" I had no idea. And where would he sleep? "Even if we did find him resting, he'd wake the moment our lips touched."

Otabia grinned in a menacing way. "Not if he drinks Liquid Lullaby."

A tingle ran through my wings. Nixie had used Liquid Lullaby to sedate Stheno and Euryale when she stole the all-seeing mirror. That plan could work. Maybe. "How would we get him to drink it? He'll be suspicious of every move I make."

"Invite him to a special dinner with you. Tell him you want to discuss his offer, to negotiate a deal. His guava champagne will be laced with Liquid Lullaby. After he's sedated, you'll have plenty of time to suck any and all memories of you from him. Then he'll long to go home to his beloved Harte."

"We'll arrive after he's passed out," Mariza said. "We can fly him to the gateway."

"Then we three," Otabia motioned to her sisters, "will deliver him back to Harte."

I tried to think of any glitches that could arise. "What if he decides to come right back?"

Otabia squared off in front of me. "Before we return him, you'll need to be operating at full power. The trinity must be complete so you can rule in the same capacity that Medusa did. You and the new rulers will be able to seal the gate. I want to be considered for the position."

My eyes bulged. "*You* want to be one of the three rulers of Rathe?"

"Why are you so surprised?"

"Because you love being a siren. It fulfills your dark side. Why would you want to care for a whole realm of sea creatures? You don't even like anyone but Mariza."

"That's not true. I do not like Mariza."

Mariza screeched, but Otabia ignored her.

"I tolerate her," Otabia said. "There's a difference."

"See?" I snickered. "I can't have a co-ruler who hates everyone."

"Why not? Stheno and Euryale hated everyone, especially themselves, yet they ruled successfully for ages."

"Not by choice."

"Then my volunteering for the position should indicate that I'll be more successful than either of them."

I eyed her suspiciously. "You'd give up feeding forever? Never hunt human men again?"

Eve and Mariza watched and listened intently, but neither said a word.

"Certainly not," Otabia scoffed. "Why would I give up one of my favorite hobbies?"

"It's not your hobby, it's part of your siren nature."

"Correct, and would I not still be a siren? Indrea won't change her form or her nature. She'll still be mer. She will still go home each night to Caspian. She isn't changing her lifestyle. Why would I need to change mine?"

"Because I can't have one of my co-rulers constantly flying off to Earth's realm to punish human men for their crimes."

"You fly off to Earth's realm all the time. Give me one good reason why I couldn't do the same."

I flinched. She had me there, and she knew it.

She smiled sinisterly. "But I do love how you're already speaking as if I have the job."

"Who would replace you, Otabia? I can't imagine anyone ever being half the siren you are."

"I told you, I wouldn't need to be replaced. I'd remain a siren and take on the additional responsibilities of a ruler."

"That's too much for one soul and you know it."

"Has it escaped your overloaded brain that conditions have changed here in Rathe? We sirens were created to be extensions of the gorgon sisters because they were sequestered to the grotto. Soon, all three rulers will be free as birds. Our siren duties will be drastically reduced."

Mariza's feathers ruffled. "Hey, where does that leave me?"

Otabia waved her talons dismissively. "Indrea will still need you for certain tasks. You can fly her wherever she needs to go."

Mariza's hands flew to her hips. "I'm not an airbus."

Otabia ignored her again. "If I'm the third ruler, Eve can assist me with any help I may require." She pointed her talon at me. "You'll still have Nixie as your mediator for conversations with Medusa. Everyone is matched up perfectly. Everyone with a purpose."

She made a valid argument. "Maybe you're right."

"Aren't I always?"

I glared at her. "That is not the kind of attitude I want any of my co-rulers to have. You need to check your oversized ego."

Her eyes lit up. "Then you will consider me?"

I let out a breath and my hands drifted open at my sides. "Even I'm surprised to say this, but yes, you're a strong contender."

"Wise decision. Wise, wise decision. Wiser if you declare me a ruler right now."

"I can't. Indrea has an equal say in this. She and I need to discuss it and agree."

"I will express my gratitude once the position is mine. When will you decide?"

"If Indrea agrees, we'll want to act as soon as possible. Like you said, the power of Rathe needs to be restored. Especially if we want to have any hope of sending Luska home."

"Yes, before he kills someone," Eve said.

I snapped my head around to look at her. "He won't kill anybody."

Mariza stepped forward. "Are you that daft? Do you think he's here to play Ring Around the Rosie? He's a beast of Harte. He will grow tired of playing cat and mouse, and when he does, he will most certainly take a life, or *lives*, to get what he wants."

I crossed my arms over my chest. "I don't believe that. He admitted I have to go to Harte willingly. Killing anyone in this realm will destroy any chance of that happening."

Otabia cackled long and loud behind me then put her hand on my shoulder. "Dear naïve and innocent Yara, if you truly believe that, you need more help than any of us can provide." Her talons dug into my chin as she turned my head to look at her. "I suggest you appoint me co-ruler before you learn how right we are and you're forced to carry that guilt for the rest of your reign."

I jerked my head out of her grip. "How do I find him to invite him to dinner?"

"We'll take care of that." Mariza fluffed her hair. "All you have to do is smile pretty and wait. The squid will take the bait."

"Go," Otabia ordered, waving her fingers to shoo me away. "Meet with Indrea and get her to agree so we can restore Rathe's power. I will prepare for your dinner date."

Eve and Mariza stepped up on either side of me. They were loyal and able bodyguards, but I didn't need them for my trip to see Indrea.

"Stay here and help Otabia," I told them. "I'll be fine alone."

Even if Luska spied on my meeting with Indrea, there would be nothing said about him or a plan to get rid of him. Our only focus would be whether or not to make Otabia our third ruler.

Indrea sat across from me. I had updated her on Medusa's instructions, which Nixie had delivered right before I'd gone looking for Treygan. All I had to do was decide on two worthy co-rulers; anything else required to restore power would be provided by Medusa or Poseidon. The only thing left to do was agree on Otabia. Indrea had been pondering her decision for too long already.

Her fingers tapped the table between us. "You're one hundred percent certain?"

"If you are, I am too."

"I don't know," Indrea wavered. "Otabia has been alive much, much longer than nearly any other creature of Rathe. I can't think of a strong reason why not to choose her, and we are severely pressed for time, but I can't imagine her wanting to rule our realm."

"It's a peculiar choice, that's for sure, but she wants it. More than I've ever known her to want anything. As self-absorbed as she may seem on the surface, she did help immensely when it came to rescuing us from Harte."

"I'm just not sure if she's capable of the kind of love and compassion a ruler should have."

"She was in love once, and it ended horribly. She swore she'd never care for anyone again, but maybe being responsible for an entire realm is the perfect medicine to heal her scars."

Indrea pressed her fingers to her lips. Her expression softened. "All right. I never imagined I'd be ruling Rathe either, so why not. Otabia it is."

Finally, a resolution to one of our many problems. "I'll have Nixie inform Medusa."

20

Koraline

Kimber and Delmar flanked me on either side as we swam to Eden's Hammock. My guilt was so thick it felt like resistance in the water. It was the longest, most painful swim of my life, and that had nothing to do with the distance or the weight of my prosthetic tail.

Delmar hadn't taken as much convincing as I'd expected. The diehard romantic in him wanted to see mine and Joel's love story continue. He said with Rathe being so unstable, turning a human should be the last of anyone's worries. He also agreed that if there was any chance Joel could help us get rid of the kraken, then getting in trouble would be worth the risk.

Kimber hadn't told him about me blackmailing her—yet. She didn't want anger and resentment present at Joel's transformation. She claimed she could put her negative feelings aside, but Delmar wouldn't be able to if he found out I had used Kimber's greatest weakness against her.

Someday I would make it up to her. I didn't know how, but I wouldn't rest until I did. A fresh surge of shame made me pump my tail harder, speeding ahead of them. The entire situation had my nerves frazzled. I had to stay focused on the miracle that Joel would be turned mer by sunset.

As we surfaced just off Lloyd's beach, I fought the pull of the current while trying to remove my tail.

"Do you need help?" Delmar asked me.

"Maybe. Can you carry me inside before I shout the news to

Joel from out here? I'm so nervous that I'm trembling."

He laughed as I pulled my prosthetic free. Kimber took it from me, her eyes shining in the sunlight, not meeting mine. Delmar scooped me into his arms and walked out of the waves. "Come on, Maiden Koraline, your true love awaits."

My heart pounded fast as we approached the house. Lloyd stepped out onto the deck and halfheartedly waved. He didn't look happy to see us. In fact, he looked upset.

Pango and Merrick didn't come out to greet us. I should have been able to sense them from here, but I couldn't. Something was wrong.

"Please let Joel be okay," I begged too quietly for anyone to hear. I squeezed Delmar's arm. "Hurry." Delmar picked up his pace as I shouted to Lloyd, "What's wrong? Where are they?"

Lloyd waited until we were on the deck to answer me. "Joel's in the hospital. He had an episode, but we got him there quickly and safely. Pango and Merrick stayed with him."

Hospital visits were normal for Joel. I could deal with that. But Lloyd looked so concerned that I was afraid to ask. "How bad was it?"

"They aren't sure if he'll be discharged."

I squirmed in Delmar's arms, wanting to stand even though I couldn't. "You mean they aren't sure when."

"No, dear, they specified *if*."

I couldn't swallow. I couldn't breathe. I stared, unblinking, as sadness filled Lloyd's eyes. Delmar said something to comfort me. Kimber may have rubbed my shoulder. It was all a blur of numbness.

"I'm sorry," Lloyd told me. "You can use my boat to visit the mainland and see him at the hospital. My wheelchair is also yours to use."

I shook my head to snap myself out of the shock. "Now. We have to go now." I jerked in Delmar's arms, angling myself toward the dock and boat, but Lloyd grabbed my arm to stop me.

"I meant tomorrow, Koraline. Visiting hours would be over

by the time you got there."

"What if something happens to him tonight?"

"Pango and Merrick are staying near the hospital in case anything happens. The doctors will call if there's a change in Joel's condition."

"But—"

"*And*," Lloyd continued, anticipating my concern and pulling a phone from his back pocket, "we have satellite phones in case he needs to call us."

"You're sure it works way out here?"

"I haven't lived here this long without a way to communicate with the rest of the world. You're welcome to call Pango and speak to him if it eases your mind." I took the phone from him and cradled it like a prized possession, willing it not to ring with unthinkable news. "You can all rest here tonight and leave first thing in the morning."

I didn't want to wait, but I also didn't want to get thrown out of a hospital for trying to break in after visiting hours. "Before sunrise," I told him. "I want to be there the moment visiting hours start."

"Of course," Lloyd said.

I looked up at Delmar. "Can we turn him in the hospital?"

His plum eyes peered down at me with the same sadness I'd seen moments ago in Lloyd. "You already know the answer to that."

My lips quivered as I fought back tears. A mer transformation had to take place in the ocean. That was a given. More importantly, the human had to be healthy enough to survive the physically and emotionally draining process. Another given that had shattered Joel's wish, and mine, into pieces of impossibility.

I had never been in a human hospital before. The energy of the place made me sad, or maybe my emotions were so low because

I didn't want to see Joel suffering. My own physical suffering certainly wasn't helping the situation.

As painful as transforming into human form was, it was necessary for me to visit Joel. Earlier that morning, when we approached land, I didn't hesitate. But the moment my tail—what was left of it—transformed into legs—what was left of them—I buckled over and cried out in agony. It felt like the bull sharks had returned and were feasting on my limbs all over again.

Delmar was beside me in an instant and channeled as much healing relief as he could. He couldn't take away all of the pain, but he took away the hot, searing feeling of phantom limbs. The frequent surges like electricity shooting up my thighs and into my back were a small price to pay to be with Joel.

I tucked my blanket around my thighs and pushed onward.

The nurse we checked in with gave me the worst look of pity. Like she thought it was so sweet and tragic that the crippled, lovesick girl was visiting her dying boyfriend. A perfect match. Both of us broken.

Pango met us in front of room 218 and moved to open the door for us.

"Wait." I threw my hand out to stop him. "I need a minute."

I inhaled a shaky breath and smoothed the wrinkles from my borrowed sundress.

Pango watched patiently. "You look gorgeous."

"I don't care how I look. I need to emotionally prepare myself for seeing him like this."

"You being here will give him strength and joy. That's the best medicine."

Pango knocked then turned the handle and winked at me. He opened the door and stepped aside so I could roll myself in.

At first, I couldn't see Joel. A curtain hanging from the ceiling hid him from my view, but I could see the end of his bed and the lumps of his feet under the sheets. Another reminder of how different we were.

I rolled myself inside and the rest of his body gradually came into view. His fingers and forearms with monitors and tubes attached, his torso reclining on the elevated mattress—and then, finally, his cute, crooked grin lit up the room.

He said my name with a gush of breath. "Koraline."

"Hi, Joel." At first I didn't even notice the tubes in his nose. They were made invisible by the light of his eyes and smile.

Pango squeezed my shoulders. "I'll give you two time alone."

After my brother had left and shut the door, I rolled forward and held Joel's hand. "I came as soon as I could. How are you feeling?"

He shrugged then blinked with heavy lids. I lifted his hand and pressed it to my lips, kissing his knuckles, praying to our gods to spare him. Closing my eyes, I fought back tears because I realized my prayers could never be answered. My gods couldn't help a human.

What if his decline was my divine punishment for what I had done to Kimber for his sake? The universe wouldn't punish both of us for my atrocity, would it? I didn't want to get Joel's hopes up, but hope was all I had to offer him. Maybe it would make him fight harder to recover. "I have news."

His eyes opened and he looked at me with a glimmer of anticipation.

"Kimber agreed." I glanced behind me at the door to make sure we were still alone and then whispered, "She agreed to turn you."

His eyes widened and he gave a gasp that turned into wheezing. The machines helping him breathe started to gurgle and pumped harder.

"Shh, calm down," I told him.

His head bobbed and his nose twitched, but he didn't reply. He stared at me with a look of utter shock.

"Joel?"

"It almost sounded . . . like you told me . . . ," he forced another breath then whispered, "I'm going to become mer."

Not exactly my words, but close enough.

I smiled and his eyes lit up. He lifted his arms, slowly, like a zombie. A ridiculously handsome zombie. "Then let's get out of here."

With a breaking heart, I faked a grin. "First, you need to rest and get your strength back."

His hands dropped back down onto the bed. The light in his eyes dimmed. "Doc says that might not happen."

I wanted to assure him it would, but I wasn't certain it was the truth, so I couldn't say the words out loud. "You're one of the strongest and most resilient souls I know."

"A Violet," he murmured.

"What about them?"

"One of them can heal me."

Sadly, I explained, "Not until you're one of us."

He rubbed his hand over his chest. "Stupid, useless lungs."

"Don't say that." I held his hand and squeezed. "Only positive thoughts right now. Law of attraction and all that."

He squeezed my hand tighter. "I'll get better. I promise."

I nodded, holding back the tears that were almost breaking free.

I worried it was the first promise Joel had ever made me that he wouldn't be able to keep.

21

My plan wasn't sitting well with Treygan, and I couldn't blame him.

We were discussing the details in Forbidden Apple Lagoon. Only sea creatures with gorgon blood in them had ever been able to enter the lagoon. Hopefully those same rules applied to krakens.

I didn't like tainting our magical place with such an ugly topic. I could have sworn the star flowers dimmed with every mention of Luska, and every crease of Treygan's brow made the apple blossoms smell less sweet. Or maybe they were more signs of Rathe's deterioration.

"If he can't remember me," I explained, "then he won't want me. I can remove any memories of whatever happened between us."

"You'd have to kiss him in order to suck the memories from his soul."

"I know."

He looked betrayed.

I held his face in my hands, staring into his indigo eyes and wishing I could erase the pain in them. "It's not like I'm doing it for any reason but to protect Rathe and send him back to Harte."

His lids fell closed for a long moment. When they opened again, the betrayal had been replaced with anger. "He attacked you. What if he hurts you or does worse in a moment of rage?"

"That won't happen."

"You're not invincible."

"The sirens will be watching. They'll jump in if anything happens." He stiffened, and I pulled him closer to me. "Nothing bad will happen."

"I don't like this."

"I don't either, but it's all we have. Unless you have another suggestion?"

He thought hard, his forehead creasing as he searched for any option other than me having to make physical contact with Luska. "None at the moment."

"Our lips touching will mean absolutely nothing. I love *you*, Treygan. He is nothing to me except a vile creature I need to banish from our world. Please be supportive of me doing my job and protecting this realm and all the souls who live here."

"The souls who live here," he quietly repeated. His jaw clenched. Our gazes stayed locked as I willed my love for him to shine through my eyes. It must have worked because he nodded and said, "I will support you for as long as I'm able."

Taken aback by his reply, I asked, "What does that mean?"

"It means what I said. As long as I'm alive, I will always support you."

"That's a strange choice of words. Should I be worried about you"—I could barely think it, much less say it—"dying?"

"I will die at some point." The words had a certain gravity, like the thought had been weighing on him for a while. "And you'll go on living without me."

It was my turn to stiffen. "Why are you saying such a horrible thing?"

"It's the truth."

I didn't want to face such an unfair inevitability. "That day won't come for a long, long time. I will love you forever. Not even death will change that."

"Death changes so many things. Including feelings you believe you'll have forever."

"Stop talking like that. I can't think about you dying. I won't. If there's a way to keep us together for eternity, then I will move heaven and ocean to do it. But we're together now, and that's what matters." I kissed him.

He pulled me closer and our kiss deepened. Longing uncoiled inside of me as his strong fingers slowly raked through my hair.

Treygan broke our kiss long enough to say, "Promise me you'll never kiss anyone else like this."

"Never in a billion years." I pushed my body against his until his back was against a tree trunk. He continued kissing me, affecting me the way no one else could. "I'm yours, and only yours. Forever."

"Stay with me." He trailed warm, soft kisses from my neck to my jaw. The kraken would never, ever come anywhere close to flooding me with the love and euphoria that Treygan did.

"Okay." I tugged on the back of his neck to move his lips closer to mine, but he resisted.

"You said you only had a few minutes before you had to go. It's been longer than a few minutes."

"The plan can wait another hour. Or two." The harder I pulled, the more he resisted me.

He looked at me from beneath heavy lids. So much love radiated from him. In a gruff voice, he said, "Clearly, I need to be the strong and sensible one right now."

He kissed my forehead, my nose, and my lips, and then he ducked out of my embrace and backed away. "Go. Carry out your plan. Induct your new rulers and rid Rathe of the kraken. You know as well as I do that this," he waved his finger between us, "shouldn't be your top priority."

"You will always be one of my top priorities."

"And you mine, but until Rathe is safe, your job as ruler comes first."

I nodded, my senses coming back to me. "Of course. I'll find you as soon as the sirens carry the kraken through the gateway and toss him back into hell where he belongs."

He smirked. "I insist on experiencing a replay of that moment so I can savor it too."

"Absolutely." I kissed his cheek then dove into the lagoon.

As I swam away, I relished the way every inch of my skin still tingled from his touch. Like he had equipped me with invincible armor made of his love. Or maybe I felt stronger because Nixie had already found Medusa and informed her of my chosen co-rulers. Perhaps power was already being restored.

Everything I did after I left the lagoon had to be a well-rehearsed show because, as I predicted, Luska was waiting for me outside of Forbidden Apple's restricted waters.

My ability to sense him was working for now, but I couldn't let him know that. I fought the urge to look behind me as he followed me underwater at a safe distance.

Step one of my multilayered plan was to see Vienna for "girl talk." Vienna wouldn't know the details, but it was better that way. I needed her reactions to be genuine so we could fool the kraken.

Nearing the selkie side of Rathe, I swam through Aurora Forest. Sprawled out below me were groves of sea auroras. They didn't look right. Normally they looked like colorful, glowing, underwater Christmas trees. Treygan had explained they were actually giant worms. Pretty worms, similar in appearance to coral, but most definitely Spirobranchus giganteus. Much smaller versions existed in Earth's tropical waters. Here in Rathe they towered over ten feet tall.

I dove down, weaving between countless tree-worms with glowing plumes that spiraled in rows. Each of them swayed and danced with the flow of water.

The last time I'd visited, their colors had been spectacular.

Turquoise and yellow, white and pink, orange and purple: count-less color combinations that looked like the handiwork of an army of sprites. Now they looked sickly, like their natural light was on a dimmer switch that had been turned down low. I gently touched one and it felt slimy.

I'm so sorry, I said to them. Hang in there. *Conditions will improve very soon.*

The best way I could help them was by sticking to my plan and ridding Rathe of Luska. I said goodbye to the suffering for-est and reluctantly swam away.

When I reached Rownan and Vienna's beach, I pulled my-self up onto an ice shelf and headed toward their front porch. I whispered my code word to the selkie standing guard and he waved me through.

Vienna was stretched out on their frosted sofa, reading a book as she absentmindedly stroked the silky fur on her shoul-der.

"Good story?" I asked.

She peeled her eyes away and stuck a leaf between pages before closing it. "At first the bratty main character annoyed the life out of me, but she's growing on me."

"Nice." Small talk accomplished. "Are Rownan and Treygan here?" I already knew they weren't. Also part of the plan.

"No, they're heading up a search party to find the kraken."

Luska felt too close for comfort. I could sense he was less than ten feet away, maybe by the window. Or maybe my nerves were shot because of the conversation I was about to have with Vienna.

I sat on the edge of her sofa and tried not to fidget. "Can I talk to you about Harte?"

She managed a sad smile. "If you must."

"Considering we weren't in our bodies while everything there happened to us, can we say it actually happened?"

A frown tugged at her face. "I'd love to say that none of it counted, but the reality is our souls experienced it, so that makes it a part of us."

"But a soul sucker ripped Sage from me. I assumed she was dead. I mean, she was severed from my body. Yet here she is." I petted her as she purred on my shoulder. "She's fine. Her death never happened."

"True, but at the time you believed it was real, correct?"

I nodded.

"You grieved for her, right?"

"Yes, it was horrible."

"Do you still recall those feelings? Can you remember the pain of losing her even though she's still here?"

I didn't want to admit it, but Vienna made a valid argument. "Yes."

Vienna spread her hands. "Exactly. The body is a vessel. Our souls are our true essence. Harte is a place that targets your soul because the essence of who we are is infinitely more powerful than our limited bodies."

I looked away.

She scooted closer to me. "I have the feeling this isn't what you wanted to hear."

"Lately, the truth is never what I want to hear."

"I'm sorry."

I didn't have to fake any emotions with my next confession. Holding my stomach, I tried pushing away the sickness that was one hundred percent genuine. "I did something horrible."

"While you were in Harte?"

"Yes. I can't tell Treygan. He'd never forgive me."

"I bet he would forgive you. One of the best things about love is that it forgives."

"Not this kind of betrayal."

She placed her hand on mine. "Let me tell you something about my time in Harte. One of those hellions deceived me into believing he was Rownan. He had me fooled for I don't know how long." She squeezed my fingers tight. "Time passed so strangely there, but it felt like years. *Years,* Yara. Can you imagine the things we did together in that time?"

I didn't reply, so she turned my face and forced me to look into her eyes. "I must have cheated on Rownan dozens of times each day. Every kiss, every touch, every—" Her pale cheeks flushed with a hint of silvery blue. "Well, you can imagine. I did things with an evil imposter of Rownan that I will never be able to forget. I'm still trying to forgive myself, but *he* forgave me right away."

I struggled to blink. "You told him?"

"I did. Rownan isn't stupid. He knew all the things I would have done if I had truly believed he was there with me."

"Did you ever get into specifics?"

She looked away, blushing deeper. "The day after we returned to Rathe. He needed to know, and as afraid as I was to tell him, it felt like the pressure of a million oceans lifted from me after I confessed."

"Did you . . . you know . . . *sleep* with the imposter?"

"Sleep with him?" She chuckled. "Oh, we did much more than sleep. We did things that proper ladies of the sea shouldn't discuss." She nudged my shoulder. "Things that are making both of us blush."

I looked away, embarrassed for her and me. "That was different. You believed he was Rownan. The imposter tricked you by—" I paused mid-sentence and covered my mouth. "Oh my gods."

"What?"

I sucked in a breath then shivered. This wasn't part of the show, but I didn't care that Luska was listening. He already knew what I was about to say, anyway. "I bet it was him. I bet the imposter of Rownan was Luska."

"What?" She shook her head and cringed. "No."

"Vienna, a little while ago he barged into Treygan's house looking exactly like Treygan. At first I was fooled, but then he got too rough with me, and I realized the truth. The kraken is a master of disguise. He can make himself look like anyone. And the fake Rownan wasn't only a master of disguise. He was a master of seduction too, right? That fits the kraken."

"But I feel nothing for him. He's seducing women left and right around here in an obvious supernatural way, yet I feel not one ounce of attraction to him."

I considered how or why that would be possible. He had the same effect on me as he did on the selkie females, even though I tried to fight it. Why wouldn't Vienna be affected? "You were in Harte longer than anyone. You were with him for years. Maybe you built up a tolerance to him or something."

All the color left her face. "Prized pet. When he called me that I thought he was insinuating that I was Rownan's pet, not his." Her eyes went wide. "I have to tell Rownan."

"That might not be a good idea."

"We don't keep secrets from each other."

Pangs of guilt slashed through me like the sharpest of selkie claws. I wished I could say the same about me and Treygan. If I could, we wouldn't be in this mess. Rathe wouldn't be in jeopardy. My loved ones wouldn't be in danger.

"I'm going to talk to him," I blurted.

"Talk to whom?"

I meant Treygan, but that would have to wait. I had to stick to the plan. "Luska, the kraken. I think he can be reasoned with. I'm sure we can make a deal that would satisfy both of us."

"Are you insane? The only thing that will satisfy him is taking you back to Harte."

"Maybe not. I think I can offer him an alternative."

"What kind of alternative?"

"I have an idea," I said vaguely. "Mutually beneficial."

"Yara, don't do anything crazy. He's dangerous."

The next part was hard to say while sounding genuine. Thank goodness I'd negotiated my ability to lie again in my deal with Medusa. It was seriously coming in handy. "I believe he's more like us than we think. Deep down, we all want the same thing: to be happy."

"I highly doubt the kraken wants to be happy."

"Perhaps he wants a different, dark kind of happy, but I can still empathize."

"Dear gods, don't run this idea by Treygan."

"I won't. This is just between Luska and me."

A subtle shadow darted away in my peripheral vision. Like a roach scurrying into hiding before you can squash it. I may have flinched a tad, but I caught myself before turning my head. I was sure it had been him standing outside the window. My siren sisters were right. He couldn't stay away from me. Let's hope they'd also be right about him taking the bait at dinner.

"I have to go," I told Vienna.

"Go where?"

"To a private dinner with Luska."

She gripped my forearm. "You cannot be alone with him."

"He won't hurt me."

"You don't know that."

I forced out my next words with something resembling confidence. "I believe that whatever we shared in Harte made him care for me. Maybe he's not the horrible monster we think he is. Maybe he's just lonely."

She looked at me as if she couldn't believe I'd be so stupid as to believe that.

I wished I could tell her I wasn't.

22

Rownan

I was tired. Tired of searching for the kraken, tired of swimming, tired of listening to everyone's theories on what was happening to Rathe. But most of all, I was tired of arguing with Vienna.

She had refused to go to Eden's Hammock like I asked. We had gone several rounds and reached a stalemate, so I left to clear my head and help with the search party.

Hours later, there was still no sign of the kraken. I was ready to go home, but the last thing I wanted was to continue fighting with Vienna, so I returned with a bouquet of Stargazer lilies.

She was sitting on our porch when I arrived.

I thanked the guards for keeping an eye on her then I greeted her with a kiss. "These are for you."

"You're very sweet." She clutched them to her chest and smelled them. "Let's go inside and catch up."

I followed her into our living room, relieved that she didn't seem angry anymore. "I'm sorry for pushing you so hard about staying in Eden's Hammock."

"You might not feel that way after I tell you about Yara's visit." She sank onto the couch in front of me, wearing her serious expression. "I need to tell you something."

"How bad is it?"

"It's an extension of something bad we've already weathered together."

I thought she was going to tell me more selkies had been seduced while I'd been out chasing my own tail. But this sounded personal. "I should sit down, shouldn't I?"

"It would probably be best."

I sat beside her on the sofa. "Bring it on."

"It's about the imposter in Harte, the one I spent intimate moments with because I believed he was you."

Taking a deep breath, I nodded for her to continue.

"I think it may have been the kraken."

The hairs on my neck stood up and my muscles tensed. "Are you serious?"

"He deceived Yara by making himself look like Treygan. She almost fell for it, except he was too rough with her." Vienna didn't realize she was making it worse by continuing. Or maybe she did, but she just had to get it out in the open. "It's the same way he acted when he was pretending to be you. I thought you were so rough and wild because Harte brought out our darker sides."

I held up my hands. "Stop. I don't want to imagine the details."

Rough and wild. The words and everything they implied ricocheted through me like a spray of bullets. Sometimes I regretted our no secrets policy.

"I'm sorry," Vienna said gingerly. "I didn't want to upset you, but I couldn't keep this from you."

"Does this mean you'll agree to go to Eden's Hammock now?"

She shook her head. "You know me better than that. I'm not going to run away while you go hunting for the kraken. Besides, Yara thinks I must have built up some kind of immunity to his powers because I was in Harte for so long. I'm not susceptible to his charm like other females. I can help."

"What if something happens to you again? How will I live with myself?"

"What if something happens to *you*?"

I kissed her forehead. "I would beg you to change your mind, but I know you won't."

"You are correct." She rested her head on my shoulder. "This is becoming a new habit of ours. Risking our lives for each other."

I couldn't bear the thought of her risking her life for anything, especially me. Luska couldn't drag Yara back to Harte against her will because she was a ruler, but what if he went after Vienna instead? Given this newest development, I had to use Lloyd's insurance policy. His wrath would be worth it as long as Vienna was safe. "I've debated whether or not to give you this, but now the answer is clear."

She sat up as I unzipped my band and pulled out the stone my father had given me. "Keep this on you at all times. It's Lloyd's, and he said it will keep you safe. And hopefully healthy."

"Healthy?"

"Our people are getting sicker."

"Sicker how?"

"The symptoms are getting worse, and they're coming right back after healing sessions. A few have even noticed patches of their fur falling out."

Her jaw went limp and she touched her hip, running her hand across her soft white fur. "How horrible. What can we do to help?"

She hadn't taken the stone yet. I was still holding it between us. "You can take this like I asked."

"If it will ease your mind, then okay." She secured it in her own band then brushed her fingertips light as snow across my bruised face. "How do you feel?"

"I'm fine. What about you?"

"Fine. But we have to help the sick."

"The elders asked me to update Yara, so I'll go see her next. Meanwhile, they're going to everyone's homes to see if there are any more outbreaks. I'm sure they'd appreciate your help if you'd like to join them."

She was already standing. "Yes, of course."

"Hang on." I grabbed her hand and pulled her back to me.

"They're worried there may be nothing that can be done to help them. There's a rumor going around that these illnesses are a result of Rathe losing Stheno and Euryale."

"A rumor?" She squinted at me. "You say that like you don't agree."

I cracked my neck and tried to stay calm. "I'm worried it's because of the kraken. So far, only our females are losing their fur, and they're all females that have gotten *friendly* with him."

Fear and worry flooded Vienna's eyes. "We need a code word. In case the kraken tries to disguise himself as you with me."

"You wouldn't be able to tell the difference now?"

"I would hope so, but I want to be sure."

I was seething at the thought of that *thing* with Vienna. He might have looked like me, and she may have believed it was me, but it wasn't. He had violated *my* Vienna, my wife. What if she also became sick because of him? I wanted to slice him into pieces and throw him into a fire pit so he could fry in hell.

"Calamari," I growled.

Vienna giggled. "Calamari is our code word?"

"Yup." Through my clenched teeth I explained, "Dead, fried squid."

I was no longer worried about sending the kraken back to Harte. I was going to kill him.

23

Everything was in place.

The dinner would be held on the beach below Sybarite's Nest, the gorgeous treehouse of my siren sisters. Otabia and Mariza monitored from above. Eve had confirmed her successful delivery of my invitation and was helping several sprites set up the food and decor.

I had allotted plenty of time for Nixie to inform Medusa who the new co-rulers were. Indrea would be waiting at Trident Rock in case she, Otabia, and I all needed to be present to seal the gateway.

"He should be arriving soon," Eve told me.

I nodded, acting like I couldn't already sense him lurking nearby. "Thank you."

She spread her wings and took off, joining her sisters above to keep a watchful eye on us. The treehouse was tall enough that they'd be out of hearing range, but with their sharp eyesight they'd be able to see if I needed help. They were impressively strong, they could fly fast, create storms, and their talons could slit throats in the blink of an eye. They were good protection.

"Thank you for helping," I told the sprites as they finished the final touches. "Go home and get some rest."

"We want to stay and help," Keeley said bravely.

"Absolutely not. I won't risk anything happening to any of you."

"We'll be careful," she assured me.

Jenna winked at me and whispered in my ear, "After he has some champagne he'll be in a good mood."

Keeley and Jenna were the only two sprites who knew about the Liquid Lullaby. Otabia put them in charge of pouring it into the correct glass. I hated that the sirens had involved the sprites at all, but Otabia figured they were so small and innocent-looking that even if Luska saw them setting up, he wouldn't suspect foul play from them. She had no right to involve them, but it was already done. A colorful spread of fruits sat on the table, along with beautiful flowers and the two flutes of champagne. They had done their jobs.

"Go home," I demanded. "That's an order."

They said their goodbyes, kissed my cheeks, and flew away. I breathed a little easier knowing they'd be safe.

I turned and stared out at the water. Would he show himself? What if he didn't? We had no backup plan. I walked slow laps around the table, mentally rehearsing my lines over and over.

I felt Luska's presence ripple over my skin the way wind does before a hard rain. I looked up to see him chest-deep in the water. From his shoulders up, he could have passed for an Indigo.

"Hello again," I said.

He smiled, and I wanted to kick myself for the excitement that rushed through me. "Hello, exquisite young ruler."

I stood still as he came out of the water. From the waist down, he looked like he was wearing black pants with a blue or purple sheen, depending on how the light hit him. But he wasn't wearing pants. The sheen was a part of him as much as my hallmarks and shimmering merfolk skin were part of me. I was certain his legs would feel like slick rubber or a snake with no scales. The thought reminded me that Sage was resting on my shoulder. I stroked her head and told her to retreat. The moment she vanished my worry about being alone with Luska intensified.

He didn't stop at a comfortable distance like any normal person would. He stepped into my personal space as if he owned it. As if he owned me. "Thank you for the dinner invitation."

I cleared my throat. "I was hoping we could come to an agreement."

"As in you agreeing to return with me?" He licked his lips.

I tried not to stare, but I couldn't tear my eyes away. He smiled as if he knew I was trying and failing to ignore his beauty. "Why don't we sit down and eat before we discuss the specifics?"

He inched so close that I had to turn my head so our lips wouldn't touch. The tip of his nose brushed against my cheek. "I don't desire food."

A warm tingle rushed through me. To stop it I envisioned being doused with ice water from the selkie side of the ocean. I would not be seduced by him.

With my head turned, I had a clear view of the table. My gaze locked on the two glasses of champagne. I walked toward them and away from Luska, feeling more relief with each step as I increased the distance between us.

Keeley and Jenna had made coasters of flowers for both drinks. The one with yellow blooms contained the Liquid Lullaby. I grabbed both flutes and offered him the dosed one. "Then at least have a drink with me."

His gaze lowered to the glass. My heart beat faster the longer he stared at it. Did he know it was drugged?

"It's guava champagne," I told him, somehow keeping my voice from trembling. "My favorite."

"Why?"

"Why what?"

His voice was calm, smooth, confident, almost amused. "Why is it your favorite?"

"Because it tastes sweet and helps me relax."

"Relax?" His brows lifted. "Do you mean it lowers your inhibitions?"

I didn't know if he meant me specifically or him too. I took a gulp of my drink. "Only if I overindulge."

"Then by all means, let us overindulge." He took his glass, dipped one finger in, and then tasted it.

Despite growing more nervous by the second, I managed to act and sound normal. "Delicious, isn't it?"

Thank the gods, he took a sip. He tilted his head as if assessing the flavor then brushed the tip of his finger on my lips. "You taste much better than this." Heat flooded my cheeks as his eyes danced over my body. "Your skin changes color with your mood."

"It's a mer trait," I explained.

"I look forward to making you light up like a rainbow." He took another sip and studied me. Even I could see that my chest and arms were turning various shades of orange and yellow.

He laughed in a deep, seductive way. It was probably the most alluring sound in the worlds. But I loved Treygan. Nothing Luska could do or say would sway me from that truth.

"Do I make you nervous, young ruler?"

"No," I lied. I took another sip and tried to keep the conversation going. I had to kill time while the champagne worked its magic. "What else do you want? What else would you accept in exchange for returning to Harte and leaving our world in peace?"

He traced the hallmarks on my neck and shoulders, giving me goosebumps. "Nothing. I won't settle for anything less than you." I stepped back out of his reach as he continued talking. "Our encounter on my beach affected me deeply. I need it again. More of it. More of you."

He drank again. Good.

I only had to play along for a tiny bit longer. "What if I agreed to scheduled visits? One every six months or so."

"What is a *month*?"

"A month," I repeated, realizing that the measurement of time didn't exist in Harte. It didn't even exist in Rathe. Some of my human tendencies were hardwired. "It's a period of about thirty days."

His brows scrunched together with confusion.

I shook my head, remembering there was no rising and setting of any sun or moon in Harte. No reigns or tide cycles like in Rathe. No way to measure time at all. He didn't understand the meaning of *days* either.

Luska's chest spasmed in a silent hiccup. He rolled his shoulders in a loose and sleepy way. "I will have you when I want you. You will have me whenever you desire. No set schedule. No creature, human or otherwise, has ever satisfied me as intensely as you." In a slower drawl, he continued, "I won't stop until I possess you the way you have possessed me."

The Liquid Lullaby was affecting him. Tentatively, I inched toward him. "Are you all right?"

The champagne flute slipped out of his hand, landing in the sand. He sank to his knees and rocked forward, but I caught him. His lids were heavy as he looked up at me. "I feel peculiar."

I had dropped my own glass to catch him, and his weight was pulling me down. I kneeled so we were face to face. "It's okay," I assured him. "I'm going to make you feel better."

And after I remove a bunch of your memories, I thought, *I'm going to ship you back to Harte.*

Cradling his face with one hand, I lifted his lips toward mine. His eyes were closed and his head was heavy. He was fading fast. Exactly as planned. I tapped into my siren side and sang three soft notes before my lips closed over his.

I bit down on his bottom lip, and his growl vibrated my teeth. I searched his mind, starting in the present, figuring I would work my way back. He groaned as his tongue slid between my lips and drew me in deeper. Even heavily sedated the guy was a master at kissing. Angry at myself for momentarily enjoying his kiss, I refocused on tapping into his memories.

Another moan of pleasure distracted me when I realized the sound was coming from me. Without me even being aware of it, he had somehow wrapped me in his arms. He seemed to be in complete control as he caressed my skin. It felt amazing. Beyond amazing. I ran my fingers through his damp hair and pressed myself against him.

A faraway shrieking of birds snapped me out of my blissful insanity.

Sirens. I'm part siren. I'm supposed to be sucking memories from him, not sucking face with him.

I bit his lip again and he pushed me down until my back was pinned against the sandy beach.

"Let me ravish you," he said much too coherently.

His hands moved too masterfully.

He wasn't sedated. Not in the slightest.

I bucked my hips and heaved him off me.

"How did you—?" I began breathlessly. "You're not—"

He was kneeling in the sand, wiping a drop of black blood from his lip. "Not as weak as you presumed? Not susceptible to your attempt to poison me and steal my memories?"

I was paralyzed with disbelief. He knew.

He licked his own blood from his fingers. "I'll admit there was a temporary rush of euphoria that weakened my control. Certainly a first for me, and I won't deny that I enjoyed it, but it was a feeble attempt at best."

Speechless, I stared at him, trying to anticipate how he might retaliate.

He leaned forward and caressed my cheek. "Young ruler, you've only glimpsed what I am capable of. What I've done so far is child's play. Don't insult me again or I'll have to teach you a difficult lesson."

I wiped my own lips with the back of my hand, trying to erase his kiss—again.

"You're the only one who has ever played hard to get with me," he said. "You must realize that makes me crave you more. Is that why you do it?"

"No!"

He stood and sauntered to the table, casually sat down, and

popped a strawberry into his mouth, followed by a couple of grapes.

I managed to stand and tried not to show how badly I was shaking. "I thought you weren't hungry?"

"I'm not," he said nonchalantly. "However, you stirred up a primal urge in me and I need to find a release. It would be rude of me to seduce another female while I still have the taste of you on my tongue."

It took a few seconds for the meaning of his words to register. I stepped forward, twitching with the urge to protect. "Stay away from my people."

He laughed, tasted a fig, and then spat it out. "They don't want me to stay away. Quite the contrary, actually. I have already seduced many selkie females. The mermaids are next, followed by the sprites."

My fists balled. "You wouldn't dare."

"Wouldn't I?" His eyes gleamed with mischief. "I don't discriminate. I corrupt everyone equally. The irony is that I don't want any of them. I only want you. Give yourself to me and the rest of the females in Rathe will be spared. We'll both get what we want."

"I am not up for negotiation."

"I'm sorry you feel that way. Since you won't cooperate, everyone else in your world is mine for the taking."

Anger boiled inside me, hot and fierce. "Why are you doing this?"

He sucked on another grape and smiled with it centered between his teeth. With a flick of his tongue, the grape disappeared and he took his time chewing. After he swallowed he replied, "Because it's fun."

"It's evil."

He rolled another grape between his lips before biting into it. "Exactly. You do know who and what I am, don't you?"

I stomped to the table and slammed my hands on the surface, gripping the edge as I leaned in until our faces were inches apart.

"What you're doing is wrong."

"In my world, right or wrong has no meaning. The only thing I care about is what satisfies me." He reached for my face, but I slashed his hand with my selkie claws. He barely flinched. His hand hovered inches from my lips as he licked the blood from it. "Be as rough with me as you like. It only increases my desire for you. Since you, no other female fully satisfies me." He lazily waved his other hand in the air. "Try as they may."

He tried touching me again, but I shoved him away with so much force I even surprised myself. The chair fell over backward, but somehow he landed on his feet. He touched his chest where hand-shaped bruises were forming. "Dear darkness, you turn me on."

"Keep this up and I will kill you," I threatened.

"You can't kill me. I'm a god of Harte."

I squinted, trying to tell if he was lying. I added it to my mental list of questions for Medusa. "I'm a ruler of Rathe. I will do whatever it takes to protect my people from you."

His dark lashes fluttered and his irises glowed with an enchanting light. For a brief moment I began slipping into a trance, but I snapped myself out of it and looked away.

"You can't win," he said, sounding amused. "I do love how hard you're trying. It makes our game more enjoyable. But in the end you will be mine."

"I will not."

He bit his bottom lip, smiling like an egotistical sadist. "I look forward to playing with you again more than you can imagine."

I shook my head and huffed. "What do I have to say or do to make you realize that you and I were a mistake and nothing will ever happen between us again?"

"There's nothing you can do or say. *Us* is inevitable."

"Yara!" a deep voice shouted from the water.

I turned, scanning the ocean. Rownan's head bobbed above the surface before he slipped under, presumably swimming toward us. A low growl simmered in my chest as I turned back to Luska.

He was gone.

I looked all around, but there was no trace of him.

Suddenly, hands braced my hips and Luska's hard body pressed against my back. I tried to jerk forward, but he held me tightly in place. A warm kiss on my neck made my knees weak.

Then, as fast as he had grabbed me, he let go of me. I spun, slashing my claws through the air, but he wasn't there.

Siren wings flapped high above me. I waved them off. I could handle him.

"Where are you, Luska?" I snarled, searching all around me. Even though I couldn't see him, I could sense him moving farther and farther away.

Rownan resurfaced and ran onto the beach. "Where is he? I just saw him."

Irritation made my skin buzz. "He's gone."

Rownan shouted at the sky, "I'm going to kill you, you soulless squid!"

"Thanks," I snapped. "I had him where I wanted him and you made him flee."

Rownan scowled at me. We both knew I was frazzled. I had no control over Luska or what he was doing, but Rownan was there in front of me, so he was easy to blame.

"From what I saw," Rownan said, "it looked like he had you where he wanted you. Not the other way around."

I rolled my eyes and collapsed into my chair, knocking the grapes off the table into the sand.

Luska's voice traveled through the air and engulfed me like a warm breeze from every direction. "You will be mine, young ruler. Lust is more powerful than love."

I sprang to my feet. "Did you hear that?"

"Hear what?"

I called out Luska's name, but he didn't answer. His energy dissipated until I no longer felt him.

I snapped at Rownan again. "Go do something useful instead of interfering with my plans and screwing up everything."

Before he could argue with me, I soared upward into Sybarite's Nest where the sirens were waiting. He called after me, but I ignored him.

The sirens' nest sat atop the tallest tree in Rathe with no climbing access to the top. That made us hopeful that Luska couldn't spy on us up there.

As if they didn't already know, I updated Otabia, Mariza, and Eve. "Well, that was a huge failure. Any other ideas?"

Eve looked away. Mariza shook her head.

Otabia paced while scanning the ocean below us. "You aren't powerful enough alone. Not for him."

"I already sent Nixie to ask Medusa for the gods' blessing to make you and Indrea rulers."

"Good. Go see if she has returned. I'll see if I can locate Luska and prevent him from adding another victim to the growing list of those he has seduced." Her black wings spread at her sides and she stepped away from me, flashing one last look of warning before flying out of the nest.

"Go to Trident Rock," I told Eve and Mariza. "Tell Indrea what happened and then help Otabia search for him. I'm in no danger."

"You can't be sure of that," Eve said.

"He was in complete control down there. If he wanted to hurt me, he would have. I'd much rather you two protect the residents of Rathe." They didn't move, so as much as I hated giving commands, I shouted, "That's an order. Go!"

They both hissed and flew away. I left right behind them, soaring off in the opposite direction. Hopefully, Medusa had told Nixie I'd chosen the right co-rulers. I needed all the power and help I could get to take down Luska.

But first I needed to see Treygan and confess my sins.

24

Koraline

In the hallway, outside of Joel's hospital room, I thanked Delmar again for trying to heal Joel.

"I'm not sure how much good I did." Delmar glanced around to make sure no nurses were in hearing range. Purple still tinted his brown irises, but it was so subtle that no human would have noticed. "I haven't mastered my ability yet, and he isn't one of us, so that limits what I can do for him."

"I still appreciate you trying to help him. And me." I rubbed the part of my legs that ached worst.

"You would have done the same for me. Do you need another session?"

I shook my head. "You've done more than enough. Go get some rest."

I owed Kimber a million times more for not ratting me out. Delmar might not be so willing to help Joel and me if he knew what I'd done.

I guiltily hugged him goodbye and went inside Joel's room.

"I'm strong enough to get out of here," Joel insisted. "I feel much better."

Between Delmar's two healing sessions Joel had slept peacefully for most of the day, but it wasn't nearly enough for a major improvement to his condition. He was faking, and I envied his ability to lie.

"The doctors want you to stay a couple more days for observation."

He glanced at the door and whispered, "What's going on in Rathe during those two days? Will the kraken be sunbathing and drinking Rum Runners while on his vacation from Harte? The sooner I get out of here, the sooner I can help."

My gaze lowered to the bed sheets. I knew he wasn't being totally selfish. He desperately wanted to be mer, but he also genuinely thought he could help, and he was willing to risk his life for the chance to prove it.

"Kimber won't turn you right now. Not after you've just been hospitalized."

"Delmar healed me."

"He did what little he could. I told you, mer healing doesn't really work on a human. Your bodies don't react to our energy the same way." It was yet another reminder that no matter how much Joel and I loved each other, we were from different worlds with different rules. "You still need to rest."

"We can wait a day if it makes Kimber feel better, but at least help me get out of here so I can do some research. I'm sure there's information that can help us in my family archives. I need to get into the vault and find something that can save the day."

The urgency in his voice made me wonder. "Why worry about that now? What changed since you were on Eden's Hammock?"

He still spoke quietly so no one would overhear. "Now Kimber is involved. I know how much her friendship means to you. If she gets in trouble for turning me, I want her to have a solid excuse. One that will let her off the hook."

My blackmail threat ricocheted through my thoughts and my stomach twisted. "What kind of excuse?"

His eyes glimmered behind his glasses. Mischief mixed with intelligence. "She can tell the Violets that I possessed knowledge of how to save Rathe from the kraken, but I wouldn't tell anyone until she turned me."

"You wouldn't do that. If you knew something, you would help."

"Of course I would. But in this situation, I can tell Kimber her turning me is conditional to sharing the information, and then when she goes before the Violets to answer for her crime, she will have a valid reason. As of right now, her only defense is she did it as a favor to you. She won't be able to lie, and turning me without permission will be a huge deal. I don't want her to get in trouble."

My gods, here he was trying to protect Kimber, someone he hardly knew, while I was threatening to singlehandedly ruin her and Delmar by betraying their secrets. He'd probably never look at me the same again if he knew how vindictive I had been. "Do you want the Violets to believe you're manipulative and used the crisis in Rathe to get what you wanted?"

"To protect you, Kimber, and Delmar from being punished? Absolutely."

Always thinking of others. It was one of the many qualities I loved about Joel. Even if his idea was crazy, made him look bad, and was a longshot, it would protect Kimber and Delmar. I owed them every ounce of protection possible.

"Okay," I conceded. "Your doctor won't like it, but we'll check you out of here today."

Joel held my hands, excited and hopeful. "The answer to saving Rathe is in the archives. I'm sure of it. I'm going to find it."

What a miracle it would be if he was right.

The sight of the bookstore made my heart quadruple in size. It's where Joel and I first met. Where our story began. The key to our happily ever after could be buried in the store's vault, collecting dust in Joel's family archives.

Pango and Joel carried my chair up the few steps to the back entrance and set me down. The door opened with a twist of Joel's key in the lock. He entered the alarm code then turned and waved me and Pango inside.

I rolled directly to Joel's office. He came up behind me, toting his oxygen tank on wheels, and opened the door to his office. As always, I inhaled deeply, savoring the aroma of all the old books and paper. A hint of saltwater mixed with mildew from some of the recovered shipwreck artifacts made it smell that much more heavenly. Like my grandmother's home. May she rest in peace.

Pango joined us and leaned on Joel's desk. "Mind if I watch you open the vault? Secret doors fascinate me."

Joel walked to the corner of his office, slid some books from a shelf, and reached for the hidden lever. The door, which was disguised as a huge framed map, slid open. Joel lifted his tank over the threshold and beckoned to me and Pango.

Surprised, Pango asked, "We're allowed to go in there?"

I smirked. I had been in Joel's vault too many times to count. He knew how much I loved looking through all of the old journals, maps, pictures, and everything else his family had taken great care in preserving.

"Yes," Joel said. "I'll need your help."

Pango rubbed his hands together with anticipation. "I love a good treasure hunt."

The three of us entered and Pango's eyes went wide with wonder as he took in the rows of bookshelves, trunks of all shapes and sizes, and more recovered artifacts. "I had no idea it would be this big. I assumed it was a closet behind a wall."

"Isn't it amazing?" I asked.

Pango nodded as he ran his fingers along the leather spines of books once owned by Joel's Great Uncle James. "Where do we even start?" he asked. "It would take months for the three of us to read through everything in here."

"You and Koraline won't be reading anything," Joel explained. "If one of you found the solution to our problems, then my plan to protect Kimber wouldn't work."

"Ahh," Pango hummed. "Handsome *and* smart." He winked at me. "I see more and more why you want to keep him around."

Joel blushed and I'm sure I did too. I changed the subject to spare us any further embarrassment. "Joel, you said you needed our help. What can we do?"

Joel adjusted the tubes in his nose and inhaled. "I remember reading something about the kraken when I was a kid." He strolled down one of the middle rows and rolled a ladder about halfway down. "I think it was in one of the journals that my great grandfather bought at an estate sale."

"Who wrote the journals?" I asked him, trying not to worry about how tired and out of breath he was.

"You'll love this. They were written by a man who claimed to remember all of his past lives." Pango and I exchanged knowing glances while Joel braced himself on a shelf. "I'm still woozy and I don't think I can make it up the ladder." He pointed to a top shelf. "In that bin, there should be seven or eight journals with red covers wrapped in plastic."

"Allow me," Pango said. At six foot five, he didn't need a ladder. He reached up and pulled down the bin of books. "Where would you like me to put them?"

"On my desk, please. I appreciate the help."

"This is a lot to read through," Pango pointed out as he carried the collection back to Joel's office.

Joel pushed his glasses up his nose and grinned at me. A burst of excitement made him look less exhausted. "But I'll bet you good money it's the most interesting reading I've done in a long time."

"Wouldn't you prefer to read outside and get some fresh air?" I asked.

"No." Joel slid into his leather office chair. "These books do not leave this room, and neither do I until I find something useful."

He gently opened the tattered cover of the first journal. Curious, I glanced at the neat handwriting that filled the browning pages.

"No peeking," he told me. "There's a whole store of books out there. Go find yourselves something to read while I figure out how to save Rathe."

25

Ink stained my skin where Luska had touched me. No matter how hard I scrubbed, faint streaks of black remained as my marks of shame.

I returned to Treygan's house and found him standing on the beach. He probably hadn't stopped worrying or imagining the worst. I landed in the sand a few feet away from him. He didn't move, only stood there staring at me.

I spoke first. "Do you want to know how it went?"

"Judging from the marks on your skin and the look on your face, I'm leaning toward not wanting to hear details."

I wrung my hands. "I failed. The Liquid Lullaby didn't work on him."

Treygan let out a breath. "At least you didn't have to kiss him."

I wiped at the streaks on my arms again.

"Yara?" He could guess the truth, but he still needed confirmation. "Did you discover it didn't work before or after you tried to take his memories?"

"After," I mumbled, still unable to look up.

"Did you remove any memories? Not that it matters. This was an all or nothing situation."

He was fishing for information on how long the kiss had lasted. I didn't know whether to laugh or cry. At least I could be truthful about that and it might make Treygan feel better.

"I didn't remove any. Didn't have the chance."

Treygan inhaled sharply. "Did he hurt you?"

"No." My next confession would definitely help him feel better. It was the only thing making me feel better about the whole fiasco. "But I hurt him."

"How?"

"Slashed him pretty deep with my selkie claws and knocked him out of a chair."

Treygan's grin was bittersweet. "He didn't retaliate?"

"That's the worst part. It seemed to excite him and make him want me more."

"Because he's a creature of absolute darkness." He hugged me to his chest, stroked my hair, and breathed me in. I wanted to stay there, curled up against his warm, strong chest forever. I wanted to pretend the kraken didn't exist. "So what now? Obviously he still intends to take you to Harte."

"That's still never going to happen."

"I couldn't agree more, but is there a new plan?"

I hadn't thought that far ahead. I needed to come clean first. I was exhausted from carrying around my dirty secret. Rownan had forgiven Vienna. All I could do was hope excessive forgiveness ran in the family.

I eased out of his arms and turned my back to him, drawing random shapes in the sand with my toes. "There's more."

He was so quiet that I looked over my shoulder to make sure he hadn't disappeared.

His worried gaze met mine. "Go on."

"Not at dinner. In Harte." I turned, trying to face him and my fear of losing him. "I'm fairly sure I cheated on you."

He blinked once, but nothing else. No lips parting, no eyes going wide in shock. His stoic expression didn't crack in the slightest. "Yes, I suspected that."

My lips sure as hell parted, and my eyes felt like they'd pop from their sockets. "Why would you suspect that?"

Much too calmly, he said, "Because when we were in Harte,

you said something about a sex-crazed kraken. Why say that if you hadn't encountered one?"

"Why didn't you ask me about it?"

"I was waiting until you were ready to discuss it. If that day ever came, it needed to be on your terms."

"How could I possibly bring up a conversation like that knowing it would hurt you?"

"I told you I never wanted to be protected from the truth."

"When did you say that?"

"In Harte."

"You expect me to remember everything you said while we were in Harte?"

"You should remember that statement because it's important to our relationship."

"I cheated on you," I blurted out again without looking at him.

"Is it truly cheating when you're under the spell of an evil creature?"

"Cheating is cheating."

"Fine, then. Call it what you want, but given the circumstances, I forgive you."

Vienna's words echoed through my mind. *One of the best things about love is that it forgives.*

Even with his forgiveness, and even though I couldn't remember the act, I still felt wretched. "You shouldn't forgive me."

He turned my face so I'd have to look at him. "Too bad. I forgive you. Completely and for good."

I tried to reply, but a sob choked me.

Treygan's brows knitted together and he pressed his forehead to mine. "Stop bottling up everything. Let go. It's just me. You're safe with me."

I shook my head. I would not cry. I would not break down. Rulers did not break down. They stayed strong.

"Cry, scream, do whatever you need to, Yara, but stop holding it all in and letting it pile up." His words were practically a whisper, but they traveled through every part of me. "It's too much for one soul to endure alone."

I had to confess to someone, and I trusted Treygan more than anyone else in my life. "I feel like I'm cracking, like I can't keep myself or this realm together in one piece."

He kissed my hands. "I understand, but maybe cracking is what you need. Cracks let the light in."

I threw my arms around his neck and let my weight fall against him.

He held me tight and stroked my hair. "We will get through this, *all* of this, together."

I wanted so badly to believe him. I savored the feeling of being safe in Treygan's arms. "I don't see how that's possible."

"Because we won't stop until we do."

"Luska won't stop either."

He pulled back and locked eyes with me again. "*He* doesn't have love on his side. We do. I will never stop loving you, Yara. I will never stop doing everything within my power to keep you safe. I will fight until the kraken is gone from here. Forever belongs to you and me. Nothing and no one will ever convince me otherwise, and I won't allow anyone to take it from us."

My wings spread and wrapped around him, enclosing us in a cocoon, even if only for a few sacred moments. His heart beat against mine and it restored some of my hope and strength.

"Come inside," he said tenderly. "You need to rest."

I eased backward, relaxing my wings and letting my grip on him loosen. "I need to summon Nixie. Hopefully she has an update on whether my choice of co-rulers has the gods' blessing."

"Who did you decide on as a third?"

"You aren't going to believe this, but Otabia."

He jerked his head back, but then a smile parted his lips. "Oddly, I can picture her as co-ruler. How did you and Indrea decide on her?"

"She nominated herself. Begged for it."

"Begged? I can't imagine Otabia begging for anything."

"Okay, more like she demanded and then made persuasive arguments about why she'd be a good choice."

"Congratulations."

Deciding on the third ruler was a step forward in restoring power to Rathe, but too many other worries prevented me from feeling any relief at solving one problem. And Treygan's well-being sat at the very top of my long Worry list. "I can't stop thinking about what you said in Forbidden Apple."

"Which part?"

"The part about me having to live without you one day."

He shook his head. "Forget about that. That was selfish of me. You have much more important things to focus on."

"I hate it too, you know. I can't even think about it." I started to choke up again. "If I lost you I would—"

"Stop it. I'm right here. We have the rest of my life left together."

I cradled his face in my hands. "I would choose you if I could. In a heartbeat, with no hesitation. If my co-rulers didn't have to be female, I would choose you over anyone."

He bit his lip and nodded. "Thank you. That means the worlds to me."

An invisible but heavy veil between us seemed to lift. We felt genuinely connected again.

He kissed my forehead. "Let's get you inside to Nixie so you can begin healing Rathe."

26

Since Yara wouldn't listen to me, I tracked down Indrea and Caspian and updated them about the growing number of sick selkies. Indrea said the number of sick merfolk was also growing. The Violets were working almost non-stop to heal everyone.

I wanted to check on Vienna, so I shadowed her and located her at Harp's Back Falls. When I arrived, the waterfalls were hardly gushing. I couldn't recall ever seeing them flow so weakly. Everywhere I looked, there were more signs of Rathe deteriorating.

Beautiful violin music filled the air. Music had a way of healing our people, so it was a brilliant idea on someone's part to put on a concert. I followed the relaxing tune to where a bunch of selkies were gathered under the moonlight watching someone play.

That someone was Vienna.

I quietly made my way through the crowd until I was closer to the front. She finished her song and everyone applauded. The crowd buzzed with conversations and started breaking up into smaller groups as Vienna set down the violin and rushed over, wrapping me in a hug.

"When did you learn to play violin?" I asked.

"In Harte."

"You found a violin in Harte?"

She looked away, ashamed. Against my better judgement, I probed further. "Vienna?"

"Let's go someplace private."

She pulled me away from the chattering crowd and into a chasm between two ice cliffs. Quietly, and without looking up at me, she said, "You gave it to me. Or, more accurately, one of the imposters gave it to me."

"Damn it," I grumbled. She had always loved violin music, but she claimed she was too busy to take lessons. "You taught yourself how to play?"

She shook her head. "No, you—*he*—taught me."

My teeth clenched at the thought of them together. "You knew I couldn't play the violin. Wasn't that a red flag that he wasn't the real me?"

"It had been years, Rownan. I wasn't even sure how long I had actually been in Harte. You—*he* said he had taken lessons. That he had been practicing every day so he could serenade me when we reunited."

"I see."

She stroked my forearms. "Please don't be angry."

"I'm not angry at you. I'm angry that you were deceived. Our relationship has been violated." And now here she was playing her beloved instrument in public for all of our kind to hear and see. Would everyone know the kraken had given her this gift? "Do you think about him when you play?"

She guffawed. "Absolutely not. I get lost in the music."

I studied her glowing face. Playing had sparked a light within her. Was it a coincidence that she suddenly revealed her newly acquired talent almost immediately after realizing the kraken was the imposter in Harte? Or was some deeper part of her reconnecting with him through the music? He had gifted her with something I never could, and that pissed me off royally.

"Row," Vienna said gently. "I know you. You're making this into something it's not. Please tell me what you're thinking."

Vienna had played exquisitely. I didn't want to say anything that might make her feel like she shouldn't play around me. I flexed my stiff fingers then waved off my concerns. "Forget it. I'm just in a bad mood because of my run-in with Yara."

"Did you tell her about the fin rot epidemic?"

"I didn't get a chance. She was having a rendezvous with the kraken when I showed up. Apparently, I ruined some big plan of hers. If I had snuck up on them instead of shouting her name, maybe I could have killed him."

Vienna stroked my cheek. "Such harsh words for such a loving soul."

"You I love, him I hate."

"Still, you're capable of anything you set your mind to, but you're not a murderer. And Luska is too powerful for you to fight alone. Promise me you won't try again."

Luska. I hated how she used his name instead of referring to him as the kraken like everyone else. "I would never make you a promise that I have no intention of keeping."

"Then at least promise me you'll never face him alone."

"I promise that I will try my best. If he finds me in a dark waterway and it's just me and him, all bets are off."

She sighed and hugged me. Resting her head on my chest, she said, "You need to apologize to Yara."

"Tell me something I don't know."

27

Nixie still hadn't shown. I had summoned her twice. What was taking her so long?

I was pacing the living room like a tiger in a cage when Rownan entered through the rivulet.

"Treygan's resting," I told him. "Go away."

"I need to speak with you. It's important."

I took a deep breath, reminding myself not to take my frustration out on him again. I peeked inside the dark resting room and saw Treygan floating peacefully. Nixie's wood panel rested against the wall, but still no sign of her spirit anywhere. Quietly, I pulled the doors shut. "Sure."

I sat at the kitchen table. Rownan sat beside me. "I apologize for interrupting you and Luska earlier."

"It's fine. I'm sorry I took it out on you. You were right. I wasn't in control of the situation."

He nodded and kept his gaze locked on me. "What's your next plan?"

"I don't know," I admitted. "I'm too weak without the strength of the trinity."

"You are not weak."

"I sure feel like it."

We sat there not speaking for a few moments until I broke the silence to ask, "Do you have any ideas?"

He semi-shrugged. "There is something, but . . ."

"Go on," I urged him. "I'm open to anything at this point."

"You won't like hearing it. Even attempting to discuss it with you is difficult."

"Uncle Lloyd always told me the hardest thing is usually the right thing."

"Lloyd." One of his eyebrows lifted. "Very well, then. Brace yourself."

I nodded.

"Is your relationship with Treygan worth risking the destruction of Rathe and everyone in it?"

"What do you mean?"

"I realize it's a brutal truth, but consider what I'm asking."

"My love for Treygan is deeper than all of the oceans combined."

He waved his hand dismissively. "That doesn't answer my question. Is the love of two people worth the lives of countless others and the destruction of a whole realm?"

Unbelievable. I leaned forward. "What if I asked you the same question about Vienna?"

"Vienna is an entirely different matter."

Rownan was trying to help, and we were all growing more frustrated and desperate, but I couldn't believe what he was implying. "Get to the point, Rownan. Say what you mean."

"You must realize Treygan is with you by default."

I couldn't have heard him right. "What?"

"He would turn any other lover to stone. You are the one exception to his curse. He's with you because you are his one and only option."

"That's not true."

"Isn't it? Tell me, if not you, who else could he choose as a partner?"

I opened my mouth to reply, but stopped. Selkies, mer, sprites, even the sirens. If any of them were to kiss Treygan, there was a chance he would turn them to stone. Not by choice, but because of who and what he was.

"And there you have it," Rownan said sadly.

My throat closed in on itself and I felt sick. How long had Rownan thought this about us? Did everyone view our relationship that way?

Otabia flew in, her dark eyes wide and furious. She landed on the table between Rownan and me. With her back to me, she raised one wing to shield me and hissed, "Stand back."

I tried leaning around her wall of black feathers. "Otabia, what's wrong with you?"

She lunged at Rownan, and he stood and lifted his hand. Otabia stopped as if she'd run into a wall. She floated upward, hovering over the kitchen table, kicking her feet. With a flick of his wrist, he threw her backward into the cabinets.

I rushed to her, helping her to her feet.

"It's him" she said. "The kraken."

As if I hadn't figured that out the moment he tossed her across the room without even touching her.

The doors to the resting room burst open and Treygan rushed in at the same moment the real Rownan and Vienna came in through the rivulet. Treygan positioned himself between me and the kraken. Rownan saw himself, or rather Luska impersonating him, and he growled like a rabid dog and charged.

Luska smiled and held up his hand again. Rownan jerked to a halt, his arms and legs still flailing, trying to get close enough to shred Luska, but Luska held him back with ease.

They looked identical. Two Rownans face to face. Such a bizarre sight.

"How do I look?" Luska asked Rownan. "Not nearly as attractive as my original packaging, but I do wear it better than you." He looked at Vienna, who stood speechless in the rivulet. "Don't you agree, my delectable pet?" He morphed back into his own humanesque form.

Rownan spewed out a string of creative expletives, but Luska ignored him.

"Yara," he said, "I may have come to you in a form that was not my own, but that does not make my words any less true. Such a relationship is not worth the loss of every soul in Rathe. Heed my warning."

He strutted out of the room while Otabia and Rownan still hovered in mid-air, squirming to break free from whatever power was holding them in place.

"Treygan, kill him!" Rownan shouted.

"If I could I would." Treygan moved to keep me covered until Luska was out of view. Seconds after Luska left the kitchen, Rownan crashed to the floor and Otabia landed gracefully on her feet.

"He's even stronger than we thought," Otabia growled.

Treygan gave a grunt of agreement then turned to face me. "Did he hurt you?"

"We just talked. He didn't try anything." *Except to convince me that you and I shouldn't be together.* But I couldn't bring myself to tell Treygan that.

He hugged me with one arm while reaching to help Rownan up with the other. "Rownan, besides your bruised pride, are you okay?"

"We're killing him," Rownan spat. "That's a promise. I will rip that bastard's head off."

Treygan focused on me again. "What was he discussing with you?"

"It wasn't important."

He kissed my forehead and I wondered if he could feel all of the self-doubt filling me to bursting.

"Yara?" Nixie called from the resting room doorway. Of course no one saw or heard her but me.

"Nixie's back," I told Treygan. My voice hitched with hope. "Time to reestablish the power of the trinity."

I slipped into the resting room with Nixie and then shut the doors behind me. My pulse was still racing from the adrenaline rush, and from the harsh truth Luska had slapped me with. I needed to push all of that aside and focus on the more important task. At least for now.

The moment I turned around, Nixie blurted out her update. "Medusa said no."

I stared at her, waiting for her to snicker and tell me she was kidding. She didn't. "What do you mean, she said no?"

"No, as in Otabia can't have the blessing of the gods." She lowered her eyes and backed away. "And neither can Indrea."

"What?" I surged forward. "How can she say no? They are both good choices."

"She said neither were the right choice."

"So who does she want me to appoint as rulers?"

Nixie still wouldn't look at me. "I asked. She said that was for you to figure out."

I grunted so loud I was sure the oceans shook. "She is impossible. Does she not realize what's happening to Rathe with every second she's wasting?" I threw my hands in the air. "Her world is falling apart, our people are getting sick, and she doesn't care. Does she want to see Rathe be destroyed?"

"Of course not," Nixie half-whispered.

"Then what am I supposed to do? I am alone and feel so helpless that I want to scream until my lungs burst."

"You're not alone. I'm here."

"Your spirit is here. I don't even get all of you."

"You get the most important part of me."

I fought back tears with everything I had. "You go to her and list every name of every damn female in this realm until she says yes to two of them."

"Believe it or not, I started to try that. Medusa said she didn't have time for childish games."

I huffed, practically choking on a combination of frustration and tears. "*She* doesn't have time for games? She could end all of this by speaking two names. Why is that so much to ask?"

"I don't know. She isn't a woman of many words. And she really sucks at explaining her reasons for anything."

"We need her to approve new rulers so we can restore power immediately."

"She said that's a big part of your problem. You're rushing your decision and choosing out of convenience instead of choosing correctly."

I raked my fingers over my scalp. "I'm rushing because Rathe's creatures are getting sicker. Our plants are dying. Our water quality is worsening. Suns and moons are fading from our sky! How much worse does she want it to get?"

"It's a tough job, Yara. It's why there are very few rulers of magical worlds."

I stood there aching to punch something. Medusa could help me—help Rathe—but she was refusing. What I couldn't understand was why.

28

Koraline

I stretched, cracking my back and shoulders. I had been reading Jules Verne for hours. Pango had alternated between flipping through books, examining Joel's collection of recovered shipwreck artifacts, and taking walks around the bookstore until he'd decided to go get us some food. Joel hadn't left his office once, not even to use the restroom.

As I watched the door and listened to an antique clock tick away each second until Pango's return with our dinner, Joel suddenly wheezed.

I glanced up with worry. He had a journal gripped in his hands and held close to his face.

"Joel?" I asked.

He was quiet. The book still hovered inches from his nose. Then he slammed it to the table, which shocked me because he usually handled old books with great care.

He finally looked at me. "I found it. The antidote to our problem. Now Kimber can turn me."

If I still had legs, I would have run over to him. "What is it?"

He placed a bookmark in the journal, shut it, and slid it in his messenger bag. "I can't tell you. Not yet."

I rolled forward. "But you really did find something? A way to send the kraken back to Harte?"

He pushed his glasses up his nose. "I'm ninety-eight percent sure I found what we need."

Joel pushed back his chair as he rose and wheeled his oxygen tank behind him. "We'll wait for Pango then take Lloyd's boat back to Eden's Hammock. My transformation can take place there."

Butterflies flitted through my stomach. This was really going to happen. Joel, the love of my life, was going to be turned mer. Things were finally starting to look bright again.

Once on Eden's Hammock, we had the excruciating chore of waiting for Pango to swim to Rathe and bring back Kimber and Delmar. My dream of Joel being transformed was so close to coming true that I worried non-stop. What if he didn't survive it? I sat on the deck, rehearsing what to say, how to say it, and contemplating when to say it.

Joel joined me on the deck. He sat beside me and studied me.

"What?" I asked.

"I love the way you constantly run your fingers through your hair then drop loose strands all over the place. You leave tiny pieces of yourself everywhere you go."

My hand stopped mid-stroke. I hadn't realized I'd been doing it until he said something. I let my hand drop into my lap and looked out at the water.

He took up where I'd left off, running his fingers through my hair. "What's the first thing we'll do after I'm turned?"

"What do you want to do?"

"Swim underwater, of course. There's a whole world down there I need to explore."

"Two worlds," I reminded him.

His eyes lit up and his smile stretched wide as he threw his head back and stared at the sky. "Rathe," he whispered. "I can't believe I'm going to see Rathe."

I stared out at the water again. If Joel's transformation failed, it would be the end for him instead of a new beginning.

"Uh-oh," Joel said. "What's wrong?"

"Why do you think something is wrong?"

"Because you're fiddling with your necklace. You always do that when something is on your mind."

I let go of my starfish pendant and placed my hands back in my lap. "We need to discuss something important."

"You mean how risky my transformation is."

"Yes. Don't misunderstand, I want to be positive—I love imagining you being mer and living in Rathe—but we also need to be realistic."

"It's going to work."

"A big part of me believes that or I wouldn't be agreeing to it, but I still need to tell you some things in case this doesn't turn out how we hope."

"No. I don't want to fuel any negative thinking."

"But I'm the one who will be left behind with the burden of things unsaid."

With a gloomy sigh, he nodded. "Fair enough."

"I know what happens when our kind die, but I have no idea what happens when humans pass. If it's anything like the way our system works, then you'll have the option to stay in limbo, to watch over the people you love."

"To watch over you," he clarified.

I started choking up. "So if that happens . . ."

"Koraline, stop. That's not going to happen."

"But if it does." I needed to get through this. "Please stay long enough for me to say goodbye. Listen to everything I need to say. If I could, I'd say it all right now, but I can't. We never really know what we needed to say until we lose the people we love."

"Of course I'll stay. I'll stay forever."

"No, that's the other condition. Limbo is hard. Don't stay to watch over me. Listen to my goodbye, know that I will always love you and I will never, ever forget you. And then when I tell you I'm finished, go to that peaceful place that waits for you beyond this world."

"What if that's not how it works for humans? What if there is no peaceful place awaiting me?"

"There has to be. We're all connected. We may have different realms and live by different rules, but we all come from the same universal source. I felt that source calling me to an ultimate home that I'm certain contains more love and joy than our limited minds can comprehend. My soul felt it, and I yearned to go, to cross over."

"But you stayed."

"Because my body was strong enough to recover." I hated what my words implied, but we had to face the truth.

Joel knew it too. "And my body isn't strong enough."

A tear threatened to fall, but I wiped it away.

"My body doesn't matter," Joel said. "My will is as strong as they come."

"No matter how strong your will, it needs an able vessel to carry on."

He smirked in a sad way. "This is the most uninspiring speech you've ever given."

"I wish with all my heart things were different. I wish you had been born mer and that the Violets could fully heal you and take away your pain."

"Being with you, I feel no pain."

We both knew that was a lie. I'd seen him suffer, battle for half a breath, and worse.

"Promise me." I brushed my fingers along his forearm. "Promise you'll do what I ask."

"Lao Tzu said, 'If you are not afraid of dying, there is nothing you cannot achieve.'"

"Yes, but Tzu also said, 'If you realize that all things change, there is nothing you will try to hold on to.'"

"I'm not ashamed to admit that I'm not evolved enough to practice that wisdom." He ran his fingers through my hair again. "Like it or not, I'm holding on to you as tightly as I can for as long as humanly, mer, or ghostly possible."

29

Rowman

Delmar shook me awake. "Joel found information about how to get rid of the kraken."

I thought I was dreaming at first, but Delmar's serious expression came into clear focus and I sat up in bed. Vienna stirred beside me. We had stayed up late discussing whether Rathe's residents should start evacuating to Earth's realm. We didn't know if it would help those who were sick, or make them worse being away from our world.

One thing we did know for sure: Vienna was going there and staying until the kraken was gone. After seeing Luska impersonate me so perfectly, right down to the exact shape and color of the bruises on my face, she was too afraid to stay in Rathe. She hadn't been able to tell us apart, and suddenly the idea that a simple code word could protect her seemed stupid. She worried he might be able to fool her again.

The thought of her staying in Eden's Hammock until Luska was dead or gone did wonders for my spirit, but after seeing him pretend to be me, I was determined to kill that demonic scum more than ever. And Delmar had just said Joel might know how to make it happen.

I rubbed my eyes and wiped my hands over my face, wincing at the tenderness of my bruises. "You're serious?"

Of course he was serious. Delmar was at our home in the middle of the night and he couldn't lie .

"Are you coming or not?" He asked me.

"Give us five minutes." I needed to wake Vienna. She might as well come with us. She had already said her goodbyes to family and friends.

Delmar patted our mattress and said, "We'll be waiting outside."

We were all gathered around Lloyd's kitchen table: Delmar and Kimber, Joel and Koraline, and Vienna and me. I sipped black coffee, trying to clear my head so I could absorb any and all information discussed. Treygan and Yara were counting on me to relay anything useful to them.

Joel started out by declaring that he wouldn't say a word until Kimber agreed to turn him mer. She sort of huffed through her nose before she nodded, and I could have sworn she rolled her eyes a little bit, but no one else seemed to notice. They were all focused on Joel.

He was still using a portable oxygen tank, and he looked terrible. I wondered if anyone truly believed he'd survive a transformation. Judging from the light practically shining through his glasses, Joel believed it wholeheartedly.

"Here's what I found," Joel began. "Luska isn't just any beast of Harte. He's a *god* of Harte."

I huffed. "That malicious piece of pond scum is a god? Says who?"

"He did tell Yara that," Delmar said. "She thought it was just his ego talking."

Joel continued. "According to my sources, Luska was appointed ruler of Harte by none other than Poseidon himself."

I looked at Joel like he'd told me I had two heads. "We're supposed to believe that?"

"Think about it," Joel said. "How was Harte created? How did all of its inhabitants end up there?"

Vienna answered. "Poseidon created Harte as a place to lock

away all of the darkness that Medusa had unleashed."

Apparently she had paid attention more than me in history classes.

"Right," Joel confirmed. "Poseidon created Harte, but who filled it? Who relocated all those dark creatures into their own realm?"

I'd never given it much thought. Harte was the creation of Poseidon and Medusa. Their power knew no limits. "I always assumed Poseidon put them there."

Joel shook his head. "Not on his own. He had help."

"From who?"

Joel apparently had a flair for the dramatic. He made deliberate eye contact with all of us before replying, "The Wrangler."

"The Wrangler?" Delmar repeated.

"Just like Yara said." Koraline murmured.

"What do you mean, Kor?" Joel asked.

She snapped out of her thoughts and focused on him. "When Yara was researching Harte, she asked if Poseidon had used a big magical net to capture all the evil. Treygan told me and we had a good chuckle about it, but neither of us knew the real answer. And now here we are, finding out her guess was mostly correct."

"Do we even know who or what a wrangler would be in regards to this situation?" I asked Joel. "Do you really mean someone literally helped Poseidon herd everything into Harte?"

"According to the legends, yes."

"Did your source say who this wrangler was?"

"Not by name, no."

"So how does that help us?"

Joel fiddled with his oxygen tank and took a few deep breaths. "Because at some point in time, the Wrangler knew how to get a whole lot of evil beasts into Harte. If we can find them, then maybe they can do it again."

I set my coffee down. "How do you suggest we find this Wrangler character from centuries ago who may or may not still be alive?"

Joel shrugged then looked at Koraline. "Maybe ask Poseidon?"

I laughed. "Ask Poseidon. Just like that. That's like us telling you to call up your creator and ask him why he gave you bad lungs."

"Rownan!" Koraline and Vienna both chided in unison.

"No harm intended," I told Joel, patting his shoulder. "Seriously, though, we have no way to communicate with Poseidon. If that's all you found to help us, then we're still stuck where we were before this meeting."

"That's not true," Lloyd said from behind me. He walked into the kitchen and leaned on the back of my chair. "Yara still has Nixie. She can ask Medusa. It's almost as good as asking Poseidon himself."

"That's a longshot," I said. "Medusa hasn't been eager to help with this mess. Far from it, actually."

Joel adjusted the tubes in his nose. "That's why I didn't stop there while researching. I found a plan B."

Everyone around the table looked as anxious as me.

"Go on," I urged.

"The agape pearl that Treygan gave Yara. Where did he find it?"

"He said he found it near the Catacombs."

"When?"

I searched my memory, but couldn't remember if he ever told me. "I'm not sure."

Joel leaned forward with a confident smile. "Most likely he discovered it—and not by accident, mind you—soon after Medusa made her decision to allow Yara to take her place."

Koraline shook her head. "Medusa hasn't let anyone take her place. She still has another pearl identical to Yara's. It's embedded in the hollow of her throat."

"Okay," Joel mused, his grin still bordering on cocky, "so maybe Yara hasn't technically replaced Medusa, but the pearl represents the transfer of power. And here's the big revelation."

Joel went from grinning to beaming. "The kraken has a pearl of his own."

My brows shot up. "Luska has a magic pearl?"

"Yes." Joel sat tall and proud. "His pearl makes him ruler of Harte the same way Yara's makes her a ruler of Rathe. The stories in the journals led me to believe that the pearl is what makes him immortal."

I hated to state the obvious. "I haven't seen any pearl anywhere on him."

Joel touched his Adam's apple. "That's because it's embedded in his throat, under the skin."

I looked up at my father, who had slowly circled the crowd while Joel talked. He knew more about sea creatures than any of us, so I asked him, "Sound legit?"

He tilted his head from side to side. "Possibly."

"I'm still unclear," Delmar said. "How does this information help us?"

I saw it so clearly, like it had already happened. My fingers twitched at the blissful thought. "I find the pearl and rip it out of him."

Vienna and Koraline snapped their heads around to look at me.

"Then he's no longer immortal," I explained. "I take away his power. Then I kill him."

Joel gave a firm nod. "Exactly."

Excitement surged so strongly inside of me that I was trembling. I practically snarled, "He's done. As soon as I tear that pearl out of him, he's done."

Joel smiled so big it lit up the whole kitchen. "There, I provided helpful information. I held up my end of the deal."

We all looked at Kimber, and after a moment of worried hesitation, she nodded.

Joel had earned his transformation.

My meetings with Nixie were starting to make me cranky. I used to look forward to them, but lately it seemed Nixie only delivered bad news from Medusa.

I stood on the top step of the resting pool, staring at Nixie's wall panel. Why was she taking so long? We should have already left for the evacuation meeting. Rathe was getting worse and so were its creatures. We needed to figure out if taking shelter in Earth's waters would make those who were sick worse or better. The elders of all species were gathering at The Divide while I waited for Nixie. Treygan and Rownan waited in the living room, giving me a few moments of much needed alone time.

I was exhausted from needing to be in multiple places at once, dealing with multiple problems that all took priority. At least if I wasn't here when Nixie returned, she wouldn't be able to deliver bad news about this Wrangler person.

I lifted one foot out of the water, torn between waiting and leaving to join the meeting. Out of the blue, I recalled the first time I awoke in a resting pool at Koraline's house on Solis. I had just been turned. I was angry, confused, trying to comprehend and accept that I had become a mermaid.

Here I stood in the same sort of pool, going through more emotional torment, except now I held the fate of an entire realm in my hands. I lowered my foot back into the water. I had to stay. Nixie might be delivering information that could help us send

Luska back to Harte.

Every soul in Rathe was counting on me to make things right. To keep them safe. I loved my new family and my new home. I had to make sacrifices to keep them safe.

A blur of red made me look up. Nixie's spirit stepped out of the wood panel.

She winked at me. "Medusa said the Wrangler still exists."

My heart seized in the best way possible. Could she actually be bringing me good news? "How and where do we find him?"

"She said Rownan knows."

"Rownan? Hang on." I threw open the double doors and waved Treygan and Rownan in. "Hurry. Nixie has news. And it might be good for a change."

"Hey!" Nixie whined.

Treygan and Rownan entered and looked at me expectantly.

"Rownan, Nixie says the Wrangler is still alive and you know where he is."

"Me?" Rownan asked. "I'd never even heard of anyone called Wrangler until Joel mentioned him."

"He must know," Nixie said. "Medusa wouldn't lie."

"Think hard," I told him. "Medusa wouldn't lie about this."

Rownan's hands opened at his sides as his shoulders shrugged to his ears. "I honestly have no memory of anyone by that name."

"Maybe you didn't meet him by name," I said, turning to Nixie. "What else did Medusa say? Where is this guy now? What does he look like?"

Nixie's eyes gleamed. "I asked both of those questions. Aren't you proud? I knew you'd want to know."

"Great job, but what did she say?"

"He lives in Harte, of course. She said he still wrangles, but only the humans who get sucked in via the Devil's Triangle."

"Is that where Rownan met him? In Harte?"

"Duh," Nixie deadpanned.

"You met him in Harte," I told Rownan.

Rownan's eye's darted upward as he wracked his brain.

I turned back to Nixie. "Tell us the rest. What did he look like?"

"Medusa said he's always smiling."

"Always smiling," I repeated. "That's it? No hair color, skin color, short or tall, nothing else except he smiles a lot?"

Nixie tapped her lip. "No, that was it. Smiling and saluting."

"Smiling and saluting is not going to help us find—"

"Saluting?" Rownan asked from behind me.

I spun around. "Does that ring a bell?"

Rownan's lips curved upward. "Yes. On our search for Vienna's body, right before we found her in that ship, there was a long-haired dude steering a ghost ship through the graveyard of planes and boats. He was smiling like a maniac and he saluted me when we made eye contact. That's him. It must be."

Part of me was elated that Rownan remembered him, but another part of me was crumbling in despair because it had just occurred to me that the information was useless.

"It doesn't matter," I murmured, shaking my head. "We can't get back into Harte. The only gateway we can pass through won't open again for months. Who knows what condition Rathe and our people will be in by then?"

The three of us shot frustrated looks at each other.

"Damn," Treygan grunted.

"We could send someone else in to find him," Rownan suggested. "A pure-blood."

"No way," I said. "You remember how difficult it was to get out. I'm not risking anyone else's life by asking someone to go there."

"What if someone were to volunteer?" a condescending voice said from above us. We all looked up. Otabia sat perched atop the open roof of the resting room, peering down at us. "*You* can't cross the gateway." Her black wings rippled. "But I can."

"Get down here," I told her. She glided down, landing in front of me. "Would you really go back into Harte to find this guy?"

"I will."

I eyed her suspiciously. "Why? You told me that place made your soul darker."

"Because it will prove my willingness to protect Rathe. If Medusa sees I helped save this realm, perhaps she will reconsider granting me a position as co-ruler."

I knew she wouldn't volunteer for selfless reasons, but I didn't blame her. "Good enough for me. I would be grateful if you would go and bring him here."

"Consider it done."

"*Can* the Wrangler enter Rathe?" Treygan asked.

"I asked that too," Nixie said. "Medusa said he's free to come and go. He stays in Harte voluntarily so he won't get bored."

"Yes," I said. "Nixie made sure."

"What if he refuses to come to Rathe?" Rownan asked.

Otabia grinned. "He won't refuse me."

She flew up and away.

Could it work? Were the pieces of this nightmarish puzzle clicking into place? I still needed information on several other crucial matters, but Treygan and Rownan couldn't know about them. "Guys, I need to speak with Nixie alone for a few minutes."

Treygan kissed my cheek. "We'll be right outside if you need us."

I shut the doors behind them and made sure they latched closed. I took a few deep breaths, contemplating whether or not I actually wanted to go through with the secret plan I had come up with. It would mean I'd have to hide things from Treygan and possibly—probably—lie to him again. Regardless, I had to have a backup plan in case this Wrangler guy couldn't help us.

Turning back to Nixie, I whispered, "Did you gather any useful information about you-know-what?"

"Whom are you talking to?" Luska's deep voice sent shivers through me.

I whipped around, shocked to see him standing in our resting pool on the same steps where I had stood minutes ago.

"Treygan!" I shouted, but my voice echoed around me.

He had enclosed us in another ink cloud. Nixie's panel rested against the wall outside of the bubble, but she was inside with us. I was certain Luska didn't know that, and I wasn't about to reveal that information.

"I'm right here with you," she said, moving to my side. "Stay strong."

I flicked my head toward the doors separating us from the living room where Treygan and Rownan waited. "They'll check on me any second and find you here."

"As if they are a threat to me."

"If you're not worried about them, then why do you need this bubble?"

"Ink cloud," he corrected. "I desired time alone with you. I couldn't have you shouting to your pathetic mate."

"I don't appreciate you invading my home again."

"This isn't your home. Your home is with me."

"No, it's not." I shook my head, glancing in disgust at his tentacle arm.

He noticed and asked, "Which version of me do you prefer?"

"Neither." I was mesmerized by the suction cups covering his tentacle. He rotated it to give me a better view, inviting me to study him. There were too many circles to count, ranging from tiny to huge.

"I've seen that look before," Luska said. "You're fascinated."

I wanted to tell him he could stick his tentacles where the sun didn't shine, but what slipped out of my mouth instead was: "Can you feel all of them?"

He grinned. "Can you feel each of your lips and fingers?"

"Of course."

"Same concept. Except all of my suckers are immensely stronger and give more pleasure."

"Yaraaa," Nixie warned. "Don't fall for his slick sexy talk."

Luska's pupils glowed that trancelike shade of dark blue. I stepped back and closed my eyes. When I opened them again, he stood directly in front of me, closer than before. Nixie stood behind him, watching me over his shoulder.

"Stay strong," she reminded me. "We'll get you out of this."

Luska leaned in as my back pressed against the ink cloud behind me. Every part of me that touched the barrier tingled in a way that warmed me to the core. I rocked forward, trying to get away from the bubble, which clearly had some sort of intoxicating effect on me. But that meant I moved closer to Luska.

My nose brushed against his bare shoulder. My gods, he smelled amazing. Crisp and cool like the air after a storm passes, but with a sweet undertone of vanilla.

"Stop smelling him!" Nixie shouted to me.

Luska spoke over her. "Don't fight what comes so naturally, young ruler."

"Stop calling me young ruler," I grumbled. "I hate it."

He dipped his head and made eye contact with me. His gaze was still intense. "What would you prefer I call you?"

"Yara," I whispered. "That's my name."

His hands clasped my hips and his lips brushed across my cheek and rested against my ear. "Yara. My stunning, powerful, intoxicating Yara."

I melted into him, unable to resist his warmth.

"Yara, snap out of it!" Nixie shouted into my other ear. "He's using his powers on you!"

I licked my lips and flexed my fingers. Every part of me felt fuzzy in the best way, like all of my stress and worries were dissolving.

"Yara," Luska purred again in my ear, pulling my body against his.

Nixie was still talking, but she sounded so far away. Part of me wondered if I should listen to her, but I didn't want to miss anything Luska said or did. Slow, simmering waves of ecstasy flooded my body. Everywhere. From my toes to my forehead. It felt as if I were being caressed by millions of tiny bubbles.

"My gods," I moaned.

"More?" His gruff voice sent more warm ripples through me.

I dug my nails into his back and pulled him closer. "Yes. More."

The ripples expanded into waves. I coiled my body around his.

"Yara!" Nixie screamed, high and shrill in my ear. "Treygan is watching you!"

My eyes flew open and I let go of Luska. He kept a firm grip on me, grinning so darkly yet so beautifully.

"Get a grip on yourself!" Nixie scolded me.

Movement in my peripheral vision made me turn my head. Treygan and Rownan were beating on the outside of the ink cloud. Every time one of them pounded on the dark, shimmery wall, bolts of light flashed through the barrier, making me squint.

"What am I doing?" I stammered.

"Losing your mind," Nixie replied at the same time Luska said, "The right thing."

I peeled myself away from him and, surprisingly, he let go of me.

"Admit it," he said, "you enjoyed every moment."

I said nothing.

He brushed his thumb along my chin. "Plenty more of that to be had in our future." He turned and looked at Treygan, who was still trying to pound his way through the protective barrier. Lights flashed around us like a strobe.

"Such a thrill for me," Luska said, "knowing he saw us."

My breath caught in my throat at the horrible thought of Treygan witnessing what we had been doing.

Luska smiled at me again as the bubble around us turned to stone. "That's my cue to leave, but I will find you soon, Yara."

The stone shattered and crashed down around me. I fell sideways into the resting pool. Between the rain of rocks and the jolt of plunging into the water, I snapped back into reality. A dreadful, awful, guilt-inducing reality.

Treygan dove into the pool, joining me beneath the surface and cradling my face in his hands. *Are you all right?*

No. I shook my head. Pieces of stone sank all around us. *I'm not all right. None of this is all right.*

Treygan tried to hug me, but I pushed away and kicked back up to the surface. He followed right behind me.

"This isn't fair." I pushed my wet hair off my face. "Not to you, not to anyone. How the hell did he get in here? How did he put me in a trance?" I thought about what Treygan must have seen. How betrayed he must have felt—again. "How can you even look at me?"

"Yara, stop," Treygan said softly. He tried pulling me to him again, but I locked my arms and pushed him away. "No! I'm an awful person, an awful partner, and an awful ruler."

"No, *he* is the awful one, not you."

"Right now I feel no better than him."

I kicked away and climbed out of the pool. I needed to get far away from that room. And far away from Treygan. I needed to get far away from everyone and everything, even myself. If only that were possible.

31

Koraline

I hadn't rested all night. I was too excited. When the sun rose, so did my worries. What if Joel wasn't strong enough to survive the transformation? We could be sentencing him to an even earlier death instead of a longer life. Was it worth the risk?

"Yes," I assured my reflection in the bathroom mirror. I splashed cold water on my face. "Because if you don't try to save him this way, then you'll never forgive yourself."

I had said it out loud, so it was the truth, but that didn't make it any less risky.

Delmar and Kimber had also stayed the night on Eden's Hammock. They'd left us after the meeting and went to Yara's old house so they wouldn't disturb anyone. Delmar said they'd be up most of the night going over the complex spells Kimber would need to cast for Joel's transformation.

I hoped they were ready. I hoped all of us were ready. I prayed that today would be the beginning of a new life for Joel.

I rolled my chair out of the bathroom and down the hall to the den. Parking myself beside the recliner where Joel slept, I held his hand. He stirred awake, and after a few moments he sucked in a deep breath. He fumbled for his glasses on the side table and shoved them onto his face. "Is it time?"

I grinned at his excitement. "Not this very second, no, but soon. I'm waking you so you can get ready for your big day. Take your time."

He flung the quilt off of him and bounded from the chair.

"I'm ready. I've never been more ready. Can we do it now?"

"Delmar and Kimber will come back when it's time. They have important preparations of their own. Besides, you have to eat breakfast. You need your strength."

He placed his hands on his stomach. "I'm too excited. I don't think I could eat anything."

"I insist you try. For me."

"Okay. Anything for you." He leaned down and kissed me. "Enjoy your last visions of me as a human. I'm going to be the dreamiest merman you've ever seen."

I smiled at his adorable confidence, but I didn't need him to be dreamy. I needed him to be alive, mer, and healthy. Was that so much to ask?

The moment had arrived.

Delmar and I treaded water beside Kimber and Joel. As much faith as I had in Kimber, I was grateful that Delmar was helping. He had successfully transformed Yara not long ago, though so much had happened since that day it felt like years had passed.

Delmar had already explained the process to Joel twice, but he reminded him one last time. "Stare into Kimber's eyes. You'll feel like you're slipping into a trance. Embrace that. If you don't, this will be much more difficult."

"Got it," Joel said, but his voice shook with nervousness. Still, he was being so brave. He removed his glasses and handed them to me. "This is the last time I'll ever speak to you as a human."

Dear gods, please don't let it be the last time he ever speaks at all. I caressed his face. "I love you. Doesn't matter whether you're human or mer."

"Thank you for giving me this gift." He took one last breath of oxygen while Delmar held his tank, and then his face slipped from my fingers as he turned to Kimber.

Her stone lips made her appear composed and calm, but I suspected she was a bundle of nerves too. I wanted to apologize to her again before she started, but no one else knew about our ugly secret. I didn't want to rouse any suspicions in Delmar, or upset her again at the start of an already delicate process. I silently apologized to her in my mind. I'd probably never stop apologizing until the day I died.

Kimber placed one hand on Joel's cheek and stared into his eyes. He blinked fast a few times. I glanced at Delmar, making sure everything was going okay. Joel's blinking slowed, his eyelids grew heavy, and his expression relaxed.

Delmar gave me a slight nod, but didn't say anything. He had warned me not to say a word once Kimber started or it could pull Joel out of the process. My lips had never been pressed together more tightly.

Kimber kept her gaze locked with Joel's and pulled him closer so they were almost nose to nose. Then she wrapped her other arm around him and pulled him beneath the water. My heart felt as if it had been pulled under too.

Delmar and I sank down with them, but I kept my movements to a minimum and drifted backward, giving them space like Delmar had instructed.

From an outsider's perspective they might have appeared to be lovers. Kimber's indigo tail wrapped around Joel's legs as they stared into each other's eyes. Their faces were so close together it could have been the moment before they shared a kiss. My soul ached at the thought of Kimber never being able to feel Delmar's lips. How I hated myself for using her disability to hurt and manipulate her.

Joel's upper body jerked and my eyes went wide with panic. Delmar held up his hand, assuring me it was okay. He had warned me there would be all sorts of spasms involved. He said it was all part of the process. Even though I had been warned, it still scared me to see it happening.

Joel's chest heaved and he clutched Kimber's arms. His

head reared back and he bucked several times. A rush of air bubbles rose above him. My heart raced so fast I thought it would explode.

More air bubbles rose above Joel. Then more and more as he convulsed violently. Was this still part of the process?

Kimber signaled to Delmar and he rushed forward to stop Joel's flailing.

What's wrong? My instincts propelled me forward.

Stay back, Koraline! Delmar shouted.

Kimber glanced my way just long enough for me to sense the panic in whatever she was telling Delmar. *Only* telling Delmar. She had closed off her sight so I couldn't hear her thoughts.

Tell me what's wrong! I squeezed Joel's glasses so hard they crumpled in my hand. I dropped them and swam forward, grabbing Joel's arm.

Joel stopped thrashing. His limbs went limp. His eyes were closed. They weren't supposed to be closed. Eyes stayed open during a transformation. That much I knew.

Panicking, I looked to Delmar for answers. He grabbed hold of Joel and rushed him to the surface.

Don't let him die, I begged, pumping my tail hard to keep up. *Please, please, please.*

Kimber's hand grasped mine, but I couldn't look at her. My focus was locked on Delmar's purple tail pumping fast above us and Joel's limp feet cutting through the water.

We broke through the surface.

"What happened?" I shouted, inhaling water.

Delmar tilted Joel's head back and performed mouth-to-mouth as he swam toward the beach.

"Dear gods, no," I cried, swimming after them. "This can't be happening."

Delmar kept breathing air into Joel's lungs even as we swam. He transitioned to legs so fast it was a blur and sprinted out of the water, carrying the love of my life in his arms. The love of my life who was now unconscious and not breathing.

Delmar laid Joel flat on the sand and continued administering CPR. I swam as far in as I could then dragged myself up the beach beside them.

"Please save him," I begged Delmar.

Kimber crawled up beside me and wrapped her arms around me. I watched for what felt like an eternity as Delmar tried over and over again to make Joel breathe. Kimber squeezed me tighter. Delmar paused to look at me, defeat creasing his tired face.

"No," I yelped. "Keep going. Don't give up on him!"

Beside me, Kimber nodded fiercely.

Delmar wiped his brow, rose up on his knees again, and pumped on Joel's chest.

Time ticked agonizingly slowly as Delmar tried again and again. Breathing, pumping, breathing, pumping. Tears streamed down my face but I couldn't blink. I wanted to move closer and give him CPR myself, but I was physically paralyzed. Every fiber of my being urged Joel to breathe. "Breathe dammit!"

His chest convulsed and he spewed a tiny bit of water from his lips.

A gasp escaped my throat.

Delmar pressed his ear to Joel's chest and closed his eyes. Relieved, he announced, "Heartbeat."

"Oh, thank heavens." My body went limp in Koraline's arms.

"He's breathing," Delmar confirmed. "Weakly, but he's breathing." He pressed his hand to Joel's cheek. "Joel, can you hear me? Wake up."

I pulled myself closer and ran my hands through Joel's wet hair. "Joel, you're okay. Wake up." I patted his cheek. "Joel, please open your eyes."

But he didn't.

Blood streaked his cheek.

"Koraline, you're bleeding," Delmar said.

I wiped my palm on my stomach and leaned over Joel, resting my head on his chest. "I'm sorry. I broke your glasses. Wake up so you can forgive me."

I listened to his weak heartbeat. Water softly gurgled in his lungs when he breathed much shallower than normal. Through my tears, Kimber's indigo eyes met mine. She watched us with pity.

What had I done? Joel's current state was my punishment for using Kimber's secret against her. No one gets away with anything in this world or any other.

"I'm so, so sorry." I hugged Joel tighter and whispered into his ear, "Please, please wake up and forgive me for all of this."

No matter what we tried or what I said, Joel didn't respond.

32

I exploded through the tide pool and landed hard on the rock floor of the grotto. My bare feet didn't feel any pain. Or maybe it was that the pain felt good. I imagined waves of frustration and anger pouring into the ground beneath me.

In the grotto, I could be alone. The only creatures small enough to get into the caves were the sprites and the sirens in bird form, and they would never enter without permission. I shook the water from my wings, unsheathed my selkie claws, and screamed at the top of my lungs—long and loud, like an injured beast. Short of having a total meltdown, screaming was all I could do to feel better.

Except I didn't feel better. I was still wound so tightly that every tendon in me could snap at any moment.

I collapsed to the floor and sat cross-legged, staring at the dirty soles of my feet. I changed my hands from selkie claws to siren talons, then to shimmering mer hands, and finally to human. No matter which form they took, they still felt helpless.

Hugging my knees to my chest, I rested my forehead against them and started humming a comforting song Uncle Lloyd used to sing to me at bedtime. I couldn't remember the words, so I made some up. Before I knew it, I was singing a siren song. Siren songs were as much a part of me as my wings. No memorization required. The eerie tone suited my mood.

I released my legs and flopped down on the ground, stretching my wings out at my sides as I studied the stalactites hanging far above me. I sang like a true siren, holding nothing back—dark, alluring, and wanting to destroy the evil male who was ruining my life and maybe my world.

As I sang, my song echoed off of the walls. Each rippling soundwave made me feel more powerful. I sang louder and louder until rocks falling in one of the tunnels caused me to snap my mouth shut.

Had I sung so loud the walls were cracking? No, I had heard Stheno and Euryale get into screaming matches that were much louder than my singing had been. I sat up and immediately sensed Luska's energy. But how? He couldn't be in the grotto.

"Hello?" I called out.

Soft footsteps echoed off the rock walls. Rounding the corner, wiping his eyes like he had been woken from sleep, was Luska.

I sprang to my feet. "How did you get in here?"

In a groggy voice he replied, "Through the entrance."

"Liar. It's too narrow for anyone bigger than a bird to fit through."

"You know nothing about cephalopods. I am extremely flexible. I can squeeze into shockingly small spaces." He strolled over to me and ran his hand down my side. "When I enter some niches it feels much better than others."

He trailed his fingers up my thigh and I slapped his hand away. "Not interested."

"You were intensely interested during our last encounter. Judging from how tired I am, I'm assuming not much time has passed." His eyebrows danced in amusement. "How long will you keep lying to yourself about your feelings for me?"

"Until you return to Harte."

"Then you admit you are lying about your feelings?"

I shook my head, replaying my reply. My stupid, mindless reply. "That's not what I meant."

"Yet it is the truth." He held out his hand. I eyed it suspiciously.

"Dance with me," he said sweetly.

"I don't dance."

"I'll lead. I'm an exceptional leader."

"No, thank you."

He dropped his hand to his side and stepped toward me. "Look at you, so drained. This realm doesn't suit you. The weight of responsibility is squelching your spirit."

"And Harte is so wonderful?" I raised my chin so he could see he didn't intimidate me.

"It is. It's mayhem and freedom to live out your darkest desires."

Without knowing how it happened, I found myself in his arms as he guided me in a series of slow steps and spins. I kept my gaze locked with his to prove I wasn't weak, but I did feel weak. And tired. He was right, I was drained. It was nice to let someone else take over, even if only for a few minutes.

As much as I didn't want to admit it, Luska was an exceptional dancer. I hated that even in Rathe, even as much as I loved Treygan, Luska still had a dangerous pull over me. More than any man or beast ever should.

"Who was that sultry creature eavesdropping on us during our last rendezvous?" His question pulled me out of my reverie.

A rock formed in my throat. He couldn't mean Nixie. She was a spirit. Only I could see and hear her. "I don't know what you're talking about."

"Ah, but you do."

My pulse hammered like my own internal stereo system. If he knew about Nixie, something bad would come of it.

"She seems better suited for an existence in Harte."

I tried to swallow, but the lump wouldn't budge.

"As you know," Luska continued, "many spirits make Harte their final home. I sensed she has a dark side that she could put to great use in my realm."

I shuddered at the thought of Nixie returning to Harte. That evil place was the reason she died. I refused to say one more word about her. Maybe he only sensed her spirit energy with us. I wouldn't confirm any of his suspicions.

"Harte is a world where she could truly spread her wings." Did he know she had wings or was that a metaphor? Had he seen her? "Perhaps if she went with us, you wouldn't feel so alone."

Change the subject, Yara, I told myself. *Keep him away from Nixie.* "I belong here in Rathe."

"Why do you believe something so preposterous?"

"It's not preposterous. This is my home. I'm Rathe's ruler. The people I love are here. I'll never leave them."

He squinted, studying me. "Now I know what I must do."

"Go back to Harte?"

"Yes. As soon as I dispose of all your reasons for staying in Rathe." He released me and walked to the tide pool.

Dread hit me as I realized what he meant by "dispose of." I rushed forward, stumbling over my own feet and splashing into the shallows of the tide pool with him. "No! Stay away from them!"

"What happens to your people is up to you."

I clutched his forearm. "Please don't hurt them."

"How I've ached to hear you beg me for what you desire."

"I am begging you for this. Please, Luska, leave them alone."

"Return to Harte with me right now, and I will grant your request."

The insane thought actually crossed my mind. In a split second, I saw myself living in that evil realm, not saying goodbye to anyone, never seeing Treygan again, how hurt and betrayed he would feel. Rathe would be safe from Luska, but Treygan would never forgive me. I'd never forgive myself. "I can't and you know that."

"Then it shall be done." He kissed me, a soft, gentle kiss, and it was over before I could resist or push him away.

He slid deeper into the tide pool as I stood there, dizzy and shell-shocked. When he swam out of sight I pulled myself together and followed him. Transforming into bird form, I zoomed through the narrow tunnel and out into the ocean.

No trace of him. Not even air bubbles left in his wake. I transformed to mer and shouted, *Luska!*

My internal voice carried through the water, but there was no reply. My wings unfurled as I raced upward and burst through the surface. I scanned both oceans from above. He couldn't have gotten far, yet I couldn't sense him or see him. No water rippling, no sign at all that he had even been there.

"Dear gods," I muttered. "Please help me."

Luska was on a mission to dispose of everyone I loved.

I had never flown so fast. I landed on the beach outside of Treygan's home. The feeling of being watched made me twitchy, but I didn't sense Luska at all. I shook off the feeling and hurried inside.

Treygan stood in his living room with Rownan. They both stopped talking as soon as they saw me.

"Oh, thank gods," I breathed. "You're all right. Luska threatened to dispose of everyone I love."

Treygan's eyes stayed locked on me, unblinking.

"Say something," I insisted.

Rownan looked away and turned his back to us, but Treygan didn't move.

"What's wrong?" I asked him.

"Maybe you should sit down."

Nothing good ever came from people telling me to sit down. "No, tell me."

He swallowed hard. "It's Nixie."

"Nixie?" I was the only one who could communicate with Nixie. How could he possibly know anything about what was going on with her? I started to walk past him to check on her, but he put a hand out to stop me. "Let me prepare you."

"Prepare me for what? You can't even see her or hear her. How would you know if anything was wrong?"

He looked at me as if I was clueless and he felt sorry for me. I pulled away and ran into the resting room. When I saw her I stopped dead in my tracks and became a statue in the doorway.

I didn't believe it. At least not for the first few seconds. Then, as the severity of the scene registered, I sank to my knees.

I had always believed that Uncle Lloyd's wall panels were indestructible. I even used one to protect his living room windows during a hurricane. I had been so ignorant, so naïve. Nothing and no one was indestructible.

Nixie's wall panel, her soul's portal, had been shattered into a billion tiny splinters of wood. I reached down and picked up one. They were everywhere, even floating in the pool.

Luska destroyed my only way of communicating with Nixie and Medusa.

Treygan kneeled beside me, trying to comfort me with his strong embrace. "Lloyd will carve another one. The kraken broke your portal of communication, but not her spirit, not your bond."

I wasn't crying. I had already told myself pretty much the same thing. Nixie would wait. Luska had cut us off from each other for maybe a week, less if Uncle Lloyd worked day and night. What made me so angry was the fact that Luska had violated Treygan's home again.

"How did he beat me here?" I mumbled to myself. I had flown so fast. How had he even had time to do such damage? I looked up at Treygan. "Were you here when it happened?"

"No. We did a quick patrol around the neighborhood. We got back right before you did."

I nodded, grateful that Treygan hadn't been here. What might Luska have done to him?

I grabbed Treygan's hands. "Please, go to Eden's Hammock." I motioned to Rownan. "Take anyone and everyone close to me. He won't be able to pass through the gateway to Earth's realm."

"I'm not going to hide like a coward," Treygan said. "I need to be here in Rathe with you."

"He's going after everyone I love. You'll be on the top of his list."

"I can protect myself."

"You can't be sure you can protect yourself when we don't even know what he's capable of."

He narrowed his eyes. He knew I was right. I hated what I was about to say, but there was no way around it. "I have no doubt he can and will kill you. Don't give him the chance."

"You handle this your way and I'll handle it mine." His hands slid out of mine.

"Since when did we become a divided team?"

"Since you lost faith in me."

I flinched. "I haven't lost faith in you."

"If that's true, then you'll support me in my decision to stay and protect my realm."

"You're not repairable," I argued, fear choking my words. "I can't ask Uncle Lloyd to carve a replacement of you."

"You won't have to."

He looked so angry and stubborn. So proud. He would never forgive me if I ordered him away like a child. The unsettling feeling of being watched made my skin crawl again, so I shook my head and reluctantly said, "Fine. Have it your way."

I scanned the room more thoroughly, searching for any sign of Luska invisibly lurking. One of the potted palms toppled on its side. Peeking out from behind some fronds was Luska's graffiti on the wall. The creepy black eye seemed to be staring directly at me. Was it possible he used it as a way to spy on us? Was it a portal for him? Is that how he beat me here?

I slowly rose, not taking my eyes off it. Rage churned in my core. I wanted revenge. In an angry voice that didn't sound like me, I said, "Eye for an eye."

Without even thinking about it, I flew forward and kicked down the wooden wall until every last bit of Luska's evil symbol was outside in Treygan's yard.

"Yara?" He wasn't trying to stop me; he was simply questioning what I was doing. My next action would speak for itself. I heaved the wood over to the beach and kindled my inner flame. Fire flew from my hands and the wood ignited, burning fast and hot.

As the smoke billowed, I turned to face the house. Rownan and Treygan stood watching me from the massive hole in the wall. I glided back inside to join them.

"I'm sorry," I told Treygan.

He held up his hands. "No apology necessary. This room needed remodeling."

Rownan smirked at me and shook his head. "Remind me never to make you angry again."

I turned and assessed the damage I had done to the wall. Treygan must have read my mind because stone began forming around the edges. I grinned and helped speed things along by creating my own stone. Together, we repaired the wall within seconds and made it stronger than before.

I didn't sense Luska anymore. I couldn't order Treygan to hide in safety on Eden's Hammock, but maybe I could assign him a job to keep him far away from the kraken. The less chance of Luska finding him, the better.

I spun to face him. "If you're staying, then I need your help."

"Name it."

"Will you check on the sprites? I'm worried Luska might go after Jenna and Keeley. Bring them and any sick sprites to Paragon Castle. And please take Rownan with you. I don't want you traveling alone."

"What will you be doing?" Treygan asked.

"Meeting with the Violets and selkie elders to decide who is sick enough to be evacuated."

"We'll see you at the castle soon." He kissed me and turned

to go, but I pulled him back and grabbed Rownan's arm with my other hand. "You two protect each other at all costs. Luska knows how much you both mean to me."

They glanced at each other, nodded, and left.

I prayed Otabia wouldn't fail in her mission to find the Wrangler. If she brought him to Rathe soon, then this nightmare could end before anyone else was "disposed of."

33

Rownan

Are we seriously going to play babysitter to sprites?

Rathe was falling apart, people were sick, and a horny hell-beast was terrorizing our world, yet here we were swimming off to fetch some sprites. What really pissed me off was that no sprite in the history of Rathe had ever needed babysitting. They might look small and cute and harmless, but when things got rough they could throw down with the best of us. Of all the creatures in Rathe, they were the least in need of protection, which was probably why Luska hadn't tried messing with them yet.

Treygan wasn't stupid. He knew as well as I did that Yara sent us on this ridiculous job to keep us off the kraken's radar.

He slowed down a little and looked at me. *We are going there, but not only for the reason Yara gave us.*

Finally, a plan. *What's brewing in that mind of yours?*

I was thinking about what you said earlier. How Joel acted like we could simply ask Poseidon about the Wrangler.

Obviously Joel isn't as smart as everyone believes.

He is extremely smart, and always seems eager to help our kind. Plus, he may have been on to something.

What do you mean?

What if Medusa and Poseidon can help us?

I laughed. *Now you're talking crazy too.*

Am I? Yara met Medusa and Poseidon when she was in the Inbetween. They aren't mythical beings that no one can communicate with. They're real, and they care about what goes on here.

I'm still not following. Poseidon is off limits to everyone but

Medusa. Nixie is the only one who can communicate with Medusa. And right now nobody can communicate with Nixie.

Incorrect. Right up until the day they left Rathe, Stheno and Euryale communicated with Medusa through the all-seeing mirror.

Lloyd had told us how he'd used a piece of the mirror to check on us in Harte, but I had no idea what else it could do. *Yara told us she tried using the mirror and it didn't work.*

Right, and why not?

I have no idea. I eyed him suspiciously. *Do you?*

I have two theories. First, maybe it's because of her mixed blood. Not enough gorgon blood in her to make it work. But maybe you or I do have enough.

I slowed. *Us?*

He doubled back and floated in front of me. *We're both half gorgon. Lloyd's blood runs through our veins. If it worked for him even after he turned human, then why shouldn't it work for us?*

Do you have the mirror?

No. I didn't want to ask Yara for a piece. She'd ask why, and I'd have to tell her. We're going to get our own piece.

How?

He motioned for me to swim with him. *Nixie broke the mirror in the grotto. There are more pieces in there. I know two helpful sprites who would be thrilled to go in and get a piece for us.*

You said you had two theories. What's the other one?

I'm wondering if Medusa didn't reply to Yara because we're still in the Eve of Poseidon.

That was an intriguing thought. Borderline insane, but intriguing nonetheless. *So you think if we tried contacting Poseidon we might get a response?*

Everyone believes Poseidon watches us closely during his reign. Doesn't it make sense that he'd be the one to reach out to right now?

Was he really buying into this idea or was it a delusion caused by desperation? *Even if we do get a piece of the mirror and you actually manage to contact him, what will you say?*

You've always believed we create our own fate.

So?

So I'm going to start following the wisdom of my brother.

How?

He stopped so suddenly I had to turn around and swim back to him. His eyes simmered with fierce determination. *I'm tired of pretending I'm a tranquil sea when I've always had a storm raging inside of me. It's my turn to be strong and unpredictable. I'm going to demand the power to send Luska back.*

I sighed inwardly and resisted the urge to smack the back of his head. I wanted to get rid of the kraken as much as he did, but a realistic plan would have been a huge help. This most definitely did not qualify.

34

Koraline

Joel was in a coma.

I had been there myself; I knew the signs. I didn't need anyone to confirm it. Nor did anyone need to tell me what I had done to the man I love. The horror of my terrible decision singed every cell in my body. But that didn't stop Caspian and Indrea from berating me.

Caspian leaned on Lloyd's table with arms so stiff I thought his bones might snap. "I never imagined you'd do something so stupid. You risked his life, Koraline. You may have *ended* his life."

I didn't reply. I had no defense.

"I won't be so coldhearted as to order you back to Rathe while he's in such an unstable condition, but I am officially warning you not to take this any further. If he wakes up, you are finished with this transformation idea. Finished, do you understand?"

I looked away.

"Koraline, swear to me that you will not attempt to continue the transformation process."

I closed my eyes and pressed the cut on my hand. "I swear that I—"

I couldn't speak the words. Transforming him was my only chance of saving him. The transformation had started. If I could finish it without risking his life, then of course I would.

Looking up into Indrea's amethyst eyes, I saw her disappointment. Her arms crossed over her chest like an impassable wall of sharp sea rock between us. "Koraline, if you can't give us your word, we will have to order you back to Rathe as well."

"That won't stop her," Caspian said. "She convinced Kimber to attempt this. She will find a way to finish it."

He was right, but I wasn't about to admit that out loud. They had already ordered Kimber and Delmar to return home. I wanted to go with them so I could take the brunt of the punishment, but I couldn't leave Joel. "What will happen to Kimber and Delmar?"

Indrea's voice was stern. "That decision is up to the other Violets. There is nothing we can do."

I squirmed in my seat. "But you're going to be the new co-ruler of Rathe. You can—"

"No, I am not," Indrea calmly cut me off. "Yara's choices were rejected. I'm still a Violet, and I have to trust my peers to decide what's best."

Ashamed, I nodded. "I understand."

Indrea rubbed her forehead then stood and opened the back door. "Lloyd, Pango, Merrick, will you join us, please?"

My stomach lurched. The last thing I wanted was to get anyone else in trouble.

They came through the door with somber faces and Pango flashed me a look of concern.

Indrea gestured to the chairs. "Please, sit down." She sounded exhausted. I opened my mouth to insist the others be left out of this, but Indrea spoke first. "Many of Rathe's residents are sick."

I stiffened. Rathe had looked a little lackluster last time I'd been there, but this sounded serious.

Caspian sat across from Pango. "We've begun the evacuation process. The sick merfolk and their caretakers will be taking refuge on Solis again."

"It's that bad?" Pango asked.

Indrea crossed her arms again, but this time it wasn't in anger. More like she was hugging herself. "Some have developed fin rot. Others are too fatigued to swim or climb out of their resting pool." My stomach knotted tighter the more she spoke. "Many of the selkies are experiencing similar symptoms. We don't know for certain whether it is caused by the loss of the ruling trinity or the presence of the kraken or both, but our water is becoming so polluted we have no choice but to evacuate the sick to purer waters."

"Earth's waters? Purer?" Merrick said incredulously.

Pango gasped. "Holy Medusa."

"What about the sprites and gorgon kin?" Lloyd asked.

"So far no serious symptoms," Indrea said.

Lloyd looked relieved. I wondered if any of the gorgons he had known were still alive. Did he miss that life? Did he miss them? Clearly he still worried about their safety.

"We're hoping once the sick are removed from the conditions in Rathe they'll improve," Caspian explained. "Violets will stay on Solis in shifts to help heal them."

"Lloyd, we hate to impose on you," Indrea said, "but we're hoping to use Yara's old house so the selkies can stay there with the air conditioning running as cold as possible. Jack offered the use of his bar, but we don't dare introduce an unknown illness to the human populace."

Lloyd shook his head. "No imposition at all. I'll cast an icing spell on the house to make their accommodations more comfortable."

We all looked surprised, even Indrea and Caspian.

Pango reached over and squeezed Lloyd's shoulder. "Aren't you just full of jaw dropping surprises?"

"That would be wonderful and greatly appreciated," Indrea said.

"Yes," Caspian agreed. "We can't thank you enough, Lloyd. We'll send help for whatever you need."

Lloyd stood and walked over to the back door, staring out at the ocean. "Sounds like what we need is to help find Yara some co-rulers."

Indrea sighed. "Easier said than done."

35

Caspian and Indrea weren't at Paragon Castle, but a guard told me they'd return soon. Treygan and Rownan hadn't arrived with the sprites yet, either. Thanking the guard, I headed for an upper floor of the castle. I didn't want to wait in an underwater room because the visibility was too bad. Another constant reminder that Rathe was getting worse.

I stood outside on a balcony, staring up at the sky. My faded sun was almost completely eclipsed by gray haze. Stheno and Euryale's were gone. Not faded. Gone. Faint rings of haze still remained where each of them had once been, but they were barely visible. The same phenomenon had occurred with the moons on the selkie side of Rathe.

On my way to the castle, I had stumbled upon a school of macawfish a few miles away from Treygan's house. They were dead. I couldn't just leave them there, so I gathered all six of them and brought them to the castle. I glanced behind me at the basket containing their bodies. I didn't know what kind of ceremony sea creatures had when someone died, but I wanted the macawfish to have a proper funeral. They mattered.

Every creature in Rathe mattered. Most were getting sick, and now some were dying. Because of me. I bowed my head and tears fell.

An Indigo guard opened the double doors behind me. "Pardon the interruption, but Treygan and Rownan are here."

"Please send them in."

I wiped my tears and turned around. A breath of relief whooshed out of me when they walked into the room. Keeley and Jenna flitted through the air on either side of them.

"Hello, Yara!" Jenna shouted happily.

Keeley made a beeline to me and landed on my shoulder, hugging my neck. "Don't worry. We're not sick."

"Thank goodness for that," I told them. "What about the rest of the sprites?"

"A few coughs and sniffles," Jenna said. "And Tucker has been getting headaches, but that's all. Nothing to worry about."

It worried me very much, but I didn't want to frighten them. I would tell Treygan about the macawfish later in private. "Did you bring the sick ones here?"

"Yes," Treygan said. "They're downstairs with some of the Violets. Jenna's not exaggerating. There really are only a few showing mild symptoms."

"Good." I rubbed my neck, feeling at least one of the knots unravel.

"You don't look so good." Keeley stroked my cheek. "Not much color left in you."

"I'm okay. Just tired."

"Get some rest," Jenna suggested. "Does wonders for us. You can rest in Echo Bayou if you'd like. I'll tell everyone to be quiet."

I grinned. "That would be lovely, but unfortunately I don't have time right now. I'll take a raincheck."

From far away, Otabia's shrill call cut through the air. She was back. Thank goodness. I stepped out onto the balcony and answered her with a siren call of my own.

"Jenna, Keeley, why don't you go downstairs with the others? Are you hungry? The kitchen staff would be happy to make you something."

"Famished!" Jenna said. "Thank you."

"We'll see you later?" Keeley asked, flying off my shoulder

and hovering in front of me.

"Yes," I assured her. "See you later."

They both kissed my cheeks and flew out of the room.

"Otabia's coming," I told Treygan and Rownan. "Let's hope she found the Wrangler."

Eve and Mariza's shadows swept over the floor as they perched high above us in the arched windows. Otabia flew in carrying a pale, transparent man with long white hair and a beard. She set him down and he looked at us in silence.

I stepped forward. "You must be the Wrangler."

He saluted me with a smile. "Indeed I am."

"Thank you so much for coming. I'm Yara." I motioned to the guys. "This is Treygan and Rownan. We're all very pleased that you're here."

"Likewise. I suppose." He clasped his hands behind his back and strolled around the room, examining the artwork on display. The room was like a small museum with pieces created from every kind of ocean material imaginable: shells, seaweed, shipwreck debris, and more. "This place sure is full of colors."

Harte was a dark and dreary place. Traveling through our realm of colorful sand and sky must have been a dramatic change for him. I wished he could see Paragon Castle the way it was supposed to be, full of sparkling sea glass and vibrant colors. Or the rays of our three suns stretched across the sky in shimmering shades of the rainbow. All of that was gone now.

Sadness drenched my words. "It used to be much brighter."

"Pardon my manners, Wrangler," Rownan said. "But are you . . . alive? You look like a ghost."

"Far from it," he replied, and I had no idea if he meant far from alive or far from a ghost. Whether he was technically alive or not didn't matter. He was here, and he might be our only hope.

"We desperately need your help," I said.

"So I've been told by that pretty black-winged creature."

I gave Otabia a nod of gratitude and she winked at me. "Otabia brought you here because we need your expertise in capturing the kraken and sending him back to Harte."

He snickered. "Was told that too."

"Can you help us?"

"That all depends. Does he want to be caught?"

What a peculiar question. "Of course he doesn't. That's why we need your help."

"If the kraken doesn't want to be caught, then there won't be any catching him. He does what he wants."

"Not in our realm, he doesn't," Treygan said.

Wrangler picked at his ghostly teeth with his ethereal pinky nail before replying. "That creature is too powerful for the likes of me to wrangle."

"But you look strong." Treygan nodded at the Wrangler's muscular arms. "And you wrangled him before and locked him in Harte."

"You flatter me, but no, I did not wrangle that beast. He was sent to rule Harte by our creator himself."

"Poseidon," Treygan said flatly.

Wrangler held up three fingers and pointed them at the sky. "The one and only."

"You must know some way to help us," I pressed. "How did you wrangle the other evil creatures?"

"I used my nets."

"What kind of nets?" Treygan asked.

"The kind I weave."

Now we were getting somewhere. Ideas were already sparking in my mind. "You weave your own nets?"

"Every good wrangler does."

I considered my next question. I had to choose my words carefully. "Can you weave us a net big and strong enough to capture the kraken?"

"I doubt anything would ever be able to contain that beast."

"Would you try? Could you weave us the strongest net you've ever made?"

He chuckled. "I'm old. And I'm rusty. A few centuries ago I

might have had enough fire left in me to attempt a feat like that, but these days, no can do." He looked at Otabia. "I do believe our business is concluded. May we proceed with our agreement?"

Treygan asked, "What agreement?"

Otabia ruffled her feathers. "The only way he'd come here was if I agreed to fly him to Earth's realm when we were finished."

"We're not finished," Treygan said.

Wrangler stroked his white beard. "You have a realistic wrangling job for me here in Rathe? If not, then we are finished. I'd like to move on to a realm where I can round up some bad beings. Black Beauty over there says there's plenty of them to be had in Earth's realm."

Rownan stood in front of him, blocking his path. "You're not leaving yet."

"Try and stop me." Wrangler kept walking, passing right through Rownan's body on his way to Otabia. "Ready, Black Beauty?"

Treygan followed and tried to touch his arm, but his hand closed on nothing as Wrangler stepped onto the balcony. Treygan turned to me and shrugged. "How am I supposed to stop a ghost?"

"We don't stop him," I said. "He's a guest, not a prisoner. Otabia, may I have a word in private before you go?"

She strutted over and we distanced ourselves from the guys so they couldn't hear us.

"Mind helping him rekindle his fire?" I whispered to her. Otabia grinned wickedly and I realized what she was thinking. "That's not what I meant! Well, maybe it is. Whatever it takes. He seems to like you."

"Of course he does. He's a male."

"Please convince him to help us. The net thing may work. It's worth a shot."

"That's all you want? Him to weave one of his nets?"

"For now, yes. But while you're being a good *hostess* to

him, perhaps you could find out if he has any other useful abilities he isn't mentioning."

"That sounds like a delectable challenge." She flicked her black hair over one shoulder. "I accept."

"Thank you. Seriously, thank you so much. I'm sorry you had to go to Harte again."

Her inky brows danced playfully. "Wasn't that bad. Besides, I brought back a sexy souvenir."

My own brows rose and I glanced over my shoulder at Wrangler. I suppose he could be considered sexy, if bearded ghostly figures qualified.

Otabia strutted over to the Wrangler and purred, "Ready?"

He replied just as flirtatiously. "If you think you can handle me."

She laughed, put her arms around him, and flew off with him toward Sybarite's Nest.

"Now what?" Treygan asked me.

"Now we pray that Otabia can change his mind." The memory of the macawfish floating lifeless in the ocean with their colorful eyes wide and staring brought back my despair. "I need you to tell me what to do for a sea creature funeral."

"Funeral?" Rownan and Treygan both asked at the same time.

Grimly, I motioned to the basket across the room. They went over and looked inside, then at each other, and finally at me.

"What happened?" Rownan asked.

"I don't know. The kraken? Rathe's deterioration?" Either way, their deaths were my doing. I glanced out at the ocean. "I have a feeling they're the first of many."

Treygan came to where I stood and held my face, silently insisting on eye contact. "We will figure this out. We will find a way to stop him."

"How many more will die before we do?" I could see my own reflection in his sad eyes. He was looking directly at the person responsible for all of this. He knew it and I knew it. His mouth opened to reply, but then his eyes flickered to the door-way. "Indrea and Caspian are here."

Several seconds later they entered. Both looked very unhap-py.

"Yara, Treygan," Indrea said curtly. "Mer meeting in Conch Hall. Now."

Rownan cleared his throat. "Treygan and I were about to leave on an important task."

"It will have to wait." Caspian's gaze locked on Treygan. "Attendance of all Indigos is mandatory."

Treygan and I exchanged concerned glances. What now?

"Wait here," Treygan told Rownan. "We'll leave as soon as the meeting is finished."

Treygan held my hand as we followed Caspian and Indrea out of the room and down a corridor to Conch Hall.

"Do you know what this is about?" I whispered to him.

"No, but for the first time ever, I'm wishing I wasn't an In-digo."

36

Koraline

You would think with all the experience Pango, Merrick, and I had with caring for and being coma patients that we'd be able to take care of Joel with no problems. But between the shock of the unsuccessful transformation and Indrea and Caspian's visit, we had been too distracted to save Joel from wetting the bed. Pango and Merrick gave him a bath while Lloyd stripped the sheets and I sat in the kitchen, crying and wondering how many more ways I could fail the man I loved.

Later, after we got Joel settled into Lloyd's recliner, Lloyd suggested moving Joel's bed into the den so I'd be able to take care of him without needing to be carried up and down the stairs to the guest room. I think he could see how much not being able to help on my own was upsetting me. It wasn't ideal, but the den had sliding doors for privacy and more room to maneuver the wheelchair, so I agreed. Pango and Merrick pushed the couch against the wall and went upstairs to dismantle the bed frame while I read some more of *Treasure Island* aloud to Joel. We were in the middle of an intense scene when someone knocked on the doors.

"Come in," I said.

Vienna peeked inside then offered a little wave and tiptoed in as if afraid she might wake Joel.

"Don't tiptoe," I told her. "Stomp, scream, make as much noise as you can. We *want* him to wake up."

She smiled. "I didn't want to disturb your time together."

I set the book down and stretched, cracking my back and

rolling my stiff neck. "It's okay. We need a break."

She held out her closed fist. "Here. I want Joel to have this."

I opened my hand and she dropped a gray stone into it. "What is it?"

"A talisman of sorts. Whoever has it is protected from harm, so I hoped maybe it would help Joel recover."

What a sweet gesture. I motioned for her to bend down and hug me. She did, and her comforting scent of winter mint wafted from her hair.

"Thank you," I told her. "He and I are both very appreciative."

Our hug was broken up by Delmar clearing his throat in the doorway.

I'd expected Caspian or Indrea to return and tell me my punishment, but instead they had sent Delmar. They must have known I'd feel worse hearing it from him.

He murmured a tired greeting and glanced at Joel. "Any improvement?"

"Not yet. How did it go with the Violets? Did you give them my statement?" I had handwritten a confession that Joel and I were to blame for everything. I begged them to pardon Delmar and Kimber for their parts in this and issue any and all punishments to me. We all knew the elders would be furious with me, but I prayed they would have mercy on my friends.

"The Violets postponed the trial until the kraken crisis is resolved."

I sighed with temporary relief.

Delmar sat on an arm of the couch and kept his gaze on Joel. I knew how he felt. Like staring at Joel might make him move, might force him to wake up. "They held a mandatory meeting for all Indigos."

"All Indigos? Why?"

His eyes met mine for only a moment before he looked away again. "One of the gorgon elders was there. He put a curse on the Indigos."

Vienna beat me to my next question. "What kind of curse?"

"They said if anyone disobeyed orders again and attempted to transform a human—" He broke off and hung his head.

"What?" I probed, thinking of Lloyd and the curse the gorgons cast on him when he was warned not to interfere in Yara's life. "They'll get sick?"

Delmar shook his head. "Death."

Vienna gasped. "They wouldn't."

I sat there in silence, the implications hitting me in wave after wave as Delmar continued. "I never thought they'd go that far, but they spoke it aloud, so it must be true. I had no say, obviously. Indrea and Caspian voted against it, but the other Violets outvoted them."

I almost tried to stand until I remembered I couldn't. "We need Yara. She's Rathe's ruler. She can override the curse."

"Yara can't enforce authority over the Violets without the agreement of all three rulers. Currently, there is no second or third."

"There has to be some way to reverse it." I could hear the desperation in my own voice. "Maybe Messina or Talus knows a counter-spell."

Delmar finally looked at me, and there was total defeat in his eyes. "There's no way to reverse it without the ruling trinity."

My mind raced. Kimber couldn't finish Joel's transformation, but maybe another Indigo could. Maybe Treygan hadn't attended the meeting. Maybe he had been off somewhere helping Yara like usual. "Was Treygan cursed too?"

"Yes. *All* Indigos attended. I'm truly sorry, Koraline, but you have to let this go for now."

I couldn't let go. Joel had been the strong one. He had said he couldn't live the wisdom of Lao Tzu, that letting go wasn't an option. Now, seeing him clinging to life, I had joined him in his philosophy.

Vienna rubbed my back, trying to comfort me as I placed the stone she had given me into Joel's hand and closed his fingers around it. I'd try anything to save him. Stones, praying for a miracle, anything.

Just like he would do for me, I was going to hold on for as long as I could.

37

Kownan

Treygan came out of the mer meeting looking like someone had stepped on his tail or peed in his resting pool. But he refused to talk about whatever had happened in there, so we headed for Trident Rock.

The chain of towering black spires loomed above us like a warning that what we were about to attempt was stupid. Or, more accurately, would never work.

Treygan swam up to the centerpiece of the rock formations, the largest one which looked like a trident. "I figure our best chance at communicating with Poseidon is here. This was his territory, where he made the gateway between here and Harte. Trident Rock means something to him."

"Whatever you say."

He pulled himself out of the water and sat on a flat rock, pulling the small piece of mirror that Jenna and Keeley took from the grotto out of his arm band. Treygan had sworn the sprites to secrecy. He wanted to make sure it worked first before telling Yara, and then he promised he'd give them credit for helping.

I followed and sat beside him. The mirror shard was the size of a small oyster shell. "I still say that thing isn't big enough to work."

"Lloyd said it only has to be large enough to show a reflection."

I rolled my eyes and waited for my brother's inevitable failure. Treygan was usually very intelligent. I couldn't understand why he believed this method of communication with Poseidon was actually possible. He was basically doing an advanced version of what every other sea creature did during the Eve of Poseidon and acting like no one else had ever thought of it before him.

He held the mirror in both hands and began chanting the spell that Lloyd had taught him. Over and over again, he spoke ancient gorgon words that I didn't understand.

I kept glancing between him and the mirror. Nothing happened. Treygan kept at it, though, and on the seventh or eighth repeat of the spell he started to get frustrated.

"Come on, Poseidon," he groaned.

I couldn't resist. "It's not working."

He glared at me and tightened his grip on the mirror. He recited his mumbo jumbo a few more times, sounding more agitated with each round. He finally stopped and I checked the mirror again. Still nothing.

Treygan set the mirror down beside him and sprang to his feet. He shouted so loud that it startled me. "Poseidon! Answer me!"

Well, this was it. He was finally losing his mind for real.

"Look, I get it," I said. "You've been trying to protect others for as long as I can remember. Hell, you spent nearly two decades ready and willing to live in the gorgon grotto with Stheno and Euryale. We all thought you were crazy back then, but this?" I stood. "Shouting at the sky is teetering on insane."

He raked his hands through his hair and paced.

"Poseidon can't hear you. Even if he could, he knows what's going on and he hasn't done anything about it, which means no help from him. The Wrangler blew us off, Medusa won't approve two new rulers, and Rathe is slowly spiraling down the drain. We need a real plan, Treygan. We need to kill the kraken before he succeeds in taking Yara back to Harte."

"That won't happen."

"What if it does?"

"It won't." He picked up the mirror and slid it back into his armband. "I'm taking it to Lloyd. He can make it work."

I grabbed his arm. "Treygan, he can make it work to see what's going on with sea creatures of Rathe. Not to communicate with our creators."

"You don't know that."

"You're wasting valuable time on this crap! If your only plan to save Yara and Rathe is to call up our creator on your magic mirror, then we're doomed."

"I *will* save them."

I let go of him and stepped back. His confidence had no substance. Not without a plan. "I know this isn't what you want to hear, but no matter how badly you want to protect her, you might lose her unless we kill that bastard. Soon."

He blinked and said nothing, so I continued.

"Our people are sick. Our oceans are mysteriously becoming more polluted than the worst of Earth's. Some of our plants and animals are dying. Who or what else has to die before you decide to take action with me?"

"He's a god, Rownan. What if we try to kill him and fail? What if he kills us? Yara would be left alone."

"That will only happen over my dead body."

"Exactly my point. I could also lose my only brother. I'm not willing to risk your life or mine."

I stood in front of him and gripped both of his shoulders. "Treygan, this is to save Yara and all of Rathe. It's more than worth the risk."

His chest rose slowly then fell, along with his reluctance. "You're right."

I relaxed. He had finally come to his senses.

"But," he added, "I have to see Lloyd first."

"Fine. I'll go with you."

"No. You'll slow me down. I'll be back soon, and I'll meet you at Paragon Castle. We'll form our plan there."

Normally I might take offense to that, but he was right. He was much a faster swimmer than me. I almost asked him to tell

Lloyd that I love him. Just in case the worst happened. "You're doing the right thing, Treygan," I said instead. "There's not a doubt in my mind."

38

Paragon Castle was bordering on chaos. Every Violet in Rathe was there to help transport the sick to Eden's Hammock. Indigos were grouping up to either guard the castle or act as escorts for the long swim to Earth's realm. Blues had been called in to help organize. The same type of procedure was happening on the selkie side of Rathe, and once again I felt horrible that I couldn't be in two places at once.

From across the room at overcrowded Conch Hall, I saw Rownan walk in and search the crowd. His eyes landed on me and he rushed over.

"Why aren't you with your people?" I asked him. "And where's Treygan?"

"Treygan's fine. He's making a quick visit to Lloyd's. I have something I need to discuss with you. And Indrea and Caspian, if possible."

I gestured to the loud crowd around us. "They're sort of busy."

"It's important," he said. "Please?"

I huffed, and then I realized how annoyed and bitchy I sounded. He was trying to help in every way he could. I had to stop being so snappy with him. Calming myself, I softened my tone. "Okay, I'll find them and meet you in Whelk Hall."

"Perfect."

I watched him walk away, wondering if he was the real thing

or if I had just been fooled again. I was ninety-eight percent sure it was Rownan, but I needed to be safe.

I motioned to Mariza and Eve. They swooped down from the rafters and landed beside me. "I didn't sense Luska, but he's fooled me before. Stay close in case that isn't really Rownan."

They nodded.

"Indrea," I called as she hurried past me. She stopped and told the Blue she'd been talking with to go on without her.

"I'm sorry to pull you away at a time like this, but Rownan is waiting for us in Whelk Hall. He needs to speak with you, Caspian, and me about something important."

"All right. Let me find Caspian."

I admired her composure. She must be stressed like never before, yet she remained so calm. That's how I should have been handling myself too.

A few minutes later, we were all gathered in Whelk Hall, looking at Rownan expectantly. Judging from his stern expression, I could tell the news wasn't good.

"What is it?"

He rubbed his goatee, glancing at all of us before he said, "Treygan and I need help with a plan."

"What plan?" I asked.

Sage hissed and rose above my head.

Rownan's lips were moving, but no sound was coming out. Mariza screeched frantically. Wings rustled above me then stopped.

Sage coiled on my shoulder, poised to strike, but I couldn't sense any threat. I stared at Rownan, who was now pounding soundlessly on an invisible barrier. He was encircled in an ink cloud.

I turned to warn everyone else, but they were all encased in ink clouds. All of them had realized it too, and they were all pressing their hands against the material, trying to find a way out. Rownan was shouting, but I couldn't hear him. Eve's and Mariza's wings were flapping and Mariza clawed at the barrier with her talons, but they were trapped.

And I still couldn't sense Luska at all. Why?

"Luska!" I yelled, slowly spinning in a circle. "Show yourself."

Sage's head darted in all directions, her tongue flickering as if she was trying to locate him by smell.

Almost as soon as I had the thought, the scent of vanilla and licorice enveloped me. I instantly relaxed. Sage uncoiled and nearly slipped down my arm, and I wondered if my eyes looked as glazed over as hers did.

From behind me, Luska whispered in my ear, "Look at them, Yara. I could crush them right now—end all of them this very instant. Like crumbling dirt between my fingers."

"Please, please don't," I begged. I knew I should be doing something. Lashing out, calling for help, trying to free the others. But my body wouldn't obey me.

He sighed and stood in front of me, no longer invisible. "I won't because I don't wish to hurt you. Not to that extreme. However, you are forcing my hand. Summoning my own Wrangler? Have you gone mad? Were you intentionally trying to anger me?"

How did he know about Wrangler? He really was angry. I could tell by his posture and the ferociousness in his tone. I'd never seen him like this before. I began trembling. "I was trying to save my people."

"You aren't taking me seriously. How do I make you understand that the longer you wait to return to Harte, the worse life will be here in Rathe?"

With a flick of his hand, the ink clouds containing Caspian, Indrea, Rownan, Eve, and Mariza all moved until they stopped in a cluster behind Luska. Then they darkened to varying shades of gray and black until I could barely see everyone inside of them.

"Please, don't hurt them," I whimpered, sounding as desperate as I felt.

Sage lolled against my shoulder as Luska lifted my chin and traced one finger over my lips. His stiff jaw relaxed and his demeanor shifted back to normal. "Stop making me act like the villain. I want to spoil you and make you delirious with ecstasy. I will honor your request because your wishes matter to me. However, I cannot allow you to keep underestimating me. I must prove to you that my threats are to be taken seriously."

The ink clouds started moving, fanning out and circling the room around us.

Luska was going to hurt one of them, I could feel it. An awful roulette wheel of souls I loved surrounded us and he was about to randomly select an unlucky victim.

"Please, Luska," I begged again, clutching his hand. "Don't do this."

"Heed my warning," he said, "or I will dispose of more beloved members of your circle."

He touched my cheek and I closed my eyes, careful not to say or do anything that might set him off. He gently kissed me then whispered against my lips, "Pity you insisted it be this way."

A hot pain shot through the back of my head. It was so intense that I cried out and fell forward against him.

Immediately, I pushed away from him and reached for the source of the burning. Before my hand found it, my eyes landed on her. A blood-curdling scream tore through me. "No! Noooo!"

Luska held up Sage in front of me like she was a piece of useless rope. Blood dripped onto the floor from her severed body. I pressed my hand to the back of my head, feeling for her. Even though I could see her detached and dangling in Luska's hand, I wanted it to be a lie. Her silver eyes were wide open and lifeless. Luska dropped her and she landed with a dreadful thud in her own pool of blood.

"No," I murmured again, falling to my knees and gathering

her in my arms. Tears welled and my throat burned with the urge to scream or sob, but I pushed all of it away.

Sage wasn't dead. She couldn't be dead. I had gone through all of this before in Harte. I wouldn't fall for it a second time.

Luska squatted in front of me. "Feel the pain of losing her, Yara. Then imagine that pain and guilt amplified by the power of several undersea volcanos. That's what will happen when I eliminate the rest of them. Do you truly want to carry that guilt for the rest of your eternal existence?"

I ran my fingers along Sage's cold scales. She wasn't dead. She couldn't be dead.

Luska petted my hair. I wanted to slash his hands off, but I couldn't do anything except hold Sage. I stared at her, holding back a flood of tears, willing her eyes to open or her spine to curve and slither up my arm.

"Call to me when you're ready to stop endangering the lives of others." Luska yanked my hair, forcing me to look up at him. "Selfishness is a trait that will suit you much better in Harte."

39

Rownan

The monster walked out of the room and my bubble prison burst. I fell to the floor then scrambled to get to Yara's side.

She was crying. Not in a normal, ugly, desperate way, but in a more worrisome way. She wasn't moving, wasn't sniffling. Tears ran down her cheeks and dripped onto the floor as she held Sage's limp body in her hands.

"Yara?" Indrea kneeled beside her, tenderly putting one arm around her shoulders.

"It's not real," Yara said. "I've been through this before. Sage isn't dead. It's an illusion."

My heart ached for her. Caspian moved behind Yara and started healing her open wound. I winced at the sight of it. Mariza, Eve, and I exchanged glances, sickened that the kraken had done this to her.

Indrea lifted Yara's chin so they made eye contact. "Sweetheart, I am so sorry. This time it is real."

"It's not." Yara croaked out the words. "Life can't be this unfair. Our gods would not be this unfair."

"This isn't the work of *our* gods," Caspian said. "This is the evilness of Harte."

"She's not dead." Yara draped Sage's body over her shoulder. Her hands shook as she held up Sage's head, trying to make her something she wasn't. "She can't be dead. She's part of me. If she's really dead then part of me died too."

Indrea held her hands open in front of Yara. "Please, let me have her. Sage deserves a proper blessing."

Yara hugged Sage's head to her chest. Tears continued streaming down her cheeks. "No. She's not dead. This isn't real."

I had no idea what to say. My determination to kill the kraken became stronger by the second, but this moment wasn't about me or my revenge. Yara needed comforting, and only one person could offer what she required.

Caspian finished healing her wound, and then I lifted Yara into my arms and turned to Eve and Mariza. "I'm taking her to Forbidden Apple Lagoon. He can't reach her there."

Mariza nodded. "I'll travel with you for protection."

"Eve, Treygan's either with Lloyd or on his way back from there. Find him and tell him to meet us at Forbidden Apple." I wanted to reach up and wipe away the single tear forming in the corner of Eve's eye, but my hands were already occupied with Yara and her river of tears. "Tell him to swim faster than ever. Yara needs him."

She flew up and out of a window. If we were going to have any hope of Yara being able to rule Rathe and beat the kraken, then it was up to Treygan to make her feel whole again.

I hadn't been to Forbidden Apple Lagoon since I was a kid. After what Treygan had told me about his time here with Yara, I considered it their place. I felt like an intruder, but at least I had good intentions.

Near the bank, beside a tree with limbs that dipped into the water, I let go of Yara. She drifted forward, making no effort to swim. Sage was draped around her neck like a scarf and Yara kept both hands on her.

"It's okay," I tried assuring her. "He can't find you here."

She floated there, eyes closed, but she was still crying. "Is Sage really gone?"

"Yes," I said quietly. "I'm so sorry."

She grabbed a tree limb and pulled herself up onto land. She sat cross-legged and put Sage in her lap, pressing one hand to the back of her head and staring at Sage's body.

I didn't know what else to say, so I sat beside her and gently pressed my shoulder against hers.

After a few minutes I said the only thing I could think of to ease some of her pain. "Treygan will be here soon."

She didn't reply, so we sat in silence, her petting Sage and me staring at the water, wishing I had the power to bring Sage back to life.

Yara reached up to the tree branches and picked a flower. She placed it on top of the ragged section where Sage had been ripped away from her. The torn scales and muscles were an ugly sight, but Yara was attempting to make it pretty.

I picked a few blossoms and added them to Yara's. Eventually, we had covered the physical ugliness of what had happened. If only the emotional wounds could be healed as easily.

After what felt like forever, Treygan arrived. He'd know what to say or do. I was at a total loss.

As I scooted away, he gave me a grateful nod. He pulled himself up onto the bank and sat facing Yara. He looked at Sage and the veins in his neck bulged as his jaw tensed. But then all of his muscles softened as he lifted Yara's chin and turned her face toward him.

"I am so, so sorry, Yamabuki."

"She's gone," Yara mumbled.

"She will always be with you. Just like Nixie. No one can take her spirit away from you."

Tears streamed down Yara's cheeks. Slowly and delicately, Treygan lifted Sage and pressed his nose to hers. He whispered words I couldn't hear and then placed her body on the ground with such tenderness that even I felt a twinge of tears burning my eyes.

He lifted Yara into his lap, cradling her like an injured child.

At first she tried squirming away. "Give her to me."

Treygan held her tight, but didn't say anything.

"I can't let go of her," Yara insisted. "She needs me."

He held on as Yara thrashed and practically tried to climb over him. She cried harder, and then got mad, pounding on his chest while desperately begging to hold Sage again. The cycle repeated several times. It was heartbreaking to watch.

After several minutes of this, Yara collapsed against Treygan's chest and sobbed long and hard. "He killed her." She clutched Treygan's shoulders and buried her face in his neck. "She was part of me and he killed her."

Every muscle in my brother's body looked like it would snap from tension. His skin swirled with shades of sadness, anger, and love.

A tear ran down my cheek and I wiped it away.

Treygan smoothed down Yara's hair and whispered to her until her sobbing turned into soft crying.

"Her spirit is here with us," he said a little louder. He spoke with so much conviction that I believed him. "I feel her. She's here with you. She always will be."

My brother. The hero.

I wished I could make everything right for him and Yara. I wished I could undo any bad or malicious things I had ever done to them. Heal any pain I'd ever caused. They deserved a happily ever after more than anyone, yet it seemed fate kept handing them one horrible blow after another.

"Everything will be okay," I told them, but not loudly enough to be heard.

I quietly slipped into the water and swam away, leaving them to their privacy. Like I said, the lagoon was their sacred place.

40

I sat there, cradled in Treygan's arms, crying until I had no more tears left.

Sage was dead. This wasn't a cruel illusion of Harte. This was my reality.

I sat up and slid out of Treygan's lap and into the lagoon. I floated a short distance away before turning around to face him. "You shouldn't be here."

He joined me in the water. His tone was so gentle. "I'm always going to be wherever you need me to be. I'm your partner, remember?"

"I'm not worthy of this. I'm not worthy of you."

"That's not true." He even floated toward me gently.

"Yes, it is."

"No," he said. How was he so calm and composed while I wanted to scream, cry, and break down? He brushed his knuckles against my cheek. "It's not the truth. You and I belong together. I spoke it out loud, so there's no denying it." He ducked his head lower so our eyes met. "I know you're devastated, but you will overcome this. The kraken will pay for what he has done."

I chuckled like a crazy person. "No, he won't. Don't you see how powerful he is? And he's not even operating at full strength. He's taking it easy on us. I'll give you one good guess who he'll kill next."

Through the water I saw Treygan's hallmarks darken and ripple. "Don't worry about me."

"I would be ecstatic if I didn't have to worry about you." Desperation tightened my vocal chords. "So help me accomplish that. Go to Eden's Hammock where he can't reach you and stay there."

He lifted his chin like a proud and brave idiot. "I told you, I refuse to run away."

"I'm not worth dying for, Treygan. Please don't be stupid. I realize I'm your only option, but you had a good life before me and you'll have one after I'm gone."

His eyes were wide below his furrowed brow. "What do you mean you're my only option?"

"You're cursed. You weren't with anyone before me because you'd turn them to stone. I'm the one exception. You don't have any other options, so you're with me by default."

"Is that what you believe?"

"It's the truth and we both know it."

He drifted backward. After a minute of tense silence his head tilted and his lips pursed. "Luska put this crazy notion in your head, didn't he?"

I focused on the water between us, fighting back more tears, or maybe rage.

Treygan eased closer to me. "Well, brace yourself, Yamabu-ki. I did have options and I still do. In case you forgot, a whole race of gorgons exists in Rathe and all of them are immune to my curse."

I scoffed. "Gorgons? You'd be attracted to monsters with serpents coming out of their heads?"

He tried staying composed, but disappointment coated his words. "Do you hear yourself? *You* are a beautiful sea monster who is grieving for your beloved serpent. Have you forgotten you're part gorgon?"

My own stupidity, along with my breath, caught in my throat. Why was I speaking so harshly about a race of creatures

I not only loved, but was a part of? I pressed my hand to my mouth. "I'm sorry. I don't know what's wrong with me. That was a wretched thing to say."

"The kraken's ugliness is seeping into you." He lifted my hand and pressed it over the anchor hallmark on his chest. "Don't let it. You're too good for that."

I thought of my conversations with Luska. "He manipulated me into doubting us. And I let him."

Treygan cradled my face in his hands. Nothing but love and devotion shone through his eyes. "I want you to always remember something. I chose you. I will always choose you. I am in love with you, body, mind, and soul. Even if every female in the worlds was offered to me, I would still, now and forever, without any doubt, choose you."

My lips parted to tell him how sorry I was for doubting him, but he silenced me with a kiss that reminded me of the strength and purity of our love. His kiss was perfect, just tender enough to ground me again after losing part of myself.

Treygan let go of me then swam to the bank to pick a few starflowers. "Give me your arm," he said as he swam back to me.

"Why?"

"Just give it to me."

He held my wrist, rotating it to expose my inner forearm. "Hold it like that, above the water."

I did as he asked while he dipped his finger in the center of one flower. He wrote an N on my arm and I gasped as the sparkling letter illuminated my skin.

He wrote the remainder of our motto—Koraline's motto—the same one we branded on our arms in Harte. *Never give up.*

I dipped my finger into the center of another flower and motioned for Treygan to give me his arm. I held it out in front of me, and in glowing stardust I wrote: *The tide will turn.*

"Written in the stars," he said. "So it must be true."

"I wish these words would stay on our arms forever."

I looked at the motto again, then at Treygan. He was more

than I could have wished for and more than I deserved.

"Believe in me," Treygan said. "Have faith in us. As long as you don't give up, love and light will win this war."

"Of course I believe in you."

Treygan's neck and shoulders relaxed. "Then we've already won."

His confidence radiated from him so strongly that the lagoon seemed to grow brighter. "You really think we can defeat him?"

He kissed my wrist and pulled me close so that our foreheads touched. Dust from the starflowers speckled his cheek, making his indigo eyes seem to sparkle. "Love can defeat him, and we have oceans of it."

I didn't want to rest, but Treygan had insisted. He pointed out that I would be useless to Rathe and myself if I had no strength left.

I floated there in the safety and tranquility of Forbidden Apple Lagoon. For the first time since the kraken's arrival, my body was fully relaxed. My mind, however, stayed alert, trying to figure out who Medusa would accept as worthy rulers and devising strategies for ridding Rathe of Luska.

Once I had some solid ideas, I eased my body awake. From the corner of my eye I saw a twinkle in the water. I pushed aside my floating hair and sat up, searching the lagoon.

The back of my neck tingled and out of habit I reached for Sage. My spirits lifted as I pulled her long, sinewy body over my shoulder, but my joy quickly sank again when I saw a vine in my hand instead of the snake I so dearly missed.

On the end of the vine was a white flower. The shimmery petals were closed.

Treygan glided through the water, approaching me with a curious stare. He carefully lifted my new vine and examined the bud. We looked at each other, and his sympathetic expression said what words couldn't. No matter how pretty the flower, it would always be an ugly reminder of Sage's death.

"Before we leave here," he said, "I need to show you something important."

I didn't understand what he meant until silver clouds passed over his irises. The calm before the storm. I had been so plagued with worry and stress that I had forgotten about one of my favorite hobbies with Treygan. Tension dissolved from my shoulders as I allowed myself to be swept away into one of Treygan's memories.

Uncle Lloyd sat at his kitchen table. Treygan leaned against the counter.

I paid close attention as they discussed information the kraken could never know about. Then Treygan outlined a plan that I didn't think would work, but I felt Treygan's confidence. He believed it would work. He and Rownan were planning an attack on the kraken, but they needed my help.

Uncle Lloyd rapped his knuckles on the table, his leg bouncing non-stop. "I don't know. This plan makes me nervous."

Treygan sat beside him. "I was against it at first too, but we're desperate. The kraken has to be stopped."

Uncle Lloyd sighed. "Make sure Rownan is with you. I gave him a stone that will hopefully protect all of you. The High Priestess said it would."

"He showed it to me. And he'll be with us."

"Good."

I pushed myself out of the memory and returned to the present moment in the lagoon. I had seen and heard enough to know my part. Yes, the plan was risky and dangerous, but it might be crazy enough to work.

Treygan still floated in front of me, holding me so I wouldn't drift away.

"Well?" he asked.

I ignored the fear tugging at my gut. "I'm in, but before we do it, I need to speak with Uncle Lloyd myself."

41

Koraline

I didn't want to leave Joel's side, but my brother had other ideas. Pretending to be deaf to my completely reasonable arguments, he had plucked me from Lloyd's wheelchair and carried me outside to get some fresh air and sunshine. And then he threatened to tie me down if I tried to crawl back into the house. I was resentfully lounging on a deck chair when he snapped his fingers in front of my face.

"Hello? Sweet sister of mine, can you return to this galaxy, please and thank you? I asked you an important question."

The sun had a halo around it. A sign of change. Would one of those changes be Joel's condition? I blinked and forced myself to stop staring at the omen above us.

"Sorry," I told Pango. "What did you ask?"

He sighed and motioned to the huge slab of wood covering half of Lloyd's back deck. "Nixie's waist and hips. Do they look accurate? Goodness knows I am not an expert in these matters."

Lloyd, Pango, Merrick, Vienna, Keeley, and Jenna had been working almost nonstop carving the new panel of Nixie. The sprites were making impressive progress on her detailed wings. Lloyd insisted only he could sculpt her face, so that left Vienna, Pango, and Merrick to sculpt the rest of her body.

I patted his hand. "She looks great. May I go back inside now?"

"No. Her corset seems sort of lopsided, but I don't know

how to fix it." With his chisel still in hand, he wiped his brow and stood. "Time for a cold beverage. Bringing fierce females back from the dead is exhausting work."

I grimaced at his casual use of the word *dead*. Joel might soon join that demographic. A little more of me died inside each time I thought about the possibility.

As Pango disappeared into the house, Lloyd joined me on the deck.

"How are you holding up, Koraline?"

I shrugged. "Still wishing for him to wake up."

"We all are."

"If he doesn't wake up . . ." I swallowed down another tiny piece of my broken heart. "If he doesn't survive this, do you think carving a portal for him would work?"

Lloyd pulled up another deck chair and sat beside me. "We could try, but I don't think we'll need to. He is going to pull through."

"I want to believe that too, but I'm also trying to be realistic."

"Don't do that." Lloyd pinched my cheek. "Too much reality dulls the spirit. Expect miracles and believe in the fantastical."

Later that evening, we were gathered at the kitchen table having dinner. Vienna and Pango tried encouraging me to eat, but I didn't have an appetite. I wanted to get back to Joel, but everyone kept insisting I take breaks. They claimed sitting at his bedside all day and night would make me feel worse instead of better.

Since they kept insisting that I needed fresh air and sunshine, I insisted Joel needed them too. From now on, Pango could carry him out onto the deck and put him in a lounger so I could sit beside him and read to him. Propping him up in a chair at the table seemed insane even to me, though, so I picked at my food and counted the minutes until I could excuse myself.

We were all startled when the kitchen door opened and Yara walked in. I should have sensed her approaching, but I hadn't felt anything. I'd have to ask Pango if he experienced the same thing. Perhaps even our powers were deteriorating along with our world.

Lloyd set down his fork. "This is a pleasant surprise. Everything okay?"

Yara looked so sad I felt a lump forming in my throat. "Everything is lightyears away from being okay."

"Anything we can help with?" Pango asked. "We're willing and able."

Yara gripped the back of her neck and looked at the floor. "Can you resurrect Sage and reattach her to me? Or give me some magic spell guaranteed to send the kraken back to Harte?"

"Sage?" Vienna stood and rushed to Yara's side. "What happened?"

We all waited in silent shock for Yara to explain, but she shook her head. "She's gone. I'm not ready to talk about it yet. I hope you can respect that."

Vienna stroked Yara's hair. "Of course we will. Oh, Yara, I'm so terribly sorry. We all know how much she meant to you."

Yara sniffled as her eyes met mine. "Forget about me. Treygan told me what happened. Has Joel woken up yet?"

I shook my head. "I'm sorry the Wrangler didn't come through."

Treygan had told us about his refusal to help. Joel's idea hadn't worked. The bad news kept pouring in, wave after wave.

"Don't rule him out yet," Yara said. "Otabia is working on him."

"So what happens next?" Pango asked her.

"Wouldn't it be wonderful if I had an answer to that question?" She rubbed her neck again and turned to Lloyd. "How's it going with the selkies?"

"Fine. They're staying at your old place."

She nodded. "Indrea said you were handling it all really well."

"Feels good to help." He motioned to all of us sitting at the table. "But they did most of the hard work."

Yara genuinely smiled as she looked at each of us. "Thank you, everyone."

We all assured her we were happy to help, and then she asked to speak to Lloyd in private. He followed her out of the kitchen and their footsteps traveled up the stairs. A door shut, and then Pango looked at me.

"Should we be worried?" he asked.

Vienna flopped back in her chair and fiddled with her napkin. "We've been worrying nonstop. Why should we stop now?"

Merrick shoved food around his plate. "After hearing about Sage, I have most certainly lost my appetite." He pushed his half-eaten meal away from him.

"Me too," Vienna agreed. "Let's get this stuff cleaned up."

I reached for my plate, but at the same time Vienna and Pango both held up their hands.

"We'll take care of this," Pango offered. "You get back to Joel."

"Yes," Vienna said. "Time seems to grow more and more precious."

She missed Rownan immensely. She had been toying with the idea of going back to Rathe, but after hearing what the kraken had done to Sage, I was pretty sure she would abandon that line of thinking.

I was certain we were all praying that Sage would be his last victim, but I had a sickening feeling that she might be the first of many.

Lloyd and Yara were upstairs for hours.

When Yara finally came down, her eyes were pink and swollen from crying. She walked out onto the back deck without a word, so I rolled myself outside to check on her. Her back was to me, but I could see her fingers trailing over the carved ridges of Nixie's new wall panel.

"We feel awful that she isn't finished yet."

"It's okay," Yara said quietly. "I've seen firsthand how much work goes into these."

I rolled myself closer, admiring the resemblance between Yara and the most powerful soul I knew of. "It's amazing how much you look like her."

She turned around. "Like who?"

"Medusa."

She huffed. "I'm nothing like Medusa."

"Don't forget you're talking to someone who saw Medusa in the Inbetween. I remember her luminous colors, the flowering vines she has for hair. Your coloring may have faded in the last few days, but you're still practically her mirror image." I reached for the flower draped over her shoulder and lifted it to my nose. "Mm, smells like apple blossoms, except sweeter."

She stepped away from the wood panel and sat in a chair. "Koraline, how much do you remember about the Inbetween?"

"A good amount. As you know, you can't easily forget an experience like that."

"Did you see Poseidon while you were there?

"Once. Sort of."

"Sort of?"

"Seeing him was like having an out of body experience while having an out of body experience. I remember feeling like I wasn't worthy of being in his presence."

"You're very worthy. Every creature of Rathe is worthy. He helped create us."

"You know what I mean."

"Do you remember if he had a pearl too?"

"You're wondering if Joel's theory about Luska's pearl is valid."

"I am."

"I do sort of recall Poseidon's Adam's apple looking silvery-black. Maybe his pearl is inside of him instead of outside like Medusa's."

Her face relaxed. "Good to know. Thank you. Treygan and Rownan are hell-bent on ripping Luska's throat open to remove it. *If* it exists."

"If they do succeed, all of this will be over, right? Luska will die?"

She sighed and looked up at the moon. "Let's hope so, because if he survives that kind of attack he'll want revenge, and he will not hold back this time."

42

Rownan

I peeked inside Treygan's resting room for the tenth time. Still empty.

"Where could Yara be?" I asked him.

Treygan pinched the bridge of his nose. "For the tenth time, I don't know. No one knows."

Eve said she had accompanied Yara back from Eden's Hammock hours ago. They had gone straight to Treygan's home because Yara said she needed to rest. Eve had taken up a guard position on the roof, and five minutes later Yara was gone.

So many merfolk were involved in the evacuation that there weren't many left to search for her, but Treygan sent whoever could be spared. I asked the selkies patrolling our side of Rathe to keep an eye out for her. No one had seen or sensed her anywhere, Treygan and I had failed at shadowing her, and Eve couldn't feel her emotions like usual.

I didn't want to say what I was thinking. If Treygan wasn't worried that Luska might have taken her, then I sure as hell didn't want to be the one to suggest it.

Otabia flew in and landed with a flurry of black feathers. She stepped side to side, back and forth, like a bird pacing a branch. "Where's Yara?"

"We don't know," Treygan sighed.

"What do you mean you don't know?"

I glared at her. "She left without telling anyone. We haven't been able to find her for the last few hours."

Otabia's ebony wings lifted high and wide. In one fluid leap, she stood face to face with Treygan. "What if she's with *him*?"

The shades of purple that had been speckling Treygan's skin since Yara disappeared started to darken. She had him worried again.

I attempted to change the subject, at least temporarily. "Where have *you* been?"

"Passed out in our nest, physically exhausted from my escapade with Wrangler."

I rolled my eyes. "Spare us the details."

Treygan's interest was piqued. "Did he agree to help?"

"Almost. We have another rendezvous planned at high tide, during which I plan to thoroughly persuade him to do more. If he is any indication, Harte males are forces to be reckoned with. I can see why Yara has succumbed to Luska's seductive powers more than once."

"Shut up, Otabia," Treygan growled.

"Don't get snippy with me because you have competition for Yara's affections. Keep her satisfied and she won't stray. But you better work extra hard. Wrangler is an expert at seduction, and he's not even a god. Imagine how much more powerful Luska must be."

"You're pushing it," Treygan told her through clenched teeth. "Get away from me before I lose control of my gorgon side."

"Is that a threat or a promise?" Otabia purred.

He threw up his hands. "Good gods, why is everyone so excited by threats and darkness? What ever happened to wanting happiness, love, and light?"

Otabia cackled. "When have I, or any other siren, ever craved light or happiness? Those needs are part of your genetic coding, not mine."

He stiffened as her words sank in. I could practically see Treygan's thoughts scrolling over his head like closed-captions. Sirens didn't require light or happiness. And Yara was part siren.

"Oh, tsk, look at that sad face," Otabia said. "You've finally realized what the rest of us have known since Yara's rise in the ranks. She isn't the ray of sunshine you fell in love with. Her dark side is undeniable and strengthening. She has needs that must be fulfilled."

I stepped forward. "Lay off, Otabia. He has enough to deal with."

Treygan didn't take his eyes off her. He leaned in so they were almost nose to nose. "In case you forgot, I have a dark side too."

"Are you confident that you can give her everything she needs?"

His lips parted, but his reply caught in his throat.

Otabia's eyebrows arched. "Mm, yes, pity your mer side won't allow you to speak the lie you so badly want to believe."

I stuck my arm between them and pushed her back to give Treygan some space. "Seriously, get out of here," I told her. "You're making things worse for him."

"I'm going. Clearly I need to find Yara and protect her since neither of you are capable."

I was done being polite. "Piss off. Now!"

She snickered as she flew away.

"Ignore her," I told Treygan. "That trip back to Harte must've made her crueler than usual."

"Yara loves me," he muttered. Then he said it again, as if trying to convince himself.

"I know she does. You know that too." Yara did love him. Everyone knew that was true. However, we also knew that in some situations love wasn't enough, but I wasn't about to point that out. Otabia had already done enough damage.

Treygan walked to the rivulet. "Wait here in case Yara returns."

"Where are you going?"

"To search for her." He waded in and I followed.

"I'm coming with you. I can help."

He almost argued, but then said, "Fine. But I'm swimming

fast, so try to keep up."

Yara wasn't at Forbidden Apple Lagoon, so we decided to check Gorgon Rock next. It was the only other place she could hide where no one else would see her. I was really hoping she'd be there so I could stop swimming at such a fast pace. My abs ached and my tail was cramping from trying to keep up with Treygan. The pathetic part was I knew he was taking it easy. We weren't swimming anywhere close to his top speed.

It was actually dangerous swimming as fast as we were, and it was kind of a miracle that we hadn't smashed into anything. Yara's sun was pathetically dim and visibility wasn't great in the murky water. That's why, as we rounded one of the outlying formations of Gorgon Rock, we almost ran straight into the kraken.

Luska's slithery dark form lurked several feet away near the grotto's small entry tunnel.

He had his back to us. He'd never see us coming.

Treygan and I exchanged looks, silently agreeing this was our chance. Yara wasn't here, but we had to try our plan now.

I surged forward, passing Treygan and hoping I could gain enough speed to rip Luska's head off in one explosion of rage.

I moved like a bullet through the water, but when I was within arm's reach of him he whipped to the side. Before I could change course, one of his tentacles wrapped around me, lifted me out of the water, and pinned me against a rock. He surfaced seconds later, dripping water. Another tentacle lifted Treygan beside me and pinned him against the rocks to my left.

Countless cups suctioned me in place. I kicked and writhed, trying to break free, but it was like a python had wrapped around me and wouldn't stop squeezing.

"Where is she?" Luska asked.

Grunting and struggling to breathe, I spat, "Like we'd tell you even if we knew."

He turned his attention to Treygan. "Ah, the young ruler's consort. I've been hoping for the opportunity to speak with you. Are you really so selfish that you would keep Yara from her destiny? If you truly loved her, you'd want the best for her."

Treygan didn't look one bit scared or even uncomfortable. He was his usual stoic self. "The best for her is me."

"She is a goddess, a powerful ruler who will live forever. Yet you expect her to settle for a relationship with a mortal."

"She makes her own choices, and she chose me."

"You won't be by her side for as long as I will. Don't you want to spare her the pain of losing you? You could do it now, before your connection is so strong that your inevitable death will destroy her."

He was playing on Treygan's greatest fears and weaknesses. How did he know to go right for his emotional jugular?

"Nothing can destroy her," Treygan argued. "She's too strong."

"She is indeed strong, and more powerful than you know. She confided in me that she holds back around you to spare your precious ego. She doesn't want to flaunt her superiority. She is capable of such greatness, yet she restrains herself so that *you* don't feel inferior. You're limiting her, holding her back from reaching her potential. How do you live with yourself knowing you cause her more harm than good?"

I flailed, trying to break free. "Treygan, don't listen to him!"

Luska leaned closer to Treygan. "If you won't do it for her, do it for all of Rathe, present and future. This realm deserves a ruler who feels free to use her full strength. You've created a situation where Yara cannot be that ruler. As long as she exists in the same realm as you, she will never be the epic soul she is destined to be."

Treygan spoke in a growl. "She already is an epic soul, and she's much too good for Harte."

Luska's eyes glowed an eerie shade of purple. "She could change Harte, bring much needed light to it. She could save two realms at once."

"Oh, come on!" I grunted and pushed against his repulsive tentacle, but it gripped me tighter and moved me farther away. "Don't let him brainwash you."

Luska continued to ignore me and address his garbage to Treygan. "Harte has never known light. My realm could thrive with her as my co-ruler. All those trapped, tortured souls; Yara could give them hope. She could better an entire realm. Are you going to be the one who stops her from achieving such greatness?"

Treygan didn't reply. I tried craning my neck to see his expression, to make sure he wasn't letting Luska get to him, but I couldn't see his face.

"It would be the most selfless gift you could ever give Yara," Luska continued. "Creatures throughout Rathe say you're known for your selflessness. If that's true, then why do you cling to her so selfishly?"

Luska was preying on all of my brother's fears and insecurities. It was like watching a ship sink with no way to stop it.

"Don't listen to him!" My voice was a whisper due to the fact my lungs were being crushed by a bastard squid.

Luska's psychotic glowing eyes returned to normal and he released Treygan into the water.

"Swim fast," Luska told him. "I will grant you a head start while I kill your brother, but once that's done I am coming for you."

I could see Treygan below me. Not floating. Not treading water. He was upright and still as a stone statue. If there's one thing I knew about my brother, it was his body language when he was furious.

Electricity filled the air. A flash of lightning pierced the sky, followed by a gust of wind. That was the sign. She was here. Yara had made it after all.

"You aren't killing my brother." Treygan's tone was cold and calm. "And I'm not swimming away from you."

Luska grinned. "Now you're depriving me of happiness as well. The chase is one of the most enjoyable parts."

Another flash of lightning. Yara was ready to attack.

Treygan sneered, almost smiling, and then calmly said, "I hope you enjoyed saying those words because they were your last."

A loud caw from the peak of Gorgon Rock made Luska and I look up. Yara soared through the sky, morphing from bird to siren and back again as she headed directly for us. Luska watched her, a curious expression on his face, his throat exposed.

My gaze dropped in time to see Treygan rushing upward on a self-created wave. He whipped out a small blade from his armband. The flashing lightning glinted off its shiny surface as he sliced through the kraken's throat, ripping away a chunk of flesh and muscle. Luska's blood, black as ink, sprayed everywhere. With a defiant roar, Treygan threw the handful far into the distance.

The tentacle holding me suddenly went slack. I slid down the rocks and splashed into the water. When I resurfaced, Luska had nearly tripled in size, casting shadows across the ocean like an ominous mountain. Yara burst through the water where Treygan had thrown the mess of flesh that hopefully contained Luska's pearl.

One of Luska's tentacles cut through the air so fast it made a whistling sound. I gasped as it collided with its target. Yara's limp body somersaulted backward until she crash-landed far away in the water.

Treygan shouted for her, but he was ensnared in another tentacle before he could get to her.

My brother's body flew past me as Luska lifted him into the air. Treygan's arms, along with the knife, were bound tight at his sides.

"Treygan!" I shouted, dodging the flailing tentacles that were keeping me at bay.

In the distance, Eve dove down from the storm clouds and

scooped up Yara's unconscious body. She flew off in the opposite direction as Luska sank into the water, pulling Treygan down with him. His head of black coral was the last part of him to disappear beneath the surface. I dove after them.

Luska's glowing eyes stared at my brother, but I could hear his thoughts too. *I warned you, but you insist on playing the hero in a game you cannot win.*

Go to hell! I shouted, trying to divert Luska's attention to me.

He chuckled. The bastard actually chuckled, and then he said again, *I warned you.*

The tentacle that held Treygan swayed to a stop above me. Rows and rows of suction cups seemed to turn inside out, changing into rows of jagged spines. My brother let out an agonized growl as Luska's menacing laugh echoed through the waves.

I screamed curses at him, torpedoing through the water at full speed. I didn't know how I'd reach Treygan, but I'd climb up the filthy kraken with my claws if needed.

Except I didn't get that far. A tentacle whipped through the water in front of me, clipping me on the shoulder and flipping me end over end.

When I managed to stop and get my bearings, Luska was below me, searching the ocean floor for the pearl Treygan had ripped from his throat. His glowing eyes found mine. *Where is it?*

He threw it as far as possible so the current can carry it away.

He snarled and swam away in the direction Treygan had thrown the pearl. I bolted upward, praying that Yara had found it and Treygan was okay.

I found my brother floating on the surface, limp and wheezing with each breath.

"Where does it hurt?" I asked, pulling him closer to me. And then I got a good look at him and felt stupid for asking. From his fins to his neck were trails of bleeding puncture wounds. "Good gods, what did he do to you?"

He couldn't answer me.

I hooked an arm under him and swam hard, pulling him with me as I put more distance between us and Luska.

"Mariza!" I shouted, hoping maybe she was hanging around to carry us to safety. But she didn't show. We were on our own.

Treygan stared straight up at the sky, his gasps becoming more labored and his chest seizing.

"Don't die. Don't let that bastard win." I swam faster, fueled by adrenaline. "I'm taking you to the Violets. They'll heal you. Hang in there. Don't die or I swear I will hunt you down and—I don't know. Just don't die."

He wheezed and trembled violently. I swam faster than ever. I had to reach the Violets in time. If the roles were reversed, Treygan would be so much quicker. He would save my life.

The High Priestess had been right all along. This time, it was my turn to save him.

43

Treygan had been in a deep sleep for hours. Rownan had gotten him to Paragon Castle in record time, but it had almost been too late. Caspian and Indrea had done several rounds of healing on him, and so had several other Violets, including Delmar. I waited in a constant state of turmoil, praying for the moment he'd wake up, but also dreading it.

Part of our plan had worked. Treygan had ripped out Luska's pearl. I was mad at myself for getting knocked unconscious so early in the fight, but at least I had managed to grab the pearl before it happened.

I wanted to hunt down Luska and kill him slowly and torturously for what he had done to Treygan. But ripping out his throat had hardly slowed him down, so what would it take to kill him? At least Treygan survived. For that, I was eternally grateful.

Rownan had tried to make me feel better by telling me about the gaping hole in Luska's throat. At least now maybe Luska couldn't speak. That might hamper his ability to manipulate everyone, but I still wanted to strangle Rownan and Treygan for jumping the gun and trying to take on the kraken alone. That was *not* part of the plan. If I hadn't gotten back from my secret meeting with the gorgon kin when I did, they both might have been killed.

That was my wake up call, even more than Sage's death had

been. Luska's threats were real. He would dispose of everyone I loved. Even if Rownan and Treygan's plan was salvageable, I refused to risk their lives again. I had to take matters into my own hands, and Treygan would hate me for it.

His eyelids fluttered open. He saw me and lifted his hand, stroking my cheek. "What happened? Did he hurt you?"

"I'm fine." I pressed his hand to my cheek and kissed his palm. "But he almost killed you."

"Almost. He didn't succeed."

"Only because of Rownan and the Violets. I've reached my breaking point, Treygan. I'm begging you, please go to Eden's Hammock and stay until this is over. He will try to kill you again."

"If he does, he'll fail again." He struggled to sit up.

I didn't think I needed to point out that his muscles were trembling just trying to stay upright. Instead, I picked up the cup beside us and held it out to him. "Drink this. You're severely dehydrated."

He downed a few gulps then set it aside and took my hands. "I love you, Yara. He doesn't. That means I win. Every time, in every faceoff, our love will make me the winner."

"This isn't a fairy tale. Good doesn't always win. If you stay here, he won't stop until you're dead and I'm broken."

His grip on my hands tightened. "How can I leave here and hide with everything that's going on?"

"I let you win that argument before. I agreed to your plan, and you almost got killed. Things are different now. I'm not asking you to hide, I'm asking you to save yourself."

"Not unless I can save you too."

With a heavy heart, I handed him the cup again. "Drink some more. It will help."

After he had finished, Eve and Mariza flew down from the windows, landing behind him.

He glanced over his shoulder at them. "Why are they here?"

"So I can say goodbye."

"Goodbye?"

When I had visited Uncle Lloyd, I'd gone over multiple scenarios with him. I was glad we had prepared for almost anything. He would know what to do when Treygan arrived. We had mapped out that route as thoroughly as the other possibilities.

"This is a no-win situation," I said, letting my fear and exhaustion creep into my voice. "If I don't go with Luska, he will continue to hurt people and ruin Rathe. My first obligation is to protect Rathe and all of its creatures. I can't keep failing at that."

"You can't—" He licked his lips and closed his eyes momentarily. "You can't protect anyone if you return to Harte."

"Wrong. I protect them by giving Luska what he wants so he'll leave Rathe. I'll choose another ruler to take my place. There are much better choices for the position anyway."

"No." He pulled me closer and pressed my hands to his chest. He tried to stare into my eyes, but I couldn't look at him. My guilt was overwhelming. "We will find a way to send him back to Harte." He squeezed my hands. "Without you."

"How?" My voice cracked. "We've tried everything we could think of and nothing works. The longer he's here, the more damage he does. He feeds on it. The more he destroys, the more he wants to destroy. I can't let it continue."

"We'll think of something else. Lloyd had other ideas." He was starting to slur his words. I hoped he wasn't so out of it he'd repeat any of Uncle Lloyd's suggestions. "You can't go with him yet. Not ever."

"I have no other choice."

"Wrong." His head lolled like his neck muscles were giving out, but he righted himself again. "You accused me of not having a choice about being with you, remember?"

I fought back tears. "This is different."

"It's not. We all have choices." He spoke slowly and deliberately. "I chose you, Yara. Now I'm asking you to choose me."

A tear ran down my cheek as I shook my head. "Do you think this is easy for me? This is a gazillion times worse than when I thought I'd be sentenced to live in the gorgon grotto for eternity. Harte terrifies me, but I have to face it to save every soul in Rathe, including you." My next words were a whisper. "Especially you."

His eyes closed for so long I thought he might have fallen asleep, but they strained open again. "Give us a couple more days. There has to be a way."

"A couple more days and Rathe might be unsalvageable. How many more will die in that time?"

"One more day."

I stood to go, but he grabbed my arm. His strength was impressive. Even as his muscles twitched, his conviction and determination didn't waver.

I needed to stay as strong as him. "You have to let me go so I can save Rathe."

He squinted at me like he was trying to read my mind, or maybe he was struggling to keep his eyes open. He unzipped his armband. "Then take this with you."

He pulled out a black pearl. A fake one. Just like we had planned. I pulled back, but he waved it closer. I shook my head, and he spoke in an infuriated voice. "You want the kraken and all of his darkness? Then you should carry his pearl and make it official."

I stared at the decoy pearl. We had strayed from our original script dramatically, but Treygan was still trying to salvage the remainder of our plan in case Luska was eavesdropping. For several breaths, I debated whether or not to join him, but I couldn't risk his life again.

"*Your* plan is no longer an option. I have to do this my way." I kissed him then bowed my head as more tears fell. "I love you so much. No matter what happens, please have faith in the fact that I love you."

He shook his head. "I don't understand."

I wanted to say so much more, but I couldn't. My new plan didn't allow it. Uncle Lloyd would make him understand. All I could do was reassure him one last time. "I do truly love you. One day you will understand."

His hand holding the black pearl quivered between us. His eyelids grew heavier, slipping down over his enlarged pupils. His head drooped forward again as he mumbled, "Everything feels wrong."

I eyed the empty cup sitting beside him. In his already weakened state, I would have thought the Liquid Lullaby would have put him out in seconds, but he had held on for several minutes. I didn't have time for this.

My wings flew open, knocking the pearl from Treygan's fingers. I didn't see where it landed, but it didn't matter. To my right, Luska, invisible and unaware that I could sense him, stood watching. He had seen everything and heard every word. He'd retrieve the black pearl and believe he was invincible. The decoy would make him less guarded.

The downside was that in order to fool Luska, I had to forsake Treygan.

He reached for me weakly and said, "Yara, don't do this."

I surged upward, hovering beyond his reach. More of my tears fell, dropping like rain onto the floor below me. "Goodbye, Treygan."

With my heart in my throat and him still reaching for me, I flew away.

44

Koraline

Joel looked so peaceful lying there. I wanted to lie down and snuggle up to him. Or grab him and shake him until his eyes opened.

"We discussed this." I pressed my fingertip along the valley between his lower lip and chin. "I know how hard it is where you are right now. I'm so torn. I don't know whether to beg you to keep fighting or tell you that it's okay to let go."

A sudden commotion startled me. The banging and shouting sounded like it was coming from the kitchen, so I backed my wheelchair away from Joel's bed and rolled out of the room.

As I approached the threshold between the kitchen and living room, I saw Mariza shoving Treygan into a chair. "Stay put. You can barely walk."

Curiosity kept me moving forward.

Eve circled behind Treygan and held him down by his shoulders. "I thought the Liquid Lullaby was supposed to knock him out for a lot longer."

"It should have," Mariza snapped. "He's too stubborn to stay down."

Treygan snarled at them. "I'll swim back the moment you leave."

Mariza waved her talons. "Yeah, yeah. Save your breath."

"I'll turn you to stone."

"No, you won't."

"To save Yara I will."

"She doesn't want you," Mariza said coldly. "She chose him."

I had no idea what was going on, but I knew better than to pick a fight with two sirens, so I parked myself in the corner with the best vantage point.

"She's only going with him to save Rathe." Treygan kept struggling to stand, but Eve held him in place.

"Her reason doesn't matter," Eve said. "Only her decision."

He tilted his head back so he could look at her. "You know this isn't right. How can you agree to keep me here?"

"It's my assignment."

"Then be ready to work hard because I refuse to stick around here and do nothing."

He wriggled free from Eve's grip, but Mariza shoved him back down so hard it broke the chair and Treygan crashed to the floor. I flinched, wanting to roll forward and help him, but he stood on his own and tried to shoulder past her. They wrestled for a moment until Mariza slammed him against a wall. Plaster broke and crumbled behind him.

I watched with my hand partially covering my eyes. This wouldn't end well.

Lloyd entered through the back door and took in the scene in a glance. "Let him go."

Mariza flashed Lloyd a glare, keeping Treygan pinned to the wall. "Yara said you'd only be needed if we couldn't control him."

"Yes, well, I'd like to end this nonsense before any more damage is done to my home."

Mariza released Treygan and he brushed himself off. "You're not going to stop me either."

Lloyd sucked in his cheeks with one brow raised, but otherwise stayed silent as Treygan walked outside and down the deck ramp to the beach.

In one long, graceful bound, Mariza crossed the room and stepped through the doorway. "I have to stop him. Yara gave us orders."

Lloyd blocked her. "I promised her I'd keep him here on Eden's Hammock. I'd never break that promise."

"Then why are you standing there?" Mariza asked. "He's almost in the water."

Lloyd tilted his head toward the beach. "Wait and see for yourself."

They stepped outside and I followed them. As I rolled onto the deck, I spotted Treygan diving beneath the surface of the breaking waves. I didn't fully understand what was happening or why. I had some guesses about what was coming, but none of them prepared me for what actually happened.

A bright green flash illuminated the water and the horizon. Treygan flew up out of the water, arms and tail flailing.

"Holy Poseidon," I muttered. Even seeing it with my own eyes, it was still hard to believe.

Treygan landed hard, but within seconds he was storming out of the shallow water onto the beach. "Are you kidding me?" he yelled.

We all turned to look at Lloyd, who stayed silent.

Treygan kept shouting as he approached. "Remove it! Whatever spell you cast to electrocute your own flesh and blood, you disable it right now."

"I will not," Lloyd said. "It's for your own protection."

My chest constricted on Treygan's behalf. From what I gathered, Yara had sent him here against his will. She was agreeing to go with the kraken to save Rathe, and now Treygan's own father was actively preventing him from trying to fix it? What a nightmare.

"You're not supposed to meddle!" Treygan yelled.

Lloyd leaned over the deck rail. "You mean I'm only supposed to meddle when it's convenient for you. Son, your head isn't on straight right now. You think you're going to race back to Rathe and take on that kraken again? Yara sent you back here which means he must have almost killed you. He won't fail if he gets a second chance at it. You can scream and be angry, but I won't lower that barrier. You're my son and I love you, and I promised Yara I'd keep you safe."

Whoa. The plot just kept thickening. Had the kraken tried to kill Treygan? I could imagine how anguished Yara must be. I'm not sure she would have ever recovered from such a loss. I said a silent thanks to our gods for Treygan's survival.

"I *will* find a way out." Treygan spread his hands at his side and we all watched as he pushed the tide back from the beach.

Farther out, the water hit an invisible wall and grew taller, piling high upon itself until it arched in a dome over the house. Lloyd's invisible barrier covered the whole island in a sphere of water. Eve and I exchanged impressed yet worried glances.

"There is no way out," Lloyd said.

Treygan let out a frustrated, angry roar that made the deck boards rumble. He dropped his hands and the water flowed down the barrier, surging back toward the beach and returning to its usual ebb and flow.

"How'd he do that?" Eve asked me.

I shrugged. Even after all these years of knowing him and witnessing what he was capable of, Treygan's power still left me speechless.

"I'm sorry," Lloyd said to Treygan. "I know how hard this is on you." He walked down the steps and joined Treygan on the beach. "Calm down and I'll explain the parts of the plan that you don't know."

I leaned forward, not wanting to miss a word.

"Yara isn't going to Harte," Lloyd explained. "She's making Luska believe that she is, but in reality she has a much different plan."

"I knew it," I muttered. Yara would never have chosen a kraken—or anyone, for that matter—over Treygan.

He didn't seem any less angry. "She can't fight him on her own. She isn't—"

"She won't be alone," Lloyd interrupted. "She's much

smarter than that."

"Has it not occurred to you or her that she won't be able to seal the gateway because power hasn't been restored? He'll come right back, more determined and vengeful than ever."

"He won't come back if he has no memories of her or Rathe."

Treygan raked his hands through his hair. "Dear gods, not this again. She already tried removing his memories and failed."

"He's weaker now without his pearl. She won't fail this time."

Treygan shook his head and turned away from his father.

"Besides," Lloyd continued, "out of all of us, Yara was the only one clearheaded enough to realize she *can't* return to Harte with Luska. Not only because he can't physically take her against her will, but also because her human blood doesn't allow her to pass through the gate."

Treygan wiped his hand over his face. Frustration radiated from him so intensely I felt it on the deck. He spun to face Lloyd again.

"Clearheaded? During this grand epiphany, did she also remember that her body isn't needed in Harte? Did she forget that only our souls experienced all the horrors while we were there?" His muscles were coiled so tight I worried they'd snap. "Did she realize that the god of a hellish realm doesn't have to *physically* drag her to Harte because he doesn't *need* her body?"

Lloyd's face paled. I was sure mine did too.

"Oh my gods," I sputtered. Could Luska steal Yara's soul?

Lloyd glanced around, trying to work out an answer. "I don't think her soul could pass through the gateway either."

"Of course it can!" Treygan roared. "The gateway rejected our human *blood*. And now she's planning to lure him to the gateway to try to remove his memories again, giving him the perfect opportunity to suck her soul from her body and disappear into Harte with her for eternity."

Lloyd turned, waving his hands frantically at Eve and Mariza. "Go. Fly as fast as you can to Yara and tell her this."

My heart raced faster than the flapping of the sirens' wings as they left without a word.

"Where's the mirror?" Treygan asked Lloyd. "I need to speak with Medusa or Poseidon."

"Son, only Stheno and Euryale could communicate with our creators using the mirror."

Treygan glared at him again. He stomped down the beach, away from us. Over his shoulder he called, "I will find a way back to her. I bet my life on it."

Rownan

As much as I didn't want to leave Rathe, I had to see Treygan and talk to him. Yara had deviated way off course from our plan. I didn't know what to do next.

By the time I reached Eden's Hammock it was the middle of the night. Lloyd's house was quiet when I entered. Everyone was either asleep or resting. Pango's blue curls could be seen floating in the stone fish tank in the living room. Merrick was beside him.

I peeked into the den to check on Joel. Koraline sat at his bedside, reading a book to him. I didn't want to disturb her, so I quietly backed out.

Time to look in on Vienna. She was staying at Yara's old house to help take care of the sick selkies. I left Lloyd's and walked up the path.

Opening the front door was like opening the door to a freezer. Dozens of selkies were asleep everywhere. The floor, sofa, loveseat, kitchen. The whole house and all the furniture had an icy sheen to it. Lloyd had frosted everything so it felt as close to home as it could get. I closed my eyes and shadowed Vienna. She was in an upstairs bedroom, so I stepped over one sleeping selkie after another and climbed the stairs, running my hands along the cold banister.

Five kids were sprawled across the king-sized bed, sleeping peacefully. Vienna was on the floor, asleep on her pelt. My nerves eased a tad seeing that she was comfortable and safe.

I tiptoed in and stretched out beside her so our faces were

level. As always, she looked like an angel. How did I get so lucky to have her as my wife? I tucked a stray hair behind her ear. She stirred, but didn't wake.

She was more than strong enough to continue living her life if I died, but we had only recently been reunited after years apart. I wanted so much more time with her. I wanted us to have children, and grandchildren. Hopefully even great-grandchildren.

We had to win this war with the kraken. We had overcome too much in the last two decades to lose each other now—again. My eyes drifted to her band and I considered taking the stone back with me for protection. At that moment, one of the kids on the bed coughed. A wet, painful-sounding cough.

Maybe Vienna hadn't gotten sick because she had the stone with her. What if all the sick selkies she was helping were contagious? Her wellbeing came before mine, so I decided she should keep it. Maybe it would help the others too.

I caressed her face. "You won't lose me, V. Even if you do, I swear on the oceans and heavens I will always find you again."

She made a soft cooing sound. I kissed the top of her head then left her room and went searching for Treygan.

I hadn't seen him at Lloyd's, so I closed my eyes and shadowed him. Within seconds, his location appeared in my mind. I followed the path that cut across the island. As I came through the palm trees and plants, I saw him sitting on the beach beside Delmar. The moon was shining bright, illuminating the water in front of them. They were deep in conversation, talking in hushed voices.

As I got closer, I heard Treygan mention something about Poseidon and then both of them went quiet. I took their silence as invitation to interrupt. "How's it going fellas?"

"As well as can be expected." Delmar sighed. He stood and brushed the sand from his shorts. "I'm heading back to the house. Rownan, good to see you. Treygan—" He glanced down at my brother, his best friend, and shook his head. "Hang in there. We'll figure out something."

He walked away and I sat beside Treygan. "Why are you still here?"

"I'm trapped. My own father imprisoned me."

"What? How? Why?"

"Yara told him to keep me here, so he cast a spell. Remember when we tried crossing the gateway at Trident Rock?"

I recalled the horrible electrocution we'd endured trying to cross the border. "He wouldn't."

"Oh, he would and he did. The barrier circles the entire island. I can swim out about twenty yards in any direction and then I get zapped and thrown back."

How seriously messed up. "They just want to make sure you stay safe."

"It's bullshit and we both know it."

"No argument there. Maybe I can talk to Lloyd. Convince him to lift the spell."

"I doubt it."

"It's still worth a try." I dug my fingers into the warm sand, already missing Rathe's cold selkie beaches.

"Did you see Eve or Mariza on your way here?" Treygan asked.

"No, why?"

"They are supposed to be delivering a crucial message to Yara."

Nothing he said via Eve or Mariza would make Yara change her mind. I didn't want to keep any secrets from him, no matter how terrible. "She's going to tell Luska she'll leave with him tomorrow at high tide."

Treygan cracked his neck. "I worry that might be truer than you think."

Not the reply I expected, but I didn't want to pry and add to his despair.

His head fell into his hands and he rubbed his forehead. "What about Luska's pearl?"

"Got it right here." I reached into my arm band and pulled

out the black pearl. The real one. I offered it to him, but he wouldn't touch it.

He took a ragged breath while studying it, and then he put his hand beneath mine and pressed my fingers closed. "Keep it. Our plan won't work now that I'm a prisoner here."

"I can do whatever needs to be done." Luska wasn't immortal anymore. Powerful, yes, but not invincible.

"No, you can't." He shook his head and gripped my shoulder. "Not this time."

He had a long history of underestimating me. I decided to keep my idea to myself so he wouldn't shoot me down or try to talk me out of it. Let's face it, death was a definite possibility in a showdown with the kraken. But I could do it. I could save our realm and Treygan's relationship with Yara. I was going to prove him wrong.

"Your mind is going a million miles an hour," he said. "I hope you're not planning anything stupid."

"Nope. Nothing stupid." I dug my fingers into the sand again. Something solid hit my hand. I picked up a small piece of mirror. Bless his stubborn and desperate heart. He was still trying to contact Poseidon.

"I know you won't stay here and do nothing. I've been debating whether or not to try talking you out of whatever scheme you're conjuring."

He didn't know Yara had promised that I could help her battle the kraken. I couldn't tell him and hurt him even worse. "Have some faith in me. For once."

"I've had faith in you for as long as I can remember." He nudged my shoulder with his. "So what time are you returning?"

"As soon as I know you're okay."

He inhaled deeply. "I will be."

I had to be sure of one thing before I left. "You'd take care of Vienna if anything happened to me, right?"

"Of course," Treygan said. "She and I could live here together on the island, sharing in the misery of how we did nothing to save our soul mates or Rathe."

"Stop saying crap like that. Vienna suffered for years and years with that cretin while she was in Harte. She has more than earned an eternal Get Out of Hell Free card. And Yara sent you here to protect you."

"Well, Yara failed at that goal." He leaned back, resting on his elbows. He meant she had hurt him by exiling him here while she faced the kraken without him. She'd broken his spirit. I could see it and hear it in every part of him. "Some things are beyond her control."

46

I fidgeted in Treygan's resting pool, trying to do exactly what Uncle Lloyd had said, going over each step again and again. He had tried to teach me how to see spirits without using a panel as a portal, but it wasn't working. I was too anxious.

Flashbacks to when I'd been sick and saw visions of my mother kept plaguing me. I could almost see her again, as an orb of light blurring back and forth above me. I clenched my eyes shut and pushed my heartache deep inside of me. My mother had passed through the Eternal Falls. She couldn't help us even if she wanted to.

The pool water subtly stirred. I opened my eyes and glanced around the room.

"Hello?" I stared at the doorway, wondering if someone would walk through or answer from the other side. Neither of those things happened.

A hint of light passed in front of me. Like a cloud of sparkling dust particles trying to form into a figure. The dim daylight from the open ceiling gave the light a pink hue. And then the pink glittering light whispered my name.

"Nixie!" Uncle Lloyd wasn't lying. It was possible.

The outline of her ethereal form became more developed as I followed Uncle Lloyd's instructions. Relax my eyes, visualize hers, hold her memory in my heart, drop any beliefs about it being impossible, and believe in the fantastical.

Nixie's ruby irises glowed in front of me. "See? You didn't need that panel to communicate with me. You never did."

"Uncle Lloyd told me, but I didn't one hundred percent believe him until right this moment."

"You've always had the ability to see spirits. You inherited it from your mother. It's why you saw her a few times when she was in spirit form watching over you."

"Why didn't you or Uncle Lloyd tell me this sooner?"

"You needed the portal to get you started. He explained it to me as spiritual training wheels. Giving you a familiar mechanism you had already successfully used seemed easier than freaking you out with one more magical fact about yourself."

I was too relieved to be annoyed, so I let it drop. "I'm so happy you're here. I would hug you right now if I could."

"It's the thought that counts." She glanced around the room and whispered, "Is Luska here?"

"Not at the moment. I was about to head over to Gorgon Rock. I have a strong hunch that he's there and I need to speak with him."

"Good. Because Rathe is falling apart and we need to get this plan rolling."

I was a bundle of nerves by the time we got to the grotto. My previous attempts at trying to lie to Luska hadn't gone so well. The thought of what he would do if he caught me lying this time left me shaking. I could only hope losing his pearl had broken his internal lie detector.

I flew through the grotto tunnels with Nixie, trying to breathe normally. When I surfaced through the tide pool, he was right there with his back to us, inking the cave walls with symbols I didn't recognize.

"I thought I'd find you here." My voice echoed through the grotto as I climbed out of the pool.

He turned around. A band of seaweed covered his neck wound. I silently prayed we had fooled him with the fake pearl. Judging from how calm he seemed, maybe we had. Or maybe he just seemed calm because he was weakening. Could we be so lucky?

His pearl had been a part of him. I wondered how I would react if someone ripped out my heart and I survived it, then later they dropped it on a floor for me to see for the first time. I imagined him retrieving the pearl, believing it was his, and sticking it back in his throat, using the seaweed to keep it in place like a bandage. We were hoping he had no experience with this type of injury so he would have no idea what to expect. It's what we had counted on when Treygan and I planned the pearl swap.

Luska motioned to one of the deeper pools farther into the main cave. He still couldn't speak. That was a good sign.

"I'm going in with you," Nixie said. "You shouldn't be alone with him."

He turned to walk away and I shook my head at her. He had seen her before. He may have already seen her again. I didn't want to make him angrier.

"Fine," she relented, "but I'll be watching from up here and I'm jumping in if it looks like you need me."

I slipped into the pool first and he followed.

When we were both underwater, I told him, *You win. I will return to Harte with you, but not until high tide.*

He narrowed his eyes. *Why wait?*

Because I can't leave without taking care of some important matters. I have to say goodbye to several people. I need to assign rulers to take my place and instruct them on what needs to be done after I'm gone.

He started to reply, but I cut him off. *In exchange for my cooperation, I want your word that you will not harm anyone else from this point on. Right now, this very second, your reign of terror ends. No more seduction, no more killing, nothing. If you keep that promise, then we leave together for Harte at high tide.*

You expect me to believe this sudden change of mind? He did sound weaker than usual. I relaxed, but only very slightly.

You should. Not once since you've been here have I lied to you about returning to Harte, or even pretended that it was an option. Now I know what you're capable of. I wouldn't lie to you knowing the consequences.

I still don't trust you.

And I don't trust you. But you said love and trust don't matter in our relationship, so I guess it's okay.

He eased closer, invading my personal space, but I didn't flinch. *If you do not keep your word and leave with me, I will immediately claim all of them.*

My face must have shown a mix of emotions. *All of what?*

The souls of those you cherish. Treygan, Rownan, Vienna, that black-winged siren corrupting my Wrangler, her blighted sisters, those two sprites you protect so fiercely, and lastly, he pointed to where Nixie's spirit watched us from above, *her.*

I had never fought so hard to keep my composure. *I'm leaving with you to spare the souls of everyone in Rathe, including my loved ones.*

Remember that when it's time for us to depart. If you fail to keep your promise, then those souls are mine to do with as I please. Whether it's to be death, an eternity in Harte, or to use as my playthings, I haven't yet decided.

You truly are an evil, soulless, bastard.

He wrapped his hand around my throat and squeezed until I couldn't breathe. *Be grateful that I am tolerant of you.*

Nixie was beside me in an instant, but there was nothing she could do. Luska pulled me toward him until our faces were millimeters apart.

If you betray me, I shall go on a killing spree that will fill Rathe's oceans with blood. I have been more than fair considering what that merboy of yours did to me. You are forever in my debt because I allowed him to live. Do not test me or I will provide you with an even more devastating demonstration of evil.

Do you understand?

I swear, Nixie growled, *if I was still alive I would rip him to shreds.*

Weakly, I replied. *I understand.*

Luska released his grip and I drifted backward, covering my aching neck. Nixie positioned herself between us as if she could stop him from hurting me again.

His close-lipped grin looked more menacing than ever as he stared at me through her ghostly form. *I look forward to seeing both of you again at high tide.*

Nixie held up her middle fingers and shoved them in his face.

He climbed out of the tide pool, but I stayed there, silent and paralyzed with fear.

That bastard. Nixie turned to face me. *Are you okay?*

I've never seen or heard him like that before.

Not that he deserves a defense, but he did have his throat ripped out. That would ruin anyone's day.

I rubbed my raw neck. *What's a surefire way to bring out the most power, strength, and determination in someone?*

Nixie shrugged. *Threaten their life?*

Wrong. Threaten the lives of their loved ones. One way or another, I would end Luska's reign of terror.

47

Koraline

Treygan stood in the doorway, clearing his throat as if I hadn't already sensed his arrival. He'd been standing there for a good three minutes watching us. I didn't know why he had come, but I hoped it wasn't so he could tell me how sorry he was. I was so utterly exhausted by the flood of pity pouring out of everyone.

Without looking at him, I said, "I never properly thanked you for saving my life."

He didn't say anything, so I turned and looked pointedly at him.

He blinked a few times as if surprised that my statement was meant for him. "The mer community saved your life with the healing ceremony."

"I never would have made it to that ceremony if it weren't for you."

One of his brows rose. He and I had never discussed the details of how I made it back to Solis after the shark attack.

"You thought I didn't know?" I continued. "Pango told me everything. You stopped the feeding frenzy. You made stone stitches to stop the bleeding. You swam me to Solis at supersonic speed so Caspian and Indrea could start healing me."

He shrugged. "It was . . ."

"You can't say it was nothing because it isn't true. You saved me, Treygan."

He pushed himself away from the doorframe and came over to stand on the opposite side of the bed. "He looks peaceful."

I studied Joel's handsome face. "I keep praying for a miracle," I said, stroking his cheek. "A few miracles, actually."

"Me too. Poseidon doesn't seem to be listening." Treygan sat on the edge of the bed, staring down at Joel. "I told him I don't even need a miracle. Simple guidance would suffice. Just a clear sign of what to do."

I grinned. "I didn't realize you spoke to Poseidon so casually."

"Conversations have a way of turning casual when they're one sided."

I knew all too well the sorrow of prayers going unanswered. "I'm sorry about Yara. If I could help you get back to her, I would."

"Thank you." Treygan tilted his head and he reached for Joel's hand. "Is that the stone Lloyd gave to Rownan?"

"Yes. Vienna gave it to us. She thought maybe it would help him."

Treygan pinched the bridge of his nose and sighed. "Leave it to Rownan to disobey vital instructions."

"What do you mean?"

"He had strict orders to keep it on him at all times. Then he goes and gives it to Vienna. Now it's here instead of in Rathe with my numbskull brother, who will probably need it more than anyone."

"I had no idea or I wouldn't have accepted it." I slid the rock free from Joel's hand to give it to Treygan, but Joel's fingers closed over mine. I shrieked and jerked with surprise. "Joel?"

He didn't react. Frantic with hope, my pulse pounding in my ears, I told Treygan, "His fingers just moved."

"Are you sure?"

"Joel," I pleaded. "I felt you move. Can you do it again?" I stared at my trembling hand resting in his. *Come on. Do it again. Wake up. Come back to me.*

Treygan started so dramatically the mattress shook. "Koraline!"

I looked up and saw Joel's eyes were open. I gasped and leaned forward. "Joel! Can you hear me?" His eyes were empty, not focusing on anything. If it had been anyone but Joel it would have been spooky. "Blink if you can hear me."

No response.

"What does this mean?" I asked Treygan.

Joel blinked, but it wasn't in response to me. He wasn't focused on either of us. He wasn't focused on anything at all.

Treygan glanced between Joel and me, his head shaking. "Joel, can you see or hear us? Blink twice for yes."

Still nothing.

"Where's Delmar?" I asked. "Maybe he can help."

Treygan didn't answer. He was silently studying Joel and tapping his bottom lip, lost in thought.

Joel blinked again. I checked his pulse. "His heartbeat is stronger. What does this mean?"

"Koraline, I think this is our sign. The miracle we were just discussing." Treygan's stern gaze penetrated me in a way that made my own heart beat even faster. "I'm going to complete Joel's transformation."

Hope swallowed me whole. Joel wasn't responding, but his eyes were open. That would be enough to continue the transformation. "Has the curse been lifted? How did you get the Violets to agree?"

He hesitated a long time before admitting, "I didn't."

Disappointment chewed up my hope and spat it out again. "I don't understand."

His indigo eyes were filled with iron determination. I was perfectly capable of reading between the lines of his insanity.

"No," I said. "That's not an option."

"It's the only option."

"A curse is in place. You'll die."

He didn't swallow, didn't flinch, didn't bat an eye. "I know."

My jaw went slack. I wanted to leap out of my wheelchair and kick his ass, but words were my only weapon. "No, you lunatic! How can you even think of doing something so deranged?"

"I've been trying to communicate with Poseidon. This is my chance. A very wise mermaid once said that we should love until it kills us because there's nothing better worth dying for."

"Don't do that. Don't use my own words against me in a situation like this."

He reached across Joel's body and held my hand. "I'm embracing your wisdom because it's true." He motioned to Joel and me. "The love you two share should be saved."

"Not at the cost of your life."

"At any cost."

Part of me was terrified that he might actually do it, while another part was so touched by him even offering. A tear ran down my cheek. "No. You're not supposed to die for someone else's love. I don't accept and neither would Joel."

"I'm not afraid of death. Yara told me what awaits us in the Inbetween."

"I know all about the Inbetween. You're not destined to see it for at least two hundred years." I leaned closer to him. "Not to mention, can you imagine Yara's suffering if you went through with it?"

"You don't understand."

"No, you don't understand! The answer is no. Right, Joel?" I turned to look at his face. His eyes were still open and vacant. "Joel would say no if he could. No, Treygan, we don't accept."

"Stop saying no. I'm so tired of everyone trying to take away my freedom to choose."

"Treygan—" My mouth opened and closed as I struggled with my disbelief. Over the last few months he had drastically changed, and I needed to remind him of that fact. "Ever since we were kids, your uncontrollable gorgon powers forced you to build walls around your heart. You let your ability to turn things to stone turn *you* to stone. None of us could break through your walls. And then Yara came. She earned a pair of wings and flew right over your walls into your internal fortress. She reached the parts of you that no other soul could. That's a miracle. That's destiny. That's every power in the universe conspiring on your behalf so you could know, *truly know*, genuine love. Whether you asked for it or not, you received the gift of love. Against all odds, in spite of all of your defenses, you were blessed by our gods. There's a reason for that. We may not know what it is right now—heck, we may never know—but it's a rare and precious thing." I pressed my hand over his. "So don't you dare give up. Don't give up on her or the love you two share."

"I'm not giving up." He smiled. The lunatic actually smiled. "Never give up. The tide will turn. That's why I'm doing it, Koraline. It's the only way I can speak with Poseidon and convince him to let me help her."

"You can't actually believe Poseidon will resurrect you just because you want to be helpful."

"When Yara died, he and Medusa granted her another chance at life."

"Only because she was destined to be one of Rathe's rulers. She had extenuating circumstances."

"My case is strong. I'll plead it until Poseidon understands how much it will benefit Rathe and Harte."

"Treygan, you're forgetting I've been to the Inbetween. I wasn't even dead, and it was still unbelievably hard for me to resist the Eternal Falls. If you're not careful, the urge to pass through to the other side will overpower your memories of life. You may not even remember your plan to ask Poseidon for help. Not to mention he'd probably laugh in your face for being so reckless."

He sighed. I prayed my reality check had squelched his delusions.

"I do know," he said. "Yara told me how difficult it was for her to remember who she was when she first arrived in the Inbetween."

"Exactly. It's too big of a gamble and odds are that you will lose."

His depression seemed to return as he simply nodded once and said, "Thank you, Koraline."

"I mean it." I hated crushing his dream of being Yara's hero during this nightmare, but his life was infinitely more important. "I may have lost my tail and legs, but I will still kick your ass if you even think about ending your life again."

"I understand. I appreciate your concern." He stood and walked away.

"That's it?" I asked. "After such a monumental conversation and this change in Joel's condition, you're leaving?"

He rubbed the back of his neck. "I'm going to find Delmar so he can help."

"That's a much better plan. Thank you."

With an unsettled feeling in the pit of my stomach, I watched Treygan leave.

Delmar suggested that I get some much needed rest while he worked his healing magic, so I got in the fish tank as soon as Pango and Merrick were out. I felt better after resting for a few hours. Physically, anyway. Emotionally, I felt pruned and shriveled. Being in my coma had been much easier than watching Joel go through his.

Pango helped me out of the tank and into my wheelchair. I was wrapping a towel around myself when I heard someone shouting from outside.

At first I thought I had imagined Joel's voice. Wishful thinking.

But then I heard Delmar yell for Lloyd.

"Where is that coming from?" Pango asked.

"Joel!" I rolled my chair through the house as fast as I could. The back door was wide open so I rolled onto the deck.

Joel stood in the surf up to his waist. Delmar was with him, and between them they carried Treygan's limp body.

"Dear gods," I gasped.

"Lloyd, Pango, help!" I screamed as loud as I could.

My fingertips grazed the bottom of Pango's shirt as he rushed past me. "Take me with you."

Lloyd was behind us in an instant. "Dammit, Treygan."

Pango lifted me out of the chair and rushed me to the beach. Pango ran fast, but it still felt like it took us so long to reach them.

I tried to call Treygan's name, but my voice caught in my throat.

Pango slowed for a moment, probably piecing together what had taken place. He set me down where the waves lapped the beach then sped ahead, splashing into the water to help.

Lloyd got there before him and took Treygan's limp body from Joel and Delmar.

"I'm sorry, Lloyd," Delmar said, his haunted gaze locked on Treygan. "He insisted. He believes they'll send him back."

"He's a fool," Lloyd snarled. "You're both fools."

Joel glanced between them and me. "What happened? I woke up and we were underwater. Treygan was passed out beside us."

Lloyd had laid Treygan flat on the sand just beyond my reach. He pressed his ear to Treygan's chest. "No, son, come on."

My hands flew to my mouth as tears blurred my eyes.

"Koraline?" Joel said frantically, kneeling beside me. "What's happening?"

Lloyd breathed into Treygan's mouth then pumped his chest several times. I reached out and held Joel's hand. My fingers, entwined with his, flew to my lips as I quietly prayed. "Please let him be okay, please, please, please."

I was so busy praying for one miracle that it took me a moment to realize another miracle had already been granted. I pulled Joel's hand from my lips and turned to look at him. "You're awake."

The sun illuminated his bare chest and I stifled a gasp. I reached up, my fingers trembling, afraid that if I touched him the miracle would disappear like a mirage. Ever so lightly, my fingertip traced a bronze image of twisting coral running along his collarbone.

In a mix of something between a whisper and a sob, I said, "You have hallmarks."

Joel looked down and a surprised sound caught in his throat. "Holy crap."

He was kneeling beside me, submerged up to the waistband of his shorts. He still had human legs, not a tail. Squinting through my blurry tears and the gentle waves, I looked closer. Glistening beneath the surface were dark red scales on his thighs.

"You're mer," I whispered.

Joel looked up at me. His eyes were so, so wide. "I'm mer."

"Oh gods." I turned my attention back to Treygan. The moment of joy for Joel was eclipsed by the sheer agony of the price we paid for his transformation. Lloyd was still aggressively performing CPR. Pango kneeled on the other side of Treygan, holding his hand and praying.

Delmar kneeled behind Lloyd and gripped his shoulders. "Lloyd, this time it's beyond your control."

"I have to try."

After many long minutes, Lloyd placed both hands on Treygan's chest and bowed his head. "Damn them and their curses."

"No," I muttered, picturing Treygan's soul at the Eternal Falls being tempted to leave us forever. "Don't give up on him, Delmar." My voice cracked with desperation. "You let him make this maniacal move, so you bring him back!"

Guilt creased his forehead, but he just shook his head. "CPR can't lift a gorgon curse. There's nothing we can do. It's in Poseidon's hands now."

The dreadful truth settled on me like an anvil. We all stared, urging, hoping, and pleading for Treygan to breathe again.

"I don't understand," Joel said. "Someone please tell me what happened to him."

"Just wait." Delmar stared at Treygan. "He said he'd convince them to send him back. He *said* so. He believed it was true."

I held my breath, watching, and waiting for another miracle. The only sound was waves breaking on the shore.

Another minute ticked by. And another.

More waves, more breaths being held, and more minutes painfully passed.

Pango began quietly crying beside me, which made me cry too.

"No." Delmar shook Treygan's arm. "Come on!"

Lloyd reached across Treygan's body and gripped Delmar's hands.

Delmar looked up at me. Tears rolled down his cheeks.

He pulled out of Lloyd's grip and shook Treygan harder. "Don't do this to us. You swore you wouldn't take no for an answer. You were supposed to come back!"

Treygan's face and body were so lifeless. I had to look away.

No one could blame Delmar for this. He was Treygan's best friend. He had always done anything Treygan asked. Why hadn't I realized Treygan still intended to follow through on his suicide mission? I could have stopped him. I *should* have stopped him.

"He's gone." Lloyd's voice hitched in a heart-obliterated groan that could only be made by a parent who had lost their child. "My firstborn is gone."

48

I stood in Sybarites Nest, mulling over what I'd just heard. If it was true, it put a serious wrinkle in my plan. Mariza and Eve looked genuinely worried about me. Even Otabia, fierce as she was, seemed concerned.

Until very recently, I had been so focused on the impossible notion of returning to Harte that I didn't stop to think about the logistics of how it would take place. Luska didn't know that Treygan, Rownan, and I had tried to enter Harte through the Trident Rock gateway and failed. My plan was based on the fact that it would reject me again.

I hadn't considered that Luska only needed my soul in Harte. My body wasn't required to pass through the gate at all.

Based on the new information—the new and terrifying curve ball that had been thrown at me—we made a change to our plan.

"You have your orders," I said to them. "Please don't let me down."

"We won't," Otabia assured me.

They flew away and I watched the three of them disappear into the gray haze.

The rest of the pieces were in place. Everyone had to do their part. Too many lives were at stake for us to screw it up.

I spread my wings, preparing to fly to the grotto, but Nixie's ruby eyes appeared in front of me, followed by the rest of her.

Sparkling red tears ran down her cheeks.

"Nixie? What's wrong?"

She looked away from me. "Joel has been turned."

My heart soared. I hadn't been able to give that situation the attention it deserved, but Koraline must have been ecstatic.

"Wait." My smile fell as fast as it had appeared. "I thought a curse had been cast. Death to any Indigo who attempted a transformation."

Nixie nodded.

A ball of fire began to burn in my belly. "No one would have disobeyed that order."

She looked away again and the fire roared into an inferno. I pictured Eden's Hammock. Where I had sent Treygan to be safe. Where he would have spent time with Koraline and Joel. My Treygan, who had been recently promoted to Indigo. My Treygan, who was the most selfless soul I knew.

"No," I murmured. "Not Treygan. He wouldn't."

She closed her eyes and sparkling, ethereal tears fell and then dissolved between us. "He did."

"Dear gods, no." My wings drooped and I swayed as the nest spun. I braced myself against a branch. Nixie had to be wrong. It had to be a mistake. "He said forever belonged to us."

"Yes, but then you chose the kraken and sent him away."

My head snapped up. "It wasn't real! You know that. I would never choose anyone besides Treygan. Uncle Lloyd must have told him. I specifically told him to tell Treygan the truth when he arrived."

"I asked what happened," she said softly. "No one could hear me."

"You saw him? You actually saw him—" I couldn't say the word *dead* out loud. How could the brightest constellation in my entire universe be gone?

Nixie nodded. "Joel's awake and healthy. Treygan is . . . the opposite."

My lungs stopped working. I couldn't feel my limbs. My

vision blurred. It took me several sickening moments to gain control of my mouth so I could speak. "Why? Why would he do this?"

"I don't know."

I sank to my knees as waves of nausea washed through me. "This can't be happening. It's a bad dream. It has to be." I clenched my eyes shut, but all I saw was Treygan's stoic, loving face. A face that Nixie was telling me I'd never see again. "Nixie, tell me it's a nightmare."

"I wish I could." She wrapped her arms around me, but I couldn't feel her.

Sobs rushed out of me. I collapsed into a fetal position, clutching my stomach as my forehead hit the floor. "He wouldn't kill himself. He wouldn't."

Nixie's silence made me cry even harder. Did Treygan die believing I had abandoned him? Did I drive him to suicide?

My stomach heaved again. I pounded my fist on the floor. All I could manage between my sobs was to say *"no"* over and over.

But it didn't matter how many times I said no. The kraken was in Rathe because of me. Treygan was dead because of me. I was a monster. A wretched, stupid, careless, world-destroying, soul-mate-killing monster.

I rolled to my side, curling myself into a ball. The tears wouldn't stop. I closed my eyes and there he was again. Perfect, loving, and gone. *Gone.*

I sucked in a breath and bolted upright. "Nixie!"

I wiped at my eyes and jumped to my feet. My shattered heart somehow managed to beat as fast as a hummingbird's wings. "He must be in the Inbetween. Tell him not to pass through the Eternal Falls. Tell him to cling to life."

She gave me a miserable look and her inner light seemed to fade. "I already did. I searched and searched, but couldn't find him."

I shook my head frantically. "No. Search again. He has to

be there!"

"No," she said sadly. "He doesn't. Most pass through the falls quickly and eagerly. I think he did too."

My heart and soul exploded into pieces all over again.

49

Rownan

I was at home, grabbing something to eat before heading out to rip Luska's head off, when Yara arrived.

She looked similar to when Sage was killed, eyes red and swollen, all color drained from her. She was broken and defeated again, except this was worse. Way worse.

Then she started talking. At first, I couldn't absorb the words. I refused to believe her.

When I realized she was serious, after she fell apart and I had to hold her up to keep her from crumbling—emotionally and physically—the reality hit me like a monsoon, tsunami, and hurricane all at the same time.

I broke things. Sliced my claws through walls. Screamed until my throat was on fire.

Yara let me.

Later, after a lot of crying, talking, and blaming ourselves, Yara told me she was returning to Harte with Luska. I couldn't tell whether she was serious or putting on another show in case Luska was spying on her. I fought with her, tried to change her mind out of respect for Treygan's memory, but she wouldn't listen. She said she had done enough damage, that too many had already died because of her. I asked her where they were meeting. She told me Gorgon Rock at high tide.

It didn't matter whether she was faking or not. If Luska was going to be at Gorgon Rock at high tide, that's where I'd wait for him. That's where I would avenge my brother's death and save Yara from spending eternity in Harte.

High tide couldn't come fast enough.

I went straight to our spot at Gorgon Rock. The spot where Treygan and I had plotted and planned as kids. The spot where only days ago we'd lain, head to head, trying to think of a way to end this mess with the kraken.

I still had some time until high tide, so I lay down on the rocky ground and stared up at the sky. Treygan was gone. My only brother was dead. Tears streamed down my temples. I wiped them away as they ran into my ears.

"You're supposed to be right here," I said to the empty space beside me. "Two heads are better than one, remember?"

More tears. More waves of fury. I would relish every second of pain I unleashed upon the kraken.

"You stare at the suns," I said aloud. "I stare at the moons."

I did my job as if Treygan were still there. I stared at the one moon left in our sky. It was dim and motionless, just like the sun on the mer side. They matched how I felt: sick. Yara's moon seemed to grow darker with each passing moment. I closed my eyes, blinking away more tears.

When I opened them again, Yara's moon looked so close to me, and so much like a silver pearl, that I had to blink several times to make sure my eyes were working properly.

I sucked in a breath. If my eyes weren't deceiving me, then I was actually staring at a silver pearl, and it was much closer than the moon. It was part of a necklace. A necklace circling the neck of my brother.

"Lying down on the job again?"

"Treygan!" I scrambled to my feet, practically knocking him backward. I stood in front of him and gripped his shoulders, stabilizing us both. I touched his arms, his chest, his head. "You're seriously standing in front of me right now?"

A proud smile spread across his face. "Told you I'd find a

way back to her."

Of course. Treygan had been trying to communicate with Poseidon at Trident Rock and with the mirror, but it hadn't worked. He'd died in a desperate attempt to get our god's attention. "You talked to Poseidon?"

"Yes."

I hugged him so hard. Then I pulled back to examine him again. "What happened?"

"I'll explain the details later. Right now, we have a kraken to deal with."

"Yara said she's meeting him here at high tide."

"Then she lied to you to keep you out of harm's way. Lloyd told me her real plan. She's laid a trap for the kraken at Trident Rock. He also told me to slap you senseless for giving this away." He placed Lloyd's gorgon stone in my hand and then smacked the back of my head. "I'm taking it easy on you because I need you in good condition so you can help me. Come on, we need to hurry."

I secured the stone in my band. "Treygan, she told me she's giving up and going to Harte, and I'm not sure it was a lie. The news of your death destroyed her."

"My death?" His brow furrowed. "How did you know about that?"

I gaped at him, replaying our conversation. I had never mentioned death. He hadn't specified how he talked to Poseidon. He thought I was shocked that he had escaped Eden's Hammock.

"Yara told me." I pointed to my puffy face and bloodshot eyes. "When have you ever seen me look like this from crying so much?"

"But no one who knew about it has left Eden's Hammock." He seemed to deflate as the truth hit him. "Nixie."

I nodded.

"Yara's not giving up," Treygan said. "She's been secretly orchestrating an all-out attack on Luska with the help of the Wrangler and the gorgons. But if she thinks I'm dead, she might do something truly drastic." He glanced around urgently. "Nix, if you're here, go to her right now. Tell her I'm not dead."

"No way would Nixie be hanging around here. Not when Yara might be about to damn herself to hell forever. She wouldn't leave Yara's side."

He grabbed me and pulled me behind him. "We're losing precious time."

He waved his hand in the air and a wave of water rose up the cliff and created a shelf. We plunged into the water and Treygan pulled me along beside him at a speed that seemed even faster than usual.

I extended my sight so he'd hear me without us needing to slow down. *I hope you have some sort of miraculous plan.*

He glanced at my band. *You still have his pearl, right?*

Yes. Why?

Because it's a requirement to us winning this war.

50

I floated on the outskirts of Trident Rock watching for Luska, wondering if he'd allow himself to be seen when he approached.

Clouds shaped like black tendrils swirled high above me. Looking closer, I saw details of suction cups. Was it another illusion or had he somehow managed to make himself a fixture in our skies?

I sensed him approaching, but couldn't see anything through the dark, cloudy water. Then a hand grabbed my leg. He pulled me under and I let him.

Hello, Yara. His long hair floated around his face. He was in his humanesque form. He didn't need to flaunt his tentacles, coral horns, or glowing eyes to remind me how powerful he was. Or maybe he didn't have those features anymore? Based on the seaweed still wrapped around his neck, I surmised that his wound hadn't healed. Hopefully, that meant his strength and abilities were still weakened.

Hello, Luska.

Shall we return home?

I almost cringed at hearing him call Harte home, but I rolled my shoulders and nodded. *It's now or never. How do we get back?*

Through the portal where I entered. He extended his hand to me and I reluctantly placed mine in it and let him pull me toward Trident Rock.

As we swam, my despair over Treygan's death and his final warning about my soul simmered inside of me. What I was about to do was for him. No matter how scared I was, I had to do it for Treygan, Rownan and Vienna, Uncle Lloyd, Nixie, Sage, my parents, and everyone else who had suffered or sacrificed themselves in an attempt to find love, happiness, or safety.

The water grew colder and darker as we approached the gateway. I was already bracing for the coming pain, certain my human blood would be rejected again.

Luska's grip tightened as we approached the shadowed waterway created by the spires of the Trident's black rocks. My skin prickled with anticipation. We reached the threshold and Luska turned to look at me.

Don't even think about turning back, he warned.

There is no turning back, I said.

We swam forward.

Electrical current ripped through me and flung me backward. My back arched so hard and fast that I was amazed my spine didn't break. Because Luska kept his grip on me, he snapped me back to him as fast as I had been jolted away. The whiplash was intense.

My flesh stung and my teeth buzzed as he yanked me closer. *Don't fight this.*

I pushed my floating hair from my face. *I didn't fight anything. A powerful force threw me backward.*

He looked at the pillars of rock then back at me. His eyes traveled up and down my body as I rubbed my neck and arms to ease the aftershocks.

Try again, he ordered. Drifting back a tad, he let go of me and motioned to the gateway. Apparently he wanted a better view so he could assess the problem.

It's going to electrocute me, I argued.

If that is true then we will rid you of your body, though it would be a pity to leave behind such a beautiful vessel. Treygan had been right. I felt as if concrete blocks were tied to me, threatening to pull me straight into hell. *Per our agreement, you will return with me one way or another. If not, your loved ones are mine to do with as I please.*

Trembling, I squared off with the gateway again. With one long, ragged exhale, I blew out all of my fear in a trail of bubbles until only determination remained. *Never give up. The tide will turn.*

With a firm pump of my tail, I swam forward.

The instant the electric current ripped through me again, I camouflaged myself. With any luck, Luska would think my disappearance meant I'd passed through the gate.

I let the force of the gateway's rejection carry me up and out of the water. It hurt like hell, but my wings unfurled and I went for altitude as he searched the threshold for me. It would buy me a few seconds, a minute at most.

I raced toward my target hidden behind a tall rock formation several spires away. My siren sisters were there, strategically positioned so I'd know exactly where to aim. Below me, I could see the crisscrossed pattern of the seafoam net the merfolk and Wrangler had weaved. I dove toward it.

Landing on the surface of the enormous net, I dug my fingertips into the foam and channeled every bit of current I'd absorbed.

I glanced over my shoulder to see Luska growing taller above the water, riding on a giant wave. He hadn't been fooled. He was searching for me.

Otabia sent category four winds whipping toward the kraken. The gorgon kin surged out from behind the cliffs where they had been hiding and waiting to do their part. The storm surge helped them move faster into place.

Countless head-snakes and slithering tails filled the current below us. Over the howling wind the sound of crackling stone tugged at my own gorgon instincts, but I needed to stay focused on my siren strength. Luska turned into a statue almost as tall as Trident Rock. The gorgon kin worked frantically to form layer upon layer of stone to keep him confined until we could get the net over him.

"Let's do this!" I shouted to the sirens.

They all reached down, each of them grabbing a corner of the net, and together we lifted it into the sky.

We sped forward, centering the massive, lightning-charged net over the petrified kraken.

"Drop it!" I shouted.

The net fell, draping over Luska like a glowing blanket.

"Ready?" I yelled to the gorgons.

Messina gave her signal for the gorgons to back off and draw their bows and arrows. Each arrow was loaded with a massive amount of the most potent Liquid Lullaby ever created.

"We'll only have a second," I reminded the sirens. "We need to move as soon as the arrows hit him."

We had already discussed how limited our window of opportunity would be. As strong as the Liquid Lullaby was, we'd still need a few minutes for it to get into his system. During those minutes we had to keep him from retaliating.

The four of us hovered, wings spanning as wide as they'd reach. Lightning flashed nonstop above us as we conjured as much current as possible. The stone exploded below us as Luska broke free.

I didn't need to command anyone. Hundreds of arrows sailed at Luska from every direction, piercing him all over. The sirens and I rushed forward as one, talons extended, injecting the already buzzing net with even more power.

Smoke billowed and Luska's tentacles sizzled as he howled in pain and struggled to rip free of the net. We kept the voltage flowing until the entire net burned so hot it ignited. I had no idea enchanted seafoam could burn like that. A sickening smell of charring flesh filled the air as one arrow-riddled tentacle reached through the flames and wrapped around my torso.

He sank below the surface, pulling me with him.

Black smoke, or maybe ink, clouded the water so thickly

that I couldn't see anything. I kicked and pulled, trying to wriggle out of his grasp, but he squeezed so tight I thought my ribs would crack.

Through the darkness his glowing eyes found mine. *You failed, Yara. Defying me was a monumental mistake. Now you and your loved ones shall burn for eternity.*

The sedative would take effect soon. I just needed to stall. *Even after my last breath, my soul will lead me back to the light. I will never stop fighting for my realm and every creature within it.*

I focused on the tentacle around me and turned it to stone at the same instant I unsheathed my selkie claws and slashed his face. My hand vibrated from the force of the impact. His left eye took the brunt of it, but I only caught a glimpse of his injuries before he turned away.

I channeled my anger like Treygan had taught me and let it explode through my torso. The stone tentacle shattered and Luska vanished. I slashed all around me with my claws, but only swiped through water.

I darted to the surface and shouted to my sisters, "He's invisible!"

I took to the air for a better view, scanning the ocean for any sign of him. I didn't know how long it would take before the Liquid Lullaby hit him, and I didn't want him seeking revenge against the gorgon kin or sirens.

The plan was for the gorgons to leave as soon as their part was done, to rush back to their enchanted homes and stay there until it was safe, but I sensed them hiding nearby. No one had left. At least they were keeping their distance.

"Where are you?" I muttered under my breath, searching until my eyes ached.

He had been out of sight for too long. With every passing second I could feel his evil brewing. What if the boatloads of Liquid Lullaby still didn't work? His threat echoed in my mind: *If you betray me, I shall go on a killing spree that will fill Rathe's oceans with blood.*

I had betrayed him and then some.

Fear and worry bubbled out of me as I screamed, "Luska, show yourself!"

51

Rownan

The sky above Trident Rock was filled with storm clouds and black spiraling tendrils of smoke. What the hell had happened? How much had we missed?

Treygan deposited me on a patch of land with several large boulders for cover. I hid behind one of them to do what he'd asked. My hands shook so badly I dropped the Serpetugon vine he'd given me. I snatched it off the ground and wrapped it tightly around my wrist. Treygan told me if I lost it, or my father's stone, we would lose this battle.

I had to stop shaking. I couldn't chance dropping the stone and have it roll away into the stormy waters. Treygan was counting on me.

Keeley and Jenna appeared out of nowhere, scaring me half to death as they landed on my shoulders.

"What are you two doing here?" I asked them.

"We're here to help," Keely said.

"You're crazy." Yara would be furious if she knew they were here risking their lives.

"Why are *you* here?" Jenna asked.

I shrugged the shoulder she stood on with her hands on her hips. "To help."

"So you're crazy too."

"Since you're here, can you do something for me?" I held up the stone Lloyd had given me. "Hold this and please don't drop it."

Keeley hovered steady in front of me, holding the rock that

was bigger than her head.

Lloyd had told Treygan precisely what to do, and Treygan had told me. I followed Treygan's instructions and tied the vine securely around the stone.

"Stay here," I told them taking the vine from Keeley. "It's getting ugly out there."

Jenna shook her tiny finger in my face. "Don't tell us what to do."

"Okay, fine. Dear gods, please let this work." I gripped the vine and stone tight in my hands and jumped into the raging sea.

Visibility underwater was worse than ever, but I swam to Trident Rock as fast as I could. As I got closer, I spotted a black tentacle sidewinding in front of me. It seemed to be blinking in and out of existence, there one second, gone the next, then back again.

The rest of Luska ascended from the ocean floor, flickering in and out of sight like his tentacle, as if he couldn't decide whether or not to be invisible.

As his head came into view, I momentarily recoiled. Half of his face was torn to shreds. His left eyeball was gone, and tattered flesh hung open where his eyelid and cheek should have been.

Well done, Yara, I thought to myself. That had to be her handiwork.

A parade of black tentacles whirled toward me at incredible speed. I tried to swim away, but two wrapped around my torso. It felt like countless piranhas biting me all over at the exact same time. I gritted my teeth as fire and ice shot through me.

I had seen what this same attack had done to Treygan. I examined the puncture wounds covering me and wondered how long I had left to live. Waves of stinging pain made me jerk and twitch.

While I could still feel my fingers, I tied the vine onto my wrist so that if someone discovered my body I'd still have what Treygan needed. I gripped the stone tighter, determined to keep it safe even as I died.

It was hard to breathe. My vision went fuzzy and my body started to convulse.

Darkness enveloped me then carried me away.

52

Things happened fast after Luska burst from the water.

One second, Otabia was on my right, searching the ocean. The next thing I knew, she was trapped in an ink bubble hovering above the stormy waves.

As I rushed toward her, another ink bubble rose out of the water directly in front of me, blocking my path. Trapped inside of it was Rownan. A pale, bleeding, convulsing Rownan with puncture wounds covering his body.

"No!" I unsheathed my selkie claws and tried ripping open the sphere of ink, but it was impenetrable.

Luska's energy approaching from behind sent chills up my spine.

I turned to face him. He was still huge, like a black mountain rising from the ocean. The dark coral on his head swayed like snakes.

My throat tightened and my heart plummeted into the waves below when I saw the others. Tentacles rose out of the water, the tip of each one wrapping around a bubble. More innocent victims were imprisoned in each one: Mariza and Eve, Keeley and Jenna, Talus and Messina, even Nixie.

"Release them!" I demanded.

Luska's eyes glowed with shades of blue and purple. I heard his thoughts in my mind as though we were still under water. *I warned you, Yara. Say farewell to them. With your next breath, I*

*will crush all of them at once. I told you there would be a price
to pay for your betrayal.*

"Please don't." I mouthed the words, not daring to breathe.
He meant it. He'd kill all of them if I so much as sniffed. It felt
as if the fate of all of Rathe hung in that one moment between in-
hale and exhale. The past, the future, countless lives, an extraor-
dinary world, all of it could be destroyed or saved. I was only
one single life, one soul, and my sacrifice could spare so many.

My wings and arms opened wide. "I'm yours. Take my
body, my soul, whatever else. Just please, *please*—I'm begging
you, Luska, don't kill them."

His evil charged the air and water all around us. Tears ran
down my cheeks as I trembled.

He returned to normal size, but his tentacles stayed in
place—ready and able to kill those I was supposed to protect.
Luska wiped his lips and drifted closer so our faces were almost
touching. He brushed away my tears.

*This is your last chance to give yourself to me. Kiss me and
surrender your soul so we can return to Harte.*

"Only if you promise to let them live."

*It's too late for Rownan, but I will spare the rest after I have
possession of your soul.*

A sob choked me as I turned to look at Rownan's lifeless
body. Why had he come here? He wasn't supposed to be anywhere near here. I couldn't stand the thought of Uncle Lloyd
losing both of his sons, so I had lied to him to protect him. And I
had failed. I had failed him, Treygan, myself, and Rathe.

There was no noise except the waves beneath us. I gazed
at each bubble, each treasured life inside, surrounding Luska
and me. All of them were trying to break through in some way.
Nixie's spirit burned such an intense shade of red that it was
almost blinding. Otabia, Mariza, and Eve clawed nonstop with
their talons. Talus and Messina were coiled to strike, their snakes
whipping frantically around their heads. Keeley and Jenna flitted
around like two lightning bugs in jars. I couldn't allow anyone

else to die.

I was out of options. My plan had failed. I had failed. He had won.

I leaned forward and pressed my lips to Luska's. The breath I'd been holding for so long was sucked out of me. His arms wrapped around me. There was nothing gentle or seductive about it. The kraken began sucking the life out of me so he could take my soul to Harte for eternity.

53

Rowan

Even in the suffocating darkness of my approaching death, I felt my brother's energy stronger than ever, like he was trying to keep me tethered to life.

My mother's peaceful face hovered above. I had always wondered if she'd be there to greet me when I died, if we'd finally be reunited. Joy rushed through me as I reached up to touch her, but she dissolved and I was alone again.

I thought of Vienna and how devastated she'd be when she learned of my death. We had only just found each other again. We were supposed to give Lloyd grandbabies. I was supposed to help Treygan and Yara with the stone he gave me. *The stone*.

While he'd been dragging me across Rathe at breakneck speed, Treygan had explained that Lloyd's gift to me was not a gorgon stone. It was the actual freaking Waterstone, a much more powerful source of protection. And it was still in my hand.

Wait, how could I still feel my hand?

I remembered my father's promise: *It will keep everyone you love safe.*

I looked around, willing my blurry vision to clear. I wasn't lying in darkness. I was encased in one of that bastard's ink bubbles.

I squeezed the Waterstone tighter and thought I heard it crack. Gray flakes tumbled away as I lifted it to check on it. I tried pulling the vine tighter to keep it together, but it seemed to be breaking apart on its own.

Blue light shined through the jagged cracks, illuminating

my hands. Tiny blue streams poured out of the stone and weaved all around me. Each stream of light connected with one of my wounds, forming an intricate glowing net. The stinging subsided and the wounds started to heal.

Lloyd knew. Maybe he didn't know exactly how or why, but he knew and he was right. The Waterstone was protecting me. Would it have done the same for Treygan when he was almost killed? I had been so careless, so stupid. This time, I was determined to do what was asked of me. Treygan, Yara, and all of Rathe were depending on me.

I sat up. Outside of my bubble, Luska had Yara wrapped in his arms. They were kissing.

"Son of a—" I jumped to my feet, wobbling on the slippery surface. "Yara, stop!"

I didn't think she could hear me, but I had to try. I sliced my claws into the inky bubble over and over, but I couldn't break free. Then I noticed the others around me. A bunch of us were trapped in bubbles, and Luska's tentacles were poised to crush us all. That's why Yara was giving herself to him. To save us.

This was no tender, loving kiss. Something was wrong beyond the obvious. I studied her more closely. It was hard to tell through the swirling ink bubble, but I could swear her hallmarks were fading and her skin was turning gray.

She looked lifeless. The way Vienna had looked when we'd found her soulless body in Harte.

The kraken was stealing Yara's soul.

"Let go of her!" I screamed, but I was trapped and no one could hear me.

I frantically searched the water in every direction. Where in the hell was Treygan?

54

I could feel myself slipping away.

Though it physically hurt to have the life drained from me, my guilt from all the death and suffering I had caused was far more excruciating. Treygan and Rownan were gone because of me. Two fearless brothers had been robbed of life because of my terrible choices. Even though they deserved so much more, I prayed they would be reunited in the Eternal Falls.

I wouldn't see them there. I'd never see any of my loved ones again because my soul would eternally belong to Luska. When he kissed me I thought maybe he would try removing my memories like I had planned to do to him. Instead, it felt like he was draining the light from me and infecting me with his darkness.

I deserved it. All of it.

Thunder rumbled so loud it caused my drooping wings to quiver. My eyes flew open, and in my peripheral vision I saw the water rise and circle around us in a waterspout connecting the ocean and sky. We hovered directly in the center of the churning funnel.

So this was how he'd take me to Harte. He was creating his own gateway.

The wind blew so fiercely it pulled us apart, breaking our kiss—if you could call such a violation a kiss. Luska's tentacles whipped around us. Thankfully, he had dropped the ink bubbles. I was on my way out of Rathe forever, but at least my loved ones were free.

Luska's hands felt like hot irons branding my skin as he held me tighter. One strong gust after another pulled at my wings, threatening to tear me from his grip. As weak and drained as I was, I was coherent enough to wonder why I could still feel what was happening to my body. If he had removed my soul, wouldn't I be having some sort of out of body experience?

Stop it, he mentally growled to me.

Stop what? This wasn't his doing?

I looked up at the wide opening of the funnel, searching the sky for my siren sisters to check if one of them was conjuring the storm. I saw nothing but thick, sooty clouds racing over us.

Before I could plead my innocence to Luska, the churning wall of water behind him began to part like a curtain. Through the crack, I saw the black spires of Trident Rock.

Something Treygan said recently came back to me. *Cracks let the light in.*

In front of Trident Rock, riding the crest of a wave and glowing like an angel, and looking fiercer than ever, was Treygan.

The electricity that had coursed through me earlier was nothing compared to the surge that reignited my heart and soul when I saw him.

But then a landslide of doubt crashed down on me. Was this one of Luska's tricks? Was I so drained that I was hallucinating? Were we already in Harte and this was a mirage meant to torture me?

Luska turned to look behind him. As soon as he saw Treygan he released his grip on me. I plummeted for a moment, extending my wings before I hit the water. I was weak and dizzy, but seeing Treygan, mirage or not, had restored some of my strength.

The churning waterspout collapsed, splashing all around me. Luska and Treygan charged each other like bloodthirsty animals and collided only yards away. An intense crack of thunder shook me to my core. Together, they tumbled in a chaotic blur of splashing tentacles and disappeared beneath the waves. I dove in to chase after them.

Countless bubbles and trails of black ink swirled in all directions. I blinked fast, fighting the rush of foul water burning my eyes. When I could finally see clearly, I was staring at two Treygans wrestling each other.

Matching indigo tails thrashed. Arms covered in identical hallmarks flailed. One of them extended his thoughts through the water. *Help me, Yara! I'm the real Treygan.*

While attempting to choke his enemy, the other one shouted, *Don't fall for it, Yara. I'm Treygan.*

I studied both of them, trying to find something that would reveal who was the imposter. What if the kraken was fooling me twice over and neither of them were Treygan?

They disappeared behind an expanding wall of churning, ink-stained water. I couldn't see anything except waves of black until one of them appeared through an explosion of dark bubbles.

Treygan, or Luska disguised as Treygan, grabbed my hand. *Kiss me so I can restore your energy.*

Could it really be my Treygan? Offering me a wave of hope in the middle of the most intense and dangerous storm of my life?

But—I couldn't find words to speak. Finally, I managed, *You died.*

I'm back. Kiss me so we can stop him! He pulled me closer and kissed me. A familiar tingling swept through my body. I relaxed into him, relishing the reprieve from the chaos around us.

Flashes of memories from Harte snaked through my mind: the demon imposters, the burning rain, the beach of bones, the ravenous lampreys filling the sky. I yearned for all of it again. My soul was on its way back there and I couldn't stop it. I didn't need to open my eyes to know I was kissing Luska. I didn't have the strength to fight him anymore.

Fire burned through my bottom lip as he bit down, trying to maintain our connection, but he was ripped away. He disappeared into the murk of ink surrounding me. Long, loud, angry growls filled the water and faded as they moved farther from me.

Where are you? I shouted.

I wasn't even sure who I was calling for. Could Treygan really be alive and here? But where was here? Were we even in Rathe anymore? Was this what it felt like to lose my soul and be cast into hell? The churning water was all I could hear. I darted up, down, left, and right, trying to see or feel anything other than the veil of black, blinding water.

Koraline's smiling face, framed by her vibrant green pigtails, appeared so vividly she almost seemed real. *Beauty is sometimes hidden under a veil of tragedy.*

The darkness was just a veil. I stopped focusing on what my eyes were telling me and evoked my other senses, searching the void for Treygan. I felt him almost immediately and swam blindly through the inky water until I reached him.

Grappling and clawing at each other, the two Treygans still looked identical. I had to make a choice. And I had to choose correctly.

Time seemed to freeze as I studied them. Same hair, same skin, same tail, same hallmarks. Then I realized Treygan had something Luska could never have, or even imitate. Light.

I closed my eyes. I had to feel what I was searching for. I had to feel the real Treygan's love and my love for him.

The connection was so powerful that even in a sea raging with the wrath of a hellish god, I felt Treygan's inner light warm every part of my being.

My eyelids fluttered, cracking open slightly as I followed the sensation to one of the two Treygans in front of me. An aura of indigo and silver light surrounded him.

My wings and hands spread wide. I summoned every ounce of physical strength I had left and channeled more strength from Treygan. Evoking all my abilities, gorgon, siren, mer, selkie, and human, I opened my eyes and turned one of the Treygans to stone.

The crackling sound of rock hardening reverberated through the water as the other Treygan let go and drifted away from the sinking statue in front of him. He darted toward me, and when he stopped, we were so close that even the rush of bubbles couldn't fit between us.

Please tell me this is real, I begged. *Tell me you're real.*

I am. I swear it on both of our lives and all of Rathe.

My heart beat faster, but my head shook involuntarily. *What if you're dead and I'm stuck in Harte and this is all a lie?*

He cradled my face in his hands. *You're not in Harte, and I won't allow him to take you back there. Once upon a time, you died too. We were both granted a second chance. And more power.*

What do you mean?

Dive in. You'll see everything you need to know.

Silver clouds passed over his pupils. White-capped waves filled his irises and I flinched. I had never seen waves in his eyes before. But I had seen them in someone else's eyes, someone important. Poseidon.

The sound of stone splintering below us startled me. Luska was already breaking free. *We don't have time.*

He gently pushed me backward, distancing us from the threat looming below. *It will only take a second. I swear I'll protect you. Now, hurry!*

The waves in his eyes looked like a tsunami. My mind felt so bleary, my body so useless, but I forced myself to take a breath and then I dove in.

I was pulled out of the exhausting turmoil and into the stillness of Treygan's soul.

Treygan stood in front of the Eternal Falls, just like I had when

I'd died and met Medusa. Except Medusa wasn't there. Poseidon towered over Treygan. He was almost as tall and wide as the waterfall itself.

Poseidon's voice resounded across the Inbetween, reaching the falls, the sky, and everything else. "Yara has let assumptions and misconceptions prevent her from making the correct choice."

Treygan stepped forward. "She's doing the best she can with the limited knowledge she's been given. Medusa has rejected her choices, but offers no real guidance."

Poseidon's silver eyes glinted then narrowed. "You protect and defend her unconditionally. You have since she was a child."

"Because I love her."

"Precisely. You and Yara can attain what Medusa and I always desired but could never have."

"Which is what?"

"A sacred and sanctified union. Pure and untainted by transgressions of divine law."

He was referring to his affair with Medusa in Athena's temple. The one act that had eternally disgraced them yet was also the spark that created all the beauty of Rathe. And the ugliness of Harte.

"You have proven time and time again your selfless dedication to Rathe and its creatures. Both you and Yara have exceeded our expectations. You love each other as much as you love Rathe, perhaps even more so."

I didn't know if it was Treygan's soul or my own that warmed at the thought. "Which is why I'm asking you to send me back and let me help her rule."

Help me rule? My own surprise blanketed Treygan's determination as Poseidon stroked his ethereal beard.

"I'll beg if I have to," Treygan said.

"Begging won't help you." He held out his hand. In his huge palm sat a silver pearl. "This will."

"You're giving that to me? Even after I ripped Luska's pearl from his throat?"

"That act may have done more harm than good, though it may yet prove useful. I commend you and Yara for your cunning, but if you do send Luska back to Harte, his pearl must go with him. As long as it remains in Rathe, he will be able to return."

Treygan let that sink in. Joel's books hadn't mentioned that crucial little detail. "Is it true that without his pearl, he isn't immortal?'"

"He is weakened, but he cannot be killed. I will not allow it. Without him, Harte would have no ruler, and eventually all of the evil within that realm would find its way back to Rathe."

"Then how do we send him back?"

"Yara has already figured that out, though she must give up on the idea of removing his memories of her. The only key she is missing is you. Once you and Yara have consecrated your bond, the strength and purity of your union will create light powerful enough to overcome his darkness."

"How do we consecrate our bond?"

"Ask any gorgon. The binding tradition originated with them."

Treygan nodded, knowing exactly which gorgon to ask. "After that, power will be restored to Rathe?"

"Once Yara chooses the third ruler, yes."

"But Medusa hasn't approved any of Yara's choices."

"Because Yara continues to ignore her instincts in this matter. It was Medusa's sisters who insisted on a female co-ruler, but they are no longer in power. Despite her beliefs to the contrary, Yara's choices are not restricted by gender or state of being."

Treygan immediately knew who he meant, and so did I. But where Treygan was feeling pure joy and excitement, I was pissed off that Medusa couldn't just tell me that in the first place.

"And when she makes her choice we'll have your blessing?"

"When the time is right."

A surge of strength and confidence made Treygan feel like

he was floating. "I'm ready."

Poseidon placed the silver pearl on the tip of his trident then touched it to Treygan's throat. The three sharp prongs glowed warm and bright. Treygan's neck felt hot, but in a glorious way. "You were born ready, Treygan. We have always known that."

He removed the trident and Treygan touched his throat. The pearl was there, hanging from a necklace that felt like seaweed. "Send me back so we can end this."

"I admire your tenacity," Poseidon said, "but before you return, I must instruct you in your newest abilities. Medusa prefers to let natural self-discovery take its course, but you have not the luxury of time."

I couldn't contain my smile. Neither could Treygan.

He pushed me out of the memory and back into the raging sea.

Oh my gods! Weak as I was, I hugged him. I had wanted this all along. He had too, but we'd never thought it was an option. *Does this mean what I think it means?*

A smile lit up his face like I had never seen before. He held my chin with one hand and touched my armband with the other. *You have your agape pearl, right?*

I always do.

Good. Will you choose me to help you rule Rathe?

Yes!

This isn't at all how I planned on proposing, but it's now or never. Want to officially be stuck with me for eternity, Yamabuki?

Of course I do. I smiled so big I thought my cheeks would tear open. I repeated what Treygan had told me so many times. *Forever belongs to you and me.*

Indeed it does.

More splintering stone snapped us out of our tender moment, and then Luska's infuriated voice echoed from below. *Yara!*

I glanced down to see tentacles racing toward us. Treygan wrapped one arm around me and a rush of water lifted us to the surface.

Rownan

Waves kept breaking over me as I searched for Luska, my brother, Yara, and anyone else who might've made it out of their ink bubbles. I thought I could see the sirens circling overhead, but my vision was still blurry.

The storm let loose with another round of intense lightning and thunder just as Yara and Treygan burst from the water and landed on the wide rock shelf at the base of Trident Rock.

I urged my aching body to swim, but I wasn't making much headway. Gratitude flooded me when Otabia snatched me out of the water and flew me the rest of the way.

We landed at Treygan's side. He instructed all of us to move behind him and stand as far back as possible. We all faced the ocean, waiting for Luska to show himself. An eerie quiet fell over Trident Rock as the storm calmed.

As far as I could see, everything was gray. Gray clouds, gray water, gray mist. Treygan's back was silver and the serpent hallmark running down his spine was steel gray. Even Yara, standing slightly to my left, looked like she'd been dipped in ashes. The monotone cloak covering our world was unsettling.

"Here he comes," Treygan said.

The water in front of him bubbled like it was boiling. Luska broke through the surface, morphing from humanesque to demented kraken, growing taller as his tentacles thrashed the air. His face was still shredded and his left eye missing.

My brother's back was to me, but I could imagine the satisfied look on his face. Yara had done that glorious damage. Too bad she didn't tear out both eyes.

Yara drew herself up and squared her shoulders, preparing to use whatever bit of strength she might have left, but Treygan stopped her.

"Please, let me do the honors. I've earned it."

"Yes, you have." She swiped her hand in Luska's direction. "He's all yours."

Treygan stepped away from the rock shelf and grew larger too, towering above all of us like a true god. His serpent hallmark began moving, and then real snakes, eight of them, emerged from his back. Sidewinding around Treygan, they struck at Luska. Each viper sank its fangs into one of Luska's tentacles and lifted him into the air.

Luska's one and only eye rolled back in his head as he struggled, and I wondered how much venom eight mer-gorgon-god-snakes could inject into one evil squid. A lot, I hoped.

Treygan's hands opened at his sides. At first I thought he had unsheathed selkie claws like mine, but then I recognized the familiar three-prong shape of tridents. Glowing tridents. With a flick of his wrists, the tridents made of light shot forward and pinned Luska to the wall of rock behind him.

I couldn't help it. I pumped my fist in the air. "Yes! Hell, yes!"

Treygan returned to his normal size along with his serpents.

Yara gazed in awe at Treygan. "That was . . . wow."

Humble as ever, Treygan sidestepped the compliments and got down to business.

"The venom won't keep him down for long." He turned to Yara, pulled her close, and raised one hand to his side. A wave rose up and encased Treygan and Yara from the waist down. They quickly glided away just above the ocean's surface like they were riding a water chariot over the smoothest road imaginable.

My brother had always been skilled at manipulating water, but now it seemed to move and support him like a natural exten-

Sacred Seas

sion of him.

"We have to follow them," I told Otabia.

She gripped me under the arms. "What in the worlds is happening?"

"I'll explain everything to you if we manage to live through this."

She carried me to Treygan and Yara's landing spot several rock formations away and set me down beside them.

"Now?" I asked Treygan.

He took Yara's hand in his. "Now."

I unwound the Serpetugon vine from around my arm, and then wrapped half around Treygan's wrist and the other half around Yara's. Just like Lloyd had done for Vienna and me. Except this ceremony was different. It would change everything.

The Waterstone hung between them, secured in the middle of the vine. Yara saw it and her eyes widened.

"Is that what I think it is?"

"One of the most powerful and important magical artifacts in existence? Yes it is. Don't do something stupid like give it away to a loved one." I finished tying the vine around her wrist and patted her on the shoulder. "Okay, I've tied the literal knots. You can tie the metaphorical one now."

Treygan grinned at Yara. "Sorry it couldn't be more romantic."

Her smile was weak but genuine. "Romance is highly overrated."

Eve and Mariza landed behind me. Mariza stepped forward and said, "The gorgon kin turned him to stone again. They're holding him off for now, but it won't last."

Keeley and Jenna buzzed past my head and tackle-hugged Treygan's shoulders.

I unzipped my arm band and pulled out the sheet of paper Treygan had given me earlier. The one our father had given him. I stared at the handwritten words. "Good gods. I can't believe I'm marrying you guys right now in the middle of all this."

Keeley squealed excitedly. "Oh my goodness! They're getting married!"

"You promised me you'd have a yellow wedding!" Jenna dipped down and kissed Yara's hair and the shriveled flower hanging over her shoulder.

"And blue," Keeley insisted. "You must have blue for good luck."

She went to work, and in seconds Yara's gray hair was streaked with sparkling yellow and blue. At least they were giving her some sort of coloring again.

Otabia hovered above us to get a better view of Trident Rock. "His stone casing is starting to crack. Whatever you're doing, you'd better do it quick."

"Do it," Yara told me. "Hurry."

I held the Waterstone in my hand and read the gorgon chant Lloyd had written out phonetically. I had no idea if I was doing it right, but there hadn't been time to recruit a full-blooded gorgon for the job. Treygan and Yara had it easy. Their vows were in English. As soon as I finished, I turned the paper around so they could read the words.

I pointed to the lines Yara needed to read. Her eyes scanned the page then her gaze locked on Treygan. "Ice and fire, dark and light, bind our souls eternally tight."

Treygan recited his part without looking. "Unbreakable like our will, as sacred as our bond, bless our love in this world and beyond."

"He's breaking free!" Otabia shouted.

I read the last few lines of gorgon just like my father had done during mine and Vienna's renewal ceremony. As soon as I finished, I let go of the Waterstone and said, "Done. Hurry up and kiss the bride."

They kissed. Passionately. Like they had all the time in the worlds.

Perhaps they did, because time seemed to stand still in that moment. A sparkling force field formed around them. The pearly-white coloring of Yara's hair and skin returned. Her hall-marks appeared again, swirling and filling with colors. As her strength returned, her shimmering wings nearly lifted her off the ground.

The Waterstone burned so hot that the remaining gorgon stone around it evaporated, revealing its true nature. A gold-en beam of light shot out of the stone and wrapped its way up Yara's arm and down her whole body, wings included. The light seemed to be illuminating her from the inside out. I couldn't tell if she was shaking from exhaustion or buzzing with power.

Next, a blue light poured from the stone and wrapped around Treygan. He radiated with the same intensity.

Jenna hugged Keeley. "Yellow and blue, yellow and blue!" they chanted together.

Treygan and Yara were in each other's arms, their eyes glued to one another. Together, they burned brighter than any sun or moon I'd ever seen.

Difficult as it probably was, Treygan broke their kiss and motioned to me. "Untie it."

I rushed forward and undid the knots as he told Yara, "You know what to do now."

"I do." Yara's smiled eclipsed Treygan's. She called to the seemingly empty sky above them, "Nixie, we choose you as our third!"

Yara lifted one hand above her head. A burst of red light il-luminated her fingers and spiraled down her arm. Treygan lifted his hand and the same red light wrapped around him. Beams of yellow, blue, and red weaved together like a braid.

The tangled light pulsed and expanded outward like a pow-erful tide, covering us, the water, and everything else as far as I could see in an ever-reaching blanket of color.

The dark clouds swirling above us dissipated and the winds calmed. The sky brightened and so did the water.

I'd say Yara looked normal again, but that wasn't true. She looked more luminous than ever, and Treygan had a glow I'd never seen before. A pink cloud of light hovered just above them, radiating power.

"Holy mackerel," Keeley squeaked.

Jenna stared in awe like the rest of us. "Has power been restored?"

I grinned so big my cheeks hurt. "It sure has. Can't you feel it?"

Otabia fluttered above us. "Celebrate later. Luska just broke free of the tridents!"

Luska roared and we all turned toward the dreadful sound. He plowed through the water with his tentacles flailing.

Yara and Treygan, still glowing, stepped off the rocks together and flew at the kraken—Yara through the air and Treygan riding a wave. Treygan cocked his arm back like he was about to deliver the blow of the centuries, but Yara beat him to it.

She pummeled Luska, delivering an epic uppercut to the eyeless side of his face. A thunderous crack shook everything so hard that I lost my balance and almost toppled over.

I recovered in time to watch Yara, Treygan, and the pink cloud that was Nixie churn around the dazed kraken like a tornado.

Blue, gold, and red cords of light wrapped around Luska, binding his tentacles tight against his body. Together, Rathe's new rulers body-slammed him onto his back at the base of Trident Rock.

I got Otabia to pick me up again and we all flew closer.

"Set me down in front of him," I said. After my brush with death, I would have liked nothing better than to get far away from those tentacles, but I still had a part to play.

I pulled out the kraken's black pearl from my armband. As roughly as possible, I ripped off his seaweed bandage and shoved the real pearl into the gaping hole in his throat, next to the fake one. "Here's your one-way ticket back to hell."

The moment I removed my hand, his throat started to heal and he swallowed.

"This isn't over!" he snarled as his face healed too, which was *really* gross to watch. "Light cannot contain me."

"We have no interest in containing you," Yara told him. "We want to *dispose* of you. Wrangler!"

A ghost ship rounded the back of Trident Rock and sailed toward us. Standing at the wheel with his silvery hair whipping behind him, our new friend saluted us.

Luska roared and thrashed again, but couldn't break free. Yara and Treygan picked him up and heaved him onto the Wrangler's ship. Even though we could see through the ship as if it were made of nothing but wispy clouds, the kraken landed with a heavy thud.

"Freakin' Harte," I grumbled. "Makes no sense."

"Return him to where he belongs," Treygan told Wrangler.

"If you fail," Otabia said, flying up to Wrangler and thrusting her chest in his face, "then we're through."

He licked his ethereal lips. "Darling, you and I will never be through. I'll be back as soon as I'm finished, and I plan to court you until you permanently swear off all other males."

He grabbed her, dipped her so low her wings almost hit the ground, and kissed her. When he set her on her feet, she was blushing. Never in my life had I ever seen her blush. Otabia and Wrangler were an item. Nothing surprised me anymore.

"Wrangler?" Yara hovered over the deck, looking down at Luska with a mix of disgust and pity. "Please, tell Stheno and Euryale that the kraken's safe return is my goodbye gift to them."

Smiling, he saluted her and Treygan again, and then he sailed his ship into the shadowed waterway between the towering black cliffs of Trident Rock. Luska kept shouting for Yara, threatening to come back for her, but as the ghost ship faded, so did Luska's voice.

Sweat dripped from my face as I continued grinning like an idiot. They did it. They saved Rathe. And they tied the knot. I'd never known two souls more worthy of a perfect ending.

I turned to the sirens, Keeley and Jenna, and the gorgon

kin who had gathered in the water around us. "In case anyone missed it, my brother and Yara got hitched! And Yara, Treygan, and Nixie are the new rulers of Rathe!"

The cheers were so loud I was sure Lloyd heard them all the way in Eden's Hammock.

56

From one of the lower landings of Gorgon Rock, I admired the new skies of Rathe. Two bright and colorful suns shone over the mer side of our ocean. Two equally bright moons illuminated the dark waters of the selkie side. Even more beautiful in my opinion were the ghostly sun and moon—ruby red with ethereal wisps of pink.

I wanted to enjoy them while they lasted. We all knew Nixie couldn't stay in the Inbetween forever. Eventually she would have to heed the pull of the Eternal Falls and we'd have to appoint another ruler in her place. But for now she was our third, and I couldn't be more pleased.

Treygan ran his hand over a section of rock wall. I admired the view of him too. His silver pearl glimmered in the sunlight. I touched my own pearl at my throat. With Uncle Lloyd's help, Treygan had made me an unbreakable necklace from Serpetugon vine.

"I agree," he told me. "It's a good place for the doorway."

I smiled, knowing what a big difference this one simple addition would make. It would bring so much happiness into our lives. "It's by far my favorite part of our project."

We were remodeling Gorgon Rock. Majorly remodeling. Soon, it would be our home. One Treygan and I designed and decorated together. The location made sense considering it was perfectly centered in the realm we now ruled together.

I glanced around, mental cogs turning. "How do you feel about changing its name?"

Treygan looked surprised. "You don't like Gorgon Rock?"

"No, that part I want to keep in honor of Medusa, Uncle Lloyd, and all other gorgons. I want to change the name of its location. I always cringe when people refer to it as The Divide. We're a united realm."

"What do you suggest its new name be?"

"Something warm and optimistic. Like Common Ground, or The Sweet Spot."

"The Sweet Spot is one hundred percent vetoed." Treygan winked at me then picked up his sketchpad. "We can consult with Nixie on a new name later. Right now I need you to look at this idea for our resting pool."

"Should we have two resting pools? In case we have a lovers' quarrel?"

"I doubt anything will be as bad as what we have already endured."

"Still," I said, mostly teasing. "Eternity is a long time to rule together."

He chuckled. "Are you sure you're ready for this kind of commitment?"

"Too late to back out now, we're already cosmically hitched."

He flashed me his humble yet godly smile. If I had ever believed one of my co-rulers could have been a male, I would have chosen Treygan from the start. Looking back, I realized he had been my first choice. In so many more ways than I ever could, he had truly earned his position. Medusa and Poseidon felt the same way, which is why they hadn't approved any of my other choices.

Without looking up from his drawings, Treygan asked, "What about a birthing pool?"

"A what?"

"A birthing pool. For when we have children."

Sacred Seas

My hands covered my stomach. I didn't know why I hadn't thought about children yet, but the suggestion caught me off guard. "Children? My gods, between you and me and all the mixed bloodlines between us, what would our children even be?"

He set down his pad and walked over to me. With both hands, he gently traced the vine hallmarks that ran along my hips. "They would be perfect."

Nixie flew down and landed beside us, interrupting the moment as usual. "They'll be spoiled little sea mutts, but I'll be here to keep them in line."

Treygan smirked. "We'd expect no less from you, Nix."

Treygan could now see and hear Nixie too. One of the perks of being a god of Rathe. It made her feel much more included and appreciated. Although sometimes, like when she nagged us about making her wall panel the focal point of our living room, I wished we'd had the foresight to negotiate a mute button on her. Still, I was glad she was in no hurry to leave us. The thought of her playing spirit nanny to our future children warmed my heart.

"Do you think they'll be able to hear and see you too?" I wondered.

"They'll inherit that ability from their mother and father. How could they not?"

Being able to see and communicate with spirits was a true gift to both of us. Treygan and I could also see and speak with Liora, Treygan's mother. Since she died giving birth to him, he had never had a chance to know her. She had watched over him for his entire life, but only Uncle Lloyd had been able to communicate with her through one of his enchanted panels. Now, much to Treygan's pure and utter joy, he and his mom had been reunited. Seeing them together did make me yearn for a reunion with my own parents, but they had both passed on. To make myself feel better, I imagined them together again and blissfully in love, which made me grateful that they weren't lingering in the Inbetween like Liora and Nixie.

Sage had also passed on. I missed her every day, but I had started to appreciate the new blooming vine that grew in her place. Every time the flower opened and exposed its shimmering silver interior, I told myself it was Sage saying hello from the other side.

"So." Nixie rubbed her hands together. "Show me where the new grand doorway is going. The first step of finalizing this happy ending is to start demolition."

57

Koraline

I sat in the sand on Lloyd's beach as the surf washed over my prosthetic tail. Watching Joel disappear beneath the waves was bittersweet. As soon as his head went under, I started the stopwatch and waited.

After almost a week of trials and training, I was convinced that what we feared was true. Joel's transformation had only half worked.

When he went into the water, scales formed on his legs, but no tail. Hallmarks covered his body and his disease seemed to be cured, but he couldn't breathe underwater or hold his breath for more than a few minutes. Sure, it was a huge improvement compared to how weak his lungs used to be, but it didn't allow for long swims deep in the ocean. We didn't even dare let him rest in the fish tank without a life vest.

Some of his memories were already starting to return. Old friends, teachers, books he'd read. Each one had been a joy for him to rediscover. I didn't know if Joel had been right about me being such a deep part of him that those memories couldn't be forgotten, or if Treygan purposefully left them as a favor to us. One to which he'd never admit.

When Joel's garnet hair came into view, I clicked the button on the stopwatch.

He swam closer and blinked water from his gorgeous eyes, which were a dark brown with ruby flecks. "How long that time?"

I read the watch. "Four minutes and eighteen seconds."

"So much for me ever being able to visit Rathe, huh?"

"Don't say that. Your abilities might be developing slower than usual. We'll give it more time and see how it goes."

He crawled over the wet sand and sat beside me. "What if nothing changes? What if I'm never able to breathe underwater the way you can?"

"Then we get you certified in Scuba."

He didn't laugh or smile like I hoped. "Scuba tanks have a time limit too."

"Joel, you're alive and healthy. You and I can be together now without hiding. Isn't that what we wanted?"

"I wanted to be mer."

"You are."

"Not the way you need me to be."

I took his hand and held it to my heart. "You are everything I need and more."

Kimber and Delmar had been pardoned for their part in Joel's transformation. The Violets didn't know what to do about Treygan—how do you punish your new god and ruler?—and they still hadn't set a date for my trial. They claimed to be too busy cleaning up after the kraken, but I wondered if Caspian and Indrea were stalling because they suspected I'd be banished from Rathe. That would be a death sentence for me unless C-weed started growing in the Catacombs again.

Joel and I had discussed what we might do if that happened—where we would live for the rest of my life, if he should close the bookstore and cut ties with his human connections. Yara had offered us her house to live in for as long as we wanted. All of the quarantined selkies had returned home to Rathe, and Yara was worried Lloyd would get lonely if everyone left him all at once. Spending what time I'd have left together on Eden's Hammock seemed like a perfectly acceptable option.

"You're not disappointed my transformation didn't work?"

Joel asked, his skin swirling with colors. I was still learning to read his mer reactions, but this one was easy. Guilt and shame. I had gotten to know those two feelings too well recently.

I gestured at my prosthetic tail. "This thing is a nuisance to swim with. Staying here saves me the exhausting commute to Rathe. I'm ecstatic to be here with you."

"What if your feelings change?" His forehead creased and I wanted to rub away the lines of sadness. "What if your trial goes well and you aren't banished to Earth? What if some day you ache to return home and I can't go with you?"

I gently stroked his face. "My home is wherever you are."

"What about Pango?"

"My brother loves it here. He'll happily visit us as much as we want. Probably more."

It wasn't the perfect ending, but it wasn't the end of our relationship or Joel's life. That's what mattered most.

Later that night, Joel and I were sitting on the porch swing at Yara's old house. My head was in Joel's lap and he was reading me the end of *Coral Island*.

He closed the book and tossed it on the floorboards at his feet. Then he stretched and let out his customary exhale, which he did every time a story ended. I settled in to hear his thoughts about the three friends sailing home.

"Do you think Ralph and his friends will ever return to—"

He stopped as Lloyd strolled up the pathway and waved to us. "Lovely evening, isn't it?"

I sat up as Joel and I both said hello and invited Lloyd to join us.

He climbed the steps and peeked through the screen door. "I'm here for the housewarming party."

"Party?" I questioned. "We aren't having a party."

"You sure about that?" He opened the screen door and went

inside.

Joel and I exchanged confused expressions. Then he lifted me and set me in my wheelchair. We went inside and rounded the wall separating the entryway from the living room.

Lloyd, Yara, Treygan, Rownan, and Vienna stood there smiling at us. Beside them, a sheet of white fabric covered the entire wall. Centered on the fabric was a big red bow.

"What's going on?" I asked. "How did you get here? We didn't even sense you or hear you come in."

"We wanted to surprise you," Yara said. "Treygan and I had a chat with the Violets. Since Joel's help was pretty instrumental in defeating the kraken, they're inclined to go easy on you for your illegal love affair. You'll still have to stand trial and face some sort of sentence, but it won't be banishment. You'll probably never be promoted to Blue, and you might be stuck doing community service for the rest of your life, but at least you'll be able to return to Rathe."

Happy tears threatened to fill my eyes but I kept them at bay while nodding. "Thank you. I look forward to also thanking them in person."

Joel held my hand and squeezed it, but I couldn't look up at him or I was sure I'd cry. I wouldn't be banished. I could return home whenever I wanted. I said a silent prayer for the mercy bestowed upon me. Joel would be able to visit my beloved world. Eventually. Hopefully.

Lloyd cleared his throat. "Speaking of community service, I've been thinking I'd like to document everything that has happened to me, and to others who have come and gone from Rathe. A sort of historical record, if you will. But I've never been a strong writer and have no experience with this sort of thing." He turned to Joel. "You and your family spent decades recording events from your history. Perhaps you and Koraline could help me and others from Rathe do the same?"

"Like memoirs?" I asked.

"Yes." Lloyd said. "I'd like everyone's story told. I feel it's important to know what transpired during this time of monumental change for Rathe."

"Sea Monster Memoirs." Joel's eyes lit up. His excitement was palpable. "I would be honored, but . . . ," he hesitated, looking at me and then back at Lloyd. "It would require time, intensive interviews, and researching multiple sources for fact checking. Those involved would have to spend a lot of time here while retelling their story."

"Maybe not." Rownan stepped closer to the sheet. "There may be a more convenient option."

He tugged on the fabric and it dropped to the floor, revealing a carved wood panel that spanned most of the wall.

My breath caught. "Gorgon Rock."

"This carving is unique," Lloyd explained with a hint of mischief in his voice. A grin tugged at his lips.

Joel held my hand and we moved closer, studying all of the panel's intricate details.

"Everyone helped carve it," Treygan said. "Lloyd did most of the work, but Yara and I chipped in, and so did Rownan and Vienna, and Pango and Merrick, and Jenna and Keeley."

"It's breathtaking." I ran my fingertips along the smooth ridges of waves. "Tell them they did an incredible job."

"Tell them yourself." Yara gently rolled my chair forward until the empty footrests touched the wood.

She urged Joel forward too. He and I apprehensively glanced at each other.

Lloyd pulled out a blue stone from his pocket and slid it into an indent in the panel. He said a few words in ancient gorgon and the stone glowed bright, lighting up the entire carving.

"Please," Lloyd said, a proud smile breaking free. "Take a closer look."

Movement at the bottom of the panel caught my eye. "Joel? Did the water just ripple?"

He hummed and leaned closer, squinting. "Rippling *and* a tail glistening in the water."

My throat tightened and my pulse quickened. "There's no way this is . . ."

I couldn't finish my sentence because it would have been a lie.

"A portal?" Joel whispered, as if afraid saying it out loud would mean someone would laugh and tell him no.

Yara spoke in a soothing voice, "Relax your eyes and open your soul."

Vienna rubbed my shoulders. "Drop any misconceptions about what's impossible."

Treygan patted Joel's back. "Expect miracles."

Rownan stepped aside while bowing. "And believe in the fantastical."

Lloyd waved his hand across the panel and it started glowing again.

The hairs on my arms rose. A colorful tunnel of light spiraled and pulled us forward. A breeze swept over my face and I closed my eyes, wishing with all my heart that it was real.

"Koraline, look!" Joel exclaimed as he rolled me forward.

My eyes flew open and tears immediately flowed. We had been transported to Gorgon Rock. The beauty of Rathe surrounded us in vivid detail. Peach and purple skies with three moons and three suns. Mer and selkie oceans that stretched for miles. *Home.*

Joel spun in a slow circle. "Is this real?"

Yara and Treygan walked through the portal behind us. They both wore ear to ear grins.

"It's real." Yara leaned down to hug me and I squeezed her tight.

Treygan shook Joel's hand and then put his arm around him and turned him to look out at Rathe again. "Welcome to your other home, Joel. Now you can come and go as you please."

I let go of Yara and held Joel's hand. "What do you think?"

He kneeled beside my chair. "It's better than I ever imagined."

We kissed, and for a moment I worried I might have actually died and passed through the Eternal Falls. Maybe this was my version of Heaven.

Rownan shouted, "Welcome home, Old Man!"

"My gods how I've missed this place." Lloyd's gruff voice made me pull back from Joel. Lloyd walked out of the portal, his eyes gleaming in a way I had never seen. After all this time, after being cursed for so long, Lloyd had also returned home to Rathe.

Vienna brushed my cheek. "I assume those are joyful tears?" I nodded.

Joel asked the question burning in my mind. "How? All due respect, Lloyd, I know you used to be a gorgon, but you've been human for decades. I didn't think you'd be able to enter Rathe."

He shrugged. "A little help from the Waterstone, and a lot of help from my son and daughter-in-law."

"New management, new rules." Yara lovingly wrapped one arm around Lloyd's waist. "None of us would be here if it weren't for him. He's helped us in more ways than I can count."

"I thought the Waterstone had been stolen," I said to Lloyd. "How did you get it?"

"An old friend returned it to me for safe keeping."

"Now it's our duty to make sure it's never stolen again." Treygan handed me my prosthetic tail. "We figured you and Joel might want to go for a swim."

Yara nodded to the oceans behind us. "They're waiting to meet Rathe's newest merman."

We turned to see sea monsters everywhere. Colorful merfolk of all ages filled the sunny mer waters. Sleek-furred selkies bobbed in their moonlit waves. The gorgon kin had slithered onto the rocky shores surrounding the mountain. Otabia, Mariza, and Eve sat perched on a cliff, smiling down at us. A swarm of sprites flew forward carrying flowers and two crowns made of twigs and vines. Jenna and Keeley placed the crowns on my head and Joel's.

Keeley kissed my nose. "Welcome back, Koraline."

Jenna kissed Joel's forehead. "Welcome home, Joel."

My heart was overflowing. My teary eyes met Yara's and she grasped my hand. Together, we looked out over the realm she and Treygan now ruled.

I figured Joel's education might as well start immediately. I told him, "We call this place The Divide."

"Really?" Joel asked, not hiding his disdain. "Not a very befitting name for the most majestic place I've ever seen. Look at all of them." He motioned to everyone surrounding us. "Gathering here as one huge family. How truly wondrous to see so many different creatures peacefully come together in one place. In this realm that so many fought for and some even died to protect. It's sacred. You should call it the Sacred Seas."

"Sacred Seas," Yara repeated, grinning at Treygan. "I love that name." She glanced at an empty space beside her. "Nixie loves it too."

Friends, old and new, called to us, urging us to join them. Joel helped me into my prosthetic tail and I slid out of my chair onto the rocky ledge.

"Go on in," I told him. "I'll be right behind you."

He kissed the top of my head then dove in. Several merfolk swam over to greet him, including Pango, Merrick, Caspian, Indrea, Delmar, and Kimber.

Kimber and I still shared our secret about my heinous blackmail, but not for long. I would confess my crime to our new rulers and serve any punishment they felt appropriate. Once Treygan and Yara knew about Kimber's desire to return her stone mouth to normal, I was certain they would find a way to grant her wish. Especially Treygan. New management, new rules. Both of us would right the wrongs we had done to Kimber. I believed that with all of my heart and soul.

Joel looked up at me from the water, his garnet hair and eyes sparkling in the sun. "You know I need a tour, right?"

I grinned wider, wondering if I would ever stop.

Before joining him, I turned to Yara and Treygan again.

"Medusa's great-great-granddaughter was right. Sometimes beauty is hidden under a veil of tragedy. But it's so worth it."

"Love until it kills you." Yara winked at me. "There's nothing better worth dying for."

At the same time, Treygan and Lloyd both looked at the empty space between them. Then Lloyd chuckled. "Liora agrees one hundred percent."

"Nixie too," Yara said.

"Me three." Treygan kissed his beaming bride. "So worth it."

THE END

Acknowledgements

Good grief, this book took forever to finish.

Heartfelt thanks to the closest members of my clan: Mom, Dad, John, Becca, Megan, Marie and Natalie. Thanks for always being there for me through all the ups and down of my writing journey.

Then, of course, I need to thank the creative peeps who helped make this book a reality:

Steve Graham, for more fabulous interior graphics.

Michelle Williams, for cover design. Good things come in threes. You did an amazing job on all the beautiful covers for this trilogy.

Rebecca Brown, my editor. I still say you should be listed as co-author of this one. I'm amazed and grateful that you didn't give up on me through this much-too-long process.

Shayne Leighton for formatting the ebook and paperback. They turned out so lovely that I want to pet every page.

RJ Walker, Jossie Marie Solheim, and Jennifer Madero for helping me name locations in this story. I didn't use your exact suggestions, but you inspired my final decisions. Told you I'd give you credit!

Most importantly, to all my readers, old and new. I can't thank you enough for supporting my books and me. For all of you who hung in there and waited years for Sacred Seas, thank you. Thank you for your patience, understanding, encouragement, and for reading "the end" even after all this time. You are the reason I didn't give up. My gratitude still is, and always will be, deeper than the oceans.

Other Books By Karen:

The Kindrily Series
(Reincarnation, soul mates, & supernatural powers.)

#1- Grasping at Eternity
#2- Taking Back Forever
#3- Fighting for Infinity

Virtual Arcana
(Virtual reality and tarot in a faraway future.)

Sign up for my newsletter to receive updates on new releases and to be entered in exclusive contests, including winning signed books.

Karen Amanda Hooper

Karen writes in sunny Florida while cuddling with her spoiled rescue bulldog and drinking green smoothies. Due to her strong Disney upbringing, she still believes in fairy tales, sprinkles magic throughout all of her novels, and found herself a real-life Peter Pan. She loves traveling to Neverland and anywhere else that will inspire more book ideas.

To learn more about Karen and her books,
visit her website at
www.KarenAmandaHooper.com